Classic Horror Stories

 National Textbook Company
a division of NTC/Contemporary Publishing Group
Lincolnwood, Illinois USA

Cover Design: Vita Jay Design
Cover illustration: Edward Gorey

Edward Gorey (1925–2000) entertained millions of readers with his wry and comic vision of mystery, murder, and mayhem. Gorey wrote and illustrated more than 100 books and illustrated many books by other authors. Today Gorey is probably best known for the delightful animated opening sequence of the PBS series "Mystery!" The cover illustration on this collection of horror stories is typical of the whimsical way in which Gorey treated creepy subjects.

Acknowledgments
The cover illustration is taken from *The Chinese Obelisks,* Copyright © 1970 Edward Gorey.
"Mrs. Amworth," is reprinted from *Visible and Invisible* by E. F. Benson, published by A. P. Watt & Son.
"The Green Scarf" by A. M. Burrage is reprinted from *Bodies and Souls,* edited by Dan Herr and Jack Wells.

After researching the copyright status of all selections reprinted in this anthology, the editors have determined that these materials are in the public domain. Every effort has been made to determine copyright owners. In the case of any omissions, the Publisher will be pleased to make suitable acknowledgment in future editions.

ISBN (student edition—hardbound): 0–8442–8098–4
ISBN (student edition—softbound): 0–8442–8099–2
ISBN (teacher's edition): 0–658–01568–0

Published by National Textbook Company,
a division of NTC/Contemporary Publishing Group, Inc.
4255 West Touhy Avenue,
Lincolnwood (Chicago), Illinois 60712–1975 U. S. A.
© 2001 NTC/Contemporary Publishing Group, Inc.
All rights reserved. No part of this book may be reproduced, stored in a retrieval system, or transmitted in any form or by any means, electronic, mechanical, photocopying, recording, or otherwise, without prior permission of the publisher.
Manufactured in the United States of America.

00 01 02 03 04 05 06 07 08 09 HP 0 9 8 7 6 5 4 3 2 1

Contents

Introduction   v

Honoré de Balzac
    The Mysterious Mansion   1

E. F. Benson
    Mrs. Amworth   13

Ambrose Bierce
    The Damned Thing   29

A. M. Burrage
    The Green Scarf   40

Wilkie Collins
    A Terribly Strange Bed   57

Charles Dickens
    The Signalman   75

Sir Arthur Conan Doyle
    The Brazilian Cat   89

Mary E. Wilkins Freeman
    The Wind in the Rose-Bush   109

Charlotte Perkins Gilman
    The Yellow Wall-paper   127

Nathaniel Hawthorne
    Young Goodman Brown   145

Lafcadio Hearn
    The Boy Who Drew Cats   160

W. H. Hodgson
    The Gateway of the Monster   165

Washington Irving
    Adventure of the German Student   186

W. W. Jacobs
    The Monkey's Paw   194

Rudyard Kipling
    The Mark of the Beast   207

Guy de Maupassant
    Vendetta   222

Edith Nesbit
    No. 17   229

Edgar Allan Poe
    The Facts in the Case of M. Valdemar   239

Robert Louis Stevenson
    The Isle of Voices   251

H. G. Wells
    The Story of the Late Mr. Elvesham   272

Edith Wharton
    The Lady's Maid's Bell   290

Introduction

Like one that on a lonesome road
Doth walk in fear and dread,
And having once turned round, walks on
And no more turns his head;
Because he knows a frightful fiend
Doth close behind him tread.

from *The Rime of the Ancient Mariner*
by Samuel Taylor Coleridge

These famous lines capture the essence of the most characteristic experience of horror in literature—a personal encounter with the ultimately terrifying. This is what horror in literature is all about: an awful something is going to get us. It's lurking under the bed (the roots of horror lie in childhood); it's behind the curtains; it's outside in the dark; it's—horror of horrors—inside us.

Human beings have experienced the sense of dread from our beginnings; from before we were human. In his classic study *Supernatural Horror in Literature,* the American writer H. P. Lovecraft says, "The oldest and strongest emotion on mankind is fear, and the oldest and strongest kind of fear is fear of the unknown." A more whimsical theory is offered in the 1993 film *Matinee*, in which a producer of low-budget horror films traces the origin of the impulse to shock to the work of paleolithic artists. He imagines a stone-age hunter who, after escaping from a mammoth, returns to his cave and paints a wildly exaggerated version of his pursuer on the wall.

Myth, legend, and folktale have always been a rich storehouse of the characters and situations typical of horror fiction: ghosts, demons, giants, ogres, dragons, monsters, werewolves, vampires, witches' sabbaths, haunted graveyards, weird forests. Homer's *Odyssey*, to take a classical example, offers a colorful catalog of horrors, including the Cyclops, a one-eyed cannibal giant; and Circe, a beautiful witch who transforms men into beasts. The American writer Nathaniel Hawthorne, who retold classical myths in several collections for children, also used a number of legendary motifs in his horror stories, including the poison damsel in "Rappaccini's Daughter" and the witches' sabbath in "Young Goodman Brown," which is included in this anthology.

Edgar Allan Poe, a genius of horror literature, exploited its whole range of themes and strategies in his fiction and poetry. The Poe story in this collection, "The Facts in the Case of M. Valdemar," brilliantly exhibits his mastery of the physical aspect of horror—in this case, sheer nastiness. Poe's fellow-American Ambrose Bierce, whose story "The Damned Thing" appears here, was another writer gifted at conveying the material side of horror.

Although every cultural tradition and period could provide examples of narratives designed to evoke shivers, the origin of the most characteristic types of modern horror fiction really begin, oddly enough, in the Age of Reason. In her essay "The Supernatural in Literature," Virginia Woolf observes, "It is worth noticing that the craving for the supernatural in literature coincided in the 18th century with a period of rationalism in thought, as if the effect of damming the human instincts at one point causes them to overflow at another." Modern horror fiction is usually traced to Horace Walpole's hugely popular novel *The Castle of Otranto* (1765). Walpole was an English aristocrat with an enthusiasm for the Middle Ages. His novel started the fashion for "Gothic" (meaning medieval) horror fiction, which featured weird landscapes, ruined castles, secret societies, supernatural events, and innocent, beautiful young heroines preyed upon by lecherous villains. Many of the most successful writers of Gothic horror have been women—from Mrs. Anne Radcliffe's *The Mysteries of Udolpho* (1794) to Anne Rice's latest vampire novel.

During the wet summer of 1816 a seminal event in the history of modern horror fiction took place. The English Romantic poets Lord Byron and Percy Shelley, Shelley's wife Mary, and Byron's physician,

John Polidori, were vacationing in Switzerland. Kept inside by a spell of bad weather, they spent the time reading German ghost stories. One night Byron proposed that they each try to write a ghost story. The others eagerly agreed, but only Mary and Dr. Polidori followed through on Byron's proposal; Mary wrote *Frankenstein* and Dr. Polidori wrote *The Vampyre*. Mary Shelley's novel stands at the beginning of the science fiction tradition, which has its own repertory of horrors. One of the preeminent figures in this tradition, H. G. Wells excelled in presenting the terrors to be found in space and time themselves. "The Story of the Late Mr. Elvesham," the Wells tale included here, is a truly nightmarish account of a young man whose life is literally stolen from him.

Polidori's novel, in which Byron himself is caricatured as the vampire, Lord Ruthven, created a vogue for stories of the undead that persisted through Bram Stoker's classic novel Dracula and right up to the present day. In "Mrs. Amworth," a vampire story included here, the English comic writer E. F. Benson creates an interesting departure from the tradition by giving his vampire the bouncy personality of a cruise director. Though most horror fiction has a very serious tone, some writers successfully take a lighter approach. Both Benson and his contemporary Edith Nesbit, whose "No. 17" appears here, were authors whose works exhibited both comedy and fantasy.

Another cultural feature of the Age of Reason in Europe was the enthusiasm for translations and imitations of *The Thousand and One Nights,* the medieval Arabic collection of popular tales drawn from a wide variety of sources, including India, Persia, and Egypt. European writers used the so-called *Arabian Nights* as a model for a variety of literary works, including satires and picaresque adventure stories, as well as tales of terror. "The mysterious East" has continued to be a fertile source of materials for writers of horror fiction. India is the source of the dangerous talisman that produces such frightful results in one of the most famous of the stories in this anthology, "The Monkey's Paw," by English writer W. W. Jacobs. India is also the background of Rudyard Kipling's story "The Mark of the Beast." Another writer who used Asian material in his work was Lafcadio Hearn, a wandering writer who lived the last years of his life in Japan. Hearn's story "The Boy Who Drew Cats," retells a famous Japanese folktale about a boy who unwittingly uses his extraordinary drawing skills to destroy a demon rat he encounters in a deserted Buddhist temple. Another wanderer, the

English writer Robert Louis Stevenson, spent his final days on the island of Samoa. He used exotic Pacific island settings in several horror stories, including, "The Isle of Voices."

The ghost story is one of the most universal and familiar forms of horror fiction. The Victorian Age, the era of Charles Dickens, was the heyday of the traditional ghost story. Dickens himself is represented here by his famous tale "The Signalman." A number of interesting variations on this traditional theme appear in this anthology, including "The Green Scarf," a story by A. M. Burrage in which a relic of the English Civil War summons up a ghost regiment of Cromwell's soldiers. The 1800s also saw the first attempts to scientifically investigate hauntings and specters—the predecessors of the Ghostbusters were already at work. W. H. Hodgson's "The Gateway of the Monster," is an example of this approach. Hodgson's story is one in a series devoted to the interesting adventures of his psychic detective, Carnacki the Ghost-Finder.

In most traditional horror stories the threat is external. A more intimate, modern form of terror comes from within. Stevenson's classic novel *Strange Case of Dr. Jekyll and Mr. Hyde* is the archetype of this kind of horror fiction. An effective example in this collection dealing with psychic phenomena is "The Yellow Wall-paper," by the American writer Charlotte Perkins Gilman.

Discussing horror fiction, Stephen King, the best known contemporary writer of this literary form, identifies the source of fear in the unknown: "what's behind the closed door." King goes on to suggest that what is *actually* behind the door or lurking at the top of the stairs is never quite as frightening as the door or the staircase itself—in other words, the *anticipation* of what is behind the door is most frightening of all. This underscores the point that what really counts in a good horror story is the atmosphere that the writer creates. All of the writers included in this anthology are masters of suspense. As you read these stories, don't hold back. Allow yourself to be transported to a variety of ghostly settings and to experience vicariously the terror those settings hold. Keep in mind the words of critic Douglas Winter: "Every horror story has a happy ending. We have a simple escape—we can just wake up and say it was all a dream."

Honoré de Balzac (1799-1850)

Born in Tours, France, into a merchant-class family, Honoré Balssa had a miserable childhood, neglected by his parents and spending six years in a gloomy boarding school. Moving with his family to Paris, he completed his studies there, earning a law degree. He suddenly decided he wanted to write, however, and spent a number of years living in near-poverty while he turned out hack writing—novels, stories, and pamphlets. An older woman befriended him, showed an interest in his work, and helped him financially.

A disastrous foray into publishing left him with debts that he would repay for the rest of his life. To escape his creditors, he lived under an assumed name. When he finally achieved some success with a novel in 1829, he tried to set himself up as a society figure and changed his name to *de Balzac* to suggest an aristocratic background. Balzac turned out a phenomenal amount of work. In 12 novels published from 1834 to 1837 he hit upon the idea of unifying his work with common themes and repeating characters. He devised the collective title of *La Comédie humaine (The Human Comedy)* and continued adding to this work, eventually including about 90 novels.

Balzac brought great powers of observation—plus a photographic memory—to his work, but he also had sympathy for describing people's feelings and motivations. He is considered by many as the originator of naturalism in the novel.

The Mysterious Mansion

About a hundred yards from the town of Vendôme, on the borders of the Loire, there is an old gray house, surmounted by very high gables, and so completely isolated that neither tanyard[1] nor shabby hostelry, such as you may find at the entrance to all small towns, exists in its immediate neighborhood.

In front of this building, overlooking the river, is a garden where the once well-trimmed box borders that used to define the walks now grow wild as they list.[2] Several willows that spring from the Loire have grown as rapidly as the hedge that encloses it, and half conceal the house. The rich vegetation of those weeds that we call foul adorns the sloping shore. Fruit trees, neglected for the last ten years, no longer yield their harvest, and their shoots form coppices. The wallfruit grows like hedges against the walls. Paths once graveled are overgrown with moss, but, to tell the truth, there is no trace of a path. From the height of the hill, to which cling the ruins of the old castle of the Dukes of Vendôme, the only spot whence the eye can plunge into this enclosure, it strikes you that, at a time not easy to determine, this plot of land was a delight of a country gentleman, who cultivated roses and tulips and practiced horticulture in general, and who was besides a lover of fine fruit. An arbor is still visible, or rather the debris of an arbor, where there is a table that time has not quite destroyed. The aspect of this garden of bygone days suggests the negative joys of peaceful, provincial life, as one might reconstruct the life of a worthy tradesman by reading the epitaph on his tombstone. As if to complete the sweetness and sadness of the ideas that possess one's soul, one of the walls displays a sundial decorated with the following commonplace Christian inscription *Ultimam cogita*.[3] The roof of this house is horribly dilapidated, the shutters are always closed, the balconies are covered with swallows' nests, the doors are perpetually shut, weeds have drawn green lines in the cracks of the flights of steps, the locks and bolts are rusty.

---

1. tanyard: tannery. They were traditionally situated away from residential areas because of the smells.
2. list: choose.
3. *Ultimam cogita:* (Latin) "Think about the end"; that is, Judgment Day.

Sun, moon, winter, summer, all in turn have worn the panelling, warped the boards, gnawed the pain. The lugubrious silence which reigns there is only broken by birds, cats, martins, rats and mice, free to course to and fro, to fight and to eat each other. Truly, here an invisible hand has graven the word *mystery*.

Should your curiosity lead you to glance at this house from the side that points to the road, you would perceive a great door which the children of the place have riddled with holes. I afterward heard that this door had been closed for the last ten years. Through the holes bored by the boys you would have observed the perfect harmony that existed between the facades of both garden and courtyard. In both the same disorder prevails. Tufts of weed encircle the paving-stones. Enormous cracks furrow the walls, round whose blackened crests twine the thousand garlands of the creeping plants. The steps are out of joint, the wire of the bell is rusted, the spouts are cracked. What fire from heaven has fallen here? What tribunal has decreed that salt should be strewn on this dwelling?[4] Has God been blasphemed, has France been here betrayed? These are the questions we ask ourselves, but get no answer from the crawling things that haunt the place. The empty and deserted house is a gigantic enigma, of which the key is lost. In bygone times it was a small fief,[5] and bears the name of the Grande Bretêche.

I inferred that I was not the only person to whom my good landlady had communicated the secret of which I was to be the sole recipient, and I prepared to listen.

"Sir," she said, "when the Emperor sent the Spanish prisoners of war and others here, the government quartered on me a young Spaniard who had been sent to Vendôme on parole.[6] Parole notwithstanding, he went out every day to show himself to the *sous-préfet*.[7] He was a Spanish grandee![8] Nothing less! His name ended in *os* and *dia*, something like Burgos de Férédia. I have his name on my books; you can read it if you like. Oh! but he was a handsome young man for a Spaniard; they are all said to be ugly. He was only five feet and a few

---

4. **salt . . . dwelling:** When Roman soldiers destroyed Carthage in the third Punic War in 146 B.C., they sowed salt on its land to prevent the growth of crops.
5. **fief** (fēf): under feudalism, inheritable land held from a lord in exchange for service.
6. **parole:** word of honor.
7. ***sous-préfet:*** (French) assistant chief of police.
8. **grandee:** nobleman of the highest rank.

inches high, but he was well grown; he had small hands that he took such care of; ah! you should have seen! He had as many brushes for his hands as a woman for her whole dressing apparatus! He had thick black hair, a fiery eye; his skin was rather bronzed, but I liked the look of it. He wore the finest linen I have ever seen on anyone, although I have had princesses staying here, and, among others, General Bertrand, the Duke and Duchess d'Abrantzs, Monsieur Decazes and the King of Spain. He didn't eat much; but his manners were so polite, so amiable, that one could not bear him a grudge. Oh! I was very fond of him, although he didn't open his lips four times in the day, and it was impossible to keep up a conversation with him. For if you spoke to him, he did not answer. It was a fad, a mania with them all, I heard say. He read his breviary[9] like a priest, he went to mass and to all the services regularly. Where did he sit! Two steps from the chapel of Madame de Merret. As he took his place there the first time he went to church, nobody suspected him of any intention in so doing. Besides, he never raised his eyes from his prayer-book, poor young man! After that, sir, in the evening he would walk on the mountains, among the castle ruins. It was the poor man's only amusement, it reminded him of the country. They say that Spain is all mountains! From the commencement of his imprisonment he stayed out late. I was anxious when I found that he did not come home before midnight; but we got accustomed to this fancy[10] of his. He took the key of the door, and we left off sitting up for him. He lodged in a house of ours in the Rue des Casernes. After that, one of our stable-men told us that in the evening, when he led the horses to the water, he thought he had seen the Spanish grandee swimming far down the river like a live fish; when he returned, I told him to take care of the rushes; he appeared vexed to have been seen in the water. At last, one day, or rather one morning, we did not find him in his room; he had not returned. After searching everywhere, I found some writing in the drawer of a table, where there were fifty gold pieces of Spain that are called doubloons and were worth about five thousand francs; and ten thousand francs' worth of diamonds in a small sealed box. The writing said that in case he did not return, he left us the money and the diamonds, on condition we paid for masses to thank God for his escape, and for his salvation. In those days my hus-

---

9. **breviary** (brē′ və rē): prayer book.
10. **fancy:** inclination.

band had not been taken from me; he hastened to seek him everywhere.

"And now for the strange part of the story. He brought home the Spaniard's clothes, that he had discovered under a big stone by the riverside near the castle, nearly opposite to the Grande Bretêche. My husband had gone there so early that no one had seen him. After reading the letter, he burned the clothes, and according to Count Férédia's desire we declared that he had escaped. The *sous préfet* sent all the gendarmerie in pursuit of him; but I trust they never caught him. Leaps believed that the Spaniard had drowned himself. I, sir, don't think so; I am more inclined to believe that he had something to do with the affair of Madame de Merret, seeing that Rosalie told me that the crucifix that her mistress thought so much of, the one she had buried with her, was of ebony and silver. Now in the beginning of his stay here, Monsieur de Freed had one in ebony and silver, and I never saw him with it later. Now sir, don't you consider that I need have no scruples about the Spaniard's fifteen thousand francs, and that I have a right to them?"

"Certainly; but you haven't tried to question Rosalie?" I said.

"Oh, yes, indeed sir, but to no purpose! The girl's like a wall. She knows something, but it is impossible to get her to talk.

After exchanging a few more words with me, my landlady left me a prey to vague and gloomy thoughts, to a romantic curiosity and a religious terror not unlike the profound impression produced on us when by night, on entering a dark church, we perceive a faint light under high arches; a vague figure glides by—the rustle of a robe or cassock is heard, and we shudder.

Suddenly the Grand Bretêche and its tall weeds, its barred windows, its rusty ironwork, its closed doors, its deserted apartments, appeared like a fantastic apparition before me. I essayed to penetrate the mysterious dwelling, and to find the knot of its dark story—the drama that had killed three persons. In my eyes Rosalie became the most interesting person in Vendôme. As I studied her, I discovered traces of secret care, despite the radiant health that shone in her plump countenance. There was in her the germ of remorse or hope; her attitude revealed a secret, like the attitude of a bigot who prays to excess, or of the infanticide who ever hears the last cry of her child. Yet her manners were rough and ingenuous—her silly smile was not that of a criminal, and could you but have seen the great kerchief that encompassed her portly bust, framed and laced in by a lilac and blue cotton gown, you would have dubbed her innocent. No, I thought, I will not leave Vendôme without learning the history of the Grande Bretêche. To gain my ends I will strike up a friendship with Rosalie, if needs be.

"Rosalie," said I one evening.

"Sir?"

"You are not married?"

She started slightly.

"Oh, I can find plenty of men when the fancy takes me to be made miserable," she said laughing.

She soon recovered from the effects of her emotion, for all women, from the great lady to the maid of the inn, possess a composure that is peculiar to them.

"You are too good-looking and well favored to be short of lovers. But tell me Rosalie, why did you take service in an inn after leaving Madame de Merrett? Did she leave you nothing to live on?"

"Oh, yes! But, sir, my place is the best in all Vendôme."

The reply was one of those that judges and lawyers would call evasive. Rosalie appeared to me to be situated in this romantic history like the square in the midst of a chessboard. She was at the heart of the truth and chief interest; she seemed to me to be bound in the very know of it. The conquest of Rosalie was no longer to be an ordinary siege—in this girl was centered the last chapter of a novel, therefore from this moment Rosalie became the object of my preference.

One morning I said to Rosalie: "Tell me all you know about Madame de Merret."

"Oh!" she replied in terror, "do not ask that of me, Monsieur Horace."

Her pretty face fell—her clear, bright color faded—and her eyes lost their innocent brightness.

"Well, then," she said, "if you must have it so, I will tell you about it; but promise to keep my secret!"

"Done! my dear girl. I must keep your secret with the honor of a thief, which is the most loyal in the world."

Were I to transcribe Rosalie's diffuse eloquence faithfully, an entire volume would scarcely contain it; so I shall abridge.

The room occupied by Madame de Merret at the Bretêche was on the ground floor. A little closet about four feet deep, built in the thickness of the wall, served as her wardrobe.

Three months before the eventful evening of which I am about to speak, Madame de Merret had been so seriously indisposed that her husband had left her to herself in her own apartment while he occupied another on the first floor.[11] By one of those chances that it is impossible to foresee, he returned home from the club (where he was accustomed to read the papers and discuss politics with the inhabitants of the place) two hours later than usual. His wife supposed him to be at home, in bed and asleep. But the invasion of France had been the subject of a most animated discussion; the billiard-match had been exciting and he had lost forty francs, an enormous sum for Vendôme, where everyone hoards and where manners are restricted within the limits of a praiseworthy modesty, which perhaps is the source of the true happiness that no Parisian covets. For some time past Monsieur de Merret had been satisfied to ask Rosalie if his wife had gone to bed; and on her reply, which was always in the affirmative, had immediately gained his own room with the good temper engendered by habit and confidence. On entering his house, he took it into his head to go and tell his wife of his misadventure, perhaps by way of consolation. At dinner he had found Madame de Merret most coquettishly attired. On his way to the club it had occurred to him that his wife was restored to health, and that her convalescence had added to her beauty. He was, as husbands are wont to be, somewhat slow in making this discovery. Instead of calling Rosalie, who was occupied just then in watching the cook and coachman play a difficult hand at brisque,[12] Monsieur de Merret went to his wife's room by the light of a lantern that he deposited on the first step of the staircase. His unmistakable step resounded under the vaulted corridor. At the moment that the count turned the handle of his wife's door, he fancied he could hear the door of the closet I spoke of close; but when he entered Madame de Merret was alone before the fireplace. The husband thought ingenuously that Rosalie was in the closet yet a suspicion that jangled in his ear put him on his guard. He looked at his wife and saw in her eyes I know not what wild and hunted expression.

"You are very late," she said. Her habitually pure, sweet voice seemed changed to him.

---

11. first floor: in Europe, the first floor is on the second level, above the ground floor.
12. brisque: an old card game.

Monsieur de Merret did not reply, for at that moment Rosalie entered. It was a thunderbolt for him. He strode about the room, passing from one window to the other, with mechanical motion and folded arms.

"Have you heard bad news, or are you unwell?" inquired his wife timidly, while Rosalie undressed her.

He kept silent.

"You can leave me," said Madame de Merret to her maid; "I will put my hair in curl papers myself."

From the expression of her husband's face she foresaw trouble, and wished to be alone with him. When Rosalie had gone, or was supposed to have gone (for she lingered in the corridor for a few minutes), Monsieur de Merret came and stood in front of his wife, and said coldly to her: "Madame, there is someone in your closet!"

She looked calmly at her husband, and replied simply: "No, sir."

This answer was heartrending to Monsieur de Merret because he did not believe it. Yet his wife had never appeared to him purer or more saintly than at that moment. He rose to open the closet door.

Madame de Merret took his hand, looked at him with an expression of melancholy, and said in a voice that betrayed singular emotion: "If you find no one there, remember this, all will be over between us!"

The extraordinary dignity of his wife's manner restored the count's profound esteem for her, and inspired him with one of those resolutions that only lack a vaster stage to become immortal.

"No," said he. "Josephine, I will not go in there. In either case it would separate us for ever. Hear me. I know how pure you are at heart, and that your life is a holy one. You would not commit a mortal sin to save your life."

At these words Madame de Merret turned a haggard gaze upon her husband.

"Here, take your crucifix," he went on. "Swear to me before God that there is no one in there; I will believe you. I will never open that door."

Madame de Merret took the crucifix and said: "I swear."

"Louder," said the husband, "and repeat, 'I swear before God that there is no one in that closet.'"

She repeated the sentence calmly.

"That will do," said Monsieur de Merret, coldly.

After a moment of silence: "I never saw this pretty toy before," he said, examining the ebony crucifix inlaid with silver and most artistically chiselled.

"I found it at Duvivier's, who bought it of a Spanish monk when the prisoners passed through Vendôme last year."

"Ah!" said Monsieur de Merret, as he replaced the crucifix on the nail, and he rang. Rosalie did not keep him waiting. Monsieur de Merret went quickly to meet her, led her to the bay window that opened on to the garden and whispered to her: "Listen! I know that Gorenflot wishes to marry you; poverty is the only drawback, and you told him that you would be his wife if he found the means to establish himself as a master mason. Well! go and fetch him, tell him to come here, with his trowel and tools. Manage not to awaken anyone in his house but himself; his fortune will be more than your desires. Above all, leave this room without babbling, otherwise—" He frowned. Rosalie went away, he recalled her. "Here, take my latchkey," he said.

"Jean!" then cried Monsieur de Merret, in tones of thunder in the corridor. Jean, who was at the same time his coachman and his confidential servant, left his game of cards and came.

"Go to bed, all of you," said his master, then, signing to him to approach, added under his breath: "When they are all asleep—asleep, d'ye hear?—you will come down and tell me."

Monsieur de Merret, who had not lost sight of his wife all the time he was giving his orders, returned quietly to her at the fireside and began to tell her of the game of billiards and the talk of the club. When Rosalie returned she found Monsieur and Madame de Merret conversing very amicably.

The count had lately had all the ceiling of his reception rooms on the ground floor repaired. Plaster of Paris is difficult to obtain in Vendôme; the carriage raises its price. The count had therefore bought a good deal, being well aware that he could find plenty of purchasers for whatever might remain over. This circumstance inspired him with the design he was about to execute.

"Sir, Gorenflot has arrived," said Rosalie in low tones.

"Show him in," replied the count in loud tones.

Madame de Merret turned rather pale, when she saw the mason.

"Gorenflot," said her husband, "go and fetch bricks from the coach-house, and bring sufficient to wall up the door of this closet; you will use the plaster I have over to coat the wall with."

Then calling Rosalie and the workman aside: "Listen Gorenflot," he said in an undertone, "you will sleep here tonight. But tomorrow you will have a passport to a foreign country, to a town to which I will direct you. I shall give you six thousand francs for your journey. You will stay ten years in that town; if you do not like it, you may establish yourself in another, provided it be in the same country. You will pass through Paris, where you will await me. There I will ensure you an additional six thousand francs by contract, which will be paid to you on your return, provided you have fulfilled the conditions of our bargain. This is the price for your absolute silence as to what you are about to do tonight. As to you, Rosalie, I will give you ten thousand francs on the day of your wedding, on condition of your marrying Gorenflot; but if you wish to marry, you must hold your tongues; or—no dowry."

"Rosalie," said Madame de Merret, "do my hair."

The husband walked calmly up and down, watching the door, the mason, and his wife, but without betraying any insulting doubts. Madame de Merret chose a moment when the workman was unloading bricks and her husband was at the other end of the room to say to Rosalie: "A thousand francs a year for you, my child, if you can tell Gorenflot to leave a chink at the bottom." Then out loud, she added coolly: "Go and help him!"

Monsieur and Madame de Merret were silent all the time that Gorenflot took to brick up the door. This silence on the part of the husband, who did not choose to furnish his wife with a pretext for saying things of a double meaning, had its purpose; on the part of Madame de Merret it was either pride or prudence. When the wall was about halfway up, the sly workman took advantage of a moment when the count's back was turned to strike a blow with his trowel in one of the glass panes of the closet-door. This act informed Madame de Merret that Rosalie had spoken to Gorenflot.

All three then saw a man's face; it was dark and gloomy with black hair and eyes of flame. Before her husband turned, the poor woman had time to make a sign to the stranger that signified hope.

At four o'clock, towards dawn, for it was the month of September, the construction was finished. The mason was handed over to the care of Jean, and Monsieur de Merret went to be in his wife's room.

On rising the following morning, he said carelessly: "The deuce! I must go to the mairie[13] for the passport." He put his hat on his head,

---

13. **mairie:** (French) town hall.

advanced three steps towards the door, altered his mind and took the crucifix.

His wife trembled for joy. "He is going to Duvivier," she thought. As soon as the count had left, Madame de Merret rang for Rosalie; then in a terrible voice: "The trowel, the trowel!" she cried, "and quick, to work! I saw how Gorenflot did it; we shall have time to make a hole and to mend it again."

In the twinkling of an eye, Rosalie brought a sort of mattock[14] to her mistress, who with unparalleled ardor set about demolishing the wall. She had already knocked out several bricks and was preparing to strike a more decisive blow when she perceived Monsieur de Merret behind her. She fainted.

"Lay Madame on her bed," said the count coldly. He had foreseen what would happen in his absence and had set a trap for his wife; he had simply written to the mayor, and had sent for Duvivier. The jeweller arrived just as the room had been put in order.

"Duvivier," inquired the count, "did you buy crucifixes of the Spaniards who passed through here?"

"No, sir."

"That will do, thank you," he said, looking at his wife like a tiger. "Jean," he added, "you will see that my meals are served in the countess's room; she is ill and I shall not leave her until she has recovered."

The cruel gentleman stayed with his wife for twenty days. In the beginning, when there were sounds in the walled closet, and Josephine attempted to implore his pity for the dying stranger, he replied, without permitting her to say a word: "You have sworn on the cross that there is no one there."

---

14. **mattock:** a tool like a pickaxe.

Discussion Questions

1. Why do you think the author begins this story with a description of the abandoned Grande Brêteche, years after the events involving Monsieur and Madame de Merret and Count Férédia?

2. Why might Rosalie tell the story to the narrator when she has refused to tell it to the landlady?

3. Describe the character of Monsieur de Merret.

4. Trace the role the crucifix plays in this story.

5. How is Monsieur de Merret able to get away with his deed?

Suggestion for Writing

Monsieur de Merret stays in his wife's rooms for 20 days to make sure she cannot rescue Count Férédia. Suppose that the husband and wife nevertheless have sufficient solitude for a few quick jottings in their diaries. Imagine that you are Monsieur or Madame de Merret and write at least four diary entries that cover those 20 days. Both husband and wife might tell of sounds coming from inside the closet and how they react to them. Madame might complain of her husband's great cruelty and despair over her lover's fate. Monsieur might congratulate himself for his cleverness and take pleasure at watching his wife's suffering.

E. F. Benson (1867-1940)

Edward F. Benson was born into a religious family; his father became Archbishop of Canterbury, and two of his brothers also became important in the Church of England. The Bensons were a literary family as well, every member of the family publishing prose and verse in magazines. Benson's education was in the classics and in archaeology, but his first book *Dodo* (1893) was a glittering comedy of manners. It became immediately and extremely popular, and Benson adapted it as a play before writing two sequels. His most memorable character, Lucia, moves in the same social circles, full of gossip, rivalry, and intense concentration on essentially petty affairs. Benson served as mayor of Rye and was honored for his literary achievements. In addition to his dozens of novels, Benson wrote short stories—including several volumes of ghost stories—plays, essays, biographies, and contemporary histories.

Mrs. Amworth

The village of Maxley, where, last summer and autumn, these strange events took place, lies on a heathery and pine-clad upland of Sussex. In all England you could not find a sweeter and saner situation. Should the wind blow from the south, it comes laden with the spices of the sea; to the east high downs protect it from the inclemencies of March; and from the west and north the breezes which reach it travel over miles of aromatic forest and heather. The village itself is insignificant enough in point of population, but rich in amenities and beauty. Halfway down the single street, with its broad road and spacious areas of grass on each side, stands the little Norman Church and the antique graveyard long disused: for the rest there are a dozen small, sedate Georgian houses, red-bricked and long-windowed, each with a square of flower garden in front, and an ampler strip behind; a score of shops, and a couple of score of thatched cottages belonging to laborers on neighboring estates, complete the entire cluster of its peaceful habitations. The general peace, however, is sadly broken on Saturdays and Sundays, for we lie on one of the main roads between London and Brighton and our quiet street becomes a race course for flying motorcars and bicycles. A notice just outside the village begging them to go slowly only seems to encourage them to accelerate their speed, for the road lies open and straight, and there is really no reason why they should do otherwise. By way of protest, therefore, the ladies of Maxley cover their noses and mouths with their handkerchiefs as they see a motor-car approaching, though, as the street is asphalted, they need not really take these precautions against dust. But late on Sunday night the horde of scorchers has passed, and we settle down again to five days of cheerful and leisurely seclusion. Railway strikes which agitate the country so much leave us undisturbed because most of the inhabitants of Maxley never leave it at all.

I am the fortunate possessor of one of these small Georgian houses, and consider myself no less fortunate in having so interesting and stimulating a neighbor as Francis Urcombe, who, the most confirmed of Maxleyites, has not slept away from his house, which stands just opposite to mine in the village street, for nearly two years, at which date, though still in middle life, he resigned his Physiological

Professorship at Cambridge University, and devoted himself to the study of those occult and curious phenomena which seem equally to concern the physician and the psychical sides of human nature. Indeed his retirement was not unconnected with his passion for the strange uncharted places that lie on the confines and borders of science, the existence of which is so stoutly denied by the more materialistic minds, for he advocated that all medical students should be obliged to pass some sort of examination in mesmerism,[1] and that one of the tripos papers[2] should be designed to test their knowledge in such subjects as appearances at time of death, haunted houses, vampirism, automatic writing,[3] and possession.

"Of course they wouldn't listen to me," ran his account of the matter, "for there is nothing that these seats of learning are so frightened of as knowledge, and the road to knowledge lies in the study of things like those. The functions of the human frame are, broadly speaking, known. They are a county, anyhow, that has been charted and mapped out. But outside that lie huge tracts of undiscovered country, which certainly exist, and the real pioneers of knowledge are those who, at the cost of being derided as credulous and superstitious, want to push on into those misty and probably perilous places. I felt that I could be of more use by setting out without compass or knapsack into the mists than by sitting in a cage like a canary and chirping about what was known. Besides, teaching is very, very bad for a man who knows himself only to be a learner: you only need to be a self-conceited ass to teach."

Here, then, in Francis Urcombe, was a delightful neighbor to one who, like myself, has an uneasy and burning curiosity about what he called the "misty and perilous places"; and this last spring we had a further and most welcome addition to our pleasant little community, in the person of Mrs. Amworth, widow of an Indian civil servant. Her husband had been a judge in the Northwest Provinces, and after his death at Peshawar she came back to England, and after a year in London found herself starving for the ampler air and sunshine of the

---

1. mesmerism: hypnotism, especially as practiced by physician Anton Mesmer (1734–1815).
2. tripos papers: honors examinations at Cambridge University.
3. automatic writing: writing thought to be produced by a medium under control of a spirit.

country to take the place of the fogs and griminess of town. She had, too, a special reason for settling in Maxley, since her ancestors up till a hundred years ago had long been native to the place, and in the old churchyard, now disused, are many gravestones bearing her maiden name of Chaston. Big and energetic, her vigorous and genial personality speedily woke Maxley up to a higher degree of sociality than it had ever known. Most of us were bachelors or spinsters or elderly folk not much inclined to exert ourselves in the expense and effort of hospitality, and hitherto the gaiety of a small tea party, with bridge afterwards and galoshes (when it was wet) to trip home in again for a solitary dinner, was about the climax of our festivities. But Mrs. Amworth showed us a more gregarious way, and set an example of luncheon parties and little dinners, which we began to follow. On other nights when no such hospitality was on foot, a lone man like myself found it pleasant to know that a call on the telephone to Mrs. Amworth's house not a hundred yards off, and an enquiry as to whether I might come over after dinner for a game of piquet[4] before bedtime, would probably evoke a response of welcome. There she would be, with a comradelike eagerness for companionship, and there was a glass of port and a cup of coffee and a cigarette and a game of piquet. She played the piano, too, in a free and exuberant manner, and had a charming voice and sang to her own accompaniment; and as the days grew long and the light lingered late, we played our game in her garden, which in the course of a few months she had turned from being a nursery for slugs and snails into a glowing patch of luxuriant blossomings. She was always cheery and jolly; she was interested in everything; and in music, in gardening, in games of all sorts was a competent performer. Everybody (with one exception) liked her, everybody felt her to bring with her the tonic of a sunny day. That one exception was Francis Urcombe; he, though he confessed he did not like her, acknowledged that he was vastly interested in her. This always seemed strange to me, for pleasant and jovial as she was, I could see nothing in her that could call forth conjecture of intrigued surmise, so healthy and unmysterious a figure did she present. But of the genuineness of Urcombe's interest there could be no doubt; one could see him watching and scrutinizing her. In matter of age, she frankly volunteered the information that she was forty-five; but her briskness, her activity, her unravaged skin, her coal-black hair,

---

4. piquet: (pi kā) game of cards for two players.

made it difficult to believe that she was not adopting an unusual device, and adding ten years on to her age instead of subtracting them.

Often, also, as our quite unsentimental friendship ripened, Mrs. Amworth would ring me up and propose her advent.[5] If I was busy writing, I was to give her, so we definitely bargained, a frank negative, and in answer I could hear her jolly laugh and her wishes for a successful evening of work. Sometimes, before her proposal arrived, Urcombe would already have stepped across from his house opposite for a smoke and a chat, and he, hearing who my intended visitor was, always urged me to beg her to come. She and I should play our piquet, said he, and he would look on, if we did not object, and learn something of the game. But I doubt whether he paid much attention to it, for nothing could be clearer than that, under that penthouse of forehead and thick eyebrows, his attention was fixed not on the cards, but on one of the players. But he seemed to enjoy an hour spent thus, and often, until one particular evening in July, he would watch her with the air of a man who has some deep problem in front of him. She, enthusiastically keen about our game, seemed not to notice his scrutiny. Then came that evening when, as I see in the light of subsequent events, began the first twitching of the veil that hid the secret horror from my eyes. I did not know it then, though I noticed that thereafter, if she rang up to propose coming round, she always asked not only if I was at leisure, but whether Mr. Urcombe was with me. If so, she said, she would not spoil the chat of two old bachelors, and laughingly wished me good night. Urcombe, on this occasion, had been with me for some half-hour before Mrs. Amworth's appearance, and had been talking to me about the medieval beliefs concerning vampirism, one of those borderland subjects which he declared had not been sufficiently studied before it had been consigned by the medical profession to the dustheap of exploded superstitions. There he sat, grim and eager, tracing with that pellucid[6] clearness which had made him in his Cambridge days so admirable a lecturer, the history of those mysterious visitations. In them all there were the same general features: one of those ghoulish spirits took up its abode in a living man or woman, conferring supernatural powers of batlike flight and glutting itself with nocturnal blood feasts. When its host died it continued to dwell in the corpse, which

---

5. **advent:** coming.
6. **pellucid:** simple in style.

remained undecayed. By day it rested, by night it left the grave and went on its awful errands. No European country in the Middle Ages seemed to have escaped them; earlier yet, parallels were to be found in Roman and Greek and in Jewish history.

"It's a large order to set all that evidence aside as being moonshine," he said. "Hundreds of totally independent witnesses in many ages have testified to the occurrence of these phenomena, and there's no explanation known to me which covers all the facts. And if you feel inclined to say, 'Why, then, if these are facts, do we not come across them now?' there are two answers I can make you. One is that there were diseases known in the Middle Ages, such as the Black Death, which were certainly existent then and which have become extinct since, but for that reason we do not assert that such diseases never existed. Just as the Black Death visited England and decimated the population of Norfolk, so here in this very district about three hundred years ago there was certainly an outbreak of vampirism, and Maxley was the center of it. My second answer is even more convincing, for I tell you that vampirism is by no means extinct now. An outbreak of it certainly occurred in India a year or two ago."

At that moment I heard my knocker plied in the cheerful and peremptory[7] manner in which Mrs. Amworth is accustomed to announce her arrival, and I went to the door to open it.

"Come in at once," I said, "and save me from having my blood curdled. Mr. Urcombe has been trying to alarm me."

Instantly her vital, voluminous presence seemed to fill the room. "Ah, but how lovely!" she said. "I delight in having my blood curdled. Go on with your ghost story, Mr. Urcombe. I adore ghost stories."

I saw that, as his habit was, he was intently observing her. "It wasn't a ghost story exactly," said he. "I was only telling our host how vampirism was not extinct yet. I was saying that there was an outbreak of it in India only a few years ago."

There was a more than perceptible pause, and I saw that, if Urcombe was observing her, she on her side was observing him with fixed eye and parted mouth. Then her jolly laugh invaded that rather tense silence.

"Oh, what a shame!" she said. "You're not going to curdle my blood at all. Where did you pick up such a tale, Mr. Urcombe? I have

---

7. peremptory: commanding.

lived for years in India and never heard a rumor of such a thing. Some storyteller in the bazaars must have invented it: they are famous at that."

I could see that Urcombe was on the point of saying something further, but checked himself.

"Ah! very likely that was it," he said.

But something had disturbed our usual peaceful sociability that night, and something had damped Mrs. Amworth's usual high spirits. She had no gusto for her piquet, and left after a couple of games. Urcombe had been silent too. Indeed he hardly spoke again till she departed.

"That was unfortunate," he said, "for the outbreak of—of a very mysterious disease, let us call it, took place at Peshawar where she and her husband were. And—"

"Well?" I asked.

"He was one of the victims of it," said he. "Naturally I had quite forgotten that when I spoke."

The summer was unseasonably hot and rainless, and Maxley suffered much from drought, and also from a plague of big black night-flying gnats, the bite of which was very irritating and virulent. They came sailing in of an evening, settling on one's skin so quietly that one perceived nothing till the sharp stab announced that one had been bitten. They did not bite the hands or face, but chose always the neck and throat for their feeding ground, and most of us, as the poison spread, assumed a temporary goiter.[8] Then about the middle of August appeared the first of those mysterious cases of illness which our local doctor attributed to the long-continued heat coupled with the bite of these venomous insects. The patient was a boy of sixteen or seventeen, the son of Mrs. Amworth's gardener, and the symptoms were an anemic pallor and a languid prostration, accompanied by great drowsiness and an abnormal appetite. He had, too, on his throat two small punctures where, so Dr. Ross conjectured, one of these great gnats had bitten him. But the odd thing was that there was no swelling or inflammation round the place where he had been bitten. The heat at this time had begun to abate, but the cooler weather failed to restore him, and the boy, in spite of the quantity of food which he so ravenously swallowed, wasted away to a skin-clad skeleton.

---

8. goiter: swelling in the neck.

I met Dr. Ross in the street one afternoon about this time, and in answer to my enquiries about his patient he said that he was afraid the boy was dying. The case, he confessed, completely puzzled him: some obscure form of pernicious anemia[9] was all he could suggest. But he wondered whether Mr. Urcombe would consent to see the boy, on the chance of his being able to throw some new light on the case, and since Urcombe was dining with me that night, I proposed to Dr. Ross to join us. He could not do this, but he said he would look in later. When he came, Urcombe at once consented to put his skill at the other's disposal, and together they went off at once. Being thus shorn of my sociable evening, I telephoned Mrs. Amworth to know if I might inflict myself on her for an hour. Her answer was a welcoming affirmative, and between piquet and music the hour lengthened itself into two. She spoke of the boy who was lying so desperately and mysteriously ill, and told me that she had often been to see him, taking him nourishing and delicate food. But today—and her kind eyes moistened as she spoke—she was afraid she had paid her last visit. Knowing the antipathy between her and Urcombe, I did not tell her that he had been called into consultation; and when I returned home she accompanied me to my door, for the sake of a breath of night air, and in order to borrow a magazine which contained an article on gardening which she wished to read.

"Ah, this delicious night air," she said, luxuriously sniffing in the coolness. "Night air and gardening are the great tonics. There is nothing so stimulating as bare contact with rich mother earth. You are never so fresh as when you have been grubbing in the soil—black hands, black nails, and boots covered with mud." She gave her great jovial laugh.

"I'm a glutton for air and earth," she said. "Positively I look forward to death, for then I shall be buried and have the kind earth all round me. No leaden caskets for me—I have given explicit directions. But what shall I do about air? Well, I suppose one can't have everything. The magazine? A thousand thanks, I will faithfully return it. Good night: garden and keep your windows open, and you won't have anemia."

"I always sleep with my windows open," said I.

I went straight up to my bedroom, of which one of the windows looks out over the street, and as I undressed I thought I heard voices

---

9. pernicious anemia: pale, weak condition, with gradual lessening in number of red blood cells.

talking outside not far away. But I paid no particular attention, put out my lights, and falling asleep plunged into the depths of a most horrible dream, distortedly suggested, no doubt, by my last words with Mrs. Amworth. I dreamed that I woke, and found that both my bedroom windows were shut. Half-suffocating, I dreamed that I sprang out of bed, and went across to open them. The blind over the first one was drawn down, and pulling it up I saw, with the indescribable horror of incipient nightmare, Mrs. Amworth's face suspended close to the pane in the darkness outside, nodding and smiling at me. Pulling down the blind again to keep that terror out, I rushed to the second window on the other side of the room, and there again was Mrs. Amworth's face. Then the panic came upon me in full blast; here was I suffocating in the airless room, and whichever window I opened Mrs. Amworth's face would float in, like those noiseless black gnats that bit before one was aware. The nightmare rose to screaming point, and with strangled yells I awoke to find my room cool and quiet with both windows open and blinds up and a half-moon high in its course, casting an oblong of tranquil light on the floor. But even when I was awake the horror persisted, and I lay tossing and turning. I must have slept long before the nightmare seized me, for now it was nearly day, and soon in the east the drowsy eyelids of morning began to lift.

I was scarcely downstairs next morning—for after the dawn I slept late—when Urcombe rang up to know if he might see me immediately. He came in, grim and preoccupied, and I noticed that he was pulling on a pipe that was not even filled.

"I want your help," he said, "and so I must tell you first of all what happened last night. I went round with the little doctor to see his patient, and found him just alive, but scarcely more. I instantly diagnosed in my own mind what this anemia, unaccountable by any other explanation, meant. The boy is the prey of a vampire."

He put his empty pipe on the breakfast table, by which I had just sat down, and folded his arms, looking at me steadily from under his overhanging brows.

"Now about last night," he said. "I insisted that he should be moved from his father's cottage into my house. As we were carrying him on a stretcher, whom should we meet but Mrs. Amworth? She expressed shocked surprise that we were moving him. Now why do you think she did that?"

With a start of horror, as I remembered my dream that night before, I felt an idea come into my mind so preposterous and unthinkable that I instantly turned it out again.

"I haven't the smallest idea," I said.

"Then listen, while I tell you about what happened later. I put out all light in the room where the boy lay, and watched. One window was a little open, for I had forgotten to close it, and about midnight I heard something outside, trying apparently to push it farther open. I guessed who it was—yes, it was full twenty feet from the ground—and I peeped round the corner of the blind. Just outside was the face of Mrs. Amworth and her hand was on the frame of the window. Very softly I crept close, and then banged the window down, and I think I just caught the tip of one of her fingers."

"But it's impossible," I cried. "How could she be floating in the air like that? And what had she come for? Don't tell me such—"

Once more, with closer grip, the remembrance of my nightmare seized me.

"I am telling you what I saw," said he. "And all night long, until it was nearly day, she was fluttering outside, like some terrible bat, trying to gain admittance. Now put together various things I have told you."

He began checking them off on his fingers.

"Number one," he said: "there was an outbreak of disease similar to that which this boy is suffering from at Peshawar, and her husband died of it. Number two: Mrs. Amworth protested against my moving the boy to my house. Number three: she, or the demon that inhabits her body, a creature powerful and deadly, tries to gain admittance. And add this, too: in medieval times there was an epidemic of vampirism here at Maxley. The vampire, so the accounts run, was found to be Elizabeth Chaston . . . I see you remember Mrs. Amworth's maiden name. Finally, the boy is stronger this morning. He would certainly not have been alive if he had been visited again. And what do you make of it?"

There was a long silence, during which I found this incredible horror assuming the hues of reality.

"I have something to add," I said, "which may or may not bear on it. You say that the—the specter went away shortly before dawn."

"Yes."

I told him of my dream, and he smiled grimly.

"Yes, you did well to awake," he said. "That warning came from your subconscious self, which never wholly slumbers, and cried out to you of deadly danger. For two reasons, then, you must help me: one to save others, the second to save yourself."

"What do you want me to do?" I asked.

"I want you first of all to help me in watching this boy, and ensuring that she does not come near him. Eventually I want you to help me in tracking the thing down, in exposing and destroying it. It is not human; it is an incarnate fiend. What steps we shall have to take I don't yet know."

It was now eleven of the forenoon, and presently I went across to his house for a twelve-hour vigil while he slept, to come on duty again that night, so that for the next twenty-four hours either Urcombe or myself was always in the room where the boy, now getting stronger every hour, was lying. The day following was Saturday and a morning of brilliant, pellucid weather, and already when I went across to his house to resume my duty the stream of motors down to Brighton had begun. Simultaneously I saw Urcombe with a cheerful face, which boded good news of his patient, coming out of his house, and Mrs. Amworth, with a gesture of salutation to me and a basket in her hand, walking up the broad strip of grass which bordered the road. There we all three met. I noticed (and saw that Urcombe noticed it, too) that one finger of her left hand was bandaged.

"Good morning to you both," said she. "And I hear your patient is doing well, Mr. Urcombe. I have come to bring him a bowl of jelly, and to sit with him for an hour. He and I are great friends. I am overjoyed at his recovery."

Urcombe paused a moment, as if making up his mind, and then shot out a pointing finger at her.

"I forbid that," he said. "You shall not sit with him or see him. And you know the reason as well as I do."

I have never seen so horrible a change pass over a human face as that which now blanched hers to the color of a gray mist. She put up her hand as if to shield herself from that pointing finger, which drew the sign of the cross in the air, and shrank back cowering on to the road. There was a wild hoot from a horn, a grinding of brakes, a shout—too late—from a passing car, and one long scream suddenly cut short. Her body rebounded from the roadway after the first wheel had gone over it, and the second followed it. It lay there, quivering and twitching, and was still.

She was buried three days afterwards in the cemetery outside Maxley, in accordance with the wishes she had told me that she had devised about her interment, and the shock which her sudden and awful death had caused to the little community began by degrees to pass off. To two people only, Urcombe and myself, the horror of it was mitigated from the first by the nature of the relief that her death brought; but, naturally enough, we kept our own counsel, and no hint of what greater horror had been thus averted was ever let slip. But, oddly enough, so it seemed to me, he was still not satisfied about something in connection with her, and would give no answer to my questions on the subject. Then as the days of a tranquil mellow September and the October that followed began to drop away like the leaves of the yellowing trees, his uneasiness relaxed. But before the entry of November the seeming tranquillity broke into hurricane.

I had been dining one night at the far end of the village, and about eleven o'clock was walking home again. The moon was of an unusual brilliance, rendering all that it shone on as distinct as in some etching. I had just come opposite the house which Mrs. Amworth had occupied, where there was a board up telling that it was to let, when I heard the click of her front gate, and the next moment I saw, with a sudden chill and quaking of my very spirit, that she stood there. Her profile, vividly illuminated, was turned to me, and I could not be mistaken in my identification of her. She appeared not to see me (indeed the shadow of the yew hedge in front of her garden enveloped me in its blackness) and she went swiftly across the road, and entered the gate of the house directly opposite. There I lost sight of her completely.

My breath was coming in short pants as if I had been running—and now indeed I ran, with fearful backward glances, along the hundred yards that separated me from my house and Urcombe's. It was to his that my flying steps took me, and the next minute I was within.

"What have you come to tell me?" he asked. "Or shall I guess?"

"You can't guess," said I.

"No; it's no guess. She has come back and you have seen her. Tell me about it."

I gave him my story.

"That's Major Pearsall's house," he said. "Come back with me there at once."

"But what can we do?" I asked.

"I've no idea. That's what we have got to find out."

A minute later, we were opposite the house. When I had passed it before, it was all dark; now lights gleamed from a couple of windows upstairs. Even as we faced it, the front door opened, and next moment Major Pearsall emerged from the gate. He saw us and stopped. "I'm on my way to Dr. Ross," he said quickly. "My wife has been taken suddenly ill. She had been in bed an hour when I came upstairs, and I found her white as a ghost and utterly exhausted. She had been to sleep, it seemed—But you will excuse me."

"One moment, Major," said Urcombe. "Was there any mark on her throat?"

"How did you guess that?" said he. "There was: one of those beastly gnats must have bitten her twice there. She was streaming with blood."

"And there's someone with her?" asked Urcombe.

"Yes, I roused her maid."

He went off, and Urcombe turned to me. "I know now what we have to do," he said. "Change your clothes, and I'll join you at your house."

"What is it?" I asked.

"I'll tell you on our way. We're going to the cemetery."

He carried a pick, a shovel, and a screwdriver when he rejoined me, and wore round his shoulders a long coil of rope. As we walked, he gave me the outlines of the ghastly hour that lay before us.

"What I have to tell you," he said, "will seem to you now too fantastic for credence, but before dawn we shall see whether it outstrips reality. By a most fortunate happening, you saw the specter, the astral body,[10] whatever you choose to call it, of Mrs. Amworth, going on its grisly business, and therefore, beyond doubt, the vampire spirit which abode in her during life animates her again in death. That is not exceptional—indeed, all these weeks since her death I have been expecting it. If I am right, we shall find her body undecayed and untouched by corruption."

"But she has been dead nearly two months," said I.

"If she had been dead two years it would still be so, if the vampire has possession of her. So remember: whatever you see done, it will be done not to her, who in the natural course would now be feeding the grasses above her grave, but to a spirit of untold evil and malignancy, which gives a phantom life to her body."

"But what shall I see done?" said I.

---

10. **astral body:** spirit form.

"I will tell you. We know that now, at this moment, the vampire clad in her mortal semblance is out; dining out. But it must get back before dawn, and it will pass into the material form that lies in her grave. We must wait for that, and then with your help I shall dig up her body. If I am right, you will look on her as she was in life, with the full vigor of the dreadful nutriment she has received pulsing in her veins. And then, when dawn has come, and the vampire cannot leave the lair of her body, I shall strike her with this" —and he pointed to his pick— "through the heart, and she, who comes to life again only with the animation the fiend gives her, she and her hellish partner will be dead indeed. Then we must bury her again, delivered at last."

We had come to the cemetery, and in the brightness of the moonshine there was no difficulty in identifying her grave. It lay some twenty yards from the small chapel in the porch of which, obscured by shadow, we concealed ourselves. From there we had a clear and open sight of the grave, and now we must wait till its infernal visitor returned home. The night was warm and windless, yet even if a freezing wind had been raging I think I should have felt nothing of it, so intense was my preoccupation as to what the night and dawn would bring. There was a bell in the turret of the chapel that struck the quarters of the hour, and it amazed me to find how swiftly the chimes succeeded one another.

The moon had long set, but a twilight of stars shone in a clear sky, when five o'clock of the morning sounded from the turret. A few minutes more passed, and then I felt Urcombe's hand softly nudging me; and looking out in the direction of his pointing finger, I saw that the form of a woman, tall and large in build, was approaching from the right. Noiselessly, with a motion more of gliding and floating than walking, she moved across the cemetery to the grave which was the center of our observation. She moved round it as if to be certain of its identity, and for a moment stood directly facing us. In the grayness to which now my eyes had grown accustomed, I could easily see her face, and recognize its features.

She drew her hand across her mouth as if wiping it, and broke into a chuckle of such laughter as made my hair stir on my head. Then she leaped onto the grave, holding her hands high above her head, and inch by inch disappeared into the earth. Urcombe's hand was laid on my arm, in an injunction to keep still, but now he removed it.

"Come," he said.

With pick and shovel and rope we went to the grave. The earth was light and sandy, and soon after six struck we had delved down to the coffin lid. With his pick he loosened the earth round it, and, adjusting the rope through the handles by which it had been lowered, we tried to raise it. This was a long and laborious business, and the light had begun to herald day in the east before we had it out, and lying by the side of the grave. With his screwdriver he loosed the fastenings of the lid, and slid it aside, and standing there we looked on the face of Mrs. Amworth. The eyes, once closed in death, were open, the cheeks were flushed with color, the red, full-lipped mouth seemed to smile.

"One blow and it is all over," he said. "You need not look."

Even as he spoke he took up the pick again, and, laying the point of it on her left breast, measured his distance. And though I knew what was coming I could not look away. . . .

He grasped the pick in both hands, raised it an inch or two for the taking of his aim, and then with full force brought it down on her breast. A fountain of blood, though she had been dead for so long, spouted high in the air, falling with the thud of a heavy splash over the shroud, and simultaneously from those red lips came one long, appalling cry, swelling up like some hooting siren, and dying away again. With that, instantaneous as a lightning flash, came the touch of corruption on her face, the color of it faded to ash, the plump cheeks fell in, the mouth dropped.

"Thank God, that's over," said he, and without pause slipped the coffin lid back into its place.

Day was coming fast now, and, working like men possessed, we lowered the coffin into its place again, and shoveled the earth over it. . . . The birds were busy with their earliest pipings as we went back to Maxley.

Discussion Questions

1. How does this story compare with other vampire tales you have read or seen dramatized?

2. Summarize Francis Urcombe's theory of knowledge known and unknown.

3. Describe Mrs. Amworth's physical appearance and behavior. Does she seem to you like a typical vampire? Why or why not?

4. What convinces Urcombe that Mrs. Amworth is an evil creature? Do you find his argument convincing? Explain.

5. Describe the destruction of Mrs. Amworth's body. Does this prove Urcombe's case against her? Explain.

Suggestion for Writing

Imagine that you are Francis Urcombe, wanting to warn the other residents of Maxley against further vampire infestation. How will you go about it? Will you call a village meeting, or speak privately to people one at a time? Will you explain your case against Mrs. Amworth—and most important, will you describe what you did to her body? Write a speech telling the villagers how to be on guard, with or without warning them specifically what they must guard against.

Ambrose Bierce (1842-1914?)

Ambrose Bierce was the youngest of a large, poor Ohio farming family. At 15 he left home and spent two years as a printer's apprentice. The only schooling he received was a year at the Kentucky Military Institute. When the Civil War broke out, he enlisted as a drummer boy, but by fighting bravely in some difficult battles he earned the honorary rank of major. He went on to write short, satiric pieces for a San Francisco weekly newspaper, was given his own column, and soon became editor of the paper. Bierce became known for his witty and merciless criticism. His fiction was distinguished by its strange, psychological twists, and some of his short stories are now considered classics. Bierce spent a number of his later years in Washington, D.C., exposing political corruption. In 1913, at the age of 71, he left to cover the Mexican Revolution and simply disappeared.

The Damned Thing

I

One Does Not Always Eat What Is on the Table

By the light of a tallow candle which had been placed on one end of a rough table a man was reading something written in a book. It was an old account book, greatly worn, and the writing was not, apparently, very legible, for the man sometimes held the page close to the flame of the candle to get a stronger light on it. The shadow of the book would then throw into obscurity a half of the room, darkening a number of faces and figures, for besides the reader, eight other men were present. Seven of them sat against the rough log walls, silent, motionless, and the room being small, not very far from the table. By extending an arm any one of them could have touched the eighth man, who lay on the table, face upward, partly covered by a sheet, his arms at his sides. He was dead.

The man with the book was not reading aloud, and no one spoke; all seemed to be waiting for something to occur; the dead man only was without expectations. From the black darkness outside came in through the aperture that served for a window, all the ever familiar noises of night in the wilderness—the long nameless note of a distant coyote; the silly pulsing thrill of tireless insects in trees, strange cries of night birds, so different from those of the birds of day; the drone of great blundering beetles, and all that mysterious chorus of small sounds that seem always to have been but half heard when they have suddenly ceased, as if conscious of an indiscretion. But nothing of all this was noted in that company, its members were not overmuch addicted to idle interest in matters of no practical importance; that was obvious in every line of their rugged faces—obvious even in the dim light of the single candle. They were evidently men of the vicinity—farmers and woodsmen.

The person reading was a trifle different; one would have said of him that he was of the world, worldly, albeit there was that in his attire which attested a certain fellowship with the organisms of his environment. His coat would hardly have passed muster in San Francisco, his footgear was not of urban origin, and the hat that lay by him on the floor (he was the only one uncovered) was such that if one had considered it as an article of mere personal adornment one would have missed its meaning. In countenance the man was rather prepossessing, with just a hint of sternness; though that he may have assumed or cultivated, as appropriate to one in authority. For he was a coroner. It was by virtue of his office that he had possession of the book in which he was reading; it had been found among the dead man's effects—in his cabin, where the inquest was now taking place.

When the coroner had finished reading he put the book into his breast pocket. At that moment the door was pushed open and a young man entered. He, clearly, was not of mountain birth and breeding: he was clad as those who dwell in cities. His clothing was dusty, however, as from travel. He had, in fact, been riding hard to attend the inquest.

The coroner nodded; no one else greeted him.

"We have waited for you," said the coroner. "It is necessary to have done with this business tonight."

The young man smiled. "I am sorry to have kept you," he said. "I went away, not to evade your summons, but to post to my newspaper an account of what I suppose I am called back to relate."

The coroner smiled.

"The account that you posted to your newspaper," he said, "differs, probably, from that which you will give her under oath."

"That," replied the other, rather hotly and with a visible flush, "is as you please. I used manifold paper[1] and I have a copy of what I sent. It was not written as news, for it is incredible, but as fiction. It may go as a part of my testimony under oath."

"But you say it is incredible."

"That is nothing to you, sir, if I also swear that it is true."

The coroner was silent for a time, his eyes upon the floor. The men about the sides of the cabin talked in whispers, but seldom withdrew their gaze from the face of the corpse. Presently the coroner lifted his eyes and said, "We will resume the inquest."

The men removed their hats. The witness was sworn.

"What is your name?" the coroner asked.

"William Harker."

---

1. **manifold paper:** carbon paper.

"Age?"

"Twenty-seven."

"You know the deceased, Hugh Morgan?"

"Yes."

"You were with him when he died?"

"Near him."

"How did that happen—your presence, I mean?"

"I was visiting him at this place to shoot and fish. A part of my purpose, however, was to study him and his odd, solitary way of life. He seemed a good model for a character in fiction. I sometimes write stories."

"I sometimes read them."

"Thank you."

"Stories in general—not yours."

Some of the jurors laughed. Against a somber background humor shows high lights. Soldiers in the interval of battle laugh easily, and a jest in the death chamber conquers by surprise.

"Relate the circumstances of this man's death," said the coroner. "You may use any notes or memoranda that you please."

The witness understood. Pulling a manuscript from his breast pocket he held it near the candle and turning the leaves until he found the passage that he wanted began to read.

II

What May Happen in a Field of Wild Oats

". . . The sun had hardly risen when we left the house. We were looking for quail, each with a shotgun, but we had only one dog. Morgan said that our best ground was beyond a certain ridge that he pointed out, and we crossed it by a trail through the *chaparral*.[2] On the other side was comparatively level ground, thickly covered with wild oats. As we emerged from the *chaparral* Morgan was but a few yards in advance. Suddenly we heard, at a little distance to our right and partly in front, a noise as of some animal thrashing about in the bushes, which we could see were violently agitated.

---

2. *chaparral* (Spanish): a thicket of bushes and shrubs.

"'We've startled a deer,' I said. 'I wish we had brought a rifle.'

"Morgan, who had stopped and was intently watching the agitated *chaparral*, said nothing, but had cocked both barrels of his gun and was holding it in readiness to aim. I thought him a trifle excited, which surprised me, for he had a reputation for exceptional coolness, even in moments of sudden and imminent peril.

"'Oh, come,' I said. 'You are not going to fill up a deer with quail shot, are you?'

"Still he did not reply, but catching a sight of his face as he turned it slightly toward me I was struck by the intensity of his look. Then I understood that we had serious business in hand, and my first conjecture was that we had "jumped" a grizzly. I advanced to Morgan's side, cocking my piece as I moved.

"The bushes were now quiet and the sounds had ceased, but Morgan was as attentive to the place as before.

"'What is it? What the devil is it?' I asked.

"'That Damned Thing!' he replied, without turning his head. His voice was husky and unnatural. He trembled visibly.

"I was about to speak further, when I observed the wild oats near the place of the disturbance moving—in the most inexplicable way. I can hardly describe it. They seemed as if stirred by a streak of wind, which not only bent them, but pressed them down—crushed them so that they did not rise, and this movement was slowly prolonging itself directly toward us.

"Nothing that I had ever seen had affected me so strangely as this unfamiliar and unaccountable phenomenon, yet I am unable to recall any sense of fear. I remember—and tell it here because, singularly enough, I recollected it then—that once in looking carelessly out an open window I momentarily mistook a small tree close at hand for one of a group of larger trees at a little distance away. It looked the same size as the others, but being more distinctly and sharply defined in mass and detail seemed out of harmony with them. It was a mere falsification of the law of aerial perspective, but it startled, almost terrified me. We so rely upon the orderly operation of familiar natural laws that any seeming suspension of them is noted as a menace to our safety, a warning of unthinkable calamity. So now the apparently causeless movement of the herbage and the slow, undeviating approach of the line of disturbance were distinctly disquieting. My companion appeared actually frightened, and I could hardly credit my senses when

I saw him suddenly throw his gun to his shoulder and fire both barrels in the agitated grain! Before the smoke of the discharge had cleared away I heard a loud savage cry—a scream like that of a wild animal—and flinging his gun upon the ground Morgan sprang away and ran swiftly from the spot. At the same moment I was thrown violently to the ground by the impact of something unseen in the smoke—some soft, heavy substance that seemed thrown against me with great force.

"Before I could get upon my feet and recover my gun, which seemed to have been struck from my hands, I heard Morgan crying out as if in mortal agony, and mingling with his cries were such hoarse, savage sounds as one hears from fighting dogs. Inexpressibly terrified, I struggled to my feet and looked in the direction of Morgan's retreat, and may heaven in mercy spare me from another sight like that! At a distance of less than thirty yards was my friend, down upon one knee, his head thrown back at a frightful angle, hatless, his long hair in disorder and his whole body in violent movement from side to side, backwards and forwards. His right arm was lifted and seemed to lack the hand—at least, I could see none. The other arm was invisible. At times, as my memory now reports this extraordinary scene, I could discern but a part of his body; it was as if he had been partly blotted out—I cannot otherwise express it—then a shifting of his position would bring it all into view again.

"All this must have occurred within a few seconds, yet in that time Morgan assumed all the postures of a determined wrestler vanquished by superior weight and strength. I saw nothing but him, and him not always distinctly. During the entire incident his shouts and curses were heard, as if through an enveloping uproar of such sounds of rage and fury as I had never heard from the throat of man or brute!

"For a moment only I stood irresolute, then throwing down my gun I ran forward to my friend's assistance. I had a vague belief that he was suffering from a fit, or some form of convulsion. Before I could reach his side he was down and quiet. All sounds had ceased but with a feeling of such terror as even these awful events had not inspired I now saw again the mysterious movement of the wild oats, prolonging itself from the trampled area about the prostrate man towards the edge of a wood. It was only when it had reached the wood that I was able to withdraw my eyes and look at my companion. He was dead."

III

A Man Though Naked May Be in Rags

The coroner rose from his seat and stood by the dead man. Lifting an edge of the sheet he pulled it away, exposing the entire body, altogether naked and showing in the candlelight a clay-like yellow. It had, however, broad maculations[3] of bluish black, obviously caused by extravasated[4] blood from contusions. The chest and sides looked as if they had been beaten with a bludgeon. There were dreadful lacerations; the skin was torn in strips and shreds.

The coroner moved round to the end of the table and undid a silk handkerchief which had been passed under the chin and knotted on the top of the head. When the handkerchief was drawn away it exposed what had been the throat. Some of the jurors who had risen to get a better view repented their curiosity and turned away their faces. Witness Harker went to the open window and leaned out across the sill, faint and sick. Dropping the handkerchief upon the dead man's neck the coroner stepped to an angle of the room and from a pile of clothing produced one garment after another, each of which he held up for a moment of inspection. All were torn, and stiff with blood. The jurors did not make a closer inspection. They seemed rather uninterested. They had, in truth, seen all this before, the only thing that was new to them being Harker's testimony.

"Gentlemen," the coroner said, "we have no more evidence, I think. Your duty has already been explained to you, if there is nothing you wish to ask you may go outside and consider your verdict."

The foreman rose—a tall, bearded man of sixty, coarsely clad.

"I should like to ask one question, Mr. Coroner," he said. "What asylum did this yer last witness escape from?"

"Mr. Harker," said the coroner gravely and tranquilly, "from what asylum did you last escape?"

Harker flushed crimson again, but said nothing, and the seven jurors rose and solemnly filed out of the cabin.

---

3. **maculations:** spots; blemishes.
4. **extravasated** (ik strav′ ə sā ted): forced to flow from normal vessels into the surrounding body tissues.

"If you have done insulting me, sir," said Harker, as soon as he and the officer were left alone with the dead man, "I suppose I am at liberty to go?"

"Yes."

Harker started to leave, but paused, with his hand on the door latch. The habit of his profession was strong in him—stronger than his sense of personal dignity. He turned about and said: "The book that you have there—I recognize it as Morgan's diary. You seemed greatly interested in it, you read in it while I was testifying. May I see it? The public would like—"

"The book will cut no figure in this matter," replied the official, slipping it into his coat pocket; "all the entries in it were made before the writer's death."

As Harker passed out of the house the jury re-entered and stood about the table on which the now covered corpse showed under the sheet with sharp definition. The foreman seated himself near the candle, produced from his breast pocket a pencil and scrap of paper and wrote rather laboriously the following verdict, which with various degrees of effort all signed. "We the jury, do find that the remains come to their death at the hands of a mountain lion, but some of us thinks, all the same, they had fits."

IV

An Explanation from the Tomb

In the diary of the late Hugh Morgan are certain interesting entries having possibly, a scientific value as suggestions. At the inquest upon his body the book was not put in evidence, possibly the coroner thought it not worthwhile to confuse the jury. The date of the first of the entries mentioned cannot be ascertained, the upper part of the leaf is torn away, the part of the entry remaining follows:

> . . . would run in a half-circle, keeping his head turned always towards the center, and again he would stand still, barking furiously. At last he ran away into the brush as fast as he could go. I thought at first that he had gone mad, but on returning to the house found no other alteration in his manner than what was obviously due to fear of punishment.

Can a dog see his nose? Do odors impress some cerebral center with images of the thing that emitted them?

September 2—Looking at the stars last night as they rose above the crest of the ridge east of the house, I observed them successively disappear—from left to right. Each was eclipsed but an instant, and only a few at the same time, but along the entire length of the ridge all that were within a degree or two of the crest were blotted out. It was as if something had passed along between them; but I could not see it, and the stars were not thick enough to define its outline. Ugh! don't like this. . .

Several weeks' entries are missing, three leaves being torn from the book.

September 27—It has been about here again—I find evidence of its presence every day. I watched again all last night in the same cover, gun in hand, double-charged with buckshot. In the morning, the fresh footprints were there, as before. Yet I would have sworn that I did not sleep—indeed, I hardly sleep at all. It is terrible, insupportable! If these amazing experiences are real I shall go mad; if they are fanciful I am mad already.

October 3—I shall not go—it shall not drive me away. No, this is my house, my land. God hates a coward.

October 5—I can stand it no longer. I have invited Harker to pass a few weeks with me—he has a level head. I can judge from his manner if he thinks me mad.

October 7—I have the solution of the mystery; it came to me last night—suddenly as by revelation. How simple—how terribly simple!

There are sounds that we cannot hear. At either end of the scale are notes that stir no chord of that imperfect instrument, the human ear. They are too high or too grave. I have observed a flock of blackbirds occupying an entire tree-top—the tops of several trees—and all in full song. Suddenly—in a moment—at absolutely the same instant—all sprang into the air and flew away. How? They could not all see one another—whole tree-tops intervened. At no point could a leader have been visible to all. There must have been a signal of warning or command, high and shrill above the din, but by me unheard. I have observed, too, the same simultaneous flight when all were silent, among not only blackbirds, but other birds—quail, for example, widely separated by bushes—even on opposite sides of a hill.

It is known to seamen that a school of whales basking or sporting on the surface of the ocean, miles apart, with the convexity[5] of the earth between, will sometimes dive at the same instant—all gone out of sight in a moment. The signal has been sounded—too grave for the ear of the sailor at the masthead and his comrades on the deck—who nevertheless feel its vibrations in the ship as the stones of a cathedral are stirred by the bass of the organ.

As with sounds, so with colors. At each end of the solar spectrum the chemist can detect the presence of what are known as "actinic" rays.[6] They represent colors—integral colors in the composition of light—which we are unable to discern. The human eye is an imperfect instrument; its range is but a few octaves of the real "chromatic scale". I am not mad; there are colors that we cannot see.

And God help me! the Damned Thing is of such a color!

---

5. **convexity:** an outward curving.
6. **actinic rays:** rays of short wavelength, including violet and ultraviolet rays, which produce chemical changes.

Discussion Questions

1. Why does William Harker write his newspaper account as fiction and yet read that account as part of his sworn testimony?

2. How do the coroner and the coroner's jury react to Harker's testimony? Why?

3. What is remarkable about the coroner's jury's verdict?

4. Describe the "Damned Thing." Take into account both Harker's and Hugh Morgan's descriptions.

5. Paraphrase Morgan's explanation of the "Damned Thing."

Suggestion for Writing

William Harker states that he wrote his newspaper account as fiction. The part he reads obviously picks up the story in the middle and then goes to the end, with Hugh Morgan's death. What do you think precedes this? What is Harker's fictional setup for this terrible death scene? Write what you think Harker might have written. He tells the coroner that it is true, and he doesn't even change Morgan's name, so perhaps his is a straightforward account of events that began when he received the invitation from Morgan to come and stay with him. What sort of explanation or warning do you imagine Morgan gave Harker before that last morning when they set out to hunt quail?

A. M. Burrage (1889-1956)

Alfred McLelland Burrage was born in Middlesex, England. While he was still in school, he began to write and to sell his stories, and thus he became a professional author at the age of 17. Burrage became a frequent contributor to periodicals of what was thought of as boys' fiction. He created a series about a character called Tufty, which proved very popular, and other series under the pen name Frank Lelland. Burrage served in France in World War I and wrote bitterly about his personal experiences in *War Is War* (1930), published under the pen name Ex-Private X. After the war Burrage contributed stories, articles, and poems to over 150 periodicals. Some of these were collected in *Some Ghost Stories* (1927) and *Someone in the Room* (1931). His efforts at longer fiction proved not so successful, and he is remembered today chiefly for his supernatural fiction.

The Green Scarf

When the Wellingford family became extinct the days of Wellingford Hall as one of the great country houses of England were already numbered. The estate passed into the hands of commercial-minded people who had no reverence for the history of a great house. The acres surrounding the hall become too valuable as building-sites to be allowed to remain as a park surrounding a country mansion. So the fat Wellingford sheep were driven elsewhere to pasture, and surveyors and architects heralded the coming of navvies[1] and builders.

All this happened many years ago. The old park became crossed and crisscrossed by new roads, and perky little villas with names like "Ivyleigh" and "Dulce Domum" sprang up like monstrous red fungi. Even these have since mellowed, and grown their own ivy and Virginia creeper, and put on airs of respectable maturity. The Hall itself, forlorn and abandoned, like some poor human wretch deserted in his old age, began slowly to crumble into decay.

Wellingford Hall was no more than an embarrassment to the new owners of the estate, who were willing to let it or sell it at the prospective tenant's or purchaser's own price; but to dispose of a great house with no land attached to it and surrounded by a garden city is no easy matter. It was too big for its environment. After some vicissitudes as a private school and the home of a small community of nuns, it was abandoned to its natural fate: "for," said one of the directors of the Wellingford Estate, Limited, a gentleman not above mixing his metaphors, "what was the sense of keeping a white elephant[2] in a state of repair?"

Three years before this present time of writing came Aubrey Vair, the painter, as poor as most other painters, a lover of old buildings and all the cobwebby branches of archaeology, and took Wellingford Hall at a weekly rental of fewer shillings than might be demanded for the use of a gardener's cottage. He knew one of the directors, and he had discovered that a few rooms in the middle of the block of buildings were still inhabitable. The directors, I suppose, wondered why anyone

---

1. **navvies:** unskilled laborers.
2. **white elephant:** something of little use or profit.

should wish to live in the damp-ridden, rat-riddles old hole, but they did not despise the shillings, and they let him come.

Vair wrote me several letters, begging me to come down and rough it with him. It was just the place for a writer he assured me; it would give me ideas. He had been searching after priests'-holes[3] and had discovered no less than five. One of the great rooms made the finest studio he had yet painted in. And really, as regards comfort, he avowed, it wasn't so bad, so long as one came there already warned to expect only the amenities of a poor bachelor establishment. And then, he added temptingly, there were the historical associations.

I already knew something about the latter, having discovered my facts in a book dealing with old English country houses. Charles the First had spent a night there during the Great Civil War. Charles the Second was supposed to have hidden there after the battle of Worcester. But best of all was the romantic tale of the capture and execution of Sir Peter Wellingford in 1649.

Briefly, Sir Peter was a proscribed Royalist who lived hunted and in hiding after the failure of the royal army. A wiser man would have crossed the Channel, but Sir Peter had a young wife at Wellingford Hall. He had often visited her in safety, and might have continued to do so, but for a traitor in his own household. This fellow, so the story went, betrayed his master by waving a green scarf from one of the windows, this being a prearranged signal to inform a detachment of Parliamentary troops that the head of the house was secretly in residence. The soldiers burst in at night, and ransacked the house before Sir Peter Wellingford was discovered in a hiding-hole—or "privacie" as the old chronicle described it. The cavalier was dragged outside and shot in his own courtyard.

Here was a story romantic enough to inveigle the fancy of most men with a grain of imagination. I fully intended to visit Wellingford Hall, but circumstances caused me to defer my intention for the first summer and it was not until the following May, when Vair had been in residence for a full year, that I paid him my deferred visit. I journeyed by road, driving myself in my small two-seater, so that Vair had no opportunity to meet me, and I had my first view of Wellingford Hall before I could be biased by his enthusiasm.

---

3. **priests'-holes:** hiding places for Catholic priests when they were outlawed during the reign of Elizabeth I (1558–1603).

Holy Writ speaks of the abomination of desolation standing where it ought not; and here was this grim, forbidding, crumbling old ruin still surrounded by its moat and standing in the midst of jerry-built[4] "Chumleighs" and "Rosemounts." It was like finding the House of Usher[5] in the middle of a new garden city. In spite of its moat the Hall had never been intended for a fortress and the bridge I crossed must have been nearly as old as the house itself.

Vair heard me coming and pushed open the great nail-studded door under the archway of the main entrance to come and greet me with a grin and a handshake. He climbed up beside me and directed me round into the yard, where there was plenty of accommodation for a dozen cars. Strangely enough, the stables and coach-houses were in better repair than the old house itself.

The hall had once been magnificent, but most of the ceiling was gone, and the oak balustrade of the staircase, having a commercial value, had been long since removed. A trail of sacking across broken paving stones pointed the way to Vair's apartments beyond. He ushered me into a fine room, in quite a reasonable state of repair, furnished with products of his speculations at country auctions. Although the month was May the weather was none too warm, and I was glad of the sight of the log fire which lent the room an additional air of comfort. Vair laughed to hear me exclaim, and asked if I were ready for tea.

He lived there, he explained, entirely alone, except that a charwoman came each morning to do the rough work and cook his one hot meal of the day.

"You won't mind putting up with cold meat and canned things of an evening?" he asked anxiously.

I hate tinned foods, but, of course, I could not say so.

After tea Vair showed me the rest of the rooms which he had made habitable, and, really, he had managed to make himself much more comfortable than I had expected. He had contrived—Heaven knows how—to learn a lot of intimate history of the old place, and knew the name by which every room had been called in the house's palmy[6] days

---

4. **jerry-built:** built poorly or of cheap materials.
5. **House of Usher:** the setting for Edgar Allan Poe's horror story "The Fall of the House of Usher." The reference suggests that the house is old, falling apart, and creepy.
6. **palmy:** prosperous.

of dignity and prosperity. My bedroom, for instance, was known as "Lady Ursula's Nursery," although history had long since forgotten who Lady Ursula was.

It was easy to see that Vair had a boyish enthusiasm for the place. He was a queer chap, with more than the average artist's share of eccentricities, and he believed in all manner of superstitions and pseudo sciences. He was one of those ageless men who might have been anything in the twenties, thirties, or forties. I happened to know that he was nearly fifty, but his thin wiriness of figure and boyish zest for life kept him youthful. Obviously his pleasure at having me down was not so much for my own sake as his. I was somebody to whom he could "show off" the house. He was clearly as proud of it as if it had been restored to its former dignity and he were the actual owner.

"For Heaven's sake, don't go about the place by yourself," he said, "or you'll break your neck. I've nearly broken mine a dozen times, and I'm beginning to know where it isn't safe to walk. It must be rather rare to find damp-rot and dry-rot in the same house, but we've got both here."

I promised faithfully that I wouldn't move without him. Even the main staircase did not appear too safe to me, but Vair assured me that it was all right.

After tea he took me over such parts of the house as it was safe to visit, but I shall make no attempt to describe most of this pilgrimage. My memory carries dreary pictures of damp and decay, of dust and dirt, and cobwebs, mouldering walls and crumbling floors. The old place must have been a warren of secret rooms and passages, and he showed me those he had discovered. All I can say is that the refugees of the bad old days must have been very uncomfortable, and those who escaped deserved to.

The large room under the roof, which we visited, had once been a secret chamber. It was called the Chapel, and here Mass had been said in defiance of the law throughout part of the sixteenth and seventeenth centuries.

"There must be a lot more secret rooms," Vair remarked. "Little Owen, who was a master at constructing such places, is known to have spent months here during the reign of Elizabeth. The house was always being raided, and the raiders had little satisfaction."

"They got the poor old cavalier," I laughed.

"Oh, yes. But he was given away, or sold, by a servant. I've shown you the place where I'm almost sure he hid—behind where the bedhead used to be in the room called the King's Chamber. We'll see if we can find some more while you're here, if you like."

It suddenly occurred to me that Vair had always called himself "sensitive," or psychic, and it was perhaps natural of me to put on the noncommittal smile of the polite sceptic and inquire if he had seen any ghosts. Rather to my surprise, he shook his head.

"No," he answered; "it isn't at all that kind of place. The house is quite friendly. I should have felt it at once if it had been otherwise."

"But I should have thought with its history—"

"Ah, it's seen troubled days, but they were always nice people who lived here. There are no dreadful legends of bloodshed and cruelty."

"There is the story of the cavalier," I objected. "Surely his ghost ought to haunt the place."

"Why? He was a good man from all accounts and he died a man's death. Only troubled or wicked people linger about the scenes of their earth-life. When he was taken out and slaughtered all the hatred and blood-lust came from *outside*. If any impressions of those spent passions remain, they're not inside the house, and I don't want them inside."

I smiled to myself, knowing that, from Vair's point of view, the house *ought* to be haunted, and his excuses for the nonappearance of a ghost struck me as ingenious but far-fetched.

"That's a pity," I said, tongue in cheek. "I quite hoped to be introduced to a Grey Lady or a Spectre Cavalier."

He frowned, knowing that I was laughing at him.

"Well, you won't be," he said, "unless—"

"Unless what?"

"Well, unless something happens to alter present conditions. If, for instance, we were to find something which someone long forgotten desired should remain hidden."

"I see."

"I doubt if you do. And I doubt if anything could be done now to disturb any of the Wellingfords in their long sleep. They seem to have been an ideal family; I haven't been able to find a word of scandal on any page of their history. Where there has once been bitterness and hatred, there you may look for ghosts. There was none here. All that came from the outside. That frenzied desire, for instance, to trap and kill a man because he had fought for his king, long after his cause was well lost; that bitter bigotry which sought to prevent folk from worshipping according to their consciences. It all came from outside, I tell you!"

Vair's voice had risen. Like most men with no particular faith, he respected all creeds, and religious intolerance always moved him to violent anger. Respect for his deadly seriousness kept my face grave.

"Do you mean just outside?" I asked.

"How do I know? And so long as they remain outside what does it matter. I assure you, I don't want them brought in." To my relief, he then veered away from a subject which was hardly within my scope of conversation. There was little of the mystic in me. All the same, when at last I retired to bed in Lady Ursula's nursery, I was glad to remember that Vair had given the house a clean bill of health in the psychic sense. By the time I had been Vair's guest for twenty-four hours I had begun to feel with him that the old ruin had a kindly and friendly atmosphere, in spite of its apparent gloom, and that this might have been the legacy of good people who had lived and died within its walls.

At the risk of giving this narrative an air of being disconnected, I must pass hurriedly over the next two or three days of my visit, for they brought forth little that is worth recording. Sometimes Vair did a little painting, and then his preoccupation drove me to my own work. We did a little fishing and sometimes walked three-quarters of a mile to the Wellingford Arms where, according to Vair, who accounted himself an expert, the bitter beer was better than the average. Sometimes we risked our necks on rickety stairs and crumbling floors, looking for more secret hiding-places, an occupation in which I soon became infected with some of Vair's schoolboy zest.

The place was quiet enough during the day, but the villas and bungalows which had marched almost to the edge of the moat made themselves audible at night. Every Lyndhurst and Balmoral seemed able to boast of a musical daughter or a powerful gramophone. The effect of sitting in one of those dignified old rooms with the windows open and hearing echoes from the musical comedies was grotesque in the extreme. Vair had evidently grown used to it, for he made no comment.

I had arrived on a Saturday, and it was on the afternoon of the Tuesday following that, between us, we made a discovery of historical interest; a discovery which we came afterwards bitterly to regret having made. We were on the first floor landing, where long windows, deep in a recess, looked out over the Wellingford Park estate, when Vair mentioned that he had never examined the window seats.

"Sliding panels," he said, "certainly have existed, but they belong mostly to fiction. They were too hard to construct and too easily discovered. Take the five hiding-places you've seen in this house. Three of them are behind fireplaces, one under the stairs, and the other must have been masked at one time by the head of a bedstead. Window seats were very often used, and this one looks likely. Let's try it."

We rapped it with our knuckles, and although it did not sound hollow, there was obviously an empty space beneath it. We pushed and tugged and teased the surface of the wood with our fingers. And suddenly I saw a crack widen, and part of the seat which had fitted into the rest of the woodwork as neatly as a drawer came away in my hands, and we stared at each other with laughter and curiosity in our eyes.

"Hallo, what's this!" Vair exclaimed.

The cavity disclosed was very small. It was obviously not the entrance to any place of concealment capable of holding a human being. I lit a match and thrust it down into the darkness. Then cheek by jowl we peered together into a cavity no more than three feet deep.

"Nothing here," I said, breaking cobwebs as I moved my wrist to and fro.

"Isn't there!" exclaimed Vair.

He brushed me aside and his arm disappeared up to the shoulder. His hand was black when he drew it forth, and an end of something like a black rag was between his fingers. It was an old piece of silk, so rotten with age that it almost crumbled under our touch; but when we had blown on it and brushed it with our fingers we saw that it owed its present color to the dirt of ages, and that it had once been green. On the instant the old tale leaped into the minds of both of us, and we exclaimed together:

"The Green Scarf!"

I forget what we said for the first minute or two. We were both excited and elated. There is some peculiar pleasure, difficult to analyze or explain, in discovering a relic which serves to corroborate some old tale or passage of ancient history. We neither of us doubted that we had discovered the green scarf by which Sir Peter Wellingford had been betrayed nearly three hundred years before.

"The traitor must have kept it here in readiness," said Vair, his eyes dancing. "And when he'd signalled he dropped it back again, and there it has lain from that day to this."

"And most likely," I added, taking the relic from his hands, "this is the very window he waved from."

The window was open and I leaned out and let the dingy rag flutter from my hand in the warm afternoon breeze.

"Don't!" said Vair sharply, and pulled me back.

The silk was so rotten with age that even the weak breeze tore it slightly, and I thought at the time that Vair's sharp "Don't!" was uttered because of the damage I had unwittingly done. It was a relic of treachery and bloodshed, but we both regarded it with a queer sort of reverence, as if it were associated with something sacred.

I should think an hour must have passed before we mentioned anything else. We were both agreed that one of us should write to a newspaper announcing our discovery and that the scarf should be cleaned by an expert and offered to a museum. One remark of Vair's struck me at the time as a little strange, but the full force of it did not come to me until some hours later.

"I wish you hadn't waved it out of the window," he said. "It's what that damned traitor did. That's what made you do it, of course—trying to re-enact part of an old tragedy."

"I don't see that it matters," I returned lightly. "Nobody saw."

He turned on me at once.

"*How do you know?*" he demanded sharply.

I could not help laughing then. "My dear fellow," I exclaimed, "are you afraid that the wife or daughter of one of your neighbors will think—"

"I wasn't thinking of *them*," he returned curtly. "When that rag was waved out of that window nearly three hundred years ago, you know what happened, you know what it brought into the house."

I thought I had caught the drift of his meaning. Vair had always declined to walk under ladders or make the thirteenth of a party, and he was unhappy for days after he had spilled the contents of a salt-cellar.

"Oh, don't be an ass, Vair," I begged. "If there's any ill luck about I give it leave to attack me and leave you alone."

He did not answer, and in a few minutes the incident had passed temporarily from my mind.

I have tried to tell this story so many times by word of mouth, and been compelled at this point to pause and hesitate, as now I am compelled to pause and think. It is not that my memory fails me; memory, indeed, serves me all too well. But hereabouts I am brought to realize the failure of my small command of words. A bad speaker can at least convey something otherwise unexpressed by look, gesture, hesitation, tone of voice. But with nothing but pen, ink, paper, and a limited vocabulary, I see little chance of giving an adequate account of what happened to us that night; of how with the twilight depression was laid upon us, straw by straw, and how with the coming of darkness horror was laid upon us, load by load.

Even before supper I found myself restless and ill at ease. Something began to weigh upon my spirit as if my mind carried the knowledge of some ordeal which I had presently to face. Of course, I put it down to an attack of "liver" and made up my mind to forget it. The intention was good, but it was unjustified by the desired result.

My discovery that Vair was suffering from a similar *malaise*[7] did not help my own case. His spirits were far below normal, and I think our mutual discovery that the other was "below form" added weight to that which was already dragging at our hearts. To make matters worse we each began to act for the other's benefit, to force laughter, to crack heavy jokes, and make cumbersome epigrams.[8] But when at twilight we lit the lamp and sat down to supper we tacitly agreed to give up pretending.

"Do you feel that there's a weight crushing you whenever there's thunder about?" Vair asked suddenly.

I was glad to think of some excuse to account for my mood, and answered quickly:

"Yes, very often. And I wouldn't mind betting there's some thunder about tonight."

Vair looked at me and seemed suddenly to change his mind over what he had been about to say.

He shook his head.

"The glass[9] hasn't gone down."

I rose from the table without apology, went to the window, pulled aside the curtains, and looked out. It was just after sunset on a very perfect May evening. There was a red glow in the west, and around this glow there was an area of sky which was almost apple-green. This merged into a very deep blue in which one or two pale stars were already beginning to play hide-and-seek.

"No," I agreed grudgingly, "there isn't a cloud in the sky. Still, storms come up very quickly."

"Yes," said Vair, "and so do other things."

---

7. ***malaise*** (ma lāz): (French) feeling of physical discomfort or uneasiness.
8. **epigram:** witty saying.
9. **glass:** barometer.

My lips moved to ask him what he meant, but I thought better of it. Whatever morbid imaginings he might be entertaining, they were scarcely likely to help my own mood. We ate in silence, continuing thus for a long time before I forced a laugh and exclaimed:

"Well, we're a jolly pair, aren't we? What the devil's the matter with us this evening? I only wish I knew."

"I only wish I didn't think I knew," he answered strangely.

"Well, what do you think—"

"I think we ought to go out somewhere tonight and stay out."

"Why? You haven't felt like this before—"

"No. And it's because I haven't felt like this before—"

He came to another sudden pause, and we looked into each other's faces for a moment before he lowered his gaze.

"Now, look here," I said, trying to keep my voice steady, "let's be as honest as we can and try to analyze this thing. I'll say it first. We're both afraid of something."

He went a step further.

"We're both afraid of the same thing," he said.

"Well, what is it, then? Let's find it out and confront it. When a horse shies at a tree you lead him up to it and show him that it's only a tree."

"If it happens to be a tree or something like a tree. But if it isn't . . . Look here, let's go out. Straight away now, while there's time. They've got bedrooms at the Wellingford Arms. Let's go and spend the night there."

With all my heart I wanted to. But Pride borrowed the voice of Reason and spoke for me.

"Oh, don't let's make fools of ourselves," I urged. "I for one don't want to truckle[10] to my nerves. If we give way like this once we shall always be doing it."

He shrugged his shoulders.

"Let's have a drink."

He brought out the whiskey. I am a temperate man with a weak head for spirits, and I admit that I exceeded my usual allowance, but it made no more difference to me than if it were water. We sat facing each other gloomily in a silence which became increasingly difficult to break.

The unusual quality of this silence had already begun to impress me when Vair mentioned it, as if my thought had communicated itself to him.

---

10. **truckle**: submit; give in.

"Don't you notice how extraordinarily still everything seems?" he asked presently.

"Yes," I agreed, and snatched suddenly at a straw. "The silence before the storm. There *is* a storm about, you see."

He shook his head.

"No," he said. "It isn't that kind of stillness."

And then, with a little leap of the heart and a tingling of the nostrils I suddenly realized a fact which seemed to me inexpressibly ugly. This stillness was not the hush of Nature before some electrical disturbance. For some time past we had heard no sound at all from the outer world. The gramophones and pianos in the little houses around us were all silent. It was the hour when at many houses on the estate hosts and guests were parting for the night, yet there was not the faint echo of a voice, nor the comfortable workaday sound of a car droning along a road. It may seem ludicrous, but I would have given a hundred pounds just then to hear the distant shunting of a train.

Vair rose suddenly, went to the window and looked out. I followed him. For some while now it had been completely dark. Overhead in a very clear sky the stars looked peacefully into our troubled eyes.

"No storm about," said Vair shortly.

He heard me catch my breath, and a moment later he was aware of what I had already perceived.

"Look! There aren't any lights! There isn't a light anywhere!"

It was true. The hour was not late, and yet from the rows of houses which began not so many yards distant, not a light was visible, nor was it possible to discern an outline of roof or chimney against the sky. We had been cut off from the lights and sounds of the outside world as completely as if we were in a cavern miles under the ground, save that our isolation—I can think of no other word—was lateral.

Vair's voice had risen high and thin. He made no effort to disguise the terror in it.

"There must be some fog about," I said; and I was so anxious lest my voice should sound like Vair's that I spoke out of the base of my chest.

"Fog! Look, man!"

I looked. Truly there was not the least sign of fog or mist. Until we raised our eyes to the sky we stared into impenetrable, featureless darkness.

Vair let the window curtains fall from his hand. He turned to me in the oppressive stillness, and his face worked until by an effort he controlled the muscles.

"Try and tell me," he said hoarsely, "*what* you've been feeling all evening."

"How can I? The same as you, I suppose!" A reminiscence of soldiering came back to me. "It's been like waiting to go over the top. A horrible aching anxiety. No, something more than that. A sense of being trapped, of being surrounded—"

"Surrounded!" He caught up the word with a cry. "That's just what you are! That's just what we both are!"

I drew him away from the curtained window.

"Surrounded? By what?" I made myself ask.

He spread out his hands and shook them helplessly.

"The Powers of Darkness, Hatred, Blood-lust, Intolerance—they were all waiting, waiting for the signal. Do you think these things die like spent matches? Do you think the black act of treachery, which brought them into this house, left nothing behind it? *They* were waiting—all these years—I tell you!" Suddenly he bared his teeth at me. "You fool, to have waved that rag at them!"

Just for a moment I felt my brain turning like a wheel, but I made a fight for my sanity and won it back.

"Look here," I said, "for God's sake don't let's behave like madmen. Let's get out of it if the house is going to affect us like this."

He stared back at me, giving me a look which I could not read.

"No," he muttered; "you wanted to stay."

"Let's go down to the Wellington Arms."

"They're closed now."

"It doesn't matter. They know you. They'll open for you."

I found myself lusting for the world beyond that unnatural girdle of darkness. The Wellingford Arms with its vulgar tin advertisements of Somebody's Beer, and Somebody Else's Whiskey, and its framed Christmas Number plates—at least there was sanity there.

But Vair suddenly turned on me the eyes of a hunted animal.

"You fool!" he burst out. "It's too late! We can't pass through *them*!"

"What do you mean?" I faltered.

"They're all around us. You know it, too. They'll break in—in their own good time—as they did before. We're trapped, I tell you!"

Against my will, and Heaven knows how hard I fought for disbelief, Vair had captured my powers of reason. In theory, if not in action, I was now prepared to follow him like a child.

"What do they want?" I stammered.

"Us! One of us or both! What did Murder and Hatred and Bloodlust ever want but sacrifice?"

He fairly spat the words at me and I seized his arm.

"Come on," I said, "we're going to get out of this. We're going to run the gauntlet."

"Ah," said Vair thickly. "If we can."

We must have crossed the hall, although I do not remember it. My next recollection is of helping Vair in his fumbling with the bolts and lock of the great door. We wrenched it open and stood looking out at an opaque wall of darkness.

I tried to force myself across the threshold, only to find myself standing rigid. As in a nightmare, my legs were shackled so that I could not move a step forward, but although terror clawed at me like a wild beast, my senses were keenly and even painfully alert.

I knew that this belt of darkness around the house was alive with whisperings and movements, with all manner of stealthiness, which lurked only just beyond the horizon of vision and the limits of hearing. And as I stood straining eyes and ears I knew that the barriers must soon break and that I should see and hear.

We stood thus a long while on the edge of the threshold we could not pass, but whether it were seconds or minutes I could not say. To us it seemed hours ere the darkness passed, melting into the living forms of men. We could *see,* and there was movement everywhere; we could *hear,* and voices were shouting orders, although the actual words eluded us. They were human voices with strange nasal intonations, snarling and shouting. Even in my extremity I remembered having heard the soldiery of Cromwell had affected a hideous nasal accent. And now the darkness was sundered[11] and shivered by a score of lights, the lights of naked torches which nodded to the rhythm of men marching. I saw the glint of them on the metal heads of pikes,[12] and on the long barrels of muskets outlined clearly now against a naked sky of stars.

---

11. **sundered:** split.
12. **pikes:** long wooden shafts with pointed steel tips.

Terror may bind a man to the spot, but another turn of the rack may torture him back into motion. So it was with us. Blind instinct alone made me slam the great door and shoot the nearest heavy bolt. I saw Vair groping for me like a tear-blinded child and I took his arm. We ran futilely back into the room we had vacated and crouched in the corner farthest from the door, while great noises like thunder began to reverberate through the house, as pike handles and musket-butts crashed sickeningly on the great outer door.

We must have taken leave of reason then, for neither Vair nor I can remember anything more until the great nail-studded door, smashed off its hinges, fell onto the broken flags of the hall with the loudest crash of all. The tramp of feet mingled with the sound of arms carelessly handled, thudding against floor and wall, and with the sharp nasal snarling of voices. In a moment it seemed they were everywhere—in the hall, on the main staircase, in the room over our heads.

Vair had all this time the grip of a madman on my wrist, and suddenly he leaned to me and screamed into my ear:

"The Chapel . . . under the roof . . . It's consecrated[13] . . . there's a chance . . . there's a chance, I tell you. . . ."

"They're on the stairs!" I cried back in despair.

"The back stairs! Come on!"

A second door in the old room gave access to a passage leading to the back stairs. Those stairs we knew to be unsafe, but ordinary human peril was something far beyond and beneath our consideration. I remember the rumble and murmur of sounds about the house as we rushed out into the passage. Footfalls and voices sounded everywhere, and musket-butts were smiting heavily against walls and stairs. As we stumbled and ran I expected at every step to be seized and overwhelmed by some horrible and nameless Power.

How we reached the attic I cannot say. The narrow, crumbling staircase creaked and swayed under us, and once I went down thigh-deep through the rotten stairs, with splinters of hard wood tearing clothes and flesh. But we were near the top ere the hunt had scented their game and sounds of pursuit began to clamor behind us.

Vair forced open the door of the little room which had once been a chapel. I blundered in over his body, which lay prone just across the threshold. He had fallen unconscious, and I had to force his legs aside

---

13. consecrated: blessed; holy.

before I could close the door. I slammed it to in the faces of vague forms which filled the passage to the stairhead, and drove home the wooden bolt inside. And then it seemed to me that our pursuers recoiled from that closed door like a great wave from the base of a cliff, and ugly cries outside died down to uneasy whisperings—and instinctively I knew that we were safe.

I must have fainted then, for I remember nothing more until I woke in the bright sunshine, Vair was sitting beside me, watching me, with a chalklike face. We hardly spoke, but sought each other's hands like frightened children.

Eventually we nerved ourselves to go downstairs into the ruin and disorder of the old house, through which, one might have thought, a whirlwind had passed during the night.

Discussion Questions

1. What was the legend concerning the capture and execution of Sir Peter Wellingford?

2. Describe the character of Aubrey Vair. What is he doing in Wellingford Hall?

3. How do the narrator and Vair come to discover the green scarf?

4. Why does the narrator wave the green scarf out of the window?

5. Explain how Vair's theory of ghosts accounts for what happens to him and the narrator that night.

Suggestion for Writing

After they find the green scarf, the narrator and Aubrey Vair agree that one of them should write to a newspaper announcing their discovery and that they should offer the scarf to a museum. In the voice of the narrator or Vair, write a letter to the editor of a newspaper or to the curator of a museum about this historic find. You will want to mention where it was discovered, of course, and probably enough of its history to explain why it is important. Will you mention—or even hint at—the events that followed?

Wilkie Collins (1824-1889)

Wilkie Collins was born in London, England, the son of a famous landscape painter. His education at a private boarding school seems not to have been taken very seriously by himself or his family, but from an early age he developed a knack for inventing tales. After an unsuccessful apprenticeship in the tea trade, he studied law and was admitted to the bar, but he proved to be as unsuited for law as for commerce. His first novel was *Antonina*, published in 1850. In 1851 he began a long friendship and collaboration with the novelist Charles Dickens. They admired each other and seem to have influenced each other's works, Collins benefitting from Dickens's skill at characterization, and Dickens picking up points from Collins's superior plot structures. Collins suffered from rheumatic gout, which in later years became so painful that he frightened away more than one secretary by groaning with pain while he was dictating. His best-known works are *The Moonstone*, an adventure involving a jewel stolen from an idol's eye, and *The Woman in White*, which has been called the first and greatest of English detective novels.

A Terribly Strange Bed

Shortly after my education at college was finished, I happened to be staying in Paris with an English friend. We were both young men then, and lived, I am afraid, rather a wild life, in the delightful city of our sojourn. One night we were idling about the neighborhood of the Palais Royal, doubtful to what amusement we should next betake ourselves. My friend proposed a visit to Frascati's, but his suggestion was not to my taste. I knew Frascati's, as the French saying is, by heart, had lost and won plenty of five-franc pieces there, merely for amusement's sake, until it was amusement no longer, and was thoroughly tired, in fact, of all the ghastly respectabilities of such a social anomaly as a respectable gambling house. "For heaven's sake," said I to my friend, "let us go somewhere where we can see a little genuine, blackguard,[1] poverty-stricken gaming, with no false gingerbread glitter thrown over it all. Let us get away from fashionable Frascati's to a house where they don't mind letting in a man with a ragged coat, or a man with no coat, ragged or otherwise." "Very well," said my friend, "we needn't go out of the Palais Royal to find such the sort of company you want. Here's the place just before us, as blackguard a place, by all report, as you could possibly wish to see." In another minute we arrived at the door, and entered the house.

When we got upstairs, and had left our hats and sticks with the doorkeeper, we were admitted into the chief gambling-room. We did not find many people assembled there. But, few as the men were who looked up at us on our entrance, they were all types—lamentably true types—of their respective classes.

We had come to see blackguards, but these men were something worse. There is a comic side, more or less appreciable, in all blackguardism—here there was nothing but tragedy—mute, weird tragedy. The quiet in the room was horrible. The thin, haggard, long-haired young man, whose sunken eyes fiercely watched the turning of the cards, never spoke; the flabby, fat-faced pimply player, who pricked his piece of pasteboard perseveringly, to register how often black won, and how often red—never spoke, the dirty wrinkled old man, with the

---

1. **blackguard** (blag´ ard): vulgar; low.

vulture eyes and the darned greatcoat, who had lost his last sou, and still looked on desperately, after he could play no longer—never spoke. Even the voice of the croupier[2] sounded as if it were strangely dulled and thickened in the atmosphere of the room. I had entered the place to laugh, but the spectacle before me was something to weep over. I soon found it necessary to take refuge in excitement from the depression of spirits which was fast stealing on me. Unfortunately, I fought the nearest excitement, by going to the table and beginning to play. Still more unfortunately, as the event will show, I won—won prodigiously, won incredibly, won at such a rate, that the regular players at the table crowded round me and, staring at my stakes with hungry, superstitious eyes, whispered to one another that the English stranger was going to break the bank.

The game was Rouge et Noir.[3] I had played at it in every city in Europe, without, however, the care or the wish to study the Theory of Chances—that philosopher's stone[4] of all gamblers! And a gambler, in the strict sense of the word, I had never been. I was heart whole from the corroding passion for play. My gaming was a mere idle amusement. I never resorted to it by necessity, because I never knew what it was to want money. I never practiced it so incessantly as to lose more than I could afford, or to gain more than I could afford, or to gain more than I could coolly pocket without being thrown off my balance by good luck. In short, I had frequented gambling tables—just as I frequented ballrooms and opera houses—because they amused me, and because I had nothing better to do with my leisure hours.

But on this occasion it was very difficult—now, for the first time in my life, I felt what the passion for play really was. My success first bewildered and then, in the most literal meaning of the word, intoxicated me. Incredible as it may appear, it is nevertheless true, that I only lost when I attempted to estimate chances, and played according to previous calculation. If I left everything to luck, and staked without any care to consideration, I was sure to win—to win in the face of every recognized probability in favor of the bank. At first, some of the men present ventured their money safely enough on my color, but I speedily

---

2. **croupier** (krü´ pē ā): person in change of a gambling table.
3. **Rouge et Noir:** (French) Red and Black, a gambling card game.
4. **philosopher's stone:** a legendary substance that was supposed to change base metals into gold or silver.

increased my stake to sums which they dared not risk. One after another they left off playing, and breathlessly looked on at my game.

Still, time after time, I staked higher and higher, and still won. The excitement in the room rose to fever pitch. The silence was interrupted by a deep-muttered chorus of oaths and exclamations, in different languages, every time the gold was shovelled across to my side of the table—even the imperturbable croupier dashed his rake on the floor in a (French) fury of astonishment at my success. But one man present preserved his self-possession, and that man was my friend. He came to my side, and whispering in English, begged me to leave the place, satisfied with what I had already gained. I must do to him the justice to say that he repeated his warnings and entreaties several times, and only left me and went away after I had rejected his advice (I was to all intents and purposes gambling drunk) in terms which rendered it impossible for him to address me again that night.

Shortly after he had gone, a hoarse voice behind me cried, "Permit me, my dear sir—permit me to restore to their proper place two Napoleons[5] which you have dropped. Wonderful luck, sir! I pledge you my word of honor, as an old soldier, in the course of my long experience in this sort of thing, I never saw such luck as yours!—never! Go on, sir—*Sacré mille bombes!*[6] Go on boldly and break the bank!"

I turned round and saw, nodding and smiling at me with inveterate civility, a tall man, dressed in a frogged and braided surtout.[7]

If I had been in my senses, I should have considered him, personally, as being rather a suspicious specimen of an old soldier. He had goggling bloodshot eyes, mangy mustachios and a broken nose. His voice betrayed a barrack-room intonation of the worst order, and he had the dirtiest pair of hands I ever saw—even in France. These little personal peculiarities exercised, however, no repelling influence on me. In the mad excitement, the reckless triumph of the moment, I was ready to "fraternize" with anybody who encouraged me in my game. I accepted the old soldier's pinch of snuff, clapped him on the back and swore he was the honestest fellow in the world—the most glorious relic of the Grand Army that I had ever met with. "Go on!" cried my military friend, snapping his fingers in ecstasy,—"Go on and win!

---

5. **Napoleons:** former gold coins of France.
6. *Sacré mille bombes:* (French) Damn it!
7. **surtout:** overcoat.

Break the bank—*Mille tonnerres!*[8] my gallant English comrade, break the bank!"

And I *did* go on—went on at such a rate that in another quarter of an hour the croupier called out: "Gentlemen! the bank has been discontinued for tonight!" All the notes and all the gold in that "bank" now lay in a heap under my hands, the whole floating capital of the gambling-house was waiting to pour into my pockets!

"Tie up the money in your pocket-handkerchief, my worthy sir," said the old soldier, as I wildly plunged my hands into my heap of gold. "Tie it up, as we used to tie a bit of dinner in the Grand Army, your winnings are too heavy for any breeches pockets that ever were sewed. There! that's it!—shovel them in, notes and all! *Credie!* what luck!—Stop! another Napoleon on the floor! Ah! *sacré petit polisson de Napoléon!*[9] Have I found thee at last? Now then, sir—two tight double knots each way with your honorable permission, and the money's safe. Feel it! feel it, fortunate sire! hard and round as a cannon ball—Ah, bah! if they had only fired such cannon balls at us at Austerlitz—*nom d'une pipe!*[10] if they only had! And now, as an ancient grenadier, as an ex-brave of the French army, what remains for me to do? I ask what? Simply this, to entreat my valued English friend to drink a bottle of champagne with me, and toast the goddess Fortune in foaming goblets before we part!"

Excellent ex-brave! Convivial ancient gambler! Champagne by all means! An English cheer for an old soldier! hurrah! hurrah! Another English cheer for the goddess Fortune! Hurrah! hurrah! hurrah!

"Bravo! the Englishman, the amiable, gracious Englishman, in whose veins circulates the vivacious blood of France! Another glass? Ah, bah!—the bottle is empty! Never mind! *Vive le vin!* I, the old soldier, order another bottle, and half a pound of *bonbons* with it!"

"No, no, ex-brave, never—ancient grenadier! *Your* bottle last time, *my* bottle this. Behold it! Toast away! The French Army!—the great Napoleon!—the present company! the croupier! the honest croupier's wife and daughters—if he has any! the ladies generally! Everybody in the world!"

By the time the second bottle of champagne was empty, I felt as if I had been drinking liquid fire—my brain seemed all aflame. No excess

---

8. *Mille tonnerres:* (French) by thunder!
9. *sacré petit palisson de Napoléon:* (French) you little rascal, Napoleon!
10. *nom d'une pipe:* (French) son of a gun!

in wine had ever had this effect on me before in my life. Was it the result of a stimulant acting upon my system when I was in a highly excited state? Was my stomach in a particularly disordered condition? Or was the champagne amazingly strong?

"Ex-brave of the French Army!" cried I, in a mad state of exhilaration, "*I* am on fire! how are *you*? You have set me on fire! Do you hear, my hero of Austerlitz? Let us have a third bottle of champagne to put the flame out!"

The old soldier wagged his head, rolled his goggled eyes, until I expected to see them slip out of their sockets, placed his dirty forefinger on the side of his dirty broken nose, solemnly ejaculated "Coffee!" and immediately ran off into the inner room.

The word pronounced by the eccentric veteran seemed to have a magical effect on the rest of the company present. With one accord they all rose to depart. Probably they had expected to profit by my intoxication, but finding that my new friend was benevolently preventing me from getting dead drunk, had now abandoned all hope of thriving pleasantly on my winnings. Whatever their motive might be, at any rate they went away in a body. When the old soldier returned and sat down again opposite me at the table, we had the room to ourselves. I could see the croupier, in a sort of vestibule which opened out of it, eating his supper in solitude. The silence was now deeper than ever.

A sudden change, too, had come over the "ex-brave". He assumed a portentuously solemn look and when he spoke to me again his speech was ornamented by no oaths, enforced by no finger-snapping, enlivened by no apostrophes or exclamations.

"Listen, my dear sir," said he, in mysteriously confidential tones, "listen to an old soldier's advice. I have been to the mistress of the house (a very charming woman, with a genius for cookery!) to impress on her the necessity of making us some particularly strong and good coffee. You must drink this coffee in order to get rid of your little amiable exaltation of spirits before you think of going home— you *must*, my good and gracious friend! With all that money to take home tonight, it is a sacred duty to yourself to have your wits about you. You are known to be a winner to an enormous extent by several gentlemen present tonight, who, in a certain point of view, are very worthy and excellent fellows, but they are mortal men, my dear sir, and they have their amiable weaknesses! Need I say more? Ah, no, no!

you understand me! Now, this is what you must do—send for a cabriolet[11] when you feel quite well again—draw up all the windows when you get into it—and tell the driver to take you home only through the large well-lighted thoroughfares. Do this, and you and your money will be safe. Do this, and tomorrow you will thank an old soldier for giving you a word of honest advice."

Just as the ex-brave ended his oration in very lachrymose tones, the coffee came in, ready poured out in two cups. My attentive friend handed me one of the cups with a bow. I was parched with thirst, and drank it off in a draught. Almost instantly afterwards, I was seized with a fit of giddiness, and felt more completely intoxicated than ever. The room whirled round and round furiously, the old soldier seemed to be regularly bobbing up and down before me like the piston of a steam engine. I was half deafened by a violent singing in my ears, a feeling of utter bewilderment, helplessness, idiocy, overcame me. I rose from my chair, holding on by the table to keep my balance, and stammered out that I felt dreadfully unwell—so unwell that I did not know how I was to go home.

"My dear friend," answered the old soldier—and even his voice seemed to be bobbing up and down as he spoke—"my dear friend, it would be madness to go home in *your* state, you would be sure to lose your money, you might be robbed and murdered with the greatest ease. *I* am going to sleep here, do *you* sleep here, too—they make up capital beds in this house—take one, sleep off the effects of the wine, and go home safely with your winnings tomorrow—tomorrow, in broad daylight."

I had but two ideas left—one, that I must never let go hold of my handkerchief of money, the other, that I must lie down somewhere immediately, and fall off into a comfortable sleep. So I agreed to the proposal about the bed, and took the offered arm of the old soldier, carrying my money with my disengaged hand. Preceded by the croupier, we passed along some passages and up a flight of stairs into the bedroom which I was to occupy. The ex-brave shook me warmly by the hand, proposed that we should breakfast together, and then, followed by the croupier, left me for the night.

I ran to the wash-hand stand, drank some of the water in my jug, poured the rest out, and plunged my face into it; then sat down in a

---

11. cabriolet (kab rē ə lā´): a small horse-drawn carriage.

chair and tried to compose myself. I soon felt better. The change for my lungs from the fetid atmosphere to the cool air of the apartment I now occupied, the almost equally refreshing change for my eyes from the glaring lights of the "salon" to the dim, quiet flicker of one bedroom candle, both aided wonderfully the restorative effects of cold water. The giddiness left me, and I began to feel a little like a reasonable being again. My first thought was of the risk of sleeping all night in a gambling-house; my second, of the still greater risk of trying to get out after the house was closed, and of going home alone at night, through the streets of Paris, with a large sum of money about me. I had slept in worse places than this on my travels; so I determined to lock, bolt and barricade my door and take my chance till the next morning.

Accordingly, I secured myself against all intrusion, looked under the bed, and into the cupboard; tried the fastening of the window, and then, satisfied that I had taken every proper precaution, pulled off my upper clothing, put my light, which was a dim one, on the hearth among a feathery litter of wood ashes, and got into bed, with the handkerchief of money under my pillow.

I soon felt that I could not go to sleep—that I could not even close my eyes. I was wide awake, and in a high fever. Every nerve of my body trembled—every one of my senses seemed to be preternaturally sharpened. I tossed and rolled, and tried every kind of position, and perseveringly sought out the cold corners of the bed, and all to no purpose. Now I thrust my arms over the clothes; now, I violently shot my legs straight out down to the bottom of the bed; now, I convulsively coiled them up as near my chin as they would go; now, I shook out my crumpled pillow, changed it to the cool side, patted it flat, and lay down quietly on my back; now, I fiercely doubled it in two, set it up on end, thrust it against the board of the bed, and tried a sitting position. Every effort was in vain, I groaned in vexation, as I felt that I was in for a sleepless night.

What could I do. I had no book to read. And yet, unless I found out some method of diverting my mind, I felt certain that I was in the condition to imagine all sorts of horrors; to rack my brain with forebodings of every possible and impossible danger; to pass the night in suffering all conceivable varieties of nervous terror.

I raised myself on my elbow, and looked about the room—which was brightened by a lovely moonlight pouring straight through the window—to see if it contained any pictures or ornaments. While my eyes wandered from wall to wall, a remembrance of LeMaistre's delightful little book, *Voyage autour de ma chambre*,[12] occurred to me. I resolved to imitate the French author, and find occupation and amusement enough to relieve the tedium of my wakefulness by making a mental inventory of every article of furniture I could see, and by following up to their sources the multitude associations which even a chair, a table or a wash-hand stand may be made to call forth.

In the nervous unsettled state of my mind at that moment, I found it much easier to make my inventory than to make my reflections, and thereupon soon gave up all hope of thinking of LeMaistre's fanciful track—or, indeed, of thinking at all. I looked about the room at different articles of furniture, and did nothing more.

There was first the bed I was lying in, a four-post bed, of all things in the world to meet with in Paris—yes, a thorough clumsy British four-poster, with the regular top lined with chintz—the regular fringed valance all around—the regular stifling unwholesome curtains, which I remembered having mechanically drawn back against the posts without particularly noticing the bed when I first got into the room. Then there was the marble-topped wash-hand stand, from which the water I had spilt, in my hurry to pour it out, was still dripping, slowly and more slowly, on to the brick floor. Then two small chairs, with my coat, waistcoat, and trousers flung on them. Then a large elbow-chair, covered with dirty-white dimity,[13] with my cravat and shirt collar thrown over the back. Then a chest of drawers with two of the brass handles off, and a tawdry, broken china inkstand placed on it by way of ornament for the top. Then the dressing table, adorned by a very small looking-glass and a very large pincushion. Then the window—an unusually large window. Then a dark old picture, which the feeble candle dimly showed me. It was the picture of a fellow in a high Spanish hat, crowned with a plume of towering feathers. A swarthy sinister ruffian, looking upward—it might be at some tall gallows on which he was going to be hanged. At any rate, he had the appearance of thoroughly deserving it.

This picture put a kind of constraint upon me to look upward too—at the top of the bed. It was a gloomy and not an interesting object,

---

12: Le Maistre . . . *Voyage autour de ma chambre*: Journey Around My Room by Antoine Le Maistre (1608–1658), French lawyer and theological writer.
13. dimity: coarse, cotton fabric.

and I looked back at the picture. I counted the feathers in the man's hat—they stood out in relief—three white, two green. I observed the crown of his hat, which was of a conical shape, according to fashion supposed to have been favored by Guido Fawkes. I wondered what he was looking up at. It couldn't be at the stars; such a desperado was neither astrologer nor astronomer. It must be the high gallows, and he was going to be hanged presently. Would the executioner come into possession of his conical-crowned hat and plume of feathers? I counted the feathers again—three white, two green.

While I still lingered over this very improving and intellectual employment, my thoughts insensibly began to wander. The moonlight shining into the room reminded me of a certain moonlight night in England—the night after a private party in a Welsh valley. Every incident of the drive homeward, through lovely scenery, which the moonlight made lovelier than ever, came back to my remembrance, though I had never given the picnic a thought for years—though, if I had *tried* to recollect it, I could certainly have recalled little or nothing of that scene long past. Of all the wonderful faculties that help to tell us that we are immortal, which speaks the sublime truth more elegantly than memory? Here was I, in a strange house of the most suspicious character, in a situation of uncertainty and even of peril, which might seem to make the cool exercise of my recollection almost out of the question, nevertheless, remembering, quite involuntarily, places, people, conversations, minute circumstances of every kind, which I had thought forgotten forever, which I could not possibly have recalled at will, even under the most favorable auspices. And what cause had produced in a moment the whole of this strange, complicated, mysterious effect? Nothing but some rays of moonlight shining in at my bedroom window.

I was still thinking of that picnic—of our merriment on the drive home—of the sentimental young lady who *would* quote *Childe Harold*[14] because it was moonlight. I was absorbed by these past scenes and past amusements, when, in an instant, the thread on which my memories hung snapped asunder, my attention immediately came back to present things more vividly than ever and I found myself, I neither knew why nor wherefore, looking hard at the picture again.

Looking for what?

---

14. *Childe Harold:* a long narrative poem by English Romantic writer George Gordon, Lord Byron (1788–1824).

Good God! The man had pulled his hat down on his brow—No! the hat itself was gone! Where was the conical crown? Where were the feathers—three white, two green? Not there? In place of the hat and feathers, what dusky object was it that now hid his forehead, his eyes, his shading hand?

Was the bed moving?

I turned on my back and looked up. Was I mad?—drunk?—dreaming?—giddy again?—or was the top of the bed really moving down—sinking slowly, regularly, silently, horribly, right down throughout the whole of its length and breadth—right down upon me as I lay underneath?

My blood seemed to stand still. A deadly paralyzing coldness stole all over me as I turned my head round on the pillow, and determined to test whether the bed-top was really moving or not by keeping my eye on the man in the picture.

The next look in that direction was enough. The dull black, frowsy outline of the valance above me was within an inch of being parallel with his waist. I still looked breathlessly. And steadily and slowly—very slowly—I saw the figure, and the line of frame below the figure, vanish, as the valance moved down before it.

I am, constitutionally, anything but timid. I have been on more than one occasion in peril of my life, and have not lost my self-possession for an instant, but when the conviction first settled on my mind that the bed top was really moving, was steadily and continuously sinking down upon me, I looked up shuddering, helpless, panic-stricken, beneath the hideous machinery for murder which was advancing closer and closer to suffocate me where I lay.

I looked up, motionless, speechless, breathless. The candle fully spent, went out, but the moonlight still brightened the room. Down and down, without pausing and without sounding, came the bed-top, and still my panic-terror seemed to bind me faster to the mattress on which I lay—down and down it sank, till the dusty color from the lining of the canopy came stealing into my nostrils.

At that final moment the instinct of self-preservation startled me out of my trance, and I moved at last. There was just room for me to roll myself sideways off the bed. As I dropped noiselessly to the floor, the edge of the murderous canopy touched me on the shoulder.

Without stopping to draw my breath, without wiping the cold sweat from my face, I rose instantly on my knees to watch the bed-top. I was literally spellbound by it. If I had heard footsteps behind me, I could not have turned round; if a means of escape had been miraculously provided for me, I could not have moved to take advantage of it. The whole life in me was, at that moment, concentrated in my eyes.

It descended—the whole canopy, with the fringe round it, came down—down—close down, so close that there was not room now to squeeze my finger between the bed-top and the bed. I felt at the sides, and discovered that what had appeared to me from beneath to be the ordinary light canopy of a four-poster bed, was in reality a thick broad mattress, that substance of which was concealed by the valance and its fringe. I looked up and saw the four posts rising hideously bare. In the middle of the bed-top was a huge wooden screw that had evidently worked it down through a hole in the ceiling, just as ordinary presses are worked down on the substance selected for compression. The frightful apparatus moved without making the faintest noise. There had been no creaking as it came down, there was not the faintest sound from the room above. Amid a dead and awful silence I beheld before me—in the nineteenth century, and in the civilized capital of France—such a machine for secret murder by suffocation as might have existed in the worst days of the Inquisition, in the lonely inns among the Hartz Mountains, in the mysterious tribunals of Westphalia! Still, as I looked at it, I could not move, I could hardly breathe, but I began to recover the power of thinking, and in a moment I discovered the murderous conspiracy framed against me in all its horror.

My cup of coffee had been drugged, and drugged too strongly. I had been saved from being smothered by having taken an overdose of some narcotic. How I had chafed and fretted at the fever-fit which had preserved my life by keeping me awake! How recklessly I had confided myself to the two wretches who had led me into this room, determined, for the sake of my winnings, to kill me in my sleep by the surest and most horrible contrivance for secretly accomplishing my destruction! How many men, winners like me, had slept, as I had proposed to sleep, in that bed, and had never been seen or heard of more? I shuddered at the bare idea of it.

But ere long, all thought was again suspended by the sight of the murderous canopy moving once more. After it had remained on the bed—as nearly as I could guess—about ten minutes, it began to move up again. The villains who worked it from above evidently believed that their purpose was now accomplished. Slowly and silently, as it descended, that horrible bed-top rose toward its former place. When it reached the upper extremities of the four posts, it reached the ceiling too. Neither hole nor screw could be seen, the bed became in appearance an ordinary bed again—the canopy an ordinary canopy—even to the most suspicious eyes.

Now, for the first time, I was able to move—to rise from my knees—to dress myself in my upper clothing—and to consider of how I should escape. If I betrayed, by the smallest noise, that the attempt to suffocate me had failed, I was certain to be murdered. Had I made any noise already? I listened intently, looking towards the door.

No! No footsteps in the passage outside—no sound of a tread, light or heavy, in the room above—absolute silence everywhere. Besides locking and bolting my door, I had moved an old wooden chest against it, which I had found under the bed. To remove this chest (my blood ran cold as I thought of what its contents *might* be!) without making some disturbance was impossible, and, moreover, to think of escaping through the house, now barred up for the night, was sheer insanity. Only one chance was left to me—the window. I stole to it on tiptoe.

My bedroom was on the first floor, above an *entresol*,[15] and looked into a back street. I raised my hand to open the window, knowing that on that action hung, by the merest hair's breadth, my chance of safety. They keep vigilant watch in a House of Murder. If any part of the frame cracked, if the hinge creaked, I was a lost man! It must have occupied me at least five minutes, reckoning by time—five *hours,* reckoning by suspense—to open that window. I succeeded in doing it silently—in doing it with all the dexterity of a housebreaker—and then looked down into the street. To leap the distance beneath me would be almost certain destruction! Next, I looked round at the sides of the house. Down the left side ran a thick waterpipe—it passed close by the outer edge of the window. The moment I saw the pipe, I knew I must be saved. My breath came and went freely for the first time since I had seen the canopy of the bed moving down upon me!

To some men the means of escape which I had discovered might have seemed difficult and dangerous enough—to me the prospect of slipping down the pipe into the street did not suggest even a thought of peril. I had always been accustomed, by the practice of gymnastics, to keep up my schoolboy powers as a daring and expert climber, and

---

15. *entresol:* (French) mezzanine; middle story.

knew that my head, hands and feet would serve me faithfully in any hazards of ascent or descent. I had already got one leg over the window-sill when I remembered the handkerchief filled with money under my pillow. I could well have afforded to leave it behind me, but I was revengefully determined that the miscreants of the gambling-house should miss their plunder as well as their victim. So I went back to the bed and tied the heavy handkerchief at my back by my cravat.

Just as I made it tight and fixed it in a comfortable place, I thought I heard a sound of breathing outside the door. The chill feeling of horror ran through me again as I listened. No! Dead silence still in the passage—I had only heard the night air blowing softly into the room. The next moment I was on the window-sill—and the next I had a firm grip on the waterpipe with my hands and knees.

I slid down into the street easily and quietly, as I thought I should, and immediately set off at the top of my speed to a branch prefecture of police, which I knew was situated in the immediate neighborhood. A sub-prefect, and several picked men among his subordinates, happened to be up, maturing, I believe some scheme for discovering the perpetrator of a mysterious murder—which all Paris was talking of just then. When I began my story, in a breathless hurry and in very bad French, I could see that the sub-prefect suspected me of being a drunken Englishman who had robbed somebody, but he soon altered his opinion as I went on, and before I had anything like concluded, he shoved all the papers before him into a drawer, put on his hat, supplied me with another (for I was bare-headed), ordered a file of soldiers, desired his followers to get ready all sorts of tools for breaking open doors and ripping up brick-flooring, and took my arm, in the most friendly and familiar manner possible, to lead me with him out of the house. I will venture to say that when the sub-prefect was a little boy, and was taken for the first time to the play, he was not half as much pleased as he was now at the job in prospect for him at the gambling-house!

Away we went through the streets, the sub-prefect cross-examining and congratulating me in the same breath as we marched at the head of our *posse comitatus*.[16] Sentinels were placed at the back and front of the house the moment we got to it and a tremendous battery of knocks

---

16. *posse comitatus:* (Latin) a body of men authorized to help keep the peace; literally, "power of the county."

was directed against the door; a light appeared at a window; I was told to conceal myself behind the police; then came more knocks, and a cry of, "Open in the name of the law!" At that terrible summons bolts and locks gave way before an invisible hand, and the moment after the sub-prefect was in the passage, confronting a waiter half-dressed and ghastly pale. This was the short dialogue which immediately took place:

"We want to see the Englishman who is sleeping in this house."

"He went away hours ago."

"He did no such thing. His friend went away, he remained. Show us to his bedroom!"

"I swear to you, Monsieur le Sous-prefect, he is not here! He—"

"I swear to you, Monsieur le garçon, he is. He slept here—he didn't find your bed comfortable—he came to us to complain of it—he is among my men—and here am I to look for a flea or two in his bedstead. Renaudin!" (calling to one of his subordinates, and pointing to the waiter) "collar that man, and tie his hands behind him. Now then, gentlemen, let us walk upstairs."

Every man and woman in the house was secured—the "old soldier" the first. Then I identified the bed in which I had slept, and then we went into the room above.

No object that was at all extraordinary appeared in any part of it. The sub-prefect looked round the place, commanded everybody to be silent, stamped twice on the floor, called for a candle, looked attentively at the spot he had stamped on, and ordered the flooring there to be carefully taken up. This was done in no time. Lights were produced, and we saw a deep raftered cavity between the floor of the room and the ceiling of the room beneath. Through this cavity there ran perpendicularly a sort of case of iron thickly greased, and inside the case appeared the screw, which communicated with the bed-top below. Extra lengths of screws, freshly oiled, levers covered with felt, all the complete upper works of a heavy press—constructed with infernal ingenuity so as to join the fixtures below, and when taken to pieces again to go into the smallest possible compass[17]—were next discovered and pulled out on the floor. After some little difficulty, the sub-prefect succeeded in putting the machinery together and, leaving his men to work it, descended with me to the bedroom. The smothering canopy was then lowered, but not so noiselessly as I had seen it lowered. When

---

17. **compass:** an enclosed area.

I mentioned this to the sub-prefect, his answer, simple as it was, had a terrible significance. "My men," said he, "are working down the bed-top for the first time—the men whose money you won were in better practice."

We left the house in the sole possession of two police agents—every one of the inmates being removed to prison on the spot. The sub-prefect, after taking down my *procès-verbal*[18] in his office, returned with me to my hotel to get my passport. "Do you think," I asked as I gave it to him, "that any men have really been smothered in that bed as they tried to smother me?"

"I have seen dozens of drowned men laid out in the morgue," answered the sub-prefect, "in whose pocket-books were found letters stating that they had committed suicide in the Seine, because they had lost everything at the gaming-table. Do I know how many of these men entered the same gambling-house as you entered?—won as *you* won?—took that bed as you took it?—slept in it?—were smothered in it?—and were privately thrown into the river, with a letter of explanation written by the murderers and placed in their pocket-books? No man can say how many or how few have suffered the fate from which you have escaped. The people of the gambling-house kept their bedstead machinery a secret from *us*—even from the police! The dead keep the rest of the secret for them. Good-night, or rather good-morning, Monsieur Faulkner! Be at my office again at nine o'clock—in the meantime, *au revoir*!"

The rest of my story is soon told. I was examined and re-examined, the gambling-house was strictly searched all through from top to bottom, the prisoners were separately interrogated and two of the less guilty among them made a confession. I discovered that the old soldier was the master of the gambling-house—justice discovered that he had been drummed out of the army as a vagabond years ago, that he had been guilty of all sorts of villainies since, that he was in possession of stolen property, which the owners identified, and that he, the croupier, another accomplice, and the woman who had made my cup of coffee, were all in the secret of the bedstead. There appeared some reason to doubt whether the inferior persons attached to the house knew anything of the suffocating machinery, and they received the benefit of that doubt by being treated simply as thieves and

---

18. *procès verbal:* official statement.

vagabonds. As for the old soldier and his two head-myrmidons,[19] they went to the galleys,[20] the woman who had drugged my coffee was imprisoned for I forget how many years, the regular attendants at the gambling-house were considered "suspicious," and placed under "surveillance," and I became, for one whole week (which is a long time), the head "lion" in Parisian society. My adventures were dramatized by three illustrious playmakers, but never saw theatrical daylight, for the censorship forbade the introduction on the stage of a correct copy of the gambling-house bedstead.

One good result was produced by my adventure, which any censorship must have approved—it cured me of ever again trying Rouge et Noir as an amusement. The sight of a green cloth with packs of cards and heaps of money on it will henceforth be forever associated in my mind with the sight of a bed-canopy descending to suffocate me in the silence and darkness of the night.

---

19. myrmidons (mur′ mə dənz): subordinates.
20: the galleys: forced service onboard ships.

Discussion Questions

1. Why do the narrator and his friend go to this particular gambling house?

2. How does the narrator describe himself as a gambler ordinarily? How does he explain his loss of control this night?

3. Who is the "old soldier"? Why do you think he behaves as he does?

4. Describe the mechanism with which the gambling-house people attempt to murder the narrator.

5. How does the narrator manage to escape being smothered?

6. What happens to the narrator's social life as a result of his adventure? What comment, if any, do you think the author is making about society?

Suggestion for Writing

"My adventure," says the narrator, "was dramatized by three illustrious playmakers . . . ." Be an illustrious playmaker and dramatize a scene from this story. You might choose the scene after the croupier closes the table, when the old soldier plies the narrator with drink and finally drugs him; or the scene where the the narrator is being escorted to his room; or any other scene that you find effective. Plays of this period tended to be melodramatic and not overly subtle. (Theaters also used very elaborate stage machinery.) Pull out all the stops and write a rip-roaring adventure scene.

Charles Dickens (1812-1870)

Charles Dickens was born into a large, poor family and educated largely at home by his mother and at a preparatory day school. He read widely. When his father was arrested and sent to prison for debt, young Dickens went to work at a bootblacking warehouse. Later he worked as a clerk in an attorney's office and then as a journalist. His first publishing success was the novel *The Pickwick Papers,* in 1836. Many of his novels were published in serial form in monthly or weekly magazines. Such titles as *Oliver Twist, The Old Curiosity Shop, A Tale of Two Cities,* and *Great Expectations* were to gain him worldwide fame and considerable wealth. His portrayals of sympathetic young people—for which he drew upon his experiences as an impoverished youth—and colorful eccentrics struck deep chords with the reading public. Dickens's lecture tours and public readings in England and the United States were greatly cheered. He continues to be regarded as one of England's great novelists, and his works continue to be widely read and presented on stage and in films. *A Christmas Carol,* for example, is given countless stagings every year at the Christmas season.

The Signalman

"Halloa! Below there!"

When he heard a voice thus calling to him, he was standing at the door of his box, with a flag in his hand, furled round its short pole. One would have thought, considering the nature of the ground, that he could not have doubted from what quarter the voice came; but instead of looking up to where I stood on the top of the steep cutting nearly over his head, he turned himself about, and looked down the line. There was something remarkable in his manner of doing so, though I could not have said for my life what. But I know it was remarkable enough to attract my notice, even though his figure was foreshortened and shadowed, down in the deep trench, and mine was high above him, so steeped in the glow of an angry sunset that I had shaded my eyes with my hand before I saw him at all.

"Halloa! Below!"

From looking down the line, he turned himself about again, and raising his eyes, saw my figure high above him.

"Is there any path by which I can come down and speak to you?"

He looked up at me without replying, and I looked down at him without pressing him too soon with a repetition of my idle question. Just then there came a vague vibration in the earth and air, quickly changing into a violent pulsation, and an oncoming rush that caused me to start back, as though it had force to draw me down. When such vapor as rose to my height from this rapid train had passed me, and was skimming away over the landscape, I looked down again, and saw him refurling the flag he had shown while the train went by.

I repeated my enquiry. After a pause, during which he seemed to regard me with fixed attention, he motioned with his rolled-up flag towards a point on my level, some to or three hundred yards distant. I called down to him, "All right!" and made for that point. There, by dint of looking closely about me, I found a rough zigzag descending path notched out, which I followed.

The cutting was extremely deep, and unusually precipitate.[1] It was made through a clammy stone, that became oozier and wetter as I went

---

1. **precipitate** (pri´ sip ə tit): steep.

down. For these reasons, I found the way long enough to give me time to recall the singular air of reluctance or compulsion with which he had pointed out the path.

When I came down low enough upon the zigzag descent to see him again, I saw that he was standing between the rails on the way by which the rain had lately passed, in an attitude as if he were waiting for me to appear. He had his left hand at his chin, and that left elbow rested on his right hand, crossed over his breast. His attitude was one of such expectation and watchfulness that I stopped for a moment, wondering at it.

I resumed my downward way, and stepping out upon the level of the railroad, and drawing nearer to him, saw that he was a dark sallow man, with a dark beard and rather heavy eyebrows. His post was in as solitary and dismal a place as ever I saw. On either side, a dripping-wet wall of jagged stone, excluding all view but a strip of sky; the perspective one way only a crooked prolongation of this great dungeon; the shorter perspective in the other direction terminating in a gloomy red light, and the gloomier entrance to a black tunnel, in whose massive architecture there was a barbarous, depressing and forbidding air. So little sunlight ever found its way to this spot that it had an earthy, deadly smell; and so much cold wind rushed through it that it struck chill to me, as if I had left the natural world.

Before he stirred, I was near enough to him to have touched him. Not even then removing his eyes from mine, he stepped back one step, and lifted his hand.

This was a lonesome post to occupy (I said), and it had riveted my attention when I looked down from up yonder. A visitor was a rarity, I should suppose; not an unwelcome rarity, I hoped? In me, he merely saw a man who had been shut up within narrow limits all his life, and who, being at last set free, had a newly awakened interest in these great works. To such purpose I spoke to him; but I am far from sure of the terms I used; for, besides that I am not happy in opening any conversation, there was something in the man that daunted me.

He directed a most curious look towards the red light near the tunnel's mouth, and looked all about it, as if something were missing from it, and then looked at me.

That light was part of his charge? Was it not?

He answered in a low voice, "Don't you know it is?"

The monstrous thought came into my mind, as I perused the fixed eyes and the saturnine[2] face, that this was a spirit, not a man. I have speculated since, whether there may have been infection in his mind.

In my turn, I stepped back. But in making the action, I detected in his eyes some latent fear of me. This put the monstrous thought to flight.

"You look at me," I said, forcing a smile, "as if you had a dread of me."

"I was doubtful," he returned, "whether I had seen you before."

"Where?"

He pointed to the red light he had looked at.

"There?" I said.

Intently watchful of me, he replied (but without a sound), "Yes."

"My good fellow, what should I do there? However, be that as it may, I never was there, you may swear."

"I think I may," he rejoined. "Yes; I am sure I may."

His manner cleared, like my own. He replied to my remarks with readiness, and in well-chosen words. He had much to do there? Yes; that was to say, he had enough responsibility to bear; but exactness and watchfulness were what was required of him, and of actual work—manual labor—he had next to none. To change that signal, to trim those lights, and to turn this iron handle now and then, was all he had to do under that head. Regarding those many long and lonely hours of which I seemed to make so much, he could only say that the routine of his life had shaped itself into that form, and he had grown used to it. He had taught himself a language down here, if only to know it by sight, and to have formed his own crude ideas of pronunciation, he could be called learning it. He had also worked at fractions and decimals, and tried a little algebra; but he was, and had been as a boy, a poor hand at figures. Was it necessary for him when on duty always to remain in that channel of damp air, and could he never rise into the sunshine between those high stone walls? Why, that depended upon times and circumstances. Under some conditions there would be less upon the line than under others, and the same held good as to certain hours of the day and night. In bright weather, he did choose occasions for getting a little above these lower shadows; but, being at all times liable to be called by his electric bell, and at such times listening for it with redoubled anxiety, the relief was less than I would suppose.

---

2. **saturnine:** gloomy.

He took me into his box, where there was a fire, a desk for an official book in which he had to make certain entries, a telegraphic instrument with its dial, face and needles, and the little bell of which he had spoken. On my trusting that he would excuse the remark that he had been well educated, and (I hoped I might say without offense) perhaps educated above that station, he observed that instances of slight incongruity in such wise would rarely be found wanting among large bodies of men; that he had heard it was so in workhouses, in the police force, even in that last desperate resource, the army; and that he knew it was so, more or less, in any great railway staff. He had been, when young (if I could believe it, sitting in that hut—he scarcely could), a student of natural philosophy, and had attended lectures; but he had run wild, misused his opportunities, gone down and never risen again. He had no complaint to offer about that. He had made his bed, and he lay upon it. It was far too late to make another.

All that I have here condensed he said in a quiet manner, with his grave dark regards divided between me and the fire. He threw in the word "sir" from time to time, and especially when he referred to his youth, as though to request me to understand that he claimed to be nothing but what I found him. He was several times interrupted by the little bell, and had to read off messages, and send replies. Once he had to stand without the door, and display a flag as a train passed, and make some verbal communication to the driver. In the discharge of his duties, I observed him to be remarkably exact and vigilant, breaking off his discourse at a syllable, and remaining silent until what he had to do was done.

In a word, I should have set this man down as one of the safest of men to be employed in that capacity, but for the circumstance that while he was speaking to me he twice broke off with a fallen color, turned his face towards the little bell when it did not ring, opened the door of the hut (which was kept shut to exclude the unhealthy damp), and looked out towards the red light near the mouth of the tunnel. On both of those occasions, he came back to the fire with the inexplicable air upon him which I had remarked, without being able to define, when we were so far asunder.[3]

Said I, when I rose to leave him, "You almost make me think that I have met with a contented man."

---

3. asunder: apart

(I am afraid I must acknowledge that I said it to lead him on.)

"I believe I used to be so," he rejoined, in the low voice in which he had first spoken; "but I am troubled, sir, I am troubled."

He would have recalled the words if he could. He had said them, however, and I took them up quickly.

"With what? What is your trouble?"

"It is very difficult to impart, sir. It is very, very difficult to speak of. If ever you make me another visit, I will try to tell you."

"But I expressly intend to make you another visit. Say, when shall it be?"

"I go off early in the morning, and I shall be on again at ten tomorrow night, sir."

"I will come at eleven."

He thanked me, and went out at the door with me. "I'll show my white light, sir," he said, in his peculiar low voice, "til you have found the way up. When you have found it, don't call out! And when you are at the top, don't call out!"

His manner seemed to make the place strike colder to me, but I said no more than, "Very well."

"And when you come down tomorrow night, don't call out! Let me ask you a parting question. What made you cry, 'Halloa! Below there!' tonight?"

"Heaven knows," said I. "I cried something to that effect—"

"Not to that effect, sir. Those were the very words, I know them well."

"I admit those were the very words. I said them, no doubt, because I saw you below."

"For no other reason?"

"What other reason could I possibly have?"

"You had no feeling that they were conveyed to you in any supernatural way?"

"No."

He wished me good-night, and held up his light. I walked by the side of the down line of rails (with a very disagreeable sensation of a train coming behind me) until I found the path. It was easier to mount than descend, and I got back to my inn without any adventure.

Punctual to my appointment, I placed my foot on the first notch of the zigzag next as the distant clocks were striking eleven. He was waiting for me at the bottom, with his white light on. "I have not called out," I said, when we came close together, "may I speak now?" "By all means, sir." "Goodnight, then, and here's my hand." "Good-night sir, and here's mine." With that we walked side by side to his box, entered it, closed the door and sat down by the fire.

"I have made up my mind, sir," he began, bending forward as soon as we were seated, and speaking in a tone but a little above a whisper, "that you shall not have to ask me twice what troubles me. I took you for someone else yesterday evening. That troubles me."

"That mistake?"

"No. That someone else."

"Who is it?"

"I don't know."

"Like me?"

"I don't know, I never saw the face. The left arm is across the face, and the right arm is waved—violently waved. This way."

I followed his action with my eyes, and it was the action of an arm gesticulating with the utmost passion and vehemence, "For God's sake, clear the way!"

"One moonlight night," said the man, "I was sitting here, when I heard a voice cry, 'Halloa! Below there!' I started up, looked from that door, and saw this someone else standing by the red light near the tunnel, waving as I just now showed you. The voice seemed hoarse with shouting, and it cried 'Look out! Look out!' And then again, 'Halloa! Below there! Look out!' I caught up my lamp, turned it on red, and ran towards the figure, calling, 'What's wrong? What has happened? Where?' It stood just outside the blackness of the tunnel. I advanced so close upon it that I wondered at its keeping the sleeve across its eyes. I ran right up to it, and had my hand stretched out to pull the sleeve away, when it was gone.

"Into the tunnel?" said I.

"No I ran on into the tunnel, five hundred yards. I stopped, and held my lamp above my head, and saw the figures of the measured distance, and saw the wet stains stealing down the walls and trickling through the arch. I ran out again faster than I had run in (for I had a mortal abhorrence of the place upon me), and I looked all round the red light with my own red light, and I went up the iron ladder to the gallery atop of it, and I came down again, and ran back here. I telegraphed both ways, 'An alarm has been given. Is anything wrong?' The answer came back, both ways, 'All's well.'"

Resisting the slow touch of a frozen finger tracing out my spine, I showed him how this figure must be a deception of his sense of sight; and how figures, originating in disease of the delicate nerves that minister to the functions of the eye, were known to have often troubled patients, some of whom had become conscious of the nature of their affliction, and had even proved it by experiments upon themselves. "As to an imaginary cry," said I, "do but listen for a moment to the wind in this unnatural valley while we speak so low, and the wild harp it makes of the telegraph wires."

That was all very well, he returned, after we had sat listening for a while, and he ought to know something of the wind and the wires—he who so often passed long winter nights there, alone and watching. But he would beg to remark that he had not finished.

I asked his pardon, and he slowly added these words, touching my arm, "Within six hours after the appearance, the memorable accident on this line happened, and within ten hours the dead and wounded were brought along through the tunnel over the spot where the figure had stood."

A disagreeable shudder crept over me, but I did my best against it. It was not to be denied, I rejoined, that this was a remarkable coincidence, calculated deeply to impress his mind. But it was unquestionable that remarkable coincidences did continually occur, and they must be taken into account in dealing with such a subject. Though to be sure I must admit, I added (for I thought I saw he was going to bring the object to bear upon me), men of common sense did not allow much for coincidences in making the ordinary calculations of life.

He again begged to remark that he had not finished.

I again begged his pardon for being betrayed into interruptions.

"This," he said, again laying his hand upon my arm, and glancing over his shoulder with hollow eyes, "was just a year ago. Six or seven months passed, and I had recovered from the surprise and shock, when one morning, as the day was breaking, I, standing at the door, looked towards the red light and saw the spectre again." He stopped, with a fixed look at me.

"Did it cry out?

"No, It was silent."

"Did it wave its arm?"

"No, It leaned against the shaft of the light, with both hands before the face. Like this."

Once more I followed his action with my eyes. It was action of mourning. I have seen such an attitude in stone figures on tombs.

"Did you go up to it?"

"I came in and sat down, partly to collect my thoughts, partly because it had turned me faint. When I went to the door again, daylight was above, and the ghost was gone."

"But nothing followed? Nothing came of this?"

He touched me on the arm with his forefinger twice or thrice, giving a ghastly nod each time: "That very day, as a train came out of the tunnel, I noticed, at a carriage window on my side, what looked like a confusion of hands and heads, and something waved. I saw it in time to signal the driver, Stop! He shut off, and put his brake on, but the train drifted past here a hundred and fifty yards or more. I ran after it, and, as I went along, heard terrible screams and cries. A beautiful young lady had died instantaneously in one of the compartments, and was brought in here and laid down on the floor between us."

Involuntarily I pushed my chair back, as I looked from the boards at which he pointed to himself.

"True, sir, True. Precisely as it happened, so I tell it you."

I could think of nothing to say to any purpose, and my mouth was very dry. The wind and the wires took up the story with a long lamenting wail.

He resumed. "Now, sir, mark this, and judge how my mind is troubled. The spectre came back a week ago. Ever since, it has been there, now and again, by fits and starts."

"At the light?"

"At the danger-light."

"What does it seem to do?"

He repeated, if possible with increased passion and vehemence, that former gesticulation of, "For God's sake, clear the way!"

Then he went on. "I have no peace or rest from it. It calls to me, for many minutes together, in an agonized manner, "Below there! Look out! Look out!" It stands waving to me. It rings my little bell—"

I caught at that. "Did it ring your bell yesterday evening when I was here and you went out the door?"

"Twice."

"Why, see," said I, "how your imagination misleads you. My eyes were on the bell, and my ears were open to the bell, and if I am a living man, it did *not* ring at those times. No, nor at any other time, except when it was rung in the natural course of physical things by the station communicating with you."

He shook his head. "I have never made a mistake as to that yet, sir. I have never confused the spectre's ring with the man's. The ghost's ring is a strange vibration in the bell that it derives from nothing else, and I have not asserted that the bell stirs to the eye. I don't wonder that you failed to hear it. But I heard it."

"And did the spectre seem to be there, when you looked out?"

"It *was* there."

"Both times?"

He repeated firmly, "Both times."

"Will you come to the door with me, and look for it now?"

He bit his underlip as though he were somewhat unwilling, but arose. I opened the door, and stood on the step, while he stood in the doorway. There was the danger-light. There was the dismal mouth of the tunnel. There were the high, wet stone walls of the cutting. There were the stars above them.

"Do you see it?" I asked him, taking particular note of his face. His eyes were prominent and strained, but not very much more so, perhaps, than my own had been when I directed them earnestly towards the same spot.

"No," he answered, "it is not there."

"Agreed," said I.

We went in again, shut the door and resumed our seats. I was thinking how best to improve this advantage, if it might be called one, when he took up the conversation in such matter-of-course way, so assuming that there could be no serious question of fact between us, that I felt myself placed in the weakest of positions.

"By this time you will fully understand, sir," he said, "that what troubles me so dreadfully is the question, What does the spectre mean?"

I was not sure, I told him, that I did fully understand.

"What is it warning against?" he said, ruminating, with his eyes on the fire, and only at times turning them on me. "What is the danger? Where is the danger? There is danger overhanging somewhere on the line. Some dreadful calamity will happen. It is not to be doubted this third time, after what has gone before. But surely this is a cruel haunting of *me*. What can *I* do?"

He pulled out his handkerchief, and wiped the drops from his heated forehead.

"If I telegraphed danger on either side of me, or on both, I can give no reason for it," he went on, wiping the palms of his hands. "I should get into trouble, and do no good. They would think I was mad. This is the way it would work: Message—'Danger! Take care!' Answer—'What Danger? Where?' Message—'Don't know. But for God's sake, take care!' They would displace me. What else could they do?"

His pain of mind was most pitiable to see. It was the mental torture of a conscientious man, oppressed beyond endurance by an unintelligible responsibility involving life.

"When it first stood under the danger-light," he went on, putting his dark hair back from his head, and drawing his hands outward across and across his temples in an extremity of feverish distress, "why not tell me where that accident was to happen—if it must happen? Why not tell me how it could be averted—if it could have been averted? When on its second coming it hid its face, why not tell me, instead, 'She is going to die. Let them keep her at home'? If it came, on those two occasions, only to show me that its warnings were true, and so to prepare me for the third, why not warn me plainly now? And I, Lord help me! A mere poor signalman on this solitary station! Why not go to somebody with credit to be believed, and power to act?"

When I saw him in this state, I saw that for the poor man's sake, as well as for the public safety, what I had to do for the time was to compose his mind. Therefore, setting aside all question of reality or unreality between us, I represented to him that whoever thoroughly discharged his duty must do well, and that at least it was his comfort that he understood his duty, though he did not understand these confounding appearances. In this effort I succeeded far better in the attempt to reason him out of his conviction. He became calm; the occupations incidentally to his post as the night advanced began to make larger demands on his attention, and I left him at two in the morning. I had offered to stay through the night, but he would not hear of it.

That I more than once looked back at the red light as I ascended the pathway, that I did not like the red light, and that I should have slept but poorly if my bed had been under it, I see no reason to conceal. Nor did I like the two sequences of the accident and the dead girl. I see no reason to conceal that either.

But what ran most in my thoughts was the consideration how ought I to act, having become the recipient of this disclosure? I had proved the man to be intelligent, vigilant, painstaking and exact but how long might he remain so, in his state of mind? Though in a subordinate position, still he held a most important trust, and would I (for instance) like to stake my own life on the chances of his continuing to execute it with precision?

Unable to overcome a feeling that there would be something treacherous in my communicating what he had told me to his superiors in the company, without first being plain with himself and proposing a middle course to him, I ultimately resolved to offer to accompany him (otherwise keeping his secret for the present) to the wisest medical practitioner we could hear of in those parts, and to take his opinion. A change in his time of duty would come round next night, he had apprised[4] me, and he would be off an hour or two after sunrise, and on again soon after sunset. I had appointed to return accordingly.

Next evening was a lovely evening, and I walked out early to enjoy it. The sun was not yet quite down when I traversed the field path near the top of the deep cutting. I would extend my walk for an hour, I said to myself, half an hour on and half an hour back, and it would then be time to go to my signalman's box.

Before pursuing my stroll, I stepped to the brink and mechanically looked down, from the point from which I had first seen him. I cannot describe the thrill that seized upon me when, close at the mouth of the tunnel, I saw the appearance of a man, with his left sleeve across his eyes, passionately waving his right arm.

The nameless horror that oppressed me passed in a moment, for in a moment I saw that this appearance of a man was a man indeed, and that there was a little group of other men, standing at a short distance, to whom he seemed to be rehearsing the gesture he made. The danger-light was not yet lighted. Against its shaft, a little low hut, entirely new to me, had been made of some wooden supports and tarpaulin. It looked no bigger than a bed.

With an irresistible sense that something was wrong, with a flashing self-reproachful fear that fatal mischief had come of my leaving the man there and causing no one to be sent to overlook or correct what he did, I descended the notched path will all the speed I could make.

"What is the matter?" I asked the men.

"Signalman killed this morning, sir."

"Not the man belonging to that box?"

---

4. **apprised:** informed.

"Yes, sir."

"Not the man I know?"

"You will recognize him sir, if you knew him," said the man who spoke for the others, solemnly uncovering his own head and raising the end of the tarpaulin, "for his face is quite composed."

"Oh, how did this happen, how did this happen?" I asked, turning from one to another as the hut closed in again.

"He was cut down by an engine, sir. No man in England knew his work better. But somehow he was not clear of the outer rail. It was just at broad day. He had struck the light, and had the lamp in his hand. As the engine came out of the tunnel, his back was towards her, and she cut him down. That man drove her, and was showing how it happened. Show the gentleman, Tom."

The man, who wore rough dark dress, stepped back to his former place at the mouth of the tunnel.

"Coming round the curve in the tunnel, sir," he said, "I saw him at the end, like as if I saw him down a perspective-glass.[5] There was not time to check speed, and I knew him to be very careful. As he didn't seem to take heed of the whistle, I shut it off when we were running down upon him, and called to him as loud as I could call."

"What did you say?"

"I said, 'Below there! Look out! Look out! For God's sake, clear the way.'"

I started.

"Ah! It was a dreadful time, sir. I never left calling to him. I put this arm before my eyes not to see, and I waved this arm to the last, but it was no use."

Without prolonging the narrative to dwell on any one of its curious circumstances more than the other, I may, in closing it, point out the coincidence that the warning of the engine-driver included, not only the words which the unfortunate signalman had repeated to me as haunting him, but also the words which I myself—not he—had attached, and that only in my own mind, to the gesticulation he had imitated.

---

5. **perspective-glass:** an optical device like a telescope.

Discussion Questions

1. Describe the setting. What part does the setting play in the events of this story?

2. What is the narrator doing in this place? Why does he involve himself in the signalman's story?

3. What two disasters does the signalman tell the narrator about that had been foretold by ghostly appearances?

4. What about the ghostly appearances now troubles the signalman?

5. How do the latest ghostly appearances seem finally to be related to the death of the signalman?

Suggestion for Writing

The narrator feels that he would be treacherous if he tells railroad officials what the signalman told him, yet he still worries that the man might be endangering his own and others' safety with his state of mind. Suppose that the narrator overcomes his worries. What would he say to the railroad officials? Write a letter to the signalman's superior, suggesting that someone needs to look into things. Will you repeat the signalman's story and risk his being thought crazy, or will you simply hint that something is wrong and risk the official's not paying attention?

Sir Arthur Conan Doyle (1859-1930)

Born in Scotland, Arthur Conan Doyle's early education was at various religious schools in England and Austria. He earned a medical degree from Edinburgh University, Scotland, and then practiced medicine in England and as a ship's doctor in the Arctic and Africa. Doyle began writing as a way to supplement his physician's income. His most famous character, Sherlock Holmes, was based on a memorable instructor he had had in Edinburgh. Eventually he abandoned medicine—at which he had never been very successful—to write full time. He was knighted in 1902 as a reward for his defense of the British cause in his book *The Great Boer War*. After the death of his son in World War I, Doyle devoted much of his time and fortune to spiritualism, writing and lecturing about the possibilities of communicating with the dead. Although Doyle preferred to be remembered for his historical novels, for which he did much research, his name will forever be linked with that of his creation, Sherlock Holmes, probably the most widely-recognized fictional detective of all time.

The Brazilian Cat

It is hard luck on a young fellow to have expensive tastes, great expectations, aristocratic connections, but no actual money in his pocket, and no profession by which he may earn any. The fact was that my father, a good, sanguine, easy-going man, had such confidence in the wealth and benevolence of his bachelor elder brother, Lord Southerton, that he took it for granted that I, his only son, would never be called upon to earn a living for myself. He imagined that if there were not a vacancy for me on the great Southerton Estates, at least there would be found some post in that diplomatic service which still remains the special preserve of our privileged classes. He died too early to realize how false his calculations had been. Neither my uncle nor the State took the slightest notice of me, or showed any interest in my career. An occasional brace of pheasants, or basket of hares, was all that ever reached me to remind me that I was heir to Otwell House and one of the richest estates in the country. In the meantime, I found myself a bachelor and man about town, living in a suite of apartments in Grosvenor Mansions, with no occupation save that of pigeon-shooting and polo-playing at Hurlingham. Month by month I realized that it was more and more difficult to get the brokers to renew my bills, or to cash any further post-obits[1] upon an unentailed property. Ruin lay right across my path, and every day I saw it clearer, nearer, and more absolutely unavoidable.

What made me feel my own poverty the more was that, apart from the great wealth of Lord Southerton, all my other relations were fairly well-to-do. The nearest of these was Everard King, my father's nephew and my own first cousin, who had spent an adventurous life in Brazil, and had now returned to this country to settle down on his fortune. We never knew how he made his money, but he appeared to have plenty of it, for he bought the estate of Greylands, near Clipton-on-the-Marsh, in Suffolk. For the first year of his residence in England he took no more notice of me than my miserly uncle; but at last one summer morning, to my very great relief and joy, I received a letter asking me

---

1. post-obits: pledges to pay debts after the death of a certain person from whom one expects to inherit money.

to come down that very day and spend a short visit at Greylands Court. I was expecting a rather long visit to Bankruptcy Court at the time, and this interruption seemed almost providential. If I could only get on terms with this unknown relative of mine, I might pull through yet. For the family credit he could not let me go entirely to the wall. I ordered my valet to pack my valise, and I set off the same evening for Clipton-on-the-Marsh.

After changing at Ipswich, a little local train deposited me at a small, deserted station lying amidst a rolling grassy country, with a sluggish and winding river curving in and out amidst the valleys, between high, silted banks, which showed that we were within reach of the tide. No carriage was awaiting me (I found afterwards that my telegram had been delayed), so I hired a dogcart at the local inn. The driver, an excellent fellow, was full of my relative's praises, and I learned from him that Mr. Everard King was already a name to conjure with in that part of the county. He had entertained the school-children, he had thrown his grounds open to visitors, he had subscribed to charities—in short, his benevolence had been so universal that my driver could only account for it on the supposition that he had parliamentary ambitions.

My attention was drawn away from my driver's panegyric[2] by the appearance of a very beautiful bird which settled on a telegraph-post beside the road. At first I thought that it was a jay, but it was larger, with a brighter plumage. The driver accounted for its presence at once by saying that it belonged to the very man whom we were about to visit. It seems that the acclimatization of foreign creatures was one of his hobbies, and that he had brought with him from Brazil a number of birds and beasts which he was endeavoring to rear in England. When once we had passed the gates of Greylands Park we had ample evidence of this taste of his. Some small spotted deer, a curious wild pig known, I believe, as a peccary, a gorgeously feathered oriole, some sort of armadillo, and a singular lumbering in-toed beast like a very fat badger, were among the creatures which I observed as we drove along the winding avenue.

Mr. Everard King, my unknown cousin, was standing in person upon the steps of his house, for he had seen us in the distance, and guessed that it was I. His appearance was very homely and benevolent, short and stout, forty-five years old, perhaps, with a round, good-humored

---

2. **panegyric** (pa nə jir′ ik): speech of praise.

face, burned brown with the tropical sun, and shot with a thousand wrinkles. He wore white linen clothes, in true planter style, with a cigar between his lips, and a large Panama hat upon the back of his head. It was such a figure as one associates with a veranda-ed bungalow, and it looked curiously out of place in front of this broad, stone English mansion, with its solid wings and its Palladio[3] pillars before the doorway.

"My dear!" he cried, glancing over his shoulder; "my dear, here is our guest! Welcome, welcome to Greylands! I am delighted to make your acquaintance, Cousin Marshall, and I take it as a great compliment that you should honor this sleepy little country place with your presence."

Nothing could be more hearty than his manner, and he set me at my ease in an instant. But it needed all his cordiality to atone for the frigidity and even rudeness of his wife, a tall, haggard woman, who came forward at his summons. She was, I believe, of Brazilian extraction, though she spoke excellent English, and I excused her manners on the score of her ignorance of our customs. She did not attempt to conceal, however, either then or afterwards, that I was no very welcome visitor at Greylands Court. Her actual words were, as a rule, courteous, but she was the possessor of a pair of particularly expressive dark eyes, and I read in them very clearly from the first that she heartily wished me back in London once more.

However, my debts were too pressing and my designs upon my wealthy relative were too vital for me to allow them to be upset by the ill-temper of his wife, so I disregarded her coldness and reciprocated the extreme cordiality of his welcome. No pains had been spared by him to make me comfortable. My room was a charming one. He implored me to tell him anything which could add to my happiness. It was on the tip of my tongue to inform him that a blank check would materially help towards that end, but I felt that it might be premature in the present state of our acquaintance. The dinner was excellent, and as we sat together afterwards over his Havanas and coffee, which later he told me was specially prepared upon his own plantation, it seemed to me that all my driver's eulogies were justified, and that I had never met a more large-hearted and hospitable man.

But, in spite of his cheery good nature, he was a man with a strong will and a fiery temper of his own. Of this I had an example upon the

---

3. **Palladio:** in the neoclassical style of Italian architect Andrea Palladio (1508–1580).

following morning. The curious aversion which Mrs. Everard King had conceived towards me was so strong, that her manner at breakfast was almost offensive. But her meaning became unmistakable when her husband had quitted the room.

"The best train in the day is at twelve-fifteen," said she.

"But I was not thinking of going today," I answered, frankly—perhaps even defiantly, for I was determined not to be driven out by this woman.

"Oh, if it rests with you—" said she, and stopped with a most insolent expression in her eyes.

"I am sure," I answered, "that Mr. Everard King would tell me if I were outstaying my welcome."

"What's this? What's this?" said a voice, and there he was in the room. He had overheard my last words, and a glance at our faces had told him the rest. In an instant his chubby, cheery face set into an expression of absolute ferocity.

"Might I trouble you to walk outside, Marshall?" said he. (I may mention that my own name is Marshall King.)

He closed the door behind me, and then, for an instant, I heard him talking in a low voice of concentrated passion to his wife. This gross breach of hospitality had evidently hit upon his tenderest point. I am no eavesdropper, so I walked out on to the lawn. Presently I heard a hurried step behind me, and there was the lady, her face pale with excitement, and her eyes red with tears.

"My husband has asked me to apologize to you, Mr. Marshall King," said she, standing with downcast eyes before me.

"Please do not say another word, Mrs. King."

Her dark eyes suddenly blazed out at me.

"You fool!" she hissed, with frantic vehemence, and turning on her heel swept back to the house.

The insult was so outrageous, so insufferable, that I could only stand staring after her in bewilderment. I was still there when my host joined me. He was his cheery, chubby self once more.

"I hope that my wife has apologized for her foolish remarks," said he.

"Oh, yes—yes, certainly!"

He put his hand through my arm and walked with me up and down the lawn.

"You must not take it seriously," said he. "It would grieve me inexpressibly if you curtailed your visit by one hour. The fact is—there is no reason why there should be any concealment between relatives—that my poor dear wife is incredibly jealous. She hates that anyone—male or female—should for an instant come between us. Her ideal is a desert island and an eternal *tête-a-tête*.⁴ That gives you the clue to her actions, which are, I confess, upon this particular point, not very far removed from mania. Tell me that you will think no more of it."

"No, no; certainly not."

"Then light this cigar and come round with me and see my little menagerie."

The whole afternoon was occupied by this inspection, which included all the birds, beasts, and even reptiles which he had imported. Some were free, some in cages, a few actually in the house. He spoke with enthusiasm of his successes and his failures, his births and his deaths, and he would cry out in his delight, like a schoolboy, when, as we walked, some gaudy bird would flutter up from the grass, or some curious beast slink into the cover. Finally he led me down a corridor which extended from one wing of the house. At the end of this there was a heavy door with a sliding shutter in it, and beside it there projected from the wall an iron handle attached to a wheel and a drum. A line of stout bars extended across the passage.

"I am about to show you the jewel of my collection," said he. "There is only one other specimen in Europe, now that the Rotterdam cub is dead. It is a Brazilian cat."

"But how does that differ from any other cat?"

"You will soon see that," said he, laughing. "Will you kindly draw that shutter and look through?"

I did so, and found that I was gazing into a large, empty room, with stone flags, and small, barred windows upon the farther wall. In the center of this room, lying in the middle of a golden patch of sunlight, there was stretched a huge creature, as large as a tiger, but as black and sleek as ebony. It was simply a very enormous and very well-kept black cat, and it cuddled up and basked in that yellow pool of light exactly as a cat would do. It was so graceful, so sinewy, and so gently and smoothly diabolical, that I could not take my eyes from the opening.

"Isn't he splendid?" said my host, enthusiastically.

"Glorious! I never saw such a noble creature."

"Some people call it a black puma, but really it is not a puma at all. That fellow is nearly eleven feet from tail to tip. Four years ago he was

---

4. *tête-á-tête* (tet ə tet´): (French) private conversation.

a little ball of black fluff, with two yellow eyes staring out of it. He was sold to me as a new-born cub up in the wild country at the head-waters of the Rio Negro.[5] They speared his mother to death after she had killed a dozen of them."

"They are ferocious, then?"

"The most absolutely treacherous and bloodthirsty creatures upon earth. You talk about a Brazilian cat to an up-country Indian, and see him get the jumps. They prefer humans to game. This fellow has never tasted living blood yet, but when he does he will be a terror. At present he won't stand anyone but me in his den. Even Baldwin, the groom, dare not go near him. As to me, I am his mother and father in one."

As he spoke he suddenly, to my astonishment, opened the door and slipped in, closing it instantly behind him. At the sound of his voice the huge, lithe creature rose, yawned and rubbed its round, black head affectionately against his side, while he patted and fondled it.

"Now, Tommy, into your cage!" said he.

The monstrous cat walked over to one side of the room and coiled itself up under a grating. Everard King came out, and taking the iron handle which I have mentioned, he began to turn it. As he did so the line of bars in the corridor began to pass through a slot in the wall and closed up the front of this grating, so as to make an effective cage. When it was in position he opened the door once more and invited me into the room, which was heavy with the pungent, musty smell peculiar to the great carnivora.[6]

"That's how we work it," said he. "We give him the run of the room for exercise, and then at night we put him in his cage. You can let him out by turning the handle from the passage, or you can, as you have seen, coop him up in the same way. No, no, you should not do that!"

I had put my hand between the bars to pat the glossy, heaving flank. He pulled it back, with a serious face.

"I assure you that he is not safe. Don't imagine that because I can take liberties with him anyone else can. He is very exclusive in his friends—aren't you, Tommy? Ah, he hears his lunch coming to him! Don't you, boy?"

A step sounded in the stone-flagged passage, and the creature had sprung to his feet, and was pacing up and down the narrow cage, his

---

5. **Rio Negro:** river in Brazil.
6. **carnivora:** flesh-eating mammals.

yellow eyes gleaming, and his scarlet tongue rippling and quivering over the white line of his jagged teeth. A groom entered with a coarse joint upon a tray, and thrust it through the bars to him. He pounced lightly upon it, carried it off to the corner, and there, holding it between his paws, tore and wrenched at it, raising his bloody muzzle every now and then to look at us. It was a malignant and yet fascinating sight.

"You can't wonder that I am fond of him, can you?" said my host, as we left the room, "especially when you consider that I have had the rearing of him. It was no joke bringing him over from the center of South America; but here he is safe and sound—and, as I have said, far the most perfect specimen in Europe. The people at the Zoo are dying to have him, but I really can't part with him. Now, I think that I have inflicted my hobby upon you long enough, so we cannot do better than follow Tommy's example, and go to our lunch."

My South American relative was so engrossed by his grounds and their curious occupants, that I hardly gave him credit at first for having any interests outside them. That he had some, and pressing ones, was soon borne in upon me by the number of telegrams which he received. They arrived at all hours, and were always opened by him with the utmost eagerness and anxiety upon his face. Sometimes I imagined that it must be the Turf, and sometimes the Stock Exchange, but certainly he had some very urgent business going forwards which was not transacted upon the Downs of Suffolk. During the six days of my visit he had never fewer than three or four telegrams a day, and sometimes as many as seven or eight.

I had occupied these six days so well, that by the end of them I had succeeded in getting upon the most cordial terms with my cousin. Every night we had sat up late in the billiard-room, he telling me the most extraordinary stories of his adventures in America—stories so desperate and reckless, that I could hardly associate them with the brown little, chubby man before me. In return, I ventured upon some of my own reminiscences of London life, which interested him so much, that he vowed he would come up to Grosvenor Mansions and stay with me. He was anxious to see the faster side of city life, and certainly, though I say it, he could not have chosen a more competent guide. It was not until the last day of my visit that I ventured to approach that which was on my mind. I told him frankly about my pecuniary difficulties and my impending ruin, and I asked his advice—

though I hoped for something more solid. He listened attentively, puffing hard at his cigar.

"But surely," said he, "you are the heir of our relative, Lord Southerton?"

"I have every reason to believe so, but he would never make me any allowance."

"No, no, I have heard of his miserly ways. My poor Marshall, your position has been a very hard one. By the way, have you heard any news of Lord Southerton's health lately?"

"He has always been in a critical condition ever since my childhood."

"Exactly—a creaking hinge, if ever there was one. Your inheritance may be a long way off. Dear me, how awkwardly situated you are!"

"I had some hopes, sir, that you, knowing all the facts, might be inclined to advance—"

"Don't say another word, my dear boy," he cried, with the utmost cordiality; "we shall talk it over tonight, and I give you my word that whatever is in my power shall be done."

I was not sorry that my visit was drawing to a close, for it is unpleasant to feel that there is one person in the house who eagerly desires your departure. Mrs. King's sallow face and forbidding eyes had become more and more hateful to me. She was no longer actively rude—her fear of her husband prevented her—but she pushed her insane jealousy to the extent of ignoring me, never addressing me, and in every way making my stay at Greylands as uncomfortable as she could. So offensive was her manner during that last day, that I should certainly have left had it not been for that interview with my host in the evening which would, I hoped, retrieve my broken fortunes.

It was very late when it occurred, for my relative, who had been receiving even more telegrams than usual during the day, went off to his study after dinner, and only emerged when the household had retired to bed. I heard him go round locking the doors, as custom was of a night, and finally he joined me in the billiard-room. His stout figure was wrapped in a dressing-gown, and he wore a pair of red Turkish slippers without any heels. Settling down into an arm-chair, he brewed himself a glass of grog, in which I could not help noticing that the whiskey considerably predominated over the water.

"My word!" said he, "what a night!"

It was, indeed. The wind was howling and screaming round the house, and the latticed windows rattled and shook as if they were coming in. The glow of the yellow lamps and the flavor of our cigars seemed the brighter and more fragrant for the contrast.

"Now, my boy," said my host, "we have the house and the night to ourselves. Let me have an idea of how your affairs stand, and I will see what can be done to set them in order. I wish to hear every detail."

Thus encouraged, I entered into a long exposition, in which all my tradesmen and creditors from my landlord to my valet, figured in turn. I had notes in my pocket-book, and I marshalled my facts, and gave, I flatter myself, a very businesslike statement of my own unbusinesslike ways and lamentable position. I was depressed, however, to notice that my companion's eyes were vacant and his attention elsewhere. When he did occasionally throw out a remark it was so entirely perfunctory and pointless, that I was sure he had not in the least followed my remarks. Every now and then he roused himself and put on some show of interest, asking me to repeat or to explain more fully, but it was always to sink once more into the same brown study.[7] At last he rose and threw the end of his cigar into the grate.

"I'll tell you what, my boy," said he. "I never had a head for figures, so you will excuse me. You must jot it all down upon paper, and let me have a note of the amount. I'll understand it when I see it in black and white."

The proposal was encouraging. I promised to do so.

"And now it's time we were in bed. By Jove, there's one o'clock striking in the hall."

The tingling of the chiming clock broke through the deep roar of the gale. The wind was sweeping past with the rush of a great river.

"I must see my cat before I go to bed," said my host. "A high wind excites him. Will you come?"

"Certainly," said I.

"Then tread softly and don't speak, for everyone is asleep."

We passed quietly down the lamp-lit Persian-rugged hall, and through the door at the farther end. All was dark in the stone corridor, but a stable lantern hung on a hook, and my host took it down and lit it. There was no grating visible in the passage, so I knew that the beast was in its cage.

"Come in!" said my relative, and opened the door.

---

7. **brown study:** deep, serious absorption in thought.

A deep growling as we entered showed that the storm had really excited the creature. In the flickering light of the lantern, we saw it, a huge black mass coiled in the corner of its den and throwing a squat, uncouth shadow upon the whitewashed wall. Its tail switched angrily among the straw.

"Poor Tommy is not in the best of tempers," said Everard King, holding up the lantern and looking in at him. "What a black devil he looks, doesn't he? I must give him a little supper to put him in a better humor. Would you mind holding the lantern for a moment?"

I took it from his hand and he stepped to the door.

"His larder is just outside here," said he. "You will excuse me for an instant won't you?" He passed out, and the door shut with a sharp metallic click behind him.

That hard crisp sound made my heart stand still. A sudden wave of terror passed over me. A vague perception of some monstrous treachery turned me cold. I sprang to the door, but there was no handle upon the inner side.

"Here!" I cried. "Let me out!"

"All right! Don't make a row!" said my host from the passage. "You've got the light all right."

"Yes, but I don't care about being locked in alone like this."

"Don't you?" I heard his hearty, chuckling laugh. "You won't be alone long."

"Let me out, sir!" I repeated angrily. "I tell you I don't allow practical jokes of this sort."

"Practical is the word," said he, with another hateful chuckle. And then suddenly I heard, amidst the roar of the storm, the creak and whine of the winch-handle turning and the rattle of the grating as it passed through the slot. Great God, he was letting loose the Brazilian cat!

In the light of the lantern I saw the bars sliding slowly before me. Already there was an opening a foot wide at the farther end. With a scream I seized the last bar with my hands and pulled with the strength of a madman. I *was* a madman with rage and horror. For a minute or more I held the thing motionless. I knew that he was straining with all his force upon the handle, and that the leverage was sure to overcome me. I gave inch by inch, my feet sliding along the stones, and all the time I begged and prayed this inhuman monster to save me from this horrible death. I conjured him by his kinship. I reminded him that I was his guest; I begged to know what harm I had ever done him. His only answers were the tugs and jerks upon the handle, each of which, in spite of all my struggles, pulled another bar through the opening. Clinging and clutching, I was dragged across the whole front of the cage, until at last, with aching wrists and lacerated fingers, I gave up the hopeless struggle. The grating clanged back as I released it, and an instant later I heard the shuffle of the Turkish slippers in the passage, and the slam of the distant door. Then everything was silent.

The creature had never moved during this time. He lay still in the corner, and his tail had ceased switching. This apparition of a man adhering to his bars and dragged screaming across him had apparently filled him with amazement. I saw his great eyes staring steadily at me. I had dropped the lantern when I seized the bars, but it still burned upon the floor, and I made a movement to grasp it, with some idea that its light might protect me. But the instant I moved, the beast gave a deep and menacing growl. I stopped and stood still, quivering with fear in every limb. The cat (if one may call so fearful a creature by so homely a name) was not more than ten feet from me. The eyes glimmered like two disks of phosphorus in the darkness. They appalled and yet fascinated me. I could not take my own eyes from them. Nature plays strange tricks with us at such moments of intensity, and those glimmering lights waxed and waned with a steady rise and fall. Sometimes they seemed to be tiny points of extreme brilliancy—little electric sparks in the black obscurity—then they would widen and widen until all that corner of the room was filled with their shifting and sinister light. And then suddenly they went out altogether.

The beast had closed its eyes. I do not know whether there may be any truth in the old idea of the dominance of the human gaze, or whether the huge cat was simply drowsy, but the fact remains that, far from showing any symptom of attacking me, it simply rested its sleek, black head upon its huge forepaws and seemed to sleep. I stood, fearing to move lest I should rouse it into malignant life once more. But at least I was able to think clearly now that the baleful eyes were off me. Here I was shut up for the night with the ferocious beast. My own instincts, to say nothing of the words of the plausible villain who laid this trap for me, warned me that the animal was as savage as its master. How could I stave it off until morning? The door was hopeless, and so were the narrow, barred windows. There was no shelter anywhere in the bare, stone- flagged room. To cry for assistance was absurd. I knew that this den was an outhouse, and that the corridor which connected it with the house was at least a hundred feet long. Besides, with the gale thundering outside, my cries were not likely to be heard. I had only my own courage and my own wits to trust to.

And then, with a fresh wave of horror, my eyes fell upon the lantern. The candle had burned low, and was already beginning to gutter. In ten minutes it would be out. I had only ten minutes then in which to do something, for I felt that if I were once left in the dark with that fearful beast I should be incapable of action. The very thought of it paralyzed me. I cast my despairing eyes round this chamber of death, and they rested upon one spot which seemed to promise I will not say safety, but less immediate and imminent danger than the open floor.

I have said that the cage had a top as well as a front, and this top was left standing when the front was wound through the slot in the wall. It consisted of bars at a few inches' interval, with stout wire netting between, and it rested upon a strong stanchion[8] at each end. It stood now as a great barred canopy over the crouching figure in the corner. The space between this iron shelf and the roof may have been from two or three feet. If I could only get up there, squeezed in between bars and ceiling, I should have only one vulnerable side. I should be safe from below, from behind, and from each side. Only on the open face of it could I be attacked. There, it is true, I had no protection whatever; but at least, I should be out of the brute's path when he began to pace about his den. He would have to come out of his way to reach me. It was now or never, for if once the light were out it would be impossible. With a gulp in my throat I sprang up, seized the iron edge of the top, and swung myself panting on to it. I writhed in face downwards, and found myself looking straight into the terrible eyes and yawning jaws of the cat. Its fetid breath came up into my face like the steam from some foul pot.

It appeared, however, to be rather curious than angry. With a sleek ripple of its long, black back it rose, stretched itself, and then rearing itself on its hind legs, with one forepaw against the wall, it raised the other, and drew its claws across the wire meshes beneath me. One sharp, white hook tore through my trousers—for I may mention that I was still in evening dress—and dug a furrow in my knee. It was not meant as an attack, but rather as an experiment, for upon my giving a

---

8. **stanchion:** an upright post or beam used as a support.

sharp cry of pain he dropped down again, and springing lightly into the room, he began walking swiftly round it, looking up every now and again in my direction. For my part I shuffled backwards until I lay with my back against the wall, screwing myself into the smallest space possible. The farther I got the more difficult it was for him to attack me.

He seemed more excited now that he had begun to move about, and he ran swiftly and noiselessly round and round the den, passing continually underneath the iron couch upon which I lay. It was wonderful to see so great a bulk passing like a shadow, with hardly the softest thudding of velvety pads. The candle was burning low—so low that I could hardly see the creature. And then, with a last flare and splutter it went out altogether. I was alone with the cat in the dark!

It helps one to face a danger when one knows that one has done all that possibly can be done. There is nothing for it then but to quietly await the result. In this case, there was no chance of safety anywhere except the precise spot where I was. I stretched myself out, therefore, and lay silently, almost breathlessly, hoping that the beast might forget my presence if I did nothing to remind him. I reckoned that it must already be two o'clock. At four it would be full dawn. I had not more than two hours to wait for daylight.

Outside, the storm was still raging, and the rain lashed continually against the little windows. Inside, the poisonous and fetid air was overpowering. I could neither hear nor see the cat. I tried to think about other things—but only one had power enough to draw my mind from my terrible position. That was the contemplation of my cousin's villainy, his unparalleled hypocrisy, his malignant hatred of me. Beneath that cheerful face there lurked the spirit of a medieval assassin. And as I thought of it I saw more clearly how cunningly the thing had been arranged. He had apparently gone to bed with the others. No doubt he had his witness to prove it. Then, unknown to them, he had slipped down, had lured me into his den and abandoned me. His story would be so simple. He had left me to finish my cigar in the billiard-room. I had gone down on my own account to have a last look at the cat. I had entered the room without observing that the cage was opened, and I had been caught. How could such a crime be brought home to him? Suspicion, perhaps—but proof, never!

How slowly those dreadful two hours went by! Once I heard a low, rasping sound, which I took to be the creature licking its own fur. Several times those greenish eyes gleamed at me through the darkness, but never in a fixed stare, and my hopes grew stronger that my presence had been forgotten or ignored. At last the least faint glimmer of light came through the windows—I first dimly saw them as two grey squares upon the black wall, then grey turned to white, and I could see my terrible companion once more. And he, alas, could see me!

It was evident to me at once that he was in a much more dangerous and aggressive mood than when I had seen him last. The cold of the morning had irritated him, and he was hungry as well. With a continual growl he paced swiftly up and down the side of the room which was farthest from my refuge, his whiskers bristling angrily, and his tail switching and lashing. As he turned at the corners his savage eyes always looked upwards at me with a dreadful menace. I knew then that he meant to kill me. Yet I found myself even at that moment admiring the sinuous grace of the devilish thing, its long, undulating, rippling movements, the gloss of its beautiful flanks, the vivid, palpitating scarlet of the glistening tongue which hung from the jet-black muzzle. And all the time that deep, threatening growl was rising and rising in an unbroken crescendo. I knew that the crisis was at hand.

It was a miserable hour to meet such a death—so cold, so comfortless, shivering in my light dress clothes upon this gridiron of torment upon which I was stretched. I tried to brace myself to it, to raise my soul above it, and at the same time, with the lucidity which comes to a perfectly desperate man, I cast round for some possible means of escape. One thing was clear to me. If that front of the cage was only back in its position once more, I could find a sure refuge behind it. Could I possibly pull it back? I hardly dared to move for fear of bringing the creature upon me. Slowly, very slowly, I put my hand forward until it grasped the edge of the front, the final bar which protruded through the wall. To my surprise it came quite easily to my jerk. Of course the difficulty of drawing it out arose from the fact that I was clinging to it. I pulled again, and three inches of it came through. It ran apparently on wheels. I pulled again . . . and then the cat sprang!

It was so quick, so sudden, that I never saw it happen. I simply heard the savage snarl, and in an instant afterwards the blazing yellow eyes, the flattened black head with its red tongue and flashing teeth, were within reach of me. The impact of the creature shook the bars upon which I lay, until I thought (as far as I could think of anything at such a moment) that they were coming down. The cat swayed there for an instant, the head and front paws quite close to me, the hind paws clawing to find a grip upon the edge of the grating. I heard the claws rasping as they clung to the wire-netting, and the breath of the beast made me sick. But its bound had been miscalculated. It could not retain its position. Slowly, grinning with rage, and scratching madly at the bars, it swung backwards and dropped heavily upon the floor. With a growl it instantly faced round to me and crouched for another spring.

I knew that the next few moments would decide my fate. The creature had learned by experience. It would not miscalculate again. I must act promptly, fearlessly, if I were to have a chance for life. In an instant I had formed my plan. Pulling off my dress-coat, I threw it down over the head of the beast. At the same moment I dropped over the edge, seized the end of the front grating, and pulled it frantically out of the wall.

It came more easily than I could have expected. I rushed across the room, bearing it with me; but, as I rushed, the accident of my position put me upon the outer side. Had it been the other way, I might have come off scathless. As it was, there was a moment's pause as I stopped it and tried to pass in through the opening which I had left. That moment was enough to give time to the creature to toss off the coat with which I had blinded him and to spring upon me. I hurled myself through the gap and pulled the rails to behind me, but he seized my leg before I could entirely withdraw it. One stroke of that huge paw tore off my calf as a shaving of wood curls off before a plane. The next moment, bleeding and fainting, I was lying among the foul straw with a line of friendly bars between me and the creature which ramped so frantically against them.

Too wounded to move, and too faint to be conscious of fear, I could only lie, more dead than alive, and watch it. It pressed its broad, black chest against the bars and angled for me with its crooked paws as I have seen a kitten do before a mouse-trap. It ripped my clothes, but, stretch as it would, it could not quite reach me. I have heard of the curious numbing effect produced by wounds from the great carnivora, and now I was destined to experience it, for I had lost all sense of personality, and was as interested in the cat's failure or success as if it were some game which I was watching. And then gradually my mind drifted away into strange vague dreams, always with that black face and red tongue coming back into them, and so I lost myself in the nirvana of delirium, the blessed relief of those who are too sorely tried.

Tracing the course of events afterwards, I conclude that I must have been insensible for about two hours. What roused me to consciousness once more was that sharp metallic click which had been the precursor of my terrible experience. It was the shooting back of the spring lock. Then, before my senses were clear enough to entirely apprehend what they saw, I was aware of the round, benevolent face of my cousin peering in through the open door. What he saw evidently amazed him. There was the cat crouching on the floor. I was stretched upon my back in my shirt-sleeves within the cage, my trousers torn to ribbons and a great pool of blood all round me. I can see his amazed face now, with the morning sunlight upon it. He peered at me, and peered again. Then he closed the door behind him, and advanced to the cage to see if I were really dead.

I cannot undertake to say what happened. I was not in a fit state to witness or to chronicle such events. I can only say that I was suddenly conscious that his face was away from me—that he was looking towards the animal.

"Good old Tommy!" he cried. "Good old Tommy!"

Then he came near the bars, with his back still towards me.

"Down, you stupid beast!" he roared. "Down, sir! Don't you know your master?"

Suddenly even in my bemuddled brain a remembrance came of those words of his when he had said that the taste of blood would turn the cat into a fiend. My blood had done it, but he was to pay the price.

"Get away!" he screamed. "Get away, you devil! Baldwin! Baldwin! Oh, my God!"

And then I heard him fall, and rise, and fall again, with a sound like the ripping of sacking. His screams grew fainter until they were lost in the worrying snarl. And then, after I thought that he was dead, I saw, as in a nightmare, a blinded, tattered, blood-soaked figure running wildly round the room—and that was the last glimpse which I had of him before I fainted once again.

I was many months in my recovery—in fact, I cannot say that I have ever recovered, for to the end of my days I shall carry a stick as a sign of my night with the Brazilian cat. Baldwin, the groom, and the other servants could not tell what had occurred, when, drawn by the death-cries of their master, they found me behind the bars, and his remains—or what they afterwards discovered to be his remains—in the clutch of the creature which he had reared. They stalled him off with hot irons, and afterwards shot him through the loophole of the door before they could finally extricate me. I was carried to my bedroom, and there, under the roof of my would-be murderer, I remained between life and death for several weeks. They had sent for a surgeon from Clipton and a nurse from London, and in a month I was able to be carried to the station, and so conveyed back once more to Grosvenor Mansions.

I have one remembrance of that illness, which might have been part of the ever-changing panorama conjured up by a delirious brain were it not so definitely fixed in my memory. One night, when the nurse was absent, the door of my chamber opened, and a tall woman in blackest mourning slipped into the room. She came across to me, and as she bent her sallow face I saw by the faint gleam of the night-light that it was the Brazilian woman whom my cousin had married. She stared intently into my face, and her expression was more kindly than I had ever seen it.

"Are you conscious?" she asked.

I feebly nodded—for I was still very weak.

"Well; then, I only wished to say to you that you have yourself to blame. Did I not do all I could for you? From the beginning I tried to drive you from the house. By every means, short of betraying my husband, I tried to save you from him. I knew that he had a reason for bringing you here. I knew that he would never let you get away again. No one knew him as I knew him, who had suffered from him so often. I did not dare to tell you all this. He would have killed me. But I did my best for you. As things have turned out, you have been the best friend that I have ever had. You have set me free, and I fancied that nothing but death would do that. I am sorry if you are hurt, but I cannot reproach myself. I told you that you were a fool—and a fool you have been." She crept out of the room, the bitter, singular woman, and I was never destined to see her again. With what remained from her husband's property she went back to her native land, and I have heard that she afterwards took the veil at Pernambuco.[9]

It was not until I had been back in London for some time that the doctors pronounced me to be well enough to do business. It was not a very welcome permission to me, for I feared that it would be the signal for an inrush of creditors; but it was Summers, my lawyer, who first took advantage of it.

"I am very glad to see that your lordship is so much better," said he. "I have been waiting a long time to offer my congratulations."

---

9. **took the veil at Pernambuco:** became a nun in a state of northeast Brazil.

"What do you mean, Summers? This is no time for joking."

"I mean what I say," he answered. "You have been Lord Southerton for the last six weeks, but we feared that it would retard your recovery if you were to learn it."

Lord Southerton! One of the richest peers in England! I could not believe my ears. And then suddenly I thought of the time which had elapsed, and how it coincided with my injuries.

"Then Lord Southerton must have died about the same time that I was hurt?"

"His death occurred upon that very day." Summers looked hard at me as I spoke, and I am convinced—for he was a very shrewd fellow—that he had guessed the true state of the case. He paused for a moment as if awaiting a confidence from me, but I could not see what was to be gained by exposing such a family scandal.

"Yes, a very curious coincidence," he continued, with the same knowing look. "Of course, you are aware that your cousin Everard King was the next heir to the estates. Now, if it had been you instead of him who had been torn to pieces by this tiger, or whatever it was, then of course he would have been Lord Southerton at the present moment."

"No doubt," said I.

"And he took such an interest in it," said Summers. "I happen to know that the late Lord Southerton's valet was in his pay, and that he used to have telegrams from him every few hours to tell him how he was getting on. That would be about the time when you were down there. Was it not strange that he should wish to be so well informed, since he knew that he was not the direct heir?"

"Very strange," said I. "And now, Summers, if you will bring me my bills and a new check book, we will begin to get things into order."

Discussion Questions

1. What does the author gain from having Marshall King narrate this story?

2. What does the setting contribute to the overall effect of the story?

3. What is Everard King's plan? What do the many telegrams he receives have to do with it?

4. Trace the apparent changes in Everard's character. How do you account for them?

5. What do you think is the greatest irony here?

Suggestion for Writing

Imagine that you are a police officer interviewing Mrs. King after the death of her husband, Everard. Ask her questions to get at the facts of what happened. Then, as Mrs. King, answer the officer's questions, being careful to give only the information that you want disclosed. Write up the interview in a Question-Answer format.

Mary E. Wilkins Freeman (1852-1930)

Mary E. Wilkins Freeman was born and raised in New England, where she spent all her life. After an education that was sketchy because of her ill health, she started writing stories and verse for children to help support her family. As secretary to Oliver Wendell Holmes, Sr., a prominent writer and physician, she became acquainted with the famous Massachusetts writers of the day. In 1891 she gained recognition for her book *A New England Nun and Other Stories*. In 1902, at age 50, she married Charles Freeman and moved to Metuchen, New Jersey, where she lived until her death. In all, Freeman wrote 238 short stories, 12 novels, 1 play, and 2 volumes of verse. Her characters were largely simple people, living frustrated lives in small New England villages; she described them simply, with no sentimentality, but with a dry sense of humor.

The Wind in the Rose-Bush

Ford Village has no railroad station, being on the other side of the river from Porter's Falls, and accessible only by the ford which gives it its name, and a ferry line.

The ferry-boat was waiting when Rebecca Flint got off the train with her bag and lunch basket. When she and her small trunk were safely embarked she sat stiff and straight and calm in the ferry boat as it shot swiftly and smoothly across stream. There was a horse attached to a light country wagon on board, and he pawed the deck uneasily. His owner stood near, with a wary eye upon him, although he was chewing, with as dully reflective an expression as a cow. Beside Rebecca sat a woman of about her own age, who kept looking at her with furtive curiosity; her husband, short and stout and saturnine, stood near her. Rebecca paid no attention to either of them. She was tall and spare and pale, the type of a spinster, yet with rudimentary lines and expressions of matronhood. She all unconsciously held her shawl, rolled up in a canvas bag, on her left hip, as if it had been a child. She wore a settled frown of dissent at life, but it was the frown of a mother who regarded life as a froward[1] child, rather than as an overwhelming fate.

The other woman continued staring at her; she was mildly stupid, except for an overdeveloped curiosity which made her at times sharp beyond belief. Her eyes glittered, red spots came on her flaccid cheeks; she kept opening her mouth to speak, making little abortive motions. Finally she could endure it no longer; she nudged Rebecca boldly.

"A pleasant day," said she.

Rebecca looked at her and nodded coldly.

"Yes, very," she assented.

"Have you come far?"

"I have come from Michigan."

"Oh!" said the woman, with awe. "It's a long way," she remarked presently.

"Yes, it is," replied Rebecca, conclusively.

Still the other woman was not daunted; there was something which she determined to know, possibly roused thereto by a vague sense of

---

1. **froward:** willful; not easily controlled.

incongruity in the other's appearance. "It's a long ways to come and leave a family," she remarked with painful shyness.

"I ain't got no family to leave," returned Rebecca shortly.

"Then you ain't—"

"No, I ain't."

"Oh!" said the woman.

Rebecca looked straight ahead at the race of the river.

It was a long ferry. Finally Rebecca herself waxed unexpectedly loquacious. She turned to the other woman and inquired if she knew John Dent's widow who lived in Ford Village. "Her husband died about three years ago," said she, by way of detail.

The woman started violently. She turned pale, then she flushed; she cast a strange glance at her husband, who was regarding both women with a sort of stolid keenness.

"Yes, I guess I do," faltered the woman finally.

"Well, his first wife was my sister," said Rebecca with the air of one imparting important intelligence.

"Was she?" responded the other woman feebly. She glanced at her husband with an expression of doubt and terror, and he shook his head forbiddingly.

"I'm going to see her, and take my niece Agnes home with me," said Rebecca.

Then the woman gave such a violent start that she noticed it.

"What is the matter?" she asked.

"Nothin', I guess," replied the woman, with eyes on her husband, who was slowly shaking his head, like a Chinese toy.[2]

"Is my niece sick?" asked Rebecca with quick suspicion.

"No, she ain't sick," replied the woman with alacrity, then she caught her breath with a gasp.

"When did you see her?"

"Let me see, I ain't seen her for some little time," replied the woman. Then she caught her breath again.

"She ought to have grown up real pretty, if she takes after my sister. She was a real pretty woman," Rebecca said wistfully.

"Yes, I guess she did grow up pretty," replied the woman in a trembling voice.

---

2. **Chinese toy:** a seated figure with a head so delicately balanced that, when touched, it continues to bob or wag for some time.

"What kind of a woman is the second wife?"

The woman glanced at her husband's warning face. She continued to gaze at him while she replied in a choking voice to Rebecca:

"I—guess she's a nice woman," she replied. "I—don't know, I—guess so. I—don't see much of her."

"I felt kind of hurt that John married again so quick," said Rebecca, "but I suppose he wanted his house kept; and Agnes wanted care. I wasn't so situated that I could take her when her mother died. I had my own mother to care for, and I was school-teaching. Now Mother has gone, and my uncle died six months ago and left me quite a little property, and I've given up my school, and I've come for Agnes. I guess she'll be glad to go with me, though I suppose her stepmother is a good woman, and has always done for her."

The man's warning shake at his wife was fairly portentous.[3]

"I guess so," said she.

"John always wrote that she was a beautiful woman," said Rebecca.

Then the ferry-boat grated on the shore.

John Dent's widow had sent a horse and wagon to meet her sister-in-law. When the woman and her husband went down the road, on which Rebecca in the wagon with her trunk soon passed them, she said reproachfully:

"Seems as if I'd ought to have told her, Thomas."

"Let her find it out herself," replied the man. "Don't you go burnin' your fingers in other folks' puddin', Maria."

"Do you s'pose she'll see anything?" asked the woman with a spasmodic shudder and a terrified roll of her eyes.

"See!" returned her husband with stolid scorn. "Better be sure there's anything to see."

"Oh, Thomas, they say—"

"Lord, ain't you found out that what they say is mostly lies?"

"But if it should be true, and she's a nervous woman, she might be scared enough to lose her wits," said his wife, staring uneasily after Rebecca's erect figure in the wagon disappearing over the crest of the hilly road.

"Wits that so easy upset ain't worth much," declared the man. "You keep out of it, Maria."

---

3. **portentous:** full of significance; warning of misfortune.

Rebecca in the meantime rode on in the wagon, beside a flaxen-headed boy, who looked to her understanding not very bright. She asked him a question and he paid no attention. She repeated it, and he responded with a bewildered and incoherent grunt. Then she let him alone, after making sure that he knew how to drive straight.

They had traveled about half a mile, passed the village square, and gone a short distance beyond, when the boy drew up with a sudden Whoa! before a very prosperous-looking house. It had been one of the aboriginal[4] cottages of the vicinity, small and white, with a roof extending over one side over a piazza,[5] and a tiny "L" jutting out in the rear, on the right hand. Now the cottage was transformed by dormer windows, a bay window on the piazzaless side, a carved railing down the front steps, and a modern hard-wood door.

"Is this John Dent's house?" asked Rebecca.

The boy was as sparing of speech as a philosopher. His only response was in flinging the reins over the horse's back, stretching out one foot to the shaft, and leaping out of the wagon, then going around to the rear for the trunk. Rebecca got out and went toward the house. Its white paint had a new gloss, its blinds were an immaculate apple green, the lawn was trimmed as smooth as velvet, and it was dotted with scrupulous groups of hydrangea and cannas.

"I always understood that John Dent was well-to-do," Rebecca reflected comfortably. "I guess Agnes will have considerable. I've got enough, but it will come in handy for her schooling. She can have advantages."

The boy dragged the trunk up the fine gravel-walk, but before he reached the steps leading up to the piazza, for the house stood on a terrace, the front door opened and a fair, frizzled head of a very large and handsome woman appeared. She held up her black silk skirt, disclosing voluminous ruffles of starched embroidery, and waited for Rebecca. She smiled placidly, her pink, double-chinned face widened and dimpled, but her blue eyes were wary and calculating. She extended her hand as Rebecca climbed the steps.

"This is Miss Flint, I suppose," said she.

"Yes, ma'am," replied Rebecca, noticing with bewilderment a curious expression compounded of fear and defiance on the other's face.

---

4. aboriginal: existing in a place from the earliest days.
5. piazza (pē at′ sə): a large covered porch, usually with columns.

"Your letter only arrived this morning," said Mrs. Dent, in a steady voice. Her great face was a uniform pink, and her china-blue eyes were at once aggressive and veiled with secrecy.

"Yes, I hardly thought you'd got my letter," replied Rebecca. "I felt as if I could not wait to hear from you before I came. I supposed you would be so situated that you could have me a little while without putting you out too much, from what John used to write me about his circumstances, and when I had that money so unexpected I felt as if I must come for Agnes. I suppose you will be willing to give her up. You know she's my own blood, and of course she's no relation to you, though you must have got attached to her. I know from her picture what a sweet girl she must be, and John always said she looked like her own mother, and Grace was a beautiful woman, if she was my sister."

Rebecca stopped and stared at the other woman in amazement and alarm. The great handsome blonde creature stood speechless, livid, gasping, with her hand to her heart, her lips parted in a horrible caricature of a smile.

"Are you sick?" cried Rebecca, drawing near. "Don't you want me to get you some water?"

Then Mrs. Dent recovered herself with a great effort. "It is nothing," she said. "I am subject to—spells. I am over it now. Won't you come in, Miss Flint?"

As she spoke, the beautiful deep-rose color suffused her face, her blue eyes met her visitor's with the opaqueness of turquoise—with a revelation of blue, but a concealment of all behind.

Rebecca followed her hostess in, and the boy, who had waited quiescently,[6] climbed the steps with the trunk. But before they entered the door a strange thing happened. On the upper terrace, close to the piazza-post, grew a great rose-bush, and on it, late in the season though it was, one small red, perfect rose.

Rebecca looked at it, and the other woman extended her hand with a quick gesture. "Don't you pick that rose," she brusquely cried.

Rebecca drew herself up with stiff dignity.

"I ain't in the habit of picking other folks' roses without leave," said she.

---

6. **quiescently** (kwē e snt lē): quietly; with no activity.

As Rebecca spoke she started violently, and lost sight of her resentment, for something singular happened. Suddenly the rosebush was agitated violently as if by a gust of wind, yet it was a remarkably still day. Not a leaf of the hydrangea standing on the terrace close to the rose trembled.

"What on earth—" began Rebecca, then she stopped with a gasp at the sight of the other woman's face. Although a face, it gave somehow the impression of a desperately clutched hand of secrecy.

"Come in!" said she in a harsh voice, which seemed to come forth from her chest with no intervention of the organs of speech. "Come into the house. I'm getting cold out here."

"What makes that rose-bush blow so when there isn't any wind?" asked Rebecca, trembling with vague horror, yet resolute.

"I don't see it is blowing," returned the woman calmly. And as she spoke, indeed the bush was quiet.

"It was blowing," declared Rebecca.

"It isn't now," said Mrs. Dent. "I can't try to account for everything that blows out-of-doors. I have too much to do."

She spoke scornfully and confidently, with defiant, unflinching eyes, first on the bush, then on Rebecca, and led the way into the house.

"It looked queer," persisted Rebecca, but she followed, and also the boy with the trunk.

Rebecca entered an interior, prosperous, even elegant, according to her simple ideas. There were Brussels carpets, lace curtains, and plenty of brilliant upholstery and polished wood.

"You're real nicely situated," remarked Rebecca, after she had become a little accustomed to her new surroundings and the two women were seated at the tea table.

Mrs. Dent stared with a hard complacency from behind her silver-plated service. "Yes, I be," said she.

"You got all the things new?" said Rebecca hesitatingly, with a jealous memory of her dead sister's bridal furnishings.

"Yes," said Mrs. Dent; "I was never one to want dead folks' things, and I had money enough of my own, so I wasn't beholden to John. I had the old duds put up at auction. They didn't bring much."

"I suppose you saved some for Agnes. She'll want some of her poor mother's things when she is grown up," said Rebecca with some indignation.

The defiant stare of Mrs. Dent's blue eyes waxed more intense. "There's a few things up garret,"[7] said she.

"She'll be likely to value them," remarked Rebecca. As she spoke she glanced at the window. "Isn't it most time for her to be coming home?" she asked.

"Most time," answered Mrs. Dent carelessly; "but when she gets over to Addie Slocum's she never knows when to come home."

"Is Addie Slocum her intimate friend?"

"Intimate as any."

"Maybe we can have her come out to see Agnes when she's living with me," said Rebecca wistfully. "I suppose she'll be likely to be homesick at first."

"Most likely," answered Mrs. Dent.

"Does she call you mother?" Rebecca asked.

"No, she calls me Aunt Emeline," replied the other woman shortly. "When did you say you were going home?"

"In about a week, I thought, if she can be ready to go as soon," answered Rebecca with a surprised look.

She reflected that she would not remain a day longer than she could help after such an inhospitable look and question.

"Oh, as far as that goes," said Mrs. Dent, "it wouldn't make any difference about her being ready. You could go home whenever you felt that you must, and she could come afterward."

"Alone?"

"Why not? She's a big girl now, and you don't have to change cars."

"My niece will go home when I do, and not travel alone, and if I can't wait here for her, in the house that used to be her mother's and my sister's home, I'll go and board somewhere," returned Rebecca with warmth.

"Oh, you can stay here as long as you want to. You're welcome," said Mrs. Dent.

Then Rebecca started. "There she is!" she declared in a trembling, exultant voice. Nobody knew how she longed to see the girl.

"She isn't as late as I thought she'd be," said Mrs. Dent, and again that curious, subtle change passed over her face and again it settled into that stony impassiveness.

Rebecca stared at the door, waiting for it to open. "Where is she?" she asked presently.

---

7. **garret:** attic.

"I guess she's stopped to take off her hat in the entry," suggested Mrs. Dent.

For answer Mrs. Dent rose with a stiff jerk and threw open the door.

"Agnes!" she called. "Agnes." Then she turned and eyed Rebecca. "She ain't there."

"I saw her pass the window," said Rebecca in bewilderment.

"You must have been mistaken."

"I know I did," persisted Rebecca.

"You couldn't have."

"I did. I saw first a shadow go over the ceiling, then I saw her in the glass there"—she pointed to a mirror over the sideboard opposite—"and then the shadow passed the window."

"How did she look in the glass?"

"Little and light-haired, with the light hair kind of tossing over her forehead."

"You couldn't have seen her."

"Was that like Agnes?"

"Like enough, but of course you didn't see her. You've been thinking so much about her that you thought you did."

"You thought *you* did."

"I thought I saw a shadow pass the window, but I must have been mistaken. She didn't come in, or we would have seen her before now. I knew it was too early for her to get home from Addie Slocum's, anyhow."

When Rebecca went to bed, Agnes had not returned. Rebecca had resolved that she would not retire until the girl came, but she was very tired, and she reasoned with herself that she was foolish. Besides, Mrs. Dent suggested that Agnes might go to the church social with Addie Slocum. When Rebecca suggested that she be sent for and told that her aunt had come, Mrs. Dent laughed meaningly.

"I guess that you'll find out that a young girl ain't so ready to leave a sociable, where there's boys, to see her aunt," said she.

"She's too young," said Rebecca incredulously and indignantly.

"She's sixteen," replied Mrs. Dent, "and she's always been great for the boys."

"She's going to school four years after I get her before she thinks of boys," declared Rebecca.

"We'll see," laughed the other woman.

After Rebecca went to bed, she lay awake a long time listening for the sound of girlish laughter and a boy's voice under her window; then she fell asleep.

The next morning she was down early. Mrs. Dent, who kept no servants, was busily preparing breakfast.

"Don't Agnes help you about breakfast?" asked Rebecca.

"No, I let her lay," replied Mrs. Dent shortly.

"What time did she get home last night?"

"She didn't get home."

"What?"

"She didn't get home. She stayed with Addie. She often does."

"Without sending you word?"

"Oh, she knew I wouldn't worry."

"When will she be home?"

"Oh, I guess she'll be along pretty soon."

Rebecca was uneasy, but she tried to conceal it, for she knew of no good reason for uneasiness. What was there to occasion alarm in the fact of one young girl staying overnight with another? She could not eat much breakfast. Afterward, she went out on the little piazza, although her hostess strove furtively to stop her.

"Why don't you go out back of the house? It's real pretty—a view over the river," she said.

"I guess I'll go out here," replied Rebecca. She had a purpose: to watch for the absent girl.

Presently Rebecca came hustling into the house through the sitting-room, into the kitchen where Mrs. Dent was cooking.

"That rose-bush!" she gasped.

Mrs. Dent turned and faced her.

"What of it?"

"It's a-blowing."

"What of it?"

"There isn't a mite of wind this morning."

Mrs. Dent turned with an immutable toss of her fair head. "If you think I can spend my time puzzling over such nonsense as—" she began, but Rebecca interrupted her with a cry and a rush to the door.

"There she is now!" she said.

She flung the door wide open, and curiously enough a breeze came in and her own gray hair tossed, and a paper blew off the table to the floor with a loud rustle, but there was nobody in sight.

"There's nobody here," Rebecca said.

She looked blankly at the other woman, who brought her rolling-pin down on a slab of pie-crust with a thud.

"I didn't hear anybody," she said calmly.

"I *saw somebody pass* that window!"

"You were mistaken again."

"I *know* I saw somebody!"

"You couldn't have. Please shut the door!"

Rebecca shut the door. She sat down beside the window and looked out on the autumnal yard, with its little curve of footpath to the kitchen door.

"What smells so strong of roses in this room?" she said presently. She sniffed hard.

"I don't smell anything but these nutmegs."

"It is not nutmeg."

"I don't smell anything else."

"Where do you suppose Agnes is?"

"Oh, perhaps she has gone over the ferry to Porter's Falls with Addie. She often does. Addie's got an aunt over there, and Addie's got a cousin, a real pretty boy."

"You suppose she's gone over there?"

"Mebbe, I shouldn't wonder."

"When should she be home?"

"Oh, not before afternoon."

Rebecca waited with all the patience she could muster. She kept reassuring herself, telling herself that it was all natural, that the other woman could not help it, but she made up her mind that if Agnes did not return that afternoon she should be sent for.

When it was four o'clock she started up with resolution. She had been furtively watching the onyx clock on the sitting-room mantel, she had timed herself. She had said that if Agnes was not home by that time she should demand that she be sent for. She rose and stood before Mrs. Dent, who looked up coolly from her embroidery.

"I've waited just as long as I'm going to," she said. "I've come 'way from Michigan to see my own sister's daughter and take her home with me. I've been here ever since yesterday—twenty-four hours—and I haven't seen her. Now I'm going to. I want her sent for."

Mrs. Dent folded her embroidery and rose.

"Well, I don't blame you," she said. "It is high time she came home. I'll go right over and get her myself."

Rebecca heaved a sigh of relief. She hardly knew what she had suspected or feared, but she knew that her position had been one of antagonism if not accusations, and she was sensible of relief.

"I wish you would," she said gratefully, and went back to her chair, while Mrs. Dent got her shawl and her little white head-tie. "I wouldn't trouble you, but I do feel as if I couldn't wait any longer to see her," she remarked apologetically.

"Oh, it ain't no trouble at all," said Mrs. Dent as she went out. "I don't blame you; you have waited long enough."

Rebecca sat at the window watching breathlessly until Mrs. Dent came stepping through the yard alone. She ran to the door and saw, hardly noticing it this time, that the rose-bush was again violently agitated, yet with no wind evident elsewhere.

"Where is she?"

Mrs. Dent laughed with still lips as she came up the steps over the terrace. "Girls will be girls," said she. "She's gone with Addie to Lincoln. Addie's got an uncle who's conductor on the train, and lives there, and he got 'em passes, and they're goin' to stay to Addie's Aunt Margaret's a few days. Mrs. Slocum said Agnes didn't have time to come over and ask me before the train went, but she took it on herself to say it would be all right, and—"

"Why hadn't she been over to tell you?" Rebecca was angry, though not suspicious. She even saw no reason for her anger.

"Oh, she was putting up grapes. She was coming over just as soon as she got the black off her hands. She heard I had company, and her hands was a sight. She was holding them over sulphur matches.

"You say she's going to stay a few days?" repeated Rebecca dazedly.

"Yes, till Thursday, Mrs. Slocum said."

"How far is Lincoln from here?"

"About fifty miles. It'll be a real treat to her. Mrs. Slocum's sister is a real nice woman."

"It is goin' to make it pretty late about my goin' home."

"If you don't feel as if you could wait, I'll get her ready and send her on just as soon as I can," Mrs. Dent said sweetly.

"I'm going to wait," said Rebecca grimly.

The two women sat down again, and Mrs. Dent took up her embroidery.

"Is there any sewing I can do for her?" Rebecca asked finally in a desperate way. "If I can get her sewing along some—"

Mrs. Dent arose with alacrity and fetched a mass of white from the closet. "Here," she said, "if you want to sew the lace on this nightgown. I was going to put her to it, but she'll be glad enough to get rid of it. She ought to have this and one more before she goes. I don't like to send her away without some good underclothing."

Rebecca snatched at the little white garment and sewed feverishly.

That night she wakened from a deep sleep a little after midnight and lay a minute trying to collect her faculties and explain to herself what she was listening to. At last she discovered that it was the then popular strain of "The Maiden's Prayer" floating up through the floor from the piano in the sitting-room below. She jumped up, threw a shawl over her nightgown, and hurried downstairs trembling. There was nobody in the sitting-room. The piano was silent. She ran to Mrs. Dent's bedroom and called hysterically:

"Emeline! Emeline!"

"What is it?" asked Mrs. Dent's voice from the bed. The voice was stern, but had a note of consciousness in it.

"Who—who was that playing 'The Maiden's Prayer' in the sitting-room, on the piano?"

"I didn't hear anybody."

"There was some one."

"I didn't hear anything."

"I tell you there was some one. But—*there ain't* anybody there."

"I didn't hear anything."

"I did—somebody playing 'The Maiden's Prayer' on the piano. Has Agnes got home? I want to know."

"Of course Agnes hasn't got home," answered Mrs. Dent with rising inflection. "Be you gone crazy over that girl? The last boat was in from Porter's Falls before we went to bed. Of course she ain't home."

"I heard—"

"You were dreaming."

"I wasn't; I was broad awake."

Rebecca went back to her chamber and kept her lamp burning all night.

The next morning her eyes upon Mrs. Dent were wary and blazing with suppressed excitement. She kept opening her mouth as if to speak, then frowning, and setting her lips hard. After breakfast she went upstairs, and came down presently with her coat and bonnet.

"Now, Emeline," she said, "I want to know where the Slocums live."

Mrs. Dent gave a strange, long, half-lidded glance at her. She was finishing her coffee.

"Why?" she asked.

"I'm going over there and find out if they have heard anything from their daughter and Agnes since they went away. I don't like what I heard last night."

"You must have been dreaming."

"It don't make any odds whether I was or not. Does she play 'The Maiden's Prayer' on the piano? I want to know."

"What if she does? She plays it a little, I believe. I don't know. She don't half play it, anyhow, and ain't got an ear."

"That wasn't half played last night. I don't like such things happening. I ain't superstitious, but I don't like it. I'm going. Where do the Slocums live?"

"You go down the road over the bridge past the old grist mill, then you turn to the left; it's the only house for half a mile. You can't miss is. It has a barn with a ship in full sail on the cupola."

"Well, I'm going. I don't feel easy."

About two hours later Rebecca returned. There were red spots on her cheeks. She looked wild. "I've been there," she said, "and there isn't a soul at home. Something has happened!"

"What has happened?"

"I don't know. Something. I had a warning last night. There wasn't a soul there. They've been sent for to Lincoln."

"Did you see anybody to ask?" asked Mrs. Dent with thinly concealed anxiety.

"I asked the woman that lives at the turn of the road. She's stone deaf. She listened while I screamed at her to know where the Slocums were, and then she said, 'Mrs. Smith doesn't live here.' I didn't see anybody on the road and that's the only house. What do you suppose it means?"

"I don't suppose it means much of anything," replied Mrs. Dent coolly. "Mr. Slocum is a conductor on the railroad, and he'd be away anyway, and Mrs. Slocum often goes early when he does, to spend the day with her sister in Porter's Falls. She'd be more likely to go away than Addie."

"And you don't think anything has happened?" Rebecca asked with diminishing distrust before the reasonableness of it.

"Land, no!"

Rebecca went upstairs to lay aside her coat and bonnet. But she came hurrying back with them still on.

"Who's been in my room?" she gasped. Her face was pale as ashes.

Mrs. Dent also paled as she regarded her.

"What do you mean?" she asked slowly.

"I found when I went upstairs that—little nightgown of—Agnes's on—the bed, laid out. It was—*laid out*. The sleeves were folded across the bosom, and there was that little red rose between them. Emeline, what is it? Emeline, what's the matter? Oh!"

Mrs. Dent was struggling for breath in great, choking gasps. She clung to the back of a chair. Rebecca, trembling herself so she could scarcely keep on her feet, got her some water.

As soon as she recovered herself Mrs. Dent regarded her with eyes full of the strangest mixture of fear and horror and hostility.

"What do you mean talking so?" she said in a hard voice.

"It *is there*."

"Nonsense. You threw it down and it fell that way."

"It was folded in my bureau drawer."

"It couldn't have been."

"Who picked that red rose?"

"Look on the bush," Mrs. Dent replied shortly.

Rebecca looked at her; her mouth gaped. She hurried out of the room. When she came back her eyes seemed to protrude. (She had in the meantime hastened upstairs, and come down with tottering steps, clinging to the banisters.)

"Now I want to know what this all means?" she demanded.

"What what means?"

"The rose is on the bush, and it's gone from the bed in my room. Is this house haunted, or what?"

"I don't know anything about a house being haunted. I don't believe in such things. Be you crazy?" Mrs. Dent spoke with gathering force. The color flashed back to her cheeks.

"No," said Rebecca shortly. "I ain't crazy yet, but I shall be if this keeps on much longer. I'm going to find out where that girl is before night."

Mrs. Dent eyed her.

"What be you going to do?"

"I'm going to Lincoln."

A faint triumphant smile overspread Mrs. Dent's large face.

"You can't," said she, "there ain't any train."

"No train?"

"No, there ain't any afternoon train from the Falls to Lincoln."

"Then I'm going over to the Slocums again tonight."

However, Rebecca did not go; such a rain came up as deterred even her resolution and she had only her best dresses with her. Then in the evening came the letter from the Michigan village which she had left nearly a week ago. It was from her cousin, a single woman, who had come to keep her house while she was away. It was a pleasant unexciting letter enough, all the first of it, and related mostly how she missed Rebecca; how she hoped she was having pleasant weather and kept her health; and how her friend Mrs. Greenaway, had come in to stay with her since she had felt lonesome the first night in the house; how she hoped Rebecca would have no objections to this, although nothing had been said about it, since she had not realized that she might be nervous alone. The cousin was painfully conscientious, hence the letter. Rebecca smiled in spite of her disturbed mind as she read it, then her eye caught the postscript. That was in a different hand, purporting to be written by the friend, Mrs. Hannah Greenaway, informing her that the cousin had fallen down the cellar stairs and broken her hip, and was in a dangerous condition, and begging Rebecca to return at once, as she herself was rheumatic and unable to nurse her properly, and no one else could be obtained.

Rebecca looked at Mrs. Dent, who had come to her room with the letter quite late; it was half-past nine, and she had gone upstairs for the night.

"Where did this come from?" she asked.

"Mr. Amblecrom brought it," she replied.

"Who's he?"

"The postmaster. He often brings letters that come on the late mail. He knows I ain't nobody to send. He brought yours about your coming. He said he and his wife came over on the ferry-boat with you."

"I remember him," Rebecca replied shortly. "There's bad news in this letter."

Mrs. Dent's face took on an expression of serious inquiry.

"Yes, my cousin Harriet has fallen down the cellar stairs—they were always dangerous—and she's broken her hip, and I've got to take the first train home tomorrow."

"You don't say so. I'm dreadfully sorry."

"No, you ain't sorry!" said Rebecca, with a look as if she leaped. "You're glad. I don't know why, but you're glad. You've wanted to get rid of me for some reason ever since I came. I don't know why. You're a strange woman. Now you've got your way, and I hope you're satisfied."

"How you talk."

Mrs. Dent spoke in a fairly injured voice, but there was a light in her eye.

"I talk the way it is. Well, I'm going tomorrow morning, and I want you, just as soon as Agnes Dent comes home, to send her out to me. Don't you wait for anything. You pack what clothes she's got, and don't wait even to mend them and you buy her ticket. I'll leave you money, and you send her along. She don't have to change cars. You start her off, when she gets home, on the next train!"

"Very well," replied the other woman. She had an expression of covert[8] amusement.

"Mind you do it."

"Very well, Rebecca."

Rebecca started on her journey the next morning. When she arrived two days later, she found her cousin in perfect health. She found, moreover, that the friend had not written the postscript in the cousin's letter. Rebecca would have returned to Ford Village the next morning, but the fatigue and nervous strain had been too much for her. She was not able to move from her bed. She had a species of low fever induced by anxiety and fatigue. But she could write, and she did, to the Slocums, and she received no answer. She also wrote to Mrs. Dent; she even sent numerous telegrams, with no response. Finally, she wrote to the postmaster, and his answer arrived by the first possible mail. The letter was short, curt, and to the purpose. Mr. Amblecrom, the postmaster, was a man of few words, and especially wary as to his expression in a letter.

"Dear madam," he wrote, "your favor rec'ed. No Slocums in Ford's Village. All dead. Addie ten years ago, her mother two years later, her father five. House vacant. Mrs. John Dent said to have neglected stepdaughter. Girl was sick. Medicine not given. Talk of taking action. Not enough evidence. House said to be haunted. Strange sights and sounds. Your niece, Agnes, died a year ago, about this time.

"Yours truly,
"Thomas Amblecrom."

---

8. **covert:** concealed.

Discussion Questions

1. Contrast the characters of Rebecca Flint and Emeline Dent.

2. Summarize the lies that Emeline tells to Rebecca. Why do you suppose she does so?

3. What seems to be the significance of the rose-bush and the wind that agitates it?

4. When Rebecca Flint crosses to Ford Village on the ferryboat, the postmaster, Mr. Amblecrom, warns his wife not to tell her anything about Agnes Dent. When he replies later to Rebecca's letter, however, Mr. Amblecrom is forthright enough about the facts, even adding that the Dent house is "said to be haunted." Why do you suppose he holds this information back until the end?

5. How is this ghost story similar to other ghost stories? How does it differ?

Suggestion for Writing

Imagine that you are Rebecca Flint. It is now some time after the events of the story, and your cousin Harriet—who has been pestering you since your return home because she thinks you have been acting strangely—asks you again what happened in Ford Village. You decide to tell her. Write the story from Rebecca's point of view, using the first person and limiting your narrative to things she saw and heard. Keep in mind that Rebecca, a former school teacher, frowns at life as at a naughty child, but that she becomes agitated enough when strange things happen, and that she has just recovered from an illness due to nervous strain. Will you tell the story honestly, or will you put your own "spin" on it?

Charlotte Perkins Gilman (1860-1935)

Charlotte Perkins Gilman developed several careers, first as a writer and then as a lecturer on issues of women's rights, socialism, and trade unionism. After a childhood of poverty and instability, caused by a neglectful father, she studied art and worked for a time as an art teacher. In 1884 she married Charles Stetson, an artist. When her only child was born the next year, she fell into a deep depression. An experimental cure by a famous doctor of "female nervous disorders" subjected her to enforced isolation, which had the effect of driving her almost insane.

She escaped both her husband and her physician by going to California and supporting herself by lecturing, editing, writing, and teaching. In 1900, having divorced Stetson, she married George Gilman; this marriage proved successful. In 1909 she founded her own monthly magazine, the *Forerunner*. The magazine, which she wrote entirely by herself, typically contained a short story, a chapter of a novel, poems, articles, and book reviews. She serialized several novels in this way.

The Yellow Wall-paper

It is very seldom that mere ordinary people like John and myself secure ancestral halls for the summer.

A colonial mansion, a hereditary estate, I would say a haunted house, and reach the height of romantic felicity,—but that would be asking too much of fate!

Still I will probably declare that there is something queer about it.

Else, why should it be let so cheaply? And why have stood so long untenanted?

John laughs at me, of course, but one expects that in marriage.

John is practical in the extreme. He has no patience with faith, an intense horror of superstition, and he scoffs openly at any talk of things not to be felt and seen and put down in figures.

John is a physician, and *perhaps*—(I would not say it to a living soul, of course, but this is dead paper and a great relief to my mind)—*perhaps* that is one reason I do not get well faster.

You see, he does not believe I am sick!

And what can one do?

If a physician of high standing, and one's own husband, assures friends and relatives that there is really nothing the matter with one but temporary nervous depression,—a slight hysterical tendency,—what is one to do?

My brother is also a physician, and also of high standing, and he says the same thing.

So I take phosphates or phosphites,—whichever it is,—and tonics, and journeys, and air, and exercise and am absolutely forbidden to "work" until I am well again.

Personally I disagree with their ideas.

Personally I believe that congenial work, with excitement and change, would do me good.

But what is one to do?

I did write for a while in spite of them; but it *does* exhaust me a good deal—having to be so sly about it; or else meet with heavy opposition.

I sometimes fancy that in my condition if I had less opposition and more society and stimulus—but John says the very worst thing I can do is to think about my condition, and I confess it always makes me feel bad.

So I will let it alone and talk about the house.

The most beautiful place! It is quite alone, standing well back from the road, quite three miles from the village. It makes me think of English places that you read about, for there are hedges, and walls and gates that lock, and lots of separate little houses for the gardeners and people.

There is a *delicious* garden! I never saw such a garden—large and shady, full of box-bordered paths, and lined with long grape-covered arbors with seats under them.

There were greenhouses, too, but they are all broken now.

There was some legal trouble, I believe, something about the heirs and co-heirs; anyhow, the place has been empty for years.

That spoils my ghostliness, I am afraid; but I don't care—there is something strange about the house—I can feel it.

I even said so to John one moonlight evening, but he said what I felt was a *draught,* and shut the window.

I get unreasonably angry with John sometimes. I'm sure I never used to be so sensitive. I think it is due to this nervous condition.

But John says if I feel so I shall neglect proper self-control; so I take pains to control myself—before him, at least, and that makes me very tired.

I don't like our room a bit. I wanted one downstairs that opened on the piazza and had roses all over the window, and such pretty, old-fashioned chintz hangings! but John would not hear of it.

He said there was only one window and not room for two beds, and no near room for him if he took another.

He is very careful and loving, and hardly lets me stir without special direction.

I have a schedule prescription for each hour in the day; he takes all care from me, and I feel so basely ungrateful not to value it more.

He said we came here solely on my account, that I was to have perfect rest and all the air I could get. "Your exercise depends on your strength, my dear," said he, "and your food somewhat on your appetite; but air, you can absorb all the time." So we took the nursery, at the top of the house.

It is a big, airy room, the whole floor nearly, with windows that look all ways, and air and sunshine galore. It was nursery first and then playground and gymnasium, I should judge; for the windows are barred for little children, and there are rings and things in the walls.

The paint and paper look as if a boys' school had used it. It is stripped off—the paper—in great patches all round the head of my bed, about as far as I can reach, and in a great place on the other side of the roof low down. I never saw a worse paper in my life.

One of those sprawling flamboyant patterns committing every artistic sin.

It is dull enough to confuse the eye in following, pronounced enough to constantly irritate, and provoke study, and when you follow the lame, uncertain curves for a little distance they suddenly commit suicide—plunge off at outrageous angles, destroy themselves in unheard-of contradictions.

The color is repellent, almost revolting; a smouldering, unclean yellow, strangely faded by the slow-turning sunlight.

It is a dull yet lurid orange in some places, a sickly sulphur tint in others.

No wonder the children hated it! I should hate it myself if I had to live in this room long.

There comes John, and I must put this away,—he hates to have me write a word.

We have been here two weeks, and I haven't felt like writing before, since that first day.

I am sitting by the window now, up in this atrocious nursery, and there is nothing to hinder my writing as much as I please, save lack of strength.

John is away all day, and even some nights when his cases are serious.

I am glad my case is not serious!

But these nervous troubles are dreadfully depressing.

John does not know how much I really suffer. He knows there is no reason to suffer, and that satisfies him.

Of course it is only nervousness. It does weigh on me so not to do my duty in any way!

I meant to be such a help to John, such a real rest and comfort, and here I am a comparative burden already!

Nobody would believe what an effort it is to do what little I am able—to dress and entertain, and order things.

It is fortunate Mary is so good with the baby. Such a dear baby!

And yet I *cannot* be with him, it makes me so nervous.

I suppose John never was nervous in his life. He laughs at me so about this wall-paper!

At first he meant to repaper the room, but afterwards he said that I was letting it get the better of me, and that nothing was worse for a nervous patient than to give way to such fancies.

He said that after the wall-paper was changed it would be the heavy bedstead, and then the barred windows, and then that gate at the head of the stairs, and so on.

"You know the place is doing you good," he said, "and really, dear, I don't care to renovate the house just for a three months' rental."

"Then do let us go downstairs," I said, "there are such pretty rooms there."

Then he took me in his arms and called me a blessed little goose, and said he would go down the cellar if I wished, and would have it whitewashed into the bargain.

But he is right enough about the beds and windows and things.

It is as airy and comfortable a room as anyone need wish, and, of course, I would not be so silly as to make him uncomfortable just for a whim.

I'm really getting quite fond of the big room, all but that horrid paper.

Out of one window I can see the garden, those mysterious deep-shaded arbors, the riotous old-fashioned flowers, and bushes and gnarly trees.

Out of another I get a lovely view of the bay and a little private wharf belonging to the estate. There is a beautiful shaded lane that runs down there from the house. I always fancy I see people walking in these numerous paths and arbors, but John has cautioned me not to give way to fancy in the least. He says that with my imaginative power and habit of story-making a nervous weakness like mine is sure to lead to all manner of excited fancies, and that I ought to use my will and good sense to check the tendency. So I try.

I think sometimes that if I were only well enough to write a little it would relieve the press of ideas and rest me.

But I find I get pretty tired when I try.

It is so discouraging not to have any advice and companionship about my work. When I get really well John says we will ask Cousin

Henry and Julia down for a long visit; but he says he would as soon put fireworks in my pillow-case as to let me have those stimulating people about now.

I wish I could get well faster.

But I must not think about that. This paper looks to me as if it *knew* what a vicious influence it had!

There is a recurrent spot where the pattern lolls like a broken neck and two bulbous eyes stare at you upside-down.

I got positively angry with the impertinence of it and the everlastingness. Up and down and sideways they crawl, and those absurd, unblinking eyes are everywhere. There is one place where two breadths didn't match, and the eyes go all up and down the line, one a little higher than the other.

I never saw so much expression in an inanimate thing before, and we all know how much expression they have!

I used to lie awake as a child and get more entertainment and terror out of blank walls and plain furniture than most children could find in a toy-store.

I remember what a kindly wink the knobs of our big old bureau used to have, and there was one chair that always seemed like a strong friend.

I used to feel that if any of the other things looked too fierce I could always hop into that chair and be safe.

The furniture in this room is no worse than inharmonious, however, for we had to bring it all from downstairs. I suppose when this was used as a playroom they had to take all the nursery things out, and no wonder! I never saw such ravages as the children have made here.

The wall-paper, as I said before, is torn off in spots, and it sticketh closer than a brother—they must have had perseverance as well as hatred.

Then the floor is scratched and gouged and splintered, the plaster itself is dug out here and there, and this great heavy bed, which is all we found in the room, looks as if it had been through the wars.

But I don't mind it a bit—only the paper.

There comes John's sister. Such a dear girl as she is, and so careful of me! I must not let her find me writing.

She is a perfect, an enthusiastic housekeeper, and hopes for no better profession. I verily believe she thinks it is the writing which made me sick!

But I can write when she is out, and see her a long way off from these windows.

There is one that commands the road, a lovely, shaded winding road, and one that just looks off over the country. A lovely country, too, full of great elms and velvet meadows.

This wall-paper has a kind of sub-pattern in a different shade, a particularly irritating one, for you can only see it in certain lights, and not clearly then.

But in the places where it isn't faded, and where the sun is just so, I can see a strange, provoking, formless sort of figure, that seems to sulk about that silly and conspicuous front design.

There's sister on the stairs!

Well, the Fourth of July is over! The people are all gone and I am tired out. John thought it might do me good to see a little company, so we just had mother and Nellie and the children down for a week.

Of course I didn't do a thing. Jennie sees to everything now.

But it tired me all the same.

John says if I don't pick up faster he shall send me to Weir Mitchell[1] in the autumn.

But I don't want to go there at all. I had a friend who was in his hands once, and she says he is just like John and my brother, only more so!

Besides, it is such an undertaking to go so far.

I don't feel as if it was worth while to turn my hand over for anything, and I'm getting dreadfully fretful and querulous.

I cry at nothing, and cry most of the time.

Of course I don't when John is here, or anybody else, but when I am alone.

And I am alone a good deal just now. John is kept in town very often by serious cases, and Jennie is good and lets me alone when I want her to.

So I walk a little in the garden or down that lovely lane, sit on the porch under the roses, and lie down up here a good deal.

I'm getting really fond of the room in spite of the wall-paper. Perhaps *because* of the wall-paper.

---

1. Weir Mitchell (1829–1914): a famous Philadelphia doctor who developed, in the 1870s, a cure for female "nervous disorders" that involved total bedrest and isolation from all stimuli. Mitchell treated Charlotte Perkins for her depression.

It dwells in my mind so!

I lie here on this great immovable bed—it is nailed down, I believe—and follow that pattern about by the hour. It is as good as gymnastics, I assure you. I start, we'll say at the bottom, down in the corner over there where it has not been touched, and I determine for the thousandth time that I *will* follow that pointless pattern to some sort of a conclusion.

I know a little of the principles of design, and I know this thing was not arranged on any laws of radiation, or alternation, or repetition, or symmetry, or anything else that I ever heard of.

It is repeated, of course, by the breadths, but not otherwise.

Looked at in one way, each breadth stands alone, the bloated curves and flourishes—a kind of "debased Romanesque"[2] with *delirium tremens*[3]—go waddling up and down in isolated columns of fatuity.

But, on the other hand, they connect diagonally, and the sprawling outlines run off in great slanting waves of optic horror, like a lot of wallowing seaweeds in full chase.

The whole thing goes horizontally, too, at least it seems so, and I exhaust myself in trying to distinguish the order of its going in that direction.

They have used a horizontal breadth for a frieze, and that adds wonderfully to the confusion.

There is one end of the room where it is almost intact, and there, when the cross-lights fade and the low sun shines directly upon it, I can almost fancy radiation, after all—the interminable grotesques seem to form around a common center and rush off in headlong plunges of equal distraction.

It makes me tired to follow it. I will take a nap, I guess.

I don't know why I should write this.

I don't want to.

I don't feel able.

And I know John would think it absurd. But I *must* say what I feel and think in some way—it is such a relief!

---

2. **Romanesque:** a style of European architecture of the 1200s and 1300s, characterized by round arches and vaults, thick walls, and interior niches.
3. *delirium tremens:* (Latin) literally, "trembling delirium," a violent state including great mental excitement, restlessness, confused speech, and hallucinations.

But the effort is getting to be greater than the relief.

Half the time now I am awfully lazy, and lie down ever so much.

John says I mustn't lose my strength, and has me take cod-liver oil and lots of tonics and things, to say nothing of ale and wine and rare meat.

Dear John! He loves me very dearly, and hates to have me sick. I tried to have a real earnest reasonable talk with him the other day, and tell him how I wished he would let me go and make a visit to Cousin Henry and Julia.

But he said I wasn't able to go, nor able to stand it after I got there; and I did not make out a very good case for myself, for I was crying before I had finished.

It is getting to be a great effort for me to think straight. Just this nervous weakness, I suppose.

And dear John gathered me up in his arms, and just carried me upstairs and laid me on the bed, and sat by me and read to me till he tired my head.

He said I was his darling and his comfort and all he had, and that I must take care of myself for his sake, and keep well.

He says no one but myself can help me out of it, that I must use my will and self-control and not let my silly fancies run away with me.

There's one comfort, the baby is well and happy, and does not have to occupy this nursery with the horrid wall-paper.

If we had not used it that blessed child would have! What a fortunate escape! Why, I wouldn't have a child of mine, an impressionable little thing, live in such a room for worlds.

I never thought of it before, but it is lucky that John kept me here, after all. I can stand it so much easier than a baby, you see.

Of course, I never mention it to them any more,—I am too wise,—but I keep watch of it all the same.

There are things in that paper that nobody knows but me, or ever will.

Behind that outside pattern the dim shapes get clearer every day.

It is always the same shape, only very numerous.

And it is like a woman stooping down and creeping about behind that pattern. I don't like it a bit. I wonder—I begin to think—I wish John would take me away from here!

It is so hard to talk with John about my case, because he is so wise, and because he loves me so.

But I tried it last night.

It was moonlight. The moon shines in all around, just as the sun does.

I hate to see it sometimes, it creeps so slowly, and always comes in by one window or another.

John was asleep and I hated to waken him, so I kept still and watched the moonlight on that undulating wall-paper till I felt creepy.

The faint figure behind seemed to shake the pattern, just as if she wanted to get out.

I got up softly and went to feel and see if the paper *did* move, and when I came back John was awake.

"What is it, little girl?" he said. "Don't go walking about like that—you'll get cold."

I thought it was a good time to talk, so I told him that I really was not gaining here, and that I wished he would take me away.

"Why, darling!" said he, "our lease will be up in three weeks, and I can't see how to leave before. The repairs are not done at home, and I cannot possibly leave town just now. Of course if you were in any danger I could and would, but you really are better, dear, whether you can see it or not. I am a doctor, dear, and I know. You are gaining flesh and color, your appetite is better. I feel really much easier about you."

"I don't weigh a bit more," said I, "nor as much; and my appetite may be better in the evening, when you are here, but it is worse in the morning, when you are away."

"Bless her little heart!" said he with a big hug; "she shall be as sick as she pleases. But now let's improve the shining hours[4] by going to sleep, and talk about it in the morning."

"And you won't go away?" I asked gloomily.

"Why, how can I, dear? It is only three weeks more and then we will take a nice little trip of a few days while Jennie is getting the house ready. Really, dear, you are better!"

"Better in body, perhaps—" I began, and stopped short, for he sat up straight and looked at me with such a stern, reproachful look that I could not say another word.

"My darling," said he, "I beg of you, for my sake and for our child's sake, as well as for your own, that you will never for one instant let

---

4. **improve the shining hours:** an allusion to Isaac Watts's poem "Against Idleness and Mischief" from *Divine Songs* (1715), which begins, "How doth the little busy bee / Improve the shining hours . . . ."

that idea enter your mind! There is nothing so dangerous, so fascinating, to a temperament like yours. It is a false and foolish fancy. Can you not trust me as a physician when I tell you so?"

So of course I said no more on that score, and we went to sleep before long. He thought I was asleep first, but I wasn't—I lay there for hours trying to decide whether that front pattern and the back pattern really did move together or separately.

On a pattern like this, by daylight, there is a lack of sequence, a defiance of law, that is a constant irritant to a normal mind.

The color is hideous enough, and unreliable enough, and infuriating enough, but the pattern is torturing.

You think you have mastered it, but just as you get well under way in following, it turns a back somersault, and there you are. It slaps you in the face, knocks you down, and tramples upon you. It is like a bad dream.

The outside pattern is a florid arabesque, reminding one of a fungus. If you can imagine a toadstool in joints, an interminable string of toadstools, budding and sprouting in endless convolutions,—why, that is something like it.

That is, sometimes!

There is one marked peculiarity about this paper, a thing nobody seems to notice but myself, and that is that it changes as the light changes.

When the sun shoots in through the east window—I always watch for that first long, straight ray—it changes so quickly that I never can quite believe it.

That is why I watch it always.

By moonlight—the moon shines in all night when there is a moon—I wouldn't know it was the same paper.

At night in any kind of light, in twilight, candlelight, lamp-light, and worst of all by moonlight, it becomes bars! The outside pattern, I mean, and the woman behind it is as plain as can be.

I didn't realize for a long time what the thing was that showed behind—that dim sub-pattern—but now I am quite sure it is a woman.

By daylight she is subdued, quiet. I fancy it is the pattern that keeps her so still. It is so puzzling. It keeps me quiet by the hour.

I lie down ever so much now. John says it is good for me, and to sleep all I can.

Indeed, he started the habit by making me lie down for an hour after each meal.

It is a very bad habit, I am convinced, for, you see, I don't sleep.

And that cultivates deceit, for I don't tell them I'm awake—oh, no!

The fact is, I am getting a little afraid of John.

He seems very queer sometimes, and even Jennie has an inexplicable look.

It strikes me occasionally, just as a scientific hypothesis, that perhaps it is the paper!

I have watched John when he did not know I was looking, and come into the room suddenly on the most innocent excuses, and I've caught him several times *looking at the paper*! And Jennie too. I caught Jennie with her hand on it once.

She didn't know I was in the room, and when I asked her in a quiet, very quiet voice, with the most restrained manner possible, what she was doing with the paper she turned around as if she had been caught stealing, and looked quite angry—asked me why I should frighten her so!

The she said that the paper stained everything it touched, and that she had found yellow smooches on all my clothes and John's, and she wished we would be more careful!

Did not that sound innocent? But I know she was studying that pattern, and I am determined that nobody shall find it out but myself!

Life is very much more exciting now than it used to be. You see I have something more to expect, to look forward to, to watch. I really do eat better, and am more quiet than I was.

John is so pleased to see me improve! He laughed a little the other day, and said I seemed to be flourishing in spite of my wall-paper.

I turned it off with a laugh. I had no intention of telling him that it was *because* of the wall-paper—he would make fun of me. He might even want to take me away.

I don't want to leave now until I have found it out. There is a week more, and I think that will be enough.

I'm feeling ever so much better! I don't sleep much at night for it is so interesting to watch developments; but I sleep a good deal in the day-time.

In the day-time it is tiresome and perplexing.

There are always new shoots on the fungus, and new shades of yellow all over it. I cannot keep count of them, though I have tried conscientiously.

It is the strangest yellow, that wall-paper! It makes me think of all the yellow things I ever saw—not beautiful ones like buttercups, but old foul, bad yellow things.

But there is something else about that paper—the smell! I noticed it the moment we came into the room, but with so much air and sun it was not bad! Now we have had a week of fog and rain, and whether the windows are open or not the smell is here.

It creeps all over the house.

I find it hovering in the dining-room, skulking in the parlor, hiding in the hall, lying in wait for me on the stairs.

It gets into my hair.

Even when I go to ride, if I turn my head suddenly and surprise it—there is that smell!

Such a peculiar odor, too! I have spent hours in trying to analyze it, to find what it smelled like.

It is not bad—at first, and very gentle, but quite the subtlest, most enduring odor I ever met.

In this damp weather it is awful. I wake up in the night and find it hanging over me.

It used to disturb me at first. I thought seriously of burning the house—to reach the smell.

But now I am used to it. The only thing I can think of that it is like is the *color* of the paper—a yellow smell!

There is a very funny mark on this wall, low down, near the mop-board. A streak that runs around the room. It goes behind every piece of furniture, except the bed, a long, straight, even *smooch,* as if it had been rubbed over and over.

I wonder how it was done and who did it, and what they did it for. Round and round and round—round and round and round—it makes me dizzy!

I really have discovered something at last.

Through watching so much at night, when it changes so, I have finally found out.

The front pattern does move—and no wonder! The woman behind shakes it!

Sometimes I think there are a great many women behind, and sometimes only one, and she crawls around fast, and her crawling shakes it all over.

Then in the very bright spots she keeps still, and in the very shady spots she just takes hold of the bars and shakes them hard.

And she is all the time trying to climb through. But nobody could climb through that pattern—it strangles so; I think that is why it has so many heads.

They get through, and then the pattern strangles them off and turns them upside-down, and makes their eyes white!

If those heads were covered or taken off it would not be half so bad.

I think that woman gets out in the day-time!

And I'll tell you why—privately—I've seen her!

I can see her out of every one of my windows!

It is the same woman, I know, for she is always creeping, and most women do not creep by daylight.

I see her in that long shaded line, creeping up and down. I see her in those dark grape arbors, creeping all around the garden.

I see her on that long road under the trees, creeping along, and when a carriage comes she hides under the blackberry vines.

I don't blame her a bit. It must be very humiliating to be caught creeping by daylight!

I always lock the door when I creep by daylight. I can't do it at night, for I know John would suspect something at once.

And John is so queer, now, that I don't want to irritate him. I wish he would take another room! Besides, I don't want anybody to get that woman out at night but myself.

I often wonder if I could see her out of all the windows at once.

But, turn as fast as I can, I can only see out of one at one time.

And though I always see her she *may* be able to creep faster than I can turn!

I have watched her sometimes away off in the open country, creeping as fast as a cloud shadow in a high wind.

If only that top pattern could be gotten off from the under one! I mean to try it, little by little.

I have found out another funny thing, but I sha'n't tell it this time! It does not do to trust people too much.

There are only two more days to get this paper off, and I believe John is beginning to notice. I don't like the look in his eyes.

And I heard him ask Jennie a lot of professional questions about me. She had a very good report to give.

She said I slept a good deal in the day-time.

John knows I don't sleep very well at night, for all I'm so quiet!

He asked me all sorts of questions, too, and pretended to be very loving and kind.

As if I couldn't see through him!

Still, I don't wonder he acts so, sleeping under this paper for three months.

It only interests me, but I feel sure John and Jennie are secretly affected by it.

Hurrah! This is the last day, but it is enough. John is to stay in town over night, and won't be out until this evening.

Jennie wanted to sleep with me—the sly thing! but I told her I should undoubtedly rest better for a night all alone.

That was clever, for really I wasn't alone a bit! As soon as it was moonlight, and that poor thing began to crawl and shake the pattern, I got up and ran to help her.

I pulled and she shook, I shook and she pulled, and before morning we had peeled off yards of that paper.

A strip about as high as my head and half-around the room.

And then when the sun came and that awful pattern began to laugh at me I declared I would finish it today!

We go away tomorrow, and they are moving all my furniture down again to leave things as they were before.

Jennie looked at the wall in amazement, but I told her merrily that I did it out of pure spite at the vicious thing.

She laughed and said she wouldn't mind doing it herself, but I must not get tired.

How she betrayed herself that time!

But I am here, and no person touches this paper but me—not *alive*!

She tried to get me out of the room—it was too patent! But I said it was so quiet and empty and clean now that I believed I would lie down again and sleep all I could; and not to wake me even for dinner—I would call when I woke.

So now she is gone, and the servants are gone, and the things are gone, and there is nothing left but that great bedstead nailed down, with the canvas mattress we found on it.

We shall sleep downstairs tonight, and take the boat home tomorrow.

I quite enjoy the room, now it is bare again.

How those children did tear about here!

This bedstead is fairly gnawed!

But I must get to work.

I have locked the door and thrown the key down into the front path.

I don't want to go out, and I don't want to have anybody come in, till John comes.

I want to astonish him.

I've got a rope up here that even Jennie did not find. If that woman does get out, and tries to get away, I can tie her!

But I forgot I could not reach far without anything to stand on!

This bed will *not* move!

I tried to lift and push it until I was lame, and then I got so angry I bit off a little piece at one corner—but it hurt my teeth.

Then I peeled off all the paper I could reach standing on the floor. It sticks horribly and the pattern just enjoys it! All those strangled heads and bulbous eyes and waddling fungus growths just shriek with derision!

I am getting angry enough to do something desperate. To jump out of the window would be admirable exercise, but the bars are too strong even to try.

Besides, I wouldn't do it. Of course not. I know well enough that a step like that is improper and might be misconstrued.

I don't like to *look* out of the windows even—there are so many of those creeping women, and they creep so fast.

I wonder if they all come out of that wall-paper, as I did?

But I am securely fastened now by my well-hidden rope—you don't get *me* out in the road there!

I suppose I shall have to get back behind the pattern when it comes night, and that is hard!

It is so pleasant to be out in this great room and creep around as I please!

I don't want to go outside. I won't even if Jennie asks me to.

For outside you have to creep on the ground, and everything is green instead of yellow.

But here I can creep smoothly on the floor, and my shoulder just fits in that long smooch around the wall, so I cannot lose my way.

Why, there's John at the door!

It is no use, young man, you can't open it!

How he does call and pound!

Now he's crying for an axe.

It would be a shame to break down that beautiful door!

"John, dear!" said I in the gentlest voice, "the key is down by the front steps, under a plantain leaf!"

That silenced him for a few moments.

Then he said—very quietly indeed, "Open the door, my darling!"

"I can't," said I. "The key is down by the front door, under a plantain leaf!"

And then I said it again, several times, very gently and slowly, and said it so often that he had to go and see, and he got it, of course, and came in. He stopped short by the door.

"What is the matter?' he cried. "For God's sake, what are you doing?"

I kept on creeping just the same, but I looked at him over my shoulder.

"I've got out at last," said I, "in spite of you and Jennie! And I've pulled off most of the paper, so you can't put me back!"

Now why should that man have fainted? But he did, and right across my path by the wall, so that I had to creep over him every time!

Discussion Questions

1. When did you first suspect the narrator's mental condition? What details does the author add as the story progresses to confirm your reaction?

2. What do you think are John's assumptions about the positions of husband and wife and of the proper relationship between them?

3. Trace the deterioration of the narrator's mental state through the ways in which she describes herself and John.

4. Discuss how the yellow wall-paper itself becomes almost another character in the story.

5. What effects does the author achieve through her choice of first-person narrative?

6. What criticism of the medical practices of the day do you find implicit in Gilman's telling of her story?

Suggestion for Writing

Imagine that you are the narrator 10 years after the incidents described in this story. You have been cured—by whatever means you choose—and now you are rereading your earlier memoir. Write a brief response to the person you once were in contrast to the person you are now. If you wish, include a description of the treatment that cured you and a critique of John's treatment that drove you to your earlier mental state.

Nathaniel Hawthorne (1804–1864)

Nathaniel Hawthorne was born in Salem, Massachusetts, where one of his ancestors had been involved in the witch hunts of the 1690s. Guilt for his ancestor's deeds haunted Hawthorne all his life and found its way into much of his writing.

Hawthorne's father, a shipmaster, died when the boy was four, and Hawthorne was brought up in a strict household where he spent much of his time in solitude. He attended Bowdoin College in Maine and returned home to write. Eventually his stories began to appear in magazines, and in 1837 he published a collection of these he called *Twice-Told Tales*. He became a leader, along with Edgar Allan Poe, in the development of the American short story. Hawthorne is best known for his novels, however. *The Scarlet Letter* (1850) and *The House of the Seven Gables* (1851) are considered classics in American literature. In both of these Hawthorne explores the effects of inherited sin.

Young Goodman Brown

Young Goodman[1] Brown came forth, at sunset, into the streets of Salem village, but put his head back, after crossing the threshold, to exchange a parting kiss with his young wife. And Faith, as the wife was aptly named, thrust own pretty head into the street, letting the wind play with the pink ribbons of her cap, while she called to Goodman Brown.

"Dearest heart," whispered she, softly and rather sadly, when her lips were close to his ear, "pr'y thee,[2] put off your journey until sunrise, and sleep in your own bed tonight. A lone woman is troubled with such dreams and such thoughts that she's afeard of herself, sometimes. Pray, tarry with me this night, dear husband, of all nights in the year."

"My love and my Faith," replied young Goodman Brown, "of all nights in the year, this one night must I tarry away from thee. My journey, as thou callest it, forth and back again, must needs be done 'twixt now and sunrise. What, my sweet pretty wife, dost thou doubt me already, and we but three months married!"

"Then, God bless you!" said Faith with the pink ribbons, "and may you find all well, when you come back."

So they parted: and the young man pursued his way, until, being about to turn the corner by the meeting-house, he looked back and saw the head of Faith still peeping after him, with a melancholy air, in spite of her pink ribbons.

"Poor little Faith!" thought he, for his heart smote[3] him. "What a wretch am I, to leave her on such an errand! She talks of dreams, too. Methought, as she spoke, there was trouble in her face, as if a dream had warned her what work is to be done tonight. But no, no! 'twould kill her to think it. Well; she's a blessed angel on earth; and after this one night, I'll cling to her skirts and follow her to heaven."

With this excellent resolve for the future, Goodman Brown felt himself justified in making more haste on his present evil purpose. He had taken a dreary road, darkened by all the gloomiest trees of the forest,

---

1. **Goodman:** a former title equivalent to *mister;* the female counterpart is *Goody.*
2. **pr'y thee:** pray thee; please.
3. **smote:** strongly affected.

which barely stood aside to let the narrow path creep through, and closed immediately behind. It was all as lonely as could be, and there is this peculiarity in such a solitude, that the traveler knows not who may be concealed by the innumerable trunks and the thick boughs overhead; so that, with lonely footsteps, he may yet be passing through an unseen multitude.

"There may be a devilish Indian behind every tree," said Goodman Brown, to himself; and he glanced fearfully behind him, as he added, "What if the devil himself should be at my very elbow?"

His head being turned back, he passed a crook of the road, and looking forward again, beheld the figure of a man, in grave and decent attire, seated at the foot of an old tree. He arose at Goodman Brown's approach, and walked onward, side by side with him.

"You are late, Goodman Brown," said he. "The clock of the Old South was striking as I came through Boston, and that is a full fifteen minutes agone."

"Faith kept me back awhile," replied the young man, with a tremor in his voice, caused by the sudden appearance of his companion, though not wholly unexpected.

It was now deep dusk in the forest, and deepest in that part of it where these two were journeying. As nearly as could be discerned, the second traveler was about fifty years old, apparently in the same rank of life as Goodman Brown, and bearing a considerable resemblance to him, though perhaps more in expression than features. Still they might have been taken for father and son. And yet, though the elder person was as simply clad as the younger, and as simple in manner too, he had an indescribable air of one who knew the world, and would not have felt abashed at the governor's dinner table, or in King William's court, were it possible that his affairs should call him thither. But the only thing about him, that could be fixed upon as remarkable, was his staff, which bore the likeness of a great black snake, so curiously wrought that it might almost be seen to twist and wriggle itself, like a living serpent. This, of course, must have been an ocular deception, assisted by the uncertain light.

"Come, Goodman Brown!" cried his fellow traveler, "this is a dull pace for the beginning of a journey. Take my staff, if you are so soon weary."

"Friend," said the other, exchanging his slow pace for a full stop; "having kept covenant by meeting thee here, it is my purpose now to return whence I came. I have scruples, touching the matter thou wot'st[4] of."

"Sayest thou so?" replied he of the serpent, smiling apart. "Let us walk on, nevertheless, reasoning as we go, and if I convince thee not, thou shalt turn back. We are but a little way in the forest yet."

"Too far, too far!" exclaimed the goodman, unconsciously resuming his walk. "My father never went into the woods on such an errand, nor his father before him. We have been a race of honest men and good Christians, since the days of the martyrs. And I be the first of the name of Brown that ever took this path, and kept—"

"Such company, thou wouldst say," observed the elder person, interpreting his pause. "Good, Goodman Brown! I have been as well acquainted with your family as ever; one among the Puritans; and that's no trifle to say. I helped your grandfather, the constable, when he lashed the Quaker woman so smartly on the streets of Salem. And it was I that brought your father a pitch-pine knot, kindled at my own hearth, to set fire to an Indian village in King Philip's[5] war. They were my good friends, both; and many a pleasant walk have we had along this path, and returned merrily after midnight. I would fain be friends with you, for their sake."

"If it be as thou sayest," replied Goodman Brown, "I marvel they never spoke of these matters. Or, verily, I marvel not, seeing that the least rumor of the sort would have driven them from New England. We are a people of prayer, and good works, to boot, and abide no such wickedness."

"Wickedness or not," said the traveler with the twisted staff, "I have a very general acquaintance here in New England. The deacons of many a church have drunk the communion wine with me; the selectmen, of divers towns, make me their chairman; and a majority of the Great and General Court are firm supporters of my interest. The governor and I, too—but these are state secrets."

"Can this be so!" cried Goodman Brown, with a stare of amazement at his undisturbed companion. "Howbeit, I have nothing to do with the governor and council; they have their own ways, and are no rule for a simple husbandman, like me. But, were I to go on with thee, how should

---

4. **wot'st:** know (archaic).
5. **King Philip's war:** King Philip was a Native American chief who led a war against the colonists in 1675.

I meet the eye of that good old man, our minister, at Salem village? Oh, his voice would make me tremble, both Sabbath day and lecture day!"

Thus far the elder traveler had listed with due gravity, but now burst into a fit of irrepressible mirth, shaking himself so violently that his snake-like staff actually seemed to wriggle in sympathy.

"Ha! ha! ha!" shouted he, again and again; then, composing himself, "Well, go on, Goodman Brown, go on; but pr'y thee, don't kill me with laughing!"

"Well, then, to end the matter at once," said Goodman Brown, considerably nettled, "there is my wife, Faith. It would break her dear little heart; and I'd rather break my own!"

"Nay, if that be the case," answered the other, "e'en go thy ways, Goodman Brown. I would not, for twenty old women like the one hobbling before us, that Faith should come to any harm."

As he spoke, he pointed his staff at a female figure on the path, in whom Goodman Brown recognized a very pious exemplary dame, who had taught him his catechism, in youth, and was still his moral and spiritual advisor, jointly with the minister and Deacon Gookin.

"A marvel, truly, that Goody Cloyse should be so far in the wilderness, at nightfall!" said he. "But, with your leave, friend, I shall take a cut through the woods, until we have left this Christian woman behind. Being a stranger to you, she might ask whom I was consorting with, and whither I was going."

"Be it so," said his fellow traveler. "Betake you to the woods, and let me keep the path."

Accordingly, the young man turned aside, but took care to watch his companion, who advanced softly along the road, until he had come within a staff's length of the old dame. She, meanwhile, was making the best of her way, with singular speed for so aged a woman, and mumbling some indistinct words, a prayer, doubtless, as she went. The traveler put forth his staff, and touched her withered neck with what seemed the serpent's tail.

"The devil!" screamed the pious old lady.

"Then Goody Cloyse knows her old friend?" observed the traveler, confronting her, and leaning on his writhing stick.

"Ah, forsooth,[6] and is it your worship, indeed?" cried the good dame. "Yea, truly it is, and in the very image of my old gossip,

---

6. forsooth: in truth (archaic).

Goodman Brown, the grandfather of the silly fellow that now is. But, would your worship believe it? My broomstick hath strangely disappeared, stolen, as I suspect, by that unhanged witch, Goody Cory, and that, too, when I was all anointed with the juice of smallage and cinquefoil and wolfsbane[7]—"

"Mingled with fine wheat and the fat of a newborn babe," said the shape of old Goodman Brown.

"Ah, your worship knows the receipt,"[8] cried the old lady, cackling aloud. "So, as I was saying, being all ready for the meeting, and no horse to ride on, I made up my mind to foot it; for they tell me, there is a nice young man to be taken to communion tonight. But now your good worship will lend me your arm, and we shall be there in a twinkling."

"That can hardly be," answered her friend. "I may not spare you my arm, Goody Cloyse, but here is my staff, if you will.

So saying, he threw it down at her feet, where, perhaps, it assumed life, being one of the rods which its owner had formerly lent to the Egyptian Magi.[9] Of this fact, however, Goodman Brown could not take cognizance. He had cast up his eyes in astonishment, and looking down again, beheld neither Goody Cloyse nor the serpentine staff, but his fellow traveler alone, who waited for him as calmly as if nothing had happened.

"That old woman taught me my catechism!" said the young man; and there was a world of meaning in this simple comment.

They continued to walk onwards, while the elder traveler exhorted his companion to make good speed and persevere in the path, discoursing so aptly that his arguments seemed rather to spring up in the bosom of his auditor[10] than to be suggested by himself. As they went, he plucked a branch of maple, to serve for a walking stick, and began to strip it of the twigs and little boughs, which were wet with evening dew. The moment his fingers touched them, they became strangely withered and dried up, as with a week's sunshine. Thus the pair proceeded, at a good free pace, until suddenly, in a gloomy hollow of the

---

7. **smallage . . . wolfsbane:** plants and herbs used in magic.
8. **receipt:** recipe.
9. **Egyptian Magi:** In Exodus 7:8–12, when Moses and Aaron beg the Egyptian Pharaoh to free the Jews from slavery, they perform a miracle by throwing down a rod that turns into a serpent; however, the Egyptian magicians turn their own rods into serpents as well by their "secret arts."
10. **auditor:** listener.

road, Goodman Brown sat himself down on the stump of a tree, and refused to go any farther.

"Friend," said he, stubbornly, "my mind is made up. Not another step will I budge on this errand. What if a wretched old woman do choose to go to the devil, when I thought she was going to heaven! Is that any reason why I should quit my dear Faith, and go after her?"

"You will think better of this, by and by," said his acquaintance, composedly. "Sit here and rest yourself awhile, and when you feel like moving again, there is my staff to help you along."

Without more words, he threw his companion the maple stick, and was as speedily out of sight as if he had vanished into the deepening gloom. The young man sat a few moments, by the roadside, applauding himself greatly, and thinking with how clear a conscience he should greet the minister, in his morning walk, nor shrink from the eye of good old Deacon Gookin. And what calm sleep would be his, that very night, which was to have been spent so wickedly, but purely and sweetly now, in the arms of Faith! Amidst these pleasant and praiseworthy meditations, Goodman Brown heard the tramp of horses along the road, and deemed it advisable to conceal himself within the verge of the forest, conscious of the guilty purpose that had brought him thither, though now so happily turned from it.

On came the hoof tramps and the voices of the riders, two grave old voices, conversing soberly as they drew near. These mingled sounds appeared to pass along the road, within a few yards of the young man's hiding place; but owing, doubtless, to the depth of the gloom at that particular spot, neither the travelers nor their steeds were visible. Though their figures brushed the small boughs by the wayside, it could not be seen that they intercepted, even for a moment, the faint gleam from the strip of bright sky, athwart which they must have passed. Goodman Brown alternately crouched and stood on tiptoe, pulling aside the branches and thrusting forth his head as far as he durst, without discerning so much as a shadow. It vexed him the more because he could have sworn, were such a thing possible, that he recognized the voices of the minister and Deacon Gookin, jogging along quietly, as they were wont to do when bound to some ordination or ecclesiastical council. While yet within hearing, one of the riders stopped to pluck a switch.

"Of the two, reverend sir," said the voice like the deacon's, "I had rather miss an ordination dinner than tonight's meeting. They tell me that some of our community are to be here from Falmouth and beyond and others from Connecticut and Rhode Island; besides several of the Indian powwows,[11] who, after their fashion, know almost as much deviltry as the best of us. Moreover, there is a goodly young woman to be taken into communion."

"Mighty well, Deacon Gookin!" replied the solemn old tones of the minister. "Spur up, or we shall be late. Nothing can be done, you know, until I get on the ground."

The hoofs clattered again, and the voices, talking so strangely in the empty air, passed on through the forest, where no church had ever gathered, nor solitary Christian prayed. Whither, then could these holy men be journeying, so deep into the heathen wilderness? Young Goodman Brown caught hold of a tree for support, being ready to sink down on the ground, faint and overburdened with the heavy sickness of his heart. He looked up to the sky, doubting whether there really was a heaven above him. Yet there was the blue arch and the stars brightening in it.

"With heaven above, and Faith below, I will stand firm against the devil!" cried Goodman Brown.

While he still gazed upward, into the deep arch of the firmament, and had lifted his hands to pray, a cloud, though no wind was stirring, hurried across the zenith,[12] and hid the brightening stars. The blue sky was still visible, except directly overhead, where this black mass of cloud was sweeping swiftly northward. Aloft in the air, as if from the depths of the cloud, came a confused and doubtful sound of voices. Once, the listener fancied that he could distinguish the accents of townspeople of his own, men and women, both pious and ungodly, many of whom he had met at the communion table, and others he had seen rioting at the tavern. The next moment, so indistinct were the sounds, he doubted whether he had heard aught but the murmur of the old forest, whispering without a wind. Then came a stronger swell of those familiar tones, heard daily in the sunshine, at Salem village, but never, until now, from a cloud of night. There was one voice, of a young woman, uttering lamentations, yet with an uncertain sorrow, and entreating for some favor, which perhaps, it would grieve her to obtain. And all the unseen multitude, both saints and sinners, seemed to encourage her onwards.

---

11. **powwows:** American Indian medicine men or priests.
12. **zenith:** the point of the sky directly overhead.

"Faith!" shouted Goodman Brown, in a voice of agony and desperation; and the echoes of the forest mocked him, crying—"Faith! Faith!" as if bewildered wretches were seeking her, all through the wilderness.

The cry of grief, rage and terror was yet piercing the night when the unhappy husband held his breath for a response. There was a scream, drowned immediately in a louder murmur of voices, fading into far-off laughter, as the dark cloud swept away, leaving the clear and silent sky above Goodman Brown. But something fluttered lightly down through the air, and caught on the branch of a tree. The young man seized it, and beheld a pink ribbon.

"My Faith is gone!" cried he, after one stupefied moment. "There is no good on earth; and sin is but a name. Come, devil! For to thee is this world given."

And maddened with despair, so that he laughed loud and long, did Goodman Brown grasp his staff and set forth again, at such a rate that he seemed to fly along the forest path rather than to walk or run. The road grew wilder and drearier and more faintly traced, and vanished at length, leaving him in the heart of the dark wilderness, still rushing onward, with the instinct that guides mortal man to evil. The whole forest was peopled with frightful sounds; the creaking of the trees, the howling of wild beasts and the yell of Indians; while sometimes the wind tolled like a distant church bell, and sometimes gave a broad roar around the traveler, as if all nature were laughing him to scorn. But he was himself the chief horror of the scene, and shrank not from its other horrors.

"Ha! ha! ha!" roared Goodman Brown, when the wind laughed at him. "Let us hear which will laugh loudest! Think not to frighten me with your deviltry! Come witch, come wizard, come Indian powwow, come devil himself! And here comes Goodman Brown. You may as well fear him as he fear you!"

In truth, all through the haunted forest, there could be nothing more frightful than the figure of Goodman Brown. On he flew, among the black pines, brandishing his staff with frenzied gestures, now giving vent to an inspiration of horrid blasphemy, and now shouting forth such laughter as set all the echoes of the forest laughing like demons around him. The fiend in his own shape is less hideous than when he rages in the breast of man. Thus sped the demoniac on his course, until, quivering among the trees, he saw a red light before him, as when the felled trunks and branches of a clearing have been set on fire and throw up their lurid blaze against the sky at the hour of midnight. He paused, in a lull of the tempest that had driven him onward, and heard the swell of what seemed a hymn, rolling solemnly from a distance, with the weight of many voices. He knew the tune; it was a familiar one in the choir of the village meeting-house. The verse died heavily away, and was lengthened by a chorus, not of human voices, but of all the sounds of the benighted wilderness, pealing in awful harmony together. Goodman Brown cried out, and his cry was lost to his own ear by its unison with the cry of the desert.

In the interval of silence, he stole forward, until the light glared full upon his eyes. At one extremity of an open space hemmed in by the dark wall of the forest, arose a rock, bearing some rude, natural resemblance either to an altar or a pulpit, and surrounded by four blazing pines, their tops aflame, their stems untouched, like candles at an evening meeting. The mass of foliage that had overgrown the summit of the rock was all on fire, blazing high into the night, and fitfully illuminating the whole field. Each pendent[13] twig and leafy festoon was in a blaze. As the red light arose and fell, a numerous congregation alternately shone forth, then disappeared in shadow, and again grew, as it were, out of the darkness, peopling the heart of the solitary woods at once.

"A grave and dark-clad company!" quoth Goodman Brown.

In truth, they were such. Among them, quivering to and fro between gloom and spendor, appeared faces that would be seen, next day, at the council board of the providence, and others which, Sabbath after Sabbath, looked devoutly heavenward, and benignantly[14] over the crowded pews, from the holiest pulpits in the land. Some affirm that the lady of the governor was there. At least, there were high dames well known to her, and wives of honored husbands, and widows, a great multitude, and ancient maidens, all of excellent repute, and fair young girls, who trembled lest their mothers should espy them. Either the sudden gleams of light, flashing over the obscure field, bedazzled Goodman Brown, or he recognized a score of the church members of Salem village, famous for their especial sanctity. Good old Deacon Gookin had arrived, and waited at the skirts of that venerable saint, his revered pastor. But, irreverently consorting with these grave,

---

13. **pendent:** overhanging.
14. **benignantly** (bi nig´ nənt lē): kindly.

reputable and pious people, these elders of the church, these chaste dames and dewy virgins, there were men of dissolute lives and women of spotted fame, wretches given over to all mean and filthy vice, and suspected even of horrid crimes. It was strange to see that the good shrank not from the wicked, nor were the sinners abashed by the saints. Scattered, also, among their pale-faced enemies, were Indian priests, or powwows, who had often scared their native forest with more hideous incantations than any known to English witchcraft.

But, where is Faith?" thought Goodman Brown; and, as hope came into his heart, he trembled.

Another verse of the hymn arose, a slow and solemn strain, such as the pious love, but joined to words which expressed all that our nature can conceive of sin, and darkly hinted at far more. Unfathomable to mere mortals is the lore of fiends. Verse after verse was sung, and still the chorus of the desert swelled between, like the deepest tone of a mighty organ. And, with the final peal of that dreadful anthem, there came a sound, as if the roaring wind, the rushing streams, the howling beasts and every other voice of the unconverted wilderness were mingling and according with the voice of guilty man, in homage to the prince of all. The four blazing pines threw up a loftier flame and obscurely discovered shapes and visages of horror on the smoke wreaths above the impious[15] assembly. At the same moment, the fire on the rock shot redly forth, and formed a glowing arch above its base, where now appeared a figure. With reverence be it spoken, the apparition bore no slight similitude, both in garb and manner, to some grave divine of the New England churches.

"Bring forth the converts!" cried a voice that echoed through the field and rolled into the forest.

At the word, Goodman Brown stepped forth from the shadow of the trees, and approached the congregation, with whom he felt a loathful brotherhood, by the sympathy of all that was wicked in his heart. He could have well nigh sworn that the shape of his own dead father beckoned him to advance, looking downward from a smoke wreath, while a woman, with dim features of despair, threw out her hand to warn him back. Was it his mother? But he had no power to retreat one step, nor to resist, even in thought, when the minister and good old Deacon Gookin seized his arms and led him to the blazing rock. Thither came

---

15. **impious** (im′ pē əs): not pious; lacking respect for God.

also the slender form of a veiled female, led between Goody Cloyse, that pious teacher of the catechism, and Martha Carrier, who had received the devil's promise to be queen of hell. A rampant hag was she! And there stood the proselytes,[16] beneath the canopy of fire.

"Welcome, my children," said the dark figure, "to the communion of your grave! Ye have found, thus young, your nature and your destiny. My children, look behind you!"

They turned; and flashing forth, as it were, in a sheet of flame, the fiend worshipers were seen; the smile of welcome gleamed darkly on every visage.

"There," resumed the sable form, "are all whom ye have reverenced from youth. Ye deemed them holier than yourselves, and shrank from your own sin, contrasting it with their lives of righteousness and prayerful aspirations heavenward. Yet here are they all in my worshiping assembly! This night it shall be granted you to know their secret deeds: how hoary[17] bearded elders of the church have whispered wanton words to the young maids of their households; how many a woman, eager for widow's weeds, has given her husband a drink at bedtime, and let him sleep his last sleep in her bosom; how beardless youths have made haste to inherit their fathers' wealth; and how fair damsels—blush not, sweet ones!—have dug little graves in the garden, and bidden me, the sole guest, to an infant's funeral. By the sympathy of your human hearts for sin, ye shall scent out all the places—whether in church, bedchamber, street, field or forest—where crime has been committed, and shall exult to behold the whole earth one stain of guilt, one mighty bloodspot. Far more than this! It shall be yours to penetrate, in every bosom, the deep mystery of sin, the fountain of all wicked arts, which inexhaustibly supplies more evil impulses than human power—than my power, at its utmost!—can make manifest in deeds. And now, my children, look upon each other."

They did so; and, by the blaze of the hell-kindled torches, the wretched man beheld his Faith, and the wife her husband, trembling before that unhallowed altar.

"Lo! There ye stand, my children," said the figure, in deep and solemn tone, almost sad, with its despairing awfulness, as if his once angelic nature could yet mourn for our miserable race. "Depending

---

16. **proselytes** (pras´ ə līts): converts to a religion.
17. **hoary:** very old.

upon one another's hearts, ye had still hoped that virtue were not all a dream. Now are ye undeceived! Evil is the nature of mankind. Evil must be your only happiness. Welcome, again, my children, to the communion of your race!"

"Welcome!" repeated the fiend worshipers, in one cry of despair and triumph.

And there they stood, the only pair, as it seemed, who were yet hesitating on the verge of wickedness, in this dark world. A basin was hollowed, naturally, in the rock. Did it contain water, reddened by the lurid light? Or was it blood? Or, perchance, a liquid flame? Herein did the Shape of Evil dip his hand and prepare to lay the mark of baptism upon their foreheads, that they might be partakers of the mystery of sin, more conscious of the secret guilt of others, both in deed and thought, than they could be of their own. The husband cast one look at his pale wife, and Faith at him. What polluted wretches would the next glance show them to each other, shuddering alike at what they disclosed and what they saw?

"Faith! Faith!" cried the husband "Look up to heaven, and resist the Wicked One!"

Whether Faith obeyed, he knew not. Hardly had he spoken than he found himself amid calm night and solitude, listening to a roar of the wind, which died heavily away through the forest. He staggered against the rock and felt it chill and damp, while a hanging twig, that had been all on fire, besprinkled his cheek with the coldest dew.

The next morning, young Goodman Brown came slowly into the street of Salem village, staring around him like a bewildered man. The good old minister was taking a walk along the graveyard, to get an appetite for breakfast and meditate his sermon, and bestowed a blessing, as he passed, on Goodman Brown. He shrank from the venerable saint, as if to avoid an anathema.[18] Old Deacon Gookin was at domestic worship, and the holy words of his prayer were heard through the open window. "What god doth the wizard pry to?" quoth Goodman Brown. Goody Cloyse, that excellent old Christian, stood in the early sunshine, at her own lattice,[19] catechizing a little girl, who had brought her a pint of morning's milk. Goodman Brown snatched away the child, as from the grasp of the fiend himself. Turning the corner by the

---

18. **anathema** (ə nath′ ə mə): curse.
19. **lattice**: window of crisscrossed wooden strips.

meeting house, he spied the head of Faith, with the pink ribbons, gazing anxiously forth, and bursting into such joy at sight of him that she skipped along the street, and almost kissed her husband before the whole village. But Goodman Brown looked sternly and sadly into her face and passed on without a greeting.

Had Goodman Brown fallen asleep in the forest, and only dreamed a wild dream of a witch meeting?

Be it so, if you will. But, alas! It was a dream of evil omen for young Goodman Brown. A stern, a sad, a darkly meditative, a distrustful, if not a desperate man, did he become from the night of that fearful dream. On the Sabbath day, when the congregation were singing a holy psalm, he could not listen, because an anthem of sin rushed loudly upon his ear and drowned all the blessed strain. When the minister spoke from the pulpit, with power and fervid eloquence and with his hand on the open Bible, of the sacred truths of our religion, and of saintlike lives and triumphant deaths, and of future bliss or misery unutterable, then did Goodman Brown turn pale, dreading lest the roof should thunder down upon the grey blasphemer and his hearers. Often, awaking suddenly at midnight, he shrank from the bosom of Faith, and at morning or eventide, when the family knelt down at prayer, he scowled, and muttered to himself, and gazed sternly at his wife and turned away. And when he had lived long, and was borne to his grave, a hoary corpse, followed by Faith, an aged woman, and children and grandchildren, a goodly procession—besides neighbors, not a few—they carved no hopeful verse upon his tombstone; for his dying hour was gloom.

Discussion Questions

1. Goodman Brown speaks of a covenant between himself and his traveling companion. What do you imagine this might have been?

2. Why is Brown so shocked to encounter his fellow townspeople in the woods? What does he think they are there for?

3. Trace Hawthorne's use of double meanings for *Faith* (faith in God and Brown's wife's name) throughout. What do these double meanings add to the story?

4. The narrator asks, "Had Goodman Brown fallen asleep in the forest, and only dreamed a wild dream of a witch meeting?" What do you think?

5. How does Brown's night in the woods affect his character and his relationships with his wife and the townspeople? Why do you think this is so?

6. Is there a moral to this story? If so, what is it?

Suggestion for Writing

The dark figure in the woods states, "Evil is the nature of mankind." Do you think it possible that if Goodman Brown had managed to deny that statement, he might not have died a gloomy man? In the voice of Goodman Brown—or of his wife, Faith—write a statement upholding the opposite position—that evil is *not* the nature of mankind. Write it as if you were speaking to the dark figure at the meeting in the woods. A debate is always more effective with specific reasons and examples. What instances of human behavior can you cite to prove your point?

Lafcadio Hearn (1850-1904)

Born on a Greek island, Lafcadio Hearn was brought at a young age to Ireland to live with his father's aunt. She sent him to a series of parochial schools and then to college in England. Hearn was a rebellious youth, however, and his aunt finally sent him to America, where he worked at various jobs until he learned the printing trade and got a job on a newspaper. His first books were literary fragments he translated from their original languages. In 1890 his *Two Years in the French West Indies* demonstrated his highly polished writing style. Traveling to Japan, he taught at a government college and then held the chair of English Literature at the Imperial University of Tokyo. Becoming a Japanese citizen, Hearn took a Japanese name and also a Japanese wife. Hearn's lifelong interest in exotic and macabre subjects is shown in the topics of his writings as well as in his delicate style.

The Boy Who Drew Cats

A long, long time ago, in a small country village in Japan, there lived a poor farmer and his wife, who were very good people. They had a number of children and found it very hard to feed them all. The elder son was strong enough when only fourteen years old to help his father, and the little girls learned to help their mother almost as soon as they could walk.

But the youngest child, a little boy, did not seem to be fit for hard work. He was very clever,—cleverer than all his brothers and sisters; but he was quite weak and small, and people said he would never grow very big. So his parents thought that it would be better for him to become a priest than to become a farmer. They took him with them to the village temple one day, and asked the good old priest who lived there if he would have their little boy for his acolyte,[1] and teach him all that a priest ought to know.

The old man spoke kindly to the lad, and asked him some hard questions. So clever were the answers that the priest agreed to take the little fellow into the temple as an acolyte, and to educate him for the priesthood.

The boy learned quickly what the old priest taught him, and was very obedient in most things. But he had one fault. He liked to draw cats during study-hours, and to draw cats even when cats ought not to have been drawn at all.

Whenever he found himself alone, he drew cats. He drew them on the margins of the priest's books and on all the screens of the temple, and on the walls, and on the pillars. Several times the priest told him this was not right; but he did not stop drawing cats. He drew them because he could not really help it. He had what is called "the genius of an *artist*," and just for that reason he was not quite fit to be an acolyte—a good acolyte should study books.

One day after he had drawn some very clever pictures of cats upon a paper screen, the old priest said to him severely: "My boy, you must go away from this temple at once. You will never make a good priest, but perhaps you will become a great artist. Now let me give you a last

---

1. acolyte (aˊ kə līt): attendant; helper, especially at religious services.

piece of advice, and be sure you never forget it. *Avoid large places at night;—keep to small!"*

The boy did not know what the priest meant by saying, "*Avoid large places;—keep to small.*" He thought and thought, while he was tying up his little bundle of clothes to go away; but he could not understand these words, and he was afraid to speak to the priest any more, except to say good-by.

He left the temple very sorrowfully, and began to wonder what he should do. If he went straight home he felt sure his father would punish him for having been disobedient to the priest; so he was afraid to go home. All at once he remembered that at the next village, twelve miles away, there was a very big temple. He had heard there were several priests at that temple; and he made up his mind to go to them and ask them to take him for their acolyte.

Now that big temple was closed up but the boy did not know this fact. The reason it had been closed up was that a goblin had frightened the priests away, and had taken possession of the place. Some brave warriors had afterward gone to the temple at night to kill the goblin, but they had never been seen alive again. Nobody had ever told these things to the boy;—so he walked all the way to the village hoping to be kindly treated by the priests.

When he got to the village it was already dark, and all the people were in bed; but he saw the big temple on a hill at the other end of the principal street, and he saw there was a light in the temple. People who tell the story say the goblin used to make that light, in order to tempt lonely travelers to ask for shelter. The boy went at once to the temple, and knocked. There was no sound inside. He knocked and knocked again; but still nobody came. At last he pushed gently at the door, and was quite glad to find that it had not been fastened. So he went in, and saw a lamp burning—but no priest.

He thought some priest would be sure to come very soon, and he sat down and waited. Then he noticed that everything in the temple was gray with dust, and thickly spun over with cobwebs. So he thought to himself that the priests would certainly like to have an acolyte, to keep the place clean. He wondered why they had allowed everything to get so dirty. What most pleased him, however, were some big white screens, good to paint cats upon. Though he was tired, he looked at once for a writing box, and found one, and ground some ink, and began to paint cats.

He painted a great many cats upon the screens; and then he began to feel very, very sleepy. He was just on the point of lying down to sleep beside one of the screens, when he suddenly remembered the words, *"Avoid large places;—keep to small!"*

The temple was very large; he was alone; and as he thought of these words—though he could not quite understand them—he began to feel for the first time a little afraid; and he resolved to look for a *small place* in which to sleep. He found a little cabinet, with a sliding door, and went into it, and shut himself up. Then he lay down and fell fast asleep.

Very late in the night he was awakened by a most terrible noise—a noise of fighting and screaming. It was so dreadful that he was afraid even to look through a chink of the little cabinet; he lay very still, holding his breath for fright.

The light that had been in the temple went out; but the awful sounds continued, and became more awful, and all the temple shook. After a long time silence came; but the boy was still afraid to move. He did not move until the light of the morning sun shone into the cabinets through the chinks of the little door.

Then he got out of his hiding place very cautiously, and looked about. The first thing he saw was that all the floor of the temple was covered with blood. And then he saw, lying dead in the middle of it, an enormous, monstrous rat—a goblin rat—bigger than a cow!

But who or what could have killed it? There was no man or other creature to be seen. Suddenly the boy observed that the mouths of all the cats he had drawn the night before, were red and wet with blood. Then he knew that the goblin had been killed by the cats which he had drawn. And then also, for the first time, he understood why the wise old priest had said to him, *"Avoid large places at night;—keep to small!"*

Afterward that boy became a very famous artist. Some of the cats which he drew are still shown to travelers in Japan.

Discussion Questions

1. What elements of a folk tale do you find in this story?

2. From the few details set forth in this story, describe the society in which it is set.

3. Is the boy a hero? Explain your answer.

4. Does fate play a role in this story? Explain your answer.

Suggestion for Writing

Imagine that you are a tour guide in the big temple where the goblin-rat was destroyed. Conduct a small group of travelers through the temple, pointing out the cabinet where the boy hid and the place on the floor where the goblin-rat was found. Also point out the screens upon which the boy painted his cats—and perhaps even the traces of blood that can still be seen on their mouths.

W. H. Hodgson (1877-1918)

Born in Essex, England, William Hope Hodgson left home at the age of thirteen. Lying about his age, he joined the crew of a ship. He spent eight years at sea, developing his interests in bodybuilding and photography and developing an intense dislike of seafaring. Later he wrote several articles for the British popular press about the harsh conditions of the lives of seamen. For several years he operated his own School of Physical Culture, a health and bodybuilding club. Some of his first published works were articles about bodybuilding and exercise. Turning to fiction, he began writing horror and sea-adventure stories, which he sold to British and American magazines, and which gave him income to allow him to devote more time to writing novels. Generally Hodgson's novels received good criticism but little popular notice. His short stories, however, earned him success with the public. In 1910, he published *Carnacki, the Ghost Finder*, the book from which this story is taken. In these tales Carnacki, an "occult detective," narrates his experiences with supernatural events both real and faked. When World War I began, Hodgson volunteered for active service and was killed near Ypres, Belgium, in 1918.

The Gateway of the Monster

In response to Carnacki's usual card of invitation to have dinner and listen to a story, I arrived promptly at Cheyne Walk, to find the three others who were always invited to these happy little times there before me. Five minutes later, Carnacki, Arkright, Jessop, Taylor and I were all engaged in the 'pleasant occupation' of dining.

"You've not been long away this time," I remarked as I finished my soup, forgetting, momentarily, Carnacki's dislike of being asked even to skirt the borders of his story until such time as he was ready. Then he would not stint[1] words.

"No," he replied with brevity and I changed the subject, remarking that I had been buying a new gun, to which piece of news he gave an intelligent nod and a smile, which I think showed a genuinely good-humored appreciation of my intentional changing of the conversation.

Later, when dinner was finished, Carnacki snugged himself comfortably down in his big chair, along with his pipe, and began his story, with very little circumlocution.[2]

"As Dodgson was remarking just now, I've only been away a short time, and for a very good reason too—I've only been away a short distance. The exact locality I am afraid I must not tell you; but it is less than twenty miles from here; rest assured, except for meaning a change of name, that won't spoil the story. And it *is* a story too! One of the most extraordinary things I have ever run against.

"I received a letter a fortnight ago from a man I will call Anderson, asking for an appointment. I arranged a time and when he turned up I found that he wished me to look into, and see whether I could not clear up, a long-standing and well-authenticated case of what he termed 'haunting.' He gave me very full particulars and, finally, as the thing seemed to present something unique, I decided to take it up.

"Two days later I drove up to the house in question late in the afternoon and discovered it a very old place, standing quite alone in its own grounds. Anderson had left a letter with the butler, I found, pleading

---

1. stint: to be sparing or economical.
2. circumlocution: use of unnecessary or evasive words.

excuses for his absence, and leaving the whole house at my disposal for my investigations.

"The butler evidently knew the object of my visit and I questioned him pretty thoroughly during dinner, which I had in rather lonely state. He is an elderly and privileged servant, and had the history of the Grey Room exact in detail. From him I learned more particulars regarding two things that Anderson had mentioned in but a casual manner. The first was that the door of the Grey Room would be heard in the dead of night to open, and slam heavily, and this even when the butler knew it was locked and the key on the bunch in his pantry. The second was that the bedclothes would always be found torn off the bed and hurled in a heap into a corner.

"But it was the door slamming that chiefly bothered the old butler. Many and many a time, he told me, had he lain awake and just shivered with fright, listening; for at night the door would be slammed time after time—thud! thud! thud! so that sleep was impossible.

"From Anderson, I knew already that the room had a history extending back over a hundred and fifty years. Three people had been strangled in it—an ancestor of his and his wife and child. This is authentic, as I had taken very great pains to make sure, so that you can imagine it was with a feeling that I had a striking case to investigate, that I went upstairs after dinner to have a look at the Grey Room.

"Peters, the butler, was in rather a state about my going, and assured me with much solemnity that in all the twenty years of his service, no one had ever entered that room after nightfall. He begged me in quite a fatherly way to wait till the morning when there could be no danger and then he could accompany me himself.

"Of course, I told him not to bother. I explained that I should do no more than look around a bit and perhaps fix a few seals. He need not fear, I was used to that sort of thing. But he shook his head when I said that.

"'There isn't many ghosts like ours, sir,' he assured me with mournful pride. And by Jove! he was right, as you will see.

"I took a couple of candles and Peters followed with his bunch of keys. He unlocked the door, but would not come inside with me. He was evidently in quite a fright and renewed his request that I would put off my examination until daylight. Of course I laughed at him, and told him he could stand sentry at the door and catch anything that came out.

"'It never comes outside, sir,' he said, in his funny old solemn manner. Somehow he managed to make me feel as if I were going to have the creeps right away. Anyway, it was one to him, you know.

"I left him there and examined the room. It is a big apartment and well furnished in the grand style, with a huge four-poster which stands with its head to the end wall. There were two candles on the mantelpiece and two on each of the three tables that were in the room. I lit the lot and after that the room felt a little less inhumanly dreary, though, mind you, it was quite fresh and well kept in every way.

"After I had taken a good look round I sealed lengths of narrow ribbon across the windows, along the walls, over the pictures, and over the fireplace and the wall-closets. All the time, as I worked, the butler stood just without the door and I could not persuade him to enter, though I jested with him a little as I stretched the ribbon and went here and there about my work. Every now and again he would say: 'You'll excuse me, I'm sure, sir; but I do wish you would come out, sir. I'm fair in a quake for you.'

"I told him he need not wait, but he was loyal enough in his way to what he considered his duty. He said he could not go away and leave me all alone there. He apologized, but made it very clear that I did not realize the danger of the room; and I could see, generally, that he was getting into a really frightened state. All the same I had to make the room so that I should know if anything material entered it, so I asked him not to bother me unless he really heard something. He was beginning to fret my nerves and the 'feel' of the room was bad enough already, without making things any nastier.

"For a time further I worked, stretching ribbons across a little above the floor and sealing them so that the merest touch would break the seals were anyone to venture into the room in the dark with the intention of playing the fool.

"All this had taken me far longer than I had anticipated and, suddenly, I heard a clock strike eleven. I had taken off my coat soon after commencing work; now however, as I had practically made an end of all that I intended to do, I walked across to the settee and picked it up. I was in the act of getting into it when the old butler's voice (he had not said a word for the last hour) came sharp and frightened: "Come out, sir, quick! There's something going to happen!' Jove! but I jumped, and then in the same moment, one of the candles on the table to the left of the bed went out. Now whether it was the wind, or what, I do not know; but just for a moment I was enough startled to make a run for the door; though I am glad to say that I pulled up before I reached it. I simply could not bunk out[3] with the butler standing there after having, as it were, read him a sort of lesson on 'bein' brave, y'know.' So I just turned right round, picked up the two candles off the mantelpiece, and walked across to the table near the bed. Well, I saw nothing. I blew out the candle that was still alight; then I went to those on the two other tables and blew them out. Then, outside the door, the old man called again: 'Oh! sir, do be told! Do be told!'

"'All right, Peters,' I said, and by Jove, my voice was not as steady as I should have liked! I made for the door and had a bid of work not to start running. I took some thundering long strides, though, as you can imagine. Near the entrance I had a sudden feeling that there was a cold wind in the room. It was almost as if the window had been suddenly opened a little. I got to the door and the old butler gave back a step, in a sort of instinctive way.

"'Collar the candles, Peters!' I said, pretty sharply, and shoved them into his hands. I turned and caught the handle and slammed the door shut with a crash. Somehow, do you know, as I did so I thought I felt something pull back on it, but it must have been only fancy. I turned the key in the lock, and then again, double-locking the door.

"I felt easier then and set to and sealed the door. In addition I put my card over the keyhole and sealed it there, after which I pocketed the key and went downstairs—with Peters who was nervous and silent, leading the way. Poor old beggar! It had not struck me until that moment that he had been enduring a considerable strain during the last two or three hours.

"About midnight I went to bed. My room lay at the end of the corridor upon which opens the door of the Grey Room. I counted the doors between it and mine and found that five rooms lay between. And I am sure you can understand that I was not sorry.

"Just as I was beginning to undress an idea came to me and I took my candle and sealing-wax and sealed the doors of all the five rooms. If any door slammed in the night, I should know just which one.

"I returned to my room, locked myself in and went to bed. I was woken suddenly from a deep sleep by a loud crash somewhere out in

---

3. **bunk out**: make a hurried escape.

the passage. I sat up in bed and listened, but heard nothing. Then I lit my candle. I was in the very act of lighting it when there came the bang of a door being violently slammed along the corridor.

"I jumped out of bed and got my revolver. I unlocked the door and went out into the passage, holding my candle high and keeping the pistol ready. Then a queer thing happened. I could not go a step towards the Grey Room. You all know I am not really a cowardly chap. I've gone into too many cases connected with ghostly things to be accused of that; but I tell you I funked[4] it, simply funked it, just like any blessed kid. There was something precious unholy in the air that night. I backed into my bedroom and shut and locked the door. Then I sat on the bed all night and listened to the dismal thudding of a door up the corridor. The sound seemed to echo through all the house.

"Daylight came at last and I washed and dressed. The door had not slammed for about an hour, and I was getting back my nerve again. I felt ashamed of myself, though in some ways it was silly, for when you're meddling with that sort of thing your nerve is bound to go, sometimes. And you just have to sit quiet and call yourself a coward until the safety of the day comes. Sometimes it is more than just cowardice, I fancy. I believe at times it is something warning you and fighting *for* you. But all the same, I always feel mean and miserable after a time like that.

"When the day came properly I opened my door, and keeping my revolver handy, went quietly along the passage. I had to pass the head of the stairs on the way, and who should I see coming up but the old butler, carrying a cup of coffee. He had merely tucked his nightshirt into his trousers and had an old pair of carpet slippers on.

"'Hullo, Peters!' I said, feeling suddenly cheerful, for I was as glad as any lost child to have a live human being close to me. 'Where are you off to with the refreshments?'

"The old man gave a start and slopped some of the coffee. He stared up at me and I could see that he looked white and done up. He came on up the stairs and held out the little tray to me.

"'I'm very thankful, indeed, sir, to see you safe and well,' he said. 'I feared one time you might risk going into the Grey Room, sir. I've lain awake all night, with the sound of the door. And when it came light I thought I'd make you a cup of coffee. I knew you would want to look at the seals—and somehow it seems safer if there's two, sir.'

---

4. **funked:** shrank back from doing or facing something.

"'Peters,' I said, 'You're a brick. This is very thoughtful of you.' And I drank the coffee. 'Come along,' I told him, and handed him back the tray. 'I'm going to have a look at what the brutes have been up to. I simply hadn't the pluck to in the night.'

"'I'm very thankful, sir,' he replied. 'Flesh and blood can do nothing, sir, against devils, and that's what's in the Grey Room after dark.'

"I examined the seals on all the doors as I went along and found them right, but when I got to the Grey Room, the seal was broken, though the visiting-card over the keyhole was untouched. I ripped it off and unlocked the door and went in, rather cautiously as you can imagine; but the whole room was empty of anything to frighten one; and there was heaps of light. I examined all my seals, and not a single one was disturbed. The old butler had followed me in, and suddenly he said, 'The bedclothes, sir!'

"I ran up to the bed and looked over, and sure enough, they were lying in the corner to the left of the bed. Jove! you can imagine how queer I felt. Something *had* been in the room. I stared for a while from the bed to the clothes on the floor. I had a feeling that I did not want to touch either. Old Peters, though, did not seem to be affected that way. He went over to the bed-coverings and was going to pick them up, as doubtless he had done every day these twenty years back, but I stopped him. I wanted nothing touched until I had finished my examination. This I must have spent a full hour over and then I let Peters straighten up the bed, after which we went out and I locked the door, for the room was getting on my nerves.

"I had a short walk and then breakfast, which made me feel more my own man. Then to the Grey Room again, and with Peters' help and that of one of the maids, I had everything taken out except the bed, even the very pictures.

"I examined the walls, floor and ceiling then, with probe, hammer and magnifying glass, but found nothing unusual. I can assure you I began to realize in very truth that some incredible thing had been loose in the room during the past night.

"I sealed up everything again and went out, locking and sealing the door as before.

"After dinner that night, Peters and I unpacked some of my stuff and I fixed up my camera and flashlight opposite to the door of the Grey Room with a string from the trigger of the flashlight to the door. You see, if the door really opened, the flashlight would blare out and there would be, possibly, a very queer picture to examine in the morning.

"The last thing I did before leaving was to uncap the lens and after that I went off to my bedroom and to bed, for I intended to be up at midnight, and to ensure this, I set my little alarm to call me; also I left my candle burning.

"The clock woke me at twelve and I got up and into my dressing-gown and slippers. I shoved my revolver into my right side-pocket and opened my door. Then I lit my darkroom lamp and withdrew the slide so that it would give a clear light. I carried it up the corridor about thirty feet and put it down on the floor, with the open side away from me, so that it would show me anything that might approach along the dark passage. Then I went back and sat in the doorway of my room, with my revolver handy, staring up the passage towards the place where I knew my camera stood outside the door of the Grey Room.

"I should think I had watched for about an hour and a half when suddenly I heard a faint noise away up the corridor. I was immediately conscious of a queer prickling sensation about the back of my head and my hands began to sweat a little. The following instant the whole end of the passage flicked into sight in the abrupt glare of the flashlight. Then came the succeeding darkness and I peered nervously up the corridor, listening tensely, and trying to find what lay beyond the faint, red glow of my dark-lamp, which now seemed ridiculously dim by contrast with the tremendous blaze of the flash-powder . . . And then, as I stooped forward, staring and listening, there came the crashing thud of the door of the Grey Room. The sound seemed to fill the whole of the large corridor and go echoing hollowly through the house. I tell you, I felt horrible—as if my bones were water. Simply beastly. Jove! how I did stare and how I listened. And then it came again, thud, thud, thud, and then a silence that was almost worse than the noise of the door, for I kept fancying that some brutal thing was stealing upon me along the corridor.

"Suddenly, my lamp was put out, and I could not see a yard before me. I realized all at once that I was doing a very silly thing, sitting there, and I jumped up. Even as I did so, I thought I heard a sound in the passage, quite near to me. I made one backward spring into my room and slammed and locked the door.

"I sat on my bed and stared at the door. I had my revolver in my hand, but it seemed an abominably useless thing. Can you understand?

I felt that there was something the other side of my door. For some unknown reason, I *knew* it was pressed up against the door, and it was soft. That was just what I thought. Most extraordinary thing to imagine, when you come to think of it!

"Presently I got hold of myself a bit and marked out a pentacle[5] hurriedly with chalk on the polished floor and there I sat in it until it was almost dawn. And all the time, away up the corridor, the door of the Grey Room thudded at solemn and horrid intervals. It was a miserable, brutal night.

"When the day began to break, the thudding of the door came gradually to an end, and at last I grabbed together my courage and went along the corridor in the half-light, to cap the lens of my camera. I can tell you, it took some doing; but if I had not gone my photograph would have been spoiled, and I was tremendously keen to save it. I got back to my room and then set to and rubbed out the five-pointed star in which I had been sitting.

"Half an hour later there was a tap at my door. It was Peters, with my coffee. When I had drunk it we both walked along to the Grey Room. As we went, I had a look at the seals on the other doors, but they were untouched. The seal on the door of the Grey Room was broken, as also was the string from the trigger of the flashlight, but the visiting-card over the keyhole was still there. I ripped it off and opened the door. Nothing unusual was to be seen, until we came to the bed; then I saw that, as on the previous day, the bedclothes had been torn off and hurled into the left-hand corner, exactly where I had seen them before. I felt very queer, but I did not forget to look at the seals—only to find that not one had been broken.

"Then I turned and looked at old Peters and he looked at me, nodding his head.

"'Let's get out of here!' I said. 'It's no place for any living human to enter without proper protection.'

"We went out then and I locked and sealed the door, again.

"After breakfast I developed the negative, but it showed only the door of the Grey Room, half opened. Then I left the house, as I wanted to get certain matters and implements that might be necessary to life and perhaps to the spirit, for I intended to spend the coming night in the Grey Room.

---

5. pentacle: a five-pointed star.

"I got back in a cab about half-past five with my apparatus, and this Peters and I carried up to the Grey Room where I piled it carefully in the center of the floor. When everything was in the room, including a cat which I had brought, I locked and sealed the door and went towards my bedroom, telling Peters I should not be down to dinner. He said, 'Yes, sir,' and went downstairs, thinking that I was going to turn in, which was what I wanted him to believe, as I knew it would have worried both himself and me if he had known what I intended.

"But I merely got my camera and flashlight from my bedroom and hurried back to the Grey Room. I entered and locked and sealed myself in and set to, for I had a lot to do before it got dark.

"First I cleared away all the ribbons across the floor; then I carried the cat, still fastened in its basket, over towards the far wall and left it. I returned then to the center of the room and measured out a space twenty-one feet in diameter, which I swept with a broom of hyssop.[6] About this I drew a circle of chalk, taking care never to step over the circle.

"Beyond this I smudged, with a bunch of garlic, a broad belt right around the chalked circle, and when this was complete I took from among my stores in the center a small jar of a certain water. I broke away the parchment and withdrew the stopper. Then, dipping my left forefinger in the little jar, I went round the circle again, making upon the floor, just within the line of chalk, the second sign of the Saaamaaa Ritual, and joining each sign most carefully with the left-handed crescent. I can tell you, I felt easier when this was done and the 'water-circle' complete.

"Then I unpacked some more of the stuff that I had brought and placed a lighted candle in the 'valley' of each crescent. After that I drew a pentacle so that each of the five points of the defensive star touched the chalk circle. In the five points of the star I placed five portions of a certain bread, each wrapped in linen; and in the five 'vales,' five opened jars of the water I had used to make the water-circle. And now I had my first protective barrier complete.

"Now anyone, except you who know something of my methods of investigation, might consider all this a piece of useless and foolish superstition; but you all remember the Black Veil case, in which I believe my life was saved by a very similar form of protection, whilst Aster, who sneered at it, and would not come inside, died.

---

6. **hyssop:** an aromatic herb used by ancient Hebrews in purification rites.

"I got the idea from the Sigsand manuscript, written, so far as I can make out, in the fourteenth century. At first, naturally, I imagined it was just an expression of the superstition of his time, and it was not until long after my first reading that it occurred to me to test his 'defense,' which I did, as I've just said, in that horrible Black Veil business. You know how *that* turned out. Later I used it several times and always I came through safe, until that Noving Fur case. It was only a partial defense there and I nearly died in the pentacle.

"After that I came across Professor Garder's *Experiments with a Medium*. When they sounded the medium with a current of a certain number of vibrations in vacuum, he lost his position—almost as if it cut him off from the immaterial. That made me think, and led eventually to the electric pentacle, which is a most marvelous defense against manifestations. I used the shape of the defensive star for this protection because I have, personally, no doubt at all but there is some extraordinary virtue in the old magic figure. Curious thing for a twentieth-century man to admit, is it not? But then, as you all know, I never did, and never will allow myself to be blinded by a little cheap laughter. I ask questions and keep my eyes open!

"In this last case I had little doubt that I had run up against an abnatural[7] monster, and I meant to take every possible care, for the danger is abominable.

"I turned now to fit the electric pentacle, setting it so that each of its points and vales coincided exactly with the points and vales of the drawn pentagram upon the floor. Then I connected up the battery and the next instant the pale blue glare from the intertwining vacuum tubes shone out.

"I glanced about me then, with something of a sigh of relief, and realized suddenly that the dusk was upon me, for the window was grey and unfriendly. Then I stared round at the big, empty room, over the double-barrier of electric and candle light, and had an abrupt, extraordinary sense of weirdness thrust upon me—in the air, you know, it seemed; as it were a sense of something inhuman impending. The room was full of the stench of bruised garlic, a smell I hate.

"I turned now to my camera, and saw that it and the flashlight were in order. Then I tested the action of my revolver carefully, though I had little thought that it would be needed. Yet, to what extent materialization

---

7. **abnatural:** unnatural.

of an abnatural creature is possible, given favorable conditions, no one can say, and I had no idea what horrible thing I was going to see or feel the presence of. I might, in the end, have to fight with a material thing. I did not know and could only be prepared. You see, I never forgot that three people had been strangled in the bed close to me, and the fierce slamming of the door I had heard myself. I had no doubt that I was investigating a dangerous and ugly case.

"By this time the night had come (though the room was very light with the burning candles), and I found myself glancing behind me constantly and then all round the room. It was nervy work waiting for that thing to come into the room.

"Suddenly I was aware of a little, cold wind sweeping over me, coming from behind. I gave one great nerve-thrill and a prickly feeling went all over the back of my head. Then I hove myself round with a sort of stiff jerk and stared straight against that queer wind. It seemed to come from the corner of the room to the left of the bed—the place where both times I had found the heap of tossed bedclothes. Yet I could see nothing unusual, no opening—nothing! . . .

"Abruptly I was aware that the candles were all a-flicker in that unnatural wind . . . I believe I just squatted there and stared in a horribly frightened, wooden way for some minutes. I shall never be able to let you know how disgustingly horrible it was sitting in that vile, cold wind! And then—flick! flick! flick! all the candles round the outer barrier went out, and there was I, locked and sealed in that room and with no light beyond the weakish blue glare of the electric pentacle.

"A time of abominable tenseness passed and still that wind blew upon me, and then suddenly I knew that something stirred in the corner to the left of the bed. I was made conscious of it rather by some inward, unused sense, than by either sight or sound, for the pale, short-radious glare of the pentacle gave but a very poor light for seeing by. Yet, as I stared, something began slowly to grow upon my sight—a moving shadow, a little darker than the surrounding shadows. I lost the thing amid the vagueness and for a moment or two I glanced swiftly from side to side with a fresh, new sense of impending danger. Then my attention was directed to the bed. All the coverings were being drawn steadily off, with a hateful, stealthy sort of motion. I heard the slow, dragging slither of the clothes, but I could see nothing of the thing that pulled. I was aware in a funny, subconscious, introspective fashion that the 'creep' had come upon me, prickling all over my head, yet I was cooler mentally than I had been for some minutes—sufficiently so to feel that my hands were sweating coldly and to shift my revolver, half-consciously, whilst I rubbed my right hand dry upon my knee, though never for an instant taking my gaze or my attention from those moving clothes.

"The faint noises from the bed ceased once and there was a most intense silence, with only the dull thudding of the blood beating in my head. Yet immediately afterwards I heard again the slurring sound of the bedclothes being dragged off the bed. In the midst of my nervous tension I remembered the camera and reached out for it, but without looking away from the bed. And then, you know, all in a moment, the whole of the bed-coverings were torn off with extraordinary violence and I heard the flump they made as they were hurled into the corner.

"There was a time of absolute quietness then for perhaps a couple of minutes and you can imagine how horrible I felt. The bedclothes had been thrown with such savageness! And then again the abominable unnaturalness of the thing that had just been done before me!

"Suddenly, over by the door, I heard a faint nose—a sort of crickling sound—and then a pitter or two upon the floor. A great nervous thrill swept over me, seeming to run up my spine and over the back of my head, for the seal that secured the door had just been broken. Something was there. I could not see the door; at least, I mean to say that it was impossible to say how much I actually saw and how much my imagination supplied. I made it out only as a continuation of the grey walls . . . And then it seemed to me that something dark and indistinct moved and wavered there among the shadows.

"Abruptly I was aware that the door was opening and with an effort I reached again for my camera; but before I could aim it, the door was slammed with a terrific crash that filled the whole room with a sort of hollow thunder. I jumped like a frightened child. There seemed such a power behind the noise, as if a vast, wanton force were 'out.' Can you understand?

"The door was not touched again; but, directly afterwards I heard the basket in which the cat lay creak. I tell you, I fairly pringled all along my back. I knew that I was going to learn definitely whether what was abroad was dangerous to life. From the cat there rose suddenly a hideous caterwaul[8] that ceased abruptly, and then—too late—I snapped

---

8. **caterwaul:** harsh cry; screech.

on the flashlight. In the great glare I saw that the basket had been overturned and the lid was wrenched open, with the cat lying half in and half out upon the floor. I saw nothing else, but I was full of the knowledge that I was in the presence of some being or thing that had power to destroy.

"During the next two or three minutes there was an odd, noticeable quietness in the room, and you must remember I was half-blinded for the time because of the flashlight, so that the whole place seemed to be pitchy dark just beyond the shine of the pentacle. I tell you it was most horrible. I just knelt there in the star and whirled round on my knees, trying to see whether anything was coming at me.

"My power of sight came gradually and I got a little hold of myself, and abruptly I saw the thing I was looking for, close to the water-circle. It was big and indistinct and wavered curiously as though the shadow of a vast spider hung suspended in the air, just beyond the barrier. It passed swiftly round the circle and seemed to probe ever towards me, but only to draw back with extraordinary jerky movements, as might a living person who touched the hot bar of a grate.

"Round and round it moved and round and round I turned. Then just opposite to one of the vales in the pentacles it seemed to pause, as though as a preliminary to a tremendous effort. It retired almost beyond the glow of the vacuum light and then came straight towards me, appearing to gather form and solidity as it came. There seemed a vast malign determination behind the movement that must succeed. I was on my knees and I jerked back, falling on to my left hand and hip, in a wild endeavor to get back from the advancing thing. With my right hand I was grabbing madly for my revolver which I had let slip. The brutal thing came with one great sweep straight over the garlic and the water-circle, almost to the vale of the pentacle. I believe I yelled. Then, just as suddenly as it had swept over, it seemed to be hurled back by some mighty, invisible force.

"It must have been some moments before I realized that I was safe, and then I got myself together in the middle of the pentacles, feeling horribly done and shaken and glancing round and round the barrier, but the thing had vanished. Yet I had learned something, for I knew now that the Grey Room was haunted by a monstrous hand.

"Suddenly, as I crouched there, I saw what had so nearly given the monster an opening through the barrier. In my movements within the pentacle I must have touched one of the jars of water, for just where the thing had made its attack the jar that guarded the 'deep' of the vale had been moved to one side and this had left one of the 'five doorways' unguarded. I put it back quickly and felt almost safe again, for I had found the cause and the defense was still good. I began to hope again that I should see the morning come in. When I saw that thing so nearly succeed I'd had an awful, weak, overwhelming feeling that the barriers could never bring me safe through the night against such a force. You can understand?

"For a long time I could not see the hand; but presently I thought I saw, once or twice, an odd wavering over among the shadows near the door. A little later, as though in a sudden fit of malignant rage, the dead body of the cat was picked up and beaten with dull, sickening blows against the solid floor. That made me feel rather queer.

"A minute afterwards the door was opened and slammed twice with tremendous force. The next instant the thing made one swift, vicious dart at me from out of the shadows. Instinctively I started sideways from it and so plucked my hand from upon the electric pentacle, where—for a wickedly careless moment—I had placed it. The monster was hurled off from the neighborhood of the pentacles, though—owing to my inconceivable foolishness—it had been enabled for a second time to pass the outer barriers. I can tell you I shook for a time with sheer funk. I moved right to the center of the pentacles again and knelt there, making myself as small and compact as possible.

"As I knelt, I began to have, presently, a vague wonder at the two 'accidents' which had so nearly allowed the brute to get at me. Was I being influenced to unconscious voluntary actions that endangered me? The thought took hold of me and I watched my every movement. Abruptly I stretched a tired leg and knocked over one of the jars of water. Some was spilled, but because of my suspicious watchfulness, I had it upright and back within the vale while yet some of the water remained. Even as I did so the vast, black half-materialized hand beat up at me out of the shadows and seemed to leap almost into my face, so nearly did it approach, but for the third time it was thrown back by some altogether enormous, over-mastering force. Yet, apart from the dazed fright in which it left me, I had for a moment that feeling of spiritual sickness, as if some delicate, beautiful, inward grace had suffered, which is felt only upon the too near approach of the abhuman and is more dreadful in a strange way than any physical pain that can be suffered. I knew by this more of the extent and closeness of the danger, and for a long time I was simply cowed by the butt-headed brutality of that force upon my spirit. I can put it no other way.

"I knelt again in the centre of the pentacles, watching myself with as much fear, almost, as the monster, for I knew now that unless I guarded myself from every sudden impulse that came to me I might simply work my own destruction. Do you see how horrible it all was?

"I spent the rest of the night in a haze of sick fright and so tense that I could not make a single movement naturally—I was in such fear that any desire for action that came to me might be prompted by the influence that I knew was at work on me. And outside of the barrier that ghastly thing went, round and round, grabbing and grabbing in the air at me. Twice more was the body of the dead cat molested. The second time I heard every bone in its body scrunch and crack. And all the time the horrible wind was blowing upon me from the corner of the room to the left of the bed.

"Then, just as the first touch of dawn came into the sky the unnatural wind ceased in a single moment and I could see no sign of the hand. The dawn came slowly and presently the wan light filled all the room and made the pale glare of the electric pentacle look more unearthly. Yet it was not until the day had fully come that I made any attempt to leave the barrier, for I did not know but that there was some method abroad in the sudden stopping of that wind to entice me from the pentacles.

"At last, when the dawn was strong and bright, I took one last look round and ran for the door. I got it unlocked in a nervous, clumsy fashion; then locked it hurriedly and went to my bedroom where I lay on the bed and tried to steady my nerves. Peters came presently with the coffee and when I had drunk it I told him I meant to have a sleep, as I had been up all night. He took the tray and went out quietly, and after I had locked my door I turned in properly and at last got to sleep.

"I woke about midday and after some lunch went up to the Grey Room. I switched off the current from the pentacle, which I had left on in my hurry; also, I removed the body of the cat. You can understand, I did not want anyone to see the poor brute.

"After that I made a very careful search of the corner where the bedclothes had been thrown. I made several holes through the woodwork and probed, but found nothing. Then it occurred to me to try with my instrument under the skirting.[9] I did so and heard my wire ring on

---

9. skirting: baseboards.

metal. I turned the hook-end of the probe that way and fished for the thing. At the second go I got it. It was a small object and I took it to the window. I found it to be a curious ring made of some greyish metal. The curious thing about it was that it was made in the form of a pentagon; that is, the same shape as the inside of the magic pentacle, but without the "mounts" which form the points of the defensive star. It was free from all chasing or engraving.

"You will understand that I was excited when I tell you that I felt sure I held in my hand the famous Luck Ring of the Anderson family which, indeed, was of all things the most intimately connected with the history of the haunting. This ring had been handed on from father to son though generations, and always—in obedience to some ancient family tradition—each son had to promise never to wear the ring. The ring, I may say, was brought home by one of the Crusaders under very peculiar circumstances, but the story is too long to go into here.

"It appears that young Sir Hulbert, an ancestor of Anderson's, made a bet one evening, in drink, you know, that he would wear the ring that night. He did so, and in the morning his wife and child were found strangled in the bed in the very room in which I stood. Many people, it would seem, thought young Sir Hulbert was guilty of having done the thing in drunken anger and he, in an attempt to prove his innocence, slept a second night in the room. He also was strangled.

"Since then no one had spent a night in the Grey Room until I did so. The ring had been lost so long that its very existence had become almost a myth, and it was most extraordinary to stand there with the actual thing in my hand, as you can understand.

"It was while I stood there looking at the ring that I got an idea. Supposing that it were, in a way, a doorway—you see what I mean? A sort of gap in the world-hedge, if I may so phrase my idea. It was a queer thought, I know, and possibly was not my own, but one of those mental nudgings from the Outside.

"You see the wind had come from that part of the room where the ring lay. I pondered the thought a lot. Then the shape—the inside of a pentacle. It had no mounts, and as the Sigsand manuscript has it: 'Thee mownts are thee Five Hills of safetie. To lack is to gyve pow'r to thee daemon; and surlie to fayvor thee Evill Thynge.' You see, the very shape of the ring was significant. I determined to test it.

"I unmade my pentacle, for it must be 'made' afresh *and around* the one to be protected. Then I went out and locked the door, after which

I left the house to get certain items, for neither 'yarbs nor fyre nor water' must be used a second time. I returned about seven-thirty and, as soon as the things I had brought had been carried up to the Grey Room, I dismissed Peters for the night, just as I had done the evening before. When he had gone downstairs I let myself into the room and locked and sealed the door. I went to the place in the center of the room where all the stuff had been packed and set to work with all my speed to construct a barrier about me and the ring.

"I do not remember whether I explained to you, but I had reasoned that if the ring were in any way a 'medium of admission,' and it were enclosed with me in the electric pentacle, it would be, to express it loosely, insulated. Do you see? The force which had visible expression as a hand would have to stay beyond the barrier which separates the ab from the normal, for the 'gateway' would be removed from accessibility.

"As I was saying, I worked with all my speed to get the barrier completed about me and the ring for it was already later than I cared to be in that room unprotected. Also, I had a feeling that there would be a vast effort made that night to regain the use of the ring. For I had the strongest conviction that the ring was a necessity to materialization. You will see whether I was right.

"I completed the barriers in about an hour and you can imagine something of the relief I felt when I saw the pale glare of the electric pentacle once more all about me. From then onwards, for about two hours, I sat quietly facing the corner from which the wind came.

"About eleven o'clock I had a queer knowledge that something was near to me, yet nothing happened for a whole hour after that. Then suddenly I felt the cold, queer wind begin to blow upon me. To my astonishment it seemed now to come from behind me and I whipped round with a hideous quake of fear. The wind met me in the face. It was flowing up from the floor close to me. I stared in a sickening maze of new frights. What on earth had I done now! The ring was there, close beside me, where I had put it. Suddenly, as I stared, bewildered, I was aware that there was something queer about the ring—funny shadowy movements and convolutions. I looked at them stupidly. And then, abruptly, I knew that the wind was blowing up at me from the ring. A queer indistinct smoke became visible to me, seeming to pour upwards through the ring and mix with the moving shadows. Suddenly I realized that I was in more than any mortal danger, for the convoluting shadows about the ring were taking shape and the deathhand was forming within the pentacle. My goodness, do you realize it? I had brought the gateway into the pentacles and the brute was coming through—pouring into the material world, as gas might pour out from the mouth of a pipe.

"I should think that I knelt for a couple of moments in a sort of stunned fright. Then with a mad, awkward movement I snatched at the ring, intending to hurl it out of the pentacles. Yet, it eluded me as though some invisible, living thing jerked it hither and thither. At last I gripped it, but in the same instant it was torn from my grasp with incredible and brutal force. A great black shadow covered it and rose into the air and came at me. I saw that it was the hand, vast and nearly perfect in form. I gave one crazy yell and jumped over the pentacles and the ring of burning candles and ran despairingly for the door. I fumbled idiotically and ineffectually with the key, and all the time I stared, with a fear that was like insanity, towards the barriers. The hand was plunging towards me; yet, even as it had been unable to pass into the pentacles when the ring was without; so, now that the ring was within, it had no power to pass out. The monster was chained, as surely as any beast would be, were chains riveted upon it.

"Even then, in that moment, I got a flash of this knowledge, but I was too utterly shaken with fright to reason and the instant I managed to get the key turned I sprang into the passage and slammed the door with a crash. I locked it and got to my room, somehow; for I was trembling so that I could hardly stand, as you can imagine. I locked myself in and managed to get the candle lit; then I lay down on the bed and kept quiet for an hour or two, and so I grew steadier.

"I got a little sleep later, but woke when Peters brought my coffee. When I had drunk it I felt altogether better and took the old man along with me to have a look into the Grey Room. I opened the door and peeped in. The candles were still burning wan against the daylight and behind them was the pale, glowing star of the electric pentacle. And there in the middle was the ring—the gateway of the monster, lying demure and ordinary.

"Nothing in the room was touched and I knew that the brute had never managed to cross the pentacles. Then I went out and locked the door.

"After a further sleep of some hours I left the house. I returned in the afternoon in a cab. I had with me an oxyhydrogen jet and two cylinders, containing the gases. I carried the things to the Grey Room and there, in the center of the electric pentacle, I erected the little furnace. Five minutes later the Luck Ring, once the luck but now the bane[10] of the Anderson family, was no more than a little splash of hot metal."

Carnacki felt in his pocket and pulled out something wrapped in tissue paper. He passed it to me. I opened it and found a small circle of greyish metal something like lead, only harder and rather brighter.

"Well," I asked, at length, after examining it and handing it round to the others, "did that stop the haunting?"

Carnacki nodded. "Yes," he said. "I slept three nights in the Grey Room before I left. Old Peters nearly fainted when he knew that I meant to, but by the third night he seemed to realize that he house was just safe and ordinary. And you know, I believe in his heart he hardly approved."

Carnacki stood up and began to shake hands. "Out you go!" he said, genially.

And, presently, we went pondering to our various homes.

---

10. **bane:** source of harm or ruin.

Discussion Questions

1. Describe the frame story for Carnacki's ghostly tale. Why do you suppose the author used this device?

2. What impression of Carnacki's character do you get from the narrator and from Carnacki's own description of the events and his reactions to them?

3. What details contribute to your impression of Carnacki's professional approach to this case?

4. Explain how Carnacki accidentally manages to trap the evil spirit.

5. In what way is the shape of the ring significant? How does this enable Carnacki to stop the hauntings?

Suggestion for Writing

Carnacki mentions the story of the murders that took place in the Grey Room 150 years ago, but he doesn't go into detail. Narrate the story of the first murders, those of Sir Hulbert's wife and child. Here are two details you will have to address: Where is the ring located in the room, and why isn't Sir Hulbert also murdered on this night? Tell the story using appropriate spooky description and dialog, if you wish.

Washington Irving (1783-1859)

Washington Irving was named after George Washington, under whom his Scots immigrant father had fought in the Revolution. The petted favorite of his ten siblings, Irving never applied himself to his education but read widely. He practiced law for a time, and for seventeen years managed his family's business in England. His comic *Knickerbocker's History of New York* launched his literary career, and *The Sketch Book* (1819–20) made him famous for the characters of Rip Van Winkle and Icabod Crane. After some years in Spain he reworked Spanish and Moorish legends into *Tales of the Alhambra* (1832). When he returned to the United States he found himself a respected man of letters. He was offered several political appointments but accepted only one—as American minister to Spain. Irving has often been called the "Father of American Literature" because, while later authors may have proved more important, he was the first to take tales and the local settings, customs, and people of the newly-formed nation and raise them to the level of art.

Adventure of the German Student

On a stormy night, in the tempestuous times of the French Revolution, a young German was returning to his lodgings, at a late hour, across the old part of Paris. The lightning gleamed, and the loud claps of thunder rattled through the lofty narrow street—but I should first tell you something about this young German.

Gottfried Wolfgang was a young man of good family. He had studied for some time at Gottingen, but being of a visionary and enthusiastic character, he had wandered into those wild and speculative doctrines which have so often bewildered German students. His secluded life, his intense application, and the singular nature of his studies, had an effect on both mind and body. His health was impaired; his imagination diseased. He had been indulging in fanciful speculations on spiritual essences until, like Swedenborg,[1] he had an ideal world of his own around him. He took up a notion, I do not know from what cause, that there was an evil influence hanging over him; an evil genius or spirit seeking to ensnare him and ensure his perdition.[2] Such an idea, working on his melancholy temperament, produced the most gloomy effects. He became haggard and desponding. His friends discovered the mental malady preying upon him, and determined that the best cure was a change of scene; he was sent, therefore, to finish his studies amidst the splendors and gayeties of Paris.

Wolfgang arrived at Paris at the breaking out of the revolution. The popular delirium at first caught his enthusiastic mind, and he was captivated by the political and philosophical theories of the day: but the scenes of blood which followed shocked his sensitive nature, disgusted him with society and the world, and made him more than ever a recluse. He shut himself up in a solitary apartment in the *Pays Latin,* the quarter of students. There, in a gloomy street not far from the monastic walls of the Sorbonne,[3] he pursued his favorite speculations. Sometimes he spent hours together in the great libraries of Paris, those catacombs of departed

---

1. **Swedenborg:** Emanuel Swedenborg (1688–1772), Swedish scientist, philosopher, and Christian mystic who held that humankind could be saved only by accepting divine truth and by being delivered from the influence and domination of evil.
2. **perdition:** damnation.
3. **Sorbonne:** the school of literature and science at the University of Paris.

authors, rummaging among their hoards of dusty and obsolete works in quest of food for his unhealthy appetite. He was, in a manner, a literary ghoul, feeding in the charnel-house[4] of decayed literature.

Wolfgang, though solitary and recluse, was an ardent temperament, but for a time it operated merely upon his imagination. He was too shy and ignorant of the world to make any advances to the fair,[5] but he was a passionate admirer of female beauty, and in his lonely chamber would often lose himself in reveries on forms and faces which he had seen, and his fancy would deck out images of loveliness far surpassing the reality.

While his mind was in this excited and sublimated state, a dream produced an extraordinary effect upon him. It was of a female face of transcendent beauty. So strong was the impression made, that he dreamt of it again and again. It haunted his thoughts by day, his slumbers by night; in fine,[6] he became passionately enamored of this shadow of a dream. This lasted so long that it became one of those fixed ideas which haunt the minds of melancholy men, and are at times mistaken for madness.

Such was Gottfried Wolfgang, and such his situation at the time I mentioned. He was returning home late one stormy night, through some of the old and gloomy streets of the *Marais,* the ancient part of Paris. The loud claps of thunder rattled among the high houses of the narrow streets. He came to the *Place de Greve,* the square where public executions are performed. The lightning quivered about the pinnacles of the ancient *Hotel de Ville,*[7] and shed flickering gleams over the open space in front. As Wolfgang was crossing the square, he shrank back with horror at finding himself close by the guillotine.[8] It was the height of the reign of terror, when this dreadful instrument of death stood ever ready, and its scaffold was continually running with the blood of the virtuous and the brave. It had that very day been actively employed in the work of carnage, and there it stood in grim array, amidst a silent and sleeping city, waiting for fresh victims.

---

4. **charnel-house:** place where dead bodies or bones are laid.
5. **the fair:** the female sex.
6. **in fine:** finally.
7. ***Hôtel de Ville:*** a municipal building.
8. **guillotine** (gi′ lə tēn): instrument of execution used especially during the French Revolution, consisting of a platform and a framework suspending a blade that descended, beheading the victim.

Wolfgang's heart sickened within him, and he was turning shuddering from the horrible engine, when he beheld a shadowy form, cowering as it were at the foot of the steps which led up to the scaffold. A succession of vivid flashes of lightning revealed it more distinctly. It was a female figure, dressed in black. She was seated on one of the lower steps of the scaffold, leaning forward, her face hid in her lap; and her long disheveled tresses hanging to the ground, streaming with the rain which fell in torrents. Wolfgang paused. There was something awful in this solitary monument of woe. The female had the appearance of being above the common order. He knew the times to be full of vicissitude,[9] and that many a fair head, which had once been pillowed on down, now wandered houseless. Perhaps this was some poor mourner whom the dreadful axe had rendered desolate, and who sat here heart-broken on the strand of existence, from which all that was dear to her had been launched into eternity.

He approached, and addressed her in the accents of sympathy. She raised her head and gazed wildly at him. What was his astonishment at beholding, by the bright glare of the lightning, the very face which had haunted him in his dreams. It was pale and disconsolate, but ravishingly beautiful.

Trembling with violent and conflicting emotions, Wolfgang again accosted her. He spoke something of her being exposed at such an hour of the night, and to the fury of such a storm, and offered to conduct her to her friends. She pointed to the guillotine with a gesture of dreadful signification.

"I have no friend on earth!" she said.

"But you have a home," said Wolfgang.

"Yes—in the grave!"

The heart of the student melted at the words.

"If a stranger dare make an offer," said he, "without danger of being misunderstood, I would offer my humble dwelling as a shelter; myself as a devoted friend. I am friendless myself in Paris, and a stranger in the land; but if my life could be of service, it is at your disposal, and should be sacrificed before harm or indignity should come to you."

There was an honest earnestness in the young man's manner that had its effect. His foreign accent, too, was in his favor; it showed him not to be a hackneyed inhabitant of Paris. Indeed, there is an eloquence

---

9. **vicissitude:** change.

in true enthusiasm that is not to be doubted. The homeless stranger confided herself implicitly to the protection of the student.

He supported her faltering steps across the Pont Neuf,[10] and by the place where the statue of Henry the Fourth had been overthrown by the populace. The storm had abated, and the thunder rumbled at a distance. All Paris was quiet; that great volcano of human passion slumbered for a while, to gather fresh strength for the next day's eruption. The student conducted his charge through the ancient streets of the *Pays Latin,* and by the dusky walls of the Sorbonne, to the great dingy hotel which he inhabited. The old portress who admitted them stared with surprise at the unusual sight of the melancholy Wolfgang with a female companion.

On entering his apartment, the student, for the first time, blushed at the scantiness and indifference to his dwelling. He had but one chamber—an old-fashioned saloon—heavily carved, and fantastically furnished with the remains of former magnificence, for it was one of those hotels in the quarter of the Luxembourg palace, which had once belonged to nobility. It was lumbered with books and papers, and all the usual apparatus of a student, and his bed stood in a recess at one end.

When lights were brought, and Wolfgang had a better opportunity of contemplating the stranger, he was more than ever intoxicated by her beauty. Her face was pale, but of a dazzling fairness, set off by a profusion of raven hair that hung clustering about it. Her eyes were large and brilliant, with a singular expression approaching almost to wildness. As far as her black dress permitted her shape to be seen, it was the perfect symmetry. Her whole appearance was highly striking, though she was dressed in the simplest style. The only thing approaching to an ornament which she wore was a broad black band around her neck, clasped by diamonds.

The perplexity now commenced with the student how to dispose of the helpless being thus thrown upon his protection. He thought of abandoning his chamber for her, and seeking shelter elsewhere. Still he was so fascinated by her charms, there seemed to be such a spell upon his thoughts and senses, that he could not tear himself from her presence. Her manner, too, was singular and unaccountable. She spoke no more of the guillotine. Her grief had abated. The attentions of the

---

10. **Pont Neuf:** in Paris, a bridge across the Seine River.

student had first won her confidence, and then, apparently, her heart. She was evidently an enthusiast like himself, and enthusiasts soon understood each other.

In the infatuation of the moment, Wolfgang avowed his passion for her. He told her the story of his mysterious dream, and how she had possessed his heart before he had even seen her. She was strangely affected by his recital, and acknowledged to have felt an impulse towards him equally unaccountable. It was the time for wild theory and wild actions. Old prejudices and superstitions were done away; every thing was under the sway of the "Goddess of Reason." Among other rubbish of the old times, the forms and ceremonies of marriage began to be considered superfluous bonds for honorable minds. Social compacts were the vogue. Wolfgang was too much of a theorist not to be tainted by the liberal doctrines of the day.

"Why should we separate?" said he: "our hearts are united; in the eyes of reason and honor we are as one. What need is there of sordid forms to bind high souls together?"

The stranger listened with emotion: she had evidently received illumination at the same school.

"You have not home nor family," continued he; "let me be every thing to you, or rather let us be every thing to one another. If form is necessary form shall be observed—there is my hand. I pledge myself to you for ever."

"For ever?" said the stranger, solemnly.

"For ever!" repeated Wolfgang.

The stranger clasped the hand extended to her: "Then I am yours," murmured she, and sank upon his bosom.

The next morning the student left his bride sleeping, and sallied forth at an early hour to seek more spacious apartments suitable to the change in his situation. When he returned, he found the stranger lying with her head hanging over the bed, and one arm thrown over it. He spoke to her, but received no reply. He advanced to awaken her from her uneasy posture. On taking her hand, it was cold—there was no pulsation—her face was pallid and ghastly. —In a word she was a corpse.

Horrified and frantic, he alarmed the house. A scene of confusion ensued. The police was summoned. As the officer of police entered the room, he started back on beholding the corpse.

"Good heaven!" cried he, "how did this woman come here?"

"Do you know anything about her?" said Wolfgang, eagerly.

"Do I?" exclaimed the officer: "she was guillotined yesterday."

He stepped forward; undid the black collar around the neck of the corpse and the head rolled on the floor!

The student burst into a frenzy. "The fiend! the fiend has gained possession of me!" shrieked he: "I am lost for ever."

They tried to soothe him, but in vain. He was possessed with the frightful belief that an evil spirit had reanimated the dead body to ensnare him. He went distracted, and died in a mad-house.

Here the old gentleman with the haunted head finished his narrative.

"And is this really a fact?" said the inquisitive gentleman.

"A fact not to be doubted," replied the other. "I had it from the best authority. The student told it to me himself. I saw him in a mad-house in Paris."

Discussion Questions

1. What does the setting—both time and place—contribute to the effects of the story?

2. What causes Wolfgang to be sent to Paris? Does this "change of scene" help him? Explain.

3. Why does Wolfgang invite the mysterious young woman home with him?

4. What has happened to the young woman by morning? What inference is the reader supposed to make?

5. How does Wolfgang interpret his encounter with the young woman? What does this do to him?

Suggestion for Writing

After Wolfgang shrieks, "I am lost for ever," those with him try "to soothe him, but in vain." Imagine that you are the police officer or Wolfgang's landlady. How would you go about soothing him? What might you say to this poor student who has undergone such a terrifying experience? Would you try to find a logical explanation or suggest that he should not be so alarmed because she was, after all, a friendly ghost? Or perhaps you would try to convince him that it was not "the fiend" but some other apparition. Write your dialog as you talk soothingly to the frenzied Wolfgang.

W. W. Jacobs (1863-1943)

William Wymark Jacobs was born in London and educated at private schools. After passing a civil service examination he became a post office clerk. From the age of 20 he enjoyed writing, mostly humorous articles, and when his first book, *Many Cargoes,* was published in 1896, he resigned soon afterward to write full time. His father was the manager of a shipping wharf, and Jacobs absorbed much of the flavor and lore of the sea. His most characteristic tales involve sailors and dock workers in amusing but exciting predicaments. A shy, quiet little man, he became known as a humorist, publishing some 20 volumes of short stories and enjoying immense popularity. His humor was quiet, producing chuckles rather than laughs, but he also produced a number of spine-chilling horror stories. After 1926 Jacobs turned his attention to the stage, writing a number of one-act comedies that are now largely forgotten. His best-known story is this one, a concise little shocker that continues to this day to be anthologized and dramatized.

The Monkey's Paw

I

Without, the night was cold and wet, but in the small parlor of Lakesnam Villa the blinds were drawn and the fire burned brightly. Father and son were at chess, the former, who possessed ideas about the game involving radical changes, putting his king into such sharp and unnecessary perils that it even provoked comment from the white-haired old lady knitting placidly by the fire.

"Hark at the wind," said Mr. White, who, having seen a fatal mistake after it was too late, was amiably desirous of preventing his son from seeing it.

"I'm listening," said the latter, grimly surveying the board as he stretched out his hand. "Check."

"I should hardly think that he'd come tonight," said his father, with his hand poised over the board.

"Mate," replied the son.

"That's the worst of living so far out," bawled Mr. White, with sudden and unlooked-for violence; "of all the beastly, slushy, out-of-the-way places to live in, this is the worst. Pathway's a bog and the road's a torrent. I don't know what people are thinking about. I suppose because only two houses on the road are let, they think it doesn't matter."

"Never mind, dear," said his wife soothingly; "perhaps you'll win the next one."

Mr. White looked up sharply, just in time to intercept a knowing glance between mother and son. The words died away on his lips, and he hid a guilty grin in his thin grey beard.

"There he is," said Herbert White, as the gate banged to loudly and heavy footsteps came towards the door.

The old man rose with hospitable haste, and opening the door, was heard condoling with the new arrival. The new arrival also condoled with himself, so that Mrs. White said, "Tut, tut!" and coughed gently as her husband entered the room, followed by a tall burly man, beady of eye and rubicund[1] of visage.

---

1. **rubicund:** reddish; ruddy.

"Sergeant-Major Morris," he said, introducing him.

The sergeant-major shook hands, and taking the proffered[2] seat by the fire, watched contentedly while his host got out whisky and tumblers and stood a small copper kettle on the fire.

At the third glass his eyes got brighter, and he began to talk, the little family circle regarding with eager interest this visitor from distant parts, as he squared his broad shoulders in the chair and spoke of strange scenes and doughty[3] deeds, of wars and plagues and strange peoples.

"Twenty-one years of it," said Mr. White, nodding at his wife and son. "When he went away he was a slip of a youth in the warehouse. Now look at him."

"He don't look to have taken much harm," said Mrs. White politely.

"I'd like to go to India myself," said the old man, "just to look round a bit, you know."

"Better where you are," said the sergeant-major, shaking his head. He put down the empty glass, and sighing softly, shook it again.

"I should like to see those old temples and fakirs[4] and jugglers," said the old man. "What was that you started telling me the other day about a monkey's paw or something, Morris?"

"Nothing," said the soldier hastily. "Leastways, nothing worth hearing."

"Monkey's paw?" said Mrs. White curiously.

"Well, it's just a bit of what you might call magic, perhaps," said the sergeant-major off-handedly.

His three listeners leaned forward eagerly. The visitor absent-mindedly put his empty glass to his lips and then set it down again. His host filled it for him.

"To look at," said the sergeant-major, fumbling in his pocket, "it's just an ordinary little paw, dried to a mummy."

He took something out of his pocket and proffered it. Mrs. White drew back with a grimace, but her son, taking it, examined it curiously.

"And what is there special about it?" inquired Mr. White, as he took it from his son, and having examined it, placed it upon the table.

"It had a spell put on it by an old fakir," said the sergeant-major, "a very holy man. He wanted to show that fate ruled people's lives, and

---

2. **proffered:** offered.
3. **doughty** (dout´ ē): brave.
4. **fakirs** (fə kirz´): Indian holy men.

that those who interfered with it did so to their sorrow. He put a spell on it so that three separate men could each have three wishes from it."

His manner was so impressive that his hearers were conscious that their light laughter jarred somewhat.

"Well, why don't you have three, sir?" said Herbert White cleverly.

The soldier regarded him in the way that middle age is wont to regard presumptuous youth. "I have," he said quietly, and his blotchy face whitened.

"And did you really have the three wishes granted?" asked Mrs. White.

"I did," said the sergeant-major, and his glass tapped against his strong teeth.

"And has anybody else wished?" enquired the old lady.

"The first man had his three wishes, yes," was the reply. "I don't know what the first two were, but the third was for death. That's how I got the paw."

His tones were so grave that a hush fell upon the group.

"If you've had your three wishes, it's no good to you now, then, Morris," said the old man at last. "What do you keep it for?"

The soldier shook his head. "Fancy, I suppose," he said slowly. "I did have some idea of selling it, but I don't think I will. It has caused enough mischief already. Besides, people won't buy. They think it's a fairy tale, some of them, and those who do think anything of it want to try it first and pay me afterwards."

"If you could have another three wishes," said the old man, eyeing him keenly, "would you have them?"

'I don't know," said the other. "I don't know."

He took the paw, and dangling it between his front finger and thumb, suddenly threw it upon the fire. White, with a slight cry, stooped down and snatched it off.

"Better let it burn," said the soldier solemnly.

"If you don't want it, Morris," said the old man, "give it to me."

"I won't," said his friend doggedly. "I threw it on the fire. If you keep it, don't blame me for what happens. Pitch it on the fire again, like a sensible man."

The other shook his head and examined his new possession closely. "How do you do it?" he inquired.

'Hold it up in your right hand and wish aloud," said the sergeant-major, "but I warn you of the consequences."

"Sounds like *The Arabian Nights*,"[5] said Mrs. White, as she rose and began to set the supper. "Don't you think you might wish for four pairs of hands for me?"

Her husband drew the talisman from his pocket, and then all three burst into laughter as the sergeant-major, with a look of alarm on his face, caught him by the arm.

"If you must wish," he said gruffly, "wish for something sensible."

Mr. White dropped it back into his pocket, and placing chairs, motioned his friend to the table. In the business of supper the talisman[6] was partly forgotten, and afterward the three sat listening in an enthralled fashion to a second installment of the soldier's adventures in India.

"If the tale about the monkey paw is not more truthful than those he has been telling us," said Herbert, as the door closed behind their guest, just in time for him to catch the last train, "we shan't make much out of it."

"Did you give him anything for it, father?" inquired Mrs. White, regarding her husband closely.

"A trifle," said he, coloring slightly. "He didn't want it, but I made him take it. And he pressed me again to throw it away."

"Likely," said Herbert, with pretended horror. "Why, we're going to be rich, and famous, and happy. Wish to be an emperor, father, to begin with; then you can't be henpecked."

He darted round the table, pursued by the maligned Mrs. White armed with an antimacassar.[7]

Mr. White took the paw from his pocket and eyed it dubiously. "I don't know what to wish for, and that's a fact," he said slowly. "It seems to me I've got all I want."

"If you only cleared the house, you'd be quite happy, wouldn't you?" said Herbert, with his hand on his shoulder. "Well, wish for two hundred pounds, then; that'll just do it."

His father, smiling shamefacedly at his own credulity, held up the talisman, as his son, with a solemn face somewhat marred by a wink at his mother, sat down at the piano and struck a few impressive chords.

---

5. *The Arabian Nights:* a collection of ancient tales from the area of Arabia, India, and Persia.
6. **talisman:** magic charm.
7. **antimacassar** (an ti mə kas′ ər): cover for the back of a chair.

"I wish for two hundred pounds!" said the old man distinctly.

A fine crash from the piano greeted the words, interrupted by a shuddering cry from the old man. His wife and son ran to him.

"It moved," he cried, with a glance of disgust at the object as it lay on the floor. "As I wished, it twisted in my hands like a snake."

"Well, I don't see the money," said his son, as he picked it up and placed it on the table, "and I bet I never shall."

"It must have been your fancy, father," said his wife, regarding him anxiously.

He shook his head. "Never mind, though; there's no harm done, but it gave me a shock all the same."

They sat down by the fire again while the two men finished their pipes. Outside, the wind was higher than ever, and the old man started nervously at the sound of a door banging upstairs. A silence unusual and depressing settled upon all three, which lasted until the old couple rose to retire for the night.

"I expect you'll find the cash tied up in a big bag in the middle of your bed," said Herbert, as he bade them good-night, "and something horrible squatting up on top of the wardrobe watching you as you pocket your ill-gotten gains."

II

In the brightness of the wintry sun the next morning as it streamed over the breakfast table Herbert laughed at his fears. There was an air of prosaic[8] wholesomeness about the room which it had lacked on the previous night, and the dirty, shriveled little paw was pitched on the sideboard with a carelessness which betokened no great belief in its virtues.

"I suppose all old soldiers are the same," said Mrs. White. "The idea of our listening to such nonsense! How could wishes be granted in these days? And if they could, how could two hundred pounds hurt you, father?"

"Might drop on his head from the sky," said the frivolous Herbert.

"Morris said the things happened so naturally," said his father, "that you might if you so wished attribute it to coincidence."

---

8. prosaic (prō zā´ ik): commonplace; dull and ordinary.

"Well, don't break into the money before I come back," said Herbert, as he rose from the table. "I'm afraid it'll turn you into a mean, avaricious[9] man, and we shall have to disown you."

His mother laughed, and following him to the door, watched him down the road, and returning to the breakfast table, was very happy at the expense of her husband's credulity. All of which did not prevent her from scurrying to the door at the postman's knock, nor prevent her from referring somewhat shortly to retired sergeant-majors of bibulous[10] habits when she found that the post brought a tailor's bill.

"Herbert will have some more of his funny remarks, I expect, when he comes home," she said, as they sat at dinner.

"I dare say," said Mr. White, pouring himself out some beer; "but for all that, the thing moved in my hand; that I'll swear to."

"You thought it did," said the old lady soothingly.

"I say it did," replied the other. "There was no thought about it; I had just—What's the matter?"

His wife made no reply. She was watching the mysterious movements of a man outside, who, peering in an undecided fashion at the house appeared to be trying to make up his mind to enter. In mental connection with the two hundred pounds, she noticed that the stranger was well dressed and wore a silk hat of glossy newness. Three times he paused at the gate, and then walked on again. The fourth time he stood with his hand upon it, and then with sudden resolution flung it open and walked up the path. Mrs. White at the same moment placed her hands behind her, and hurriedly unfastening the strings of her apron, put that useful article of apparel beneath the cushion of her chair.

She brought the stranger, who seemed ill at ease, into the room. He gazed furtively at Mrs. White, and listened in a preoccupied fashion as the old lady apologized for the appearance of the room, and her husband's coat, a garment which he usually reserved for the garden. She then waited as patiently as her sex would permit for him to broach his business, but he was at first strangely silent.

"I—was asked to call," he said at last, and stooped and picked a piece of cotton from his trousers. "I come from Maw and Meggins."

The old lady started. "Is anything the matter?" she asked breathlessly. "Has anything happened to Herbert? What is it? What is it?"

---

9. **avaricious** (av ə rish´ əs): greedy.
10. **bibulous:** fond of alcoholic liquor.

Her husband interposed. "There, there, mother," he said hastily. "Sit down, and don't jump to conclusions. You've not brought bad news, I'm sure, sir," and he eyed the other wistfully.

"I'm sorry—" began the visitor.

"Is he hurt?" demanded the mother.

The visitor bowed in assent. "Badly hurt," he said quietly, "but he is not in any pain."

"Oh, thank God!" said the old woman, clasping her hands. "Thank God for that! Thank—"

She broke off suddenly as the sinister meaning of the assurance dawned upon her and she saw the awful confirmation of her fears in the other's averted face. She caught her breath, and turning to her slower-witted husband, laid her trembling old hand upon his. There was a long silence.

"He was caught in the machinery," said the visitor at length, in a low voice.

"Caught in the machinery," repeated Mr. White, in a dazed fashion, "yes."

He sat staring blankly out the window, and taking his wife's hand between his own, pressed it as he had been wont to do in their old courting days nearly forty years before.

"He was the only one left to us," he said, turning gently to the visitor. "It is hard."

The other coughed, and rising, walked slowly to the window. "The firm wished me to convey their sincere sympathy with you in your great loss," he said, without looking round. "I beg that you will understand that I am only their servant and merely obeying orders."

There was no reply; the old woman's face was white, her eyes staring, and her breath inaudible; on the husband's face was a look such as his friend the sergeant might have carried into his first action.

"I was to say that Maw and Meggins disclaim all responsibility," continued the other. "They admit to no liability at all, but in consideration of your son's services they wish to present you with a certain sum as compensation."

Mr White dropped his wife's hand, and rising to his feet, gazed with a look of horror at his visitor. His dry lips shaped the words, "How much?"

"Two hundred pounds," was the answer.

Unconscious of his wife's shriek, the old man smiled faintly, put out his hands like a sightless man, and dropped, a senseless heap, to the floor.

III

In the huge new cemetery, some two miles distant, the old people buried their dead, and came back to a house steeped in shadow and silence. It was all over so quickly that at first they could hardly realize it, and remained in a state of expectation as though of something else to happen—something else which was to lighten this load, too heavy for old hearts to bear.

But the days passed, and expectation gave place to resignation—the hopeless resignation of the old, sometimes miscalled apathy. Sometimes they hardly exchanged a word, for now they had nothing to talk about, and their days were long to weariness.

It was about a week after that that the old man, waking suddenly in the night, stretched out his hand and found himself alone. The room was in darkness, and the sound of subdued weeping came from the window. He raised himself in bed and listened.

"Come back," he said tenderly. "You will be cold."

"It is colder for my son," said the old woman, and wept afresh.

The sound of her sobs died away on his ears. The bed was warm, and his eyes heavy with sleep. He dozed fitfully, and then slept until a sudden wild cry from his wife awoke him with a start.

"The monkey's paw!" she cried wildly. "The monkey's paw!"

He started up in alarm. "Where? Where is it? What's the matter?"

She came stumbling across the room toward him. "I want it," she said quietly. "You've not destroyed it?"

"It's in the parlor, on the bracket," he replied, marveling. "Why?"

She cried and laughed together, and bending over, kissed his cheek.

"I only just though of it," she said hysterically. "Why didn't I think of it before? Why didn't you think of it?"

"Think of what?" he questioned.

"The other two wishes," she replied rapidly. "We've only had one."

"Was not that enough?" he demanded fiercely.

"No," she cried triumphantly; "we'll have one more. Go down and get it quickly, and wish our boy alive again."

The man sat up in bed and flung the bedclothes from his quaking limbs. "Good God, you are mad!" he cried, aghast.

"Get it," she panted; "get it quickly, and wish—Oh, my boy, my boy!"

Her husband struck a match and lit the candle. "Get back to bed," he said unsteadily. "You don't know what you are saying."

"We had the first wish granted," said the old woman feverishly; "why not the second?"

"A coincidence," stammered the old man.

"Go and get it and wish," cried the old woman, and dragged him towards the door.

He went down in the darkness, and felt his way to the parlor, and then to the mantel piece. The talisman was in its place, and a horrible fear that the unspoken wish might bring his mutilated son before him ere he could escape from the room seized upon him, and he caught his breath as he found that he had lost the direction of the door. His brow cold with sweat, he felt his way round the table, and groped along the wall until he found himself in the small passage with the unwholesome thing in his hand.

Even his wife's face seemed changed as he entered the room. It was white and expectant, and to his fears seemed to have an unnatural look upon it. He was afraid of her.

"Wish!" she cried, in a strong voice.

"It is foolish and wicked," he faltered.

"Wish!" repeated his wife.

He raised his hand. "I wish my son alive again."

The talisman fell to the floor, and he regarded it shudderingly. Then he sank trembling into a chair as the old woman, with burning eyes, walked to the window and raised the blind.

He sat until he was chilled with the cold, glancing occasionally at the figure of the old woman peering through the window. The candle end, which had burnt below the rim of the china candlestick, was throwing pulsating shadows on the ceiling and walls, until, with a flicker larger than the rest, it expired. The old man, with an unspeakable sense of relief at the failure of the talisman, crept back to his bed, and a minute or two afterwards the old woman came silently and apathetically beside him.

Neither spoke, but both lay silently listening to the ticking of the clock. A stair creaked, and a squeaky mouse scurried noisily through the wall. The darkness was oppressive, and after lying for some time screwing up his courage, the husband took the box of matches, and striking one, went downstairs for a candle.

At the foot of the stairs the match went out, and he paused to strike another, and at the same moment a knock, so quiet and stealthy as to be scarcely audible, sounded on the front door.

The matches fell from his hand. He stood motionless, his breath suspended until the knock was repeated. Then he turned and fled swiftly back to the bedroom, and closed the door behind him. A third knock sounded through the house.

"*What's that?*" cried the old woman, starting up.

"A rat," said the old man, in shaking tones—"a rat. It passed me on the stairs."

His wife sat up in bed listening. A loud knock resounded through the house.

"It's Herbert!" she screamed. "It's Herbert!"

She ran to the door, but her husband was before her, and catching her by the arm, held her tightly.

"What are you going to do?" he whispered hoarsely.

"It's my boy; it's Herbert!" she cried, struggling mechanically. "I forgot it was two miles away. What are you holding me for? Let go. I must open the door."

"For God's sake, don't let it in," cried the old man, trembling.

"You're afraid of your own son," she cried, struggling. "Let me go. I'm coming, Herbert; I'm coming."

There was another knock, and another. The old woman with a sudden wrench broke free and ran from the room. Her husband followed to the landing, and called after her appealingly as she hurried downstairs. He heard the chain rattle back and the bottom bolt drawn slowly and stiffly from the socket. Then the old woman's voice, strained and panting.

"The top bolt," she cried loudly. "Come down. I can't reach it."

But her husband was on his hands and knees groping wildly on the floor in search of the paw. If he could only find it before the thing outside got in. A perfect fusillade[11] of knocks reverberated through the house, and he heard the scraping of a chair as his wife put it down in the passage against the door. He heard the creaking of the bolt as it

---

11. **fusillade** (fyu′ sə lād): series of rapid and continuous noises.

came slowly back, and at the same moment he found the monkey's paw, and frantically breathed his third and last wish.

The knocking ceased suddenly, although the echoes of it were still in the house. He heard the chair drawn back and the door opened. A cold wind rushed up the staircase, and a long loud wail of disappointment and misery from his wife gave him courage to run down to her side, and then to the gate beyond. The street lamp flickering opposite shone on a quiet and deserted road.

Discussion Questions

1. Recount the history of the monkey's paw to the point where Mr. White rescues it from the fire. What does Mr. White hope from it?

2. How does Herbert himself contribute to the situation that brings about his death?

3. Explain the irony that accompanies Mr. White's receiving the $200.

4. What is Mr. White's second wish? Why does he do so?

5. The narrator does not tell Mr. White's third "frantically breathed" wish. What do you suppose it is? Why do you think he does so?

Suggestion for Writing

Could the Whites have gotten what they wanted without being visited by disaster? Write a brief essay in which you explain that it was the way Mr. White *worded* his wish that resulted in such a tragic outcome. Suggest a way that Mr. White could have wished for $200 safely or suggest a more sensible wish for him to have made. As an alternative, write about how Mrs. White could have wished for her son back again without conjuring up the horror that Mr. White finally wishes back into its grave.

Rudyard Kipling (1865-1936)

Rudyard Kipling was born in India, where his father was a professor of architecture at a British art school, but was sent at age five to England for his education. Beaten and bullied by his guardians, he suffered ill health until rescued by his parents; he was then sent to a military academy to prepare for the civil service. Returning to India, Kipling worked as a newspaper reporter, also contributing poems and sketches to various publications. In 1886 he published *Departmental Ditties and Other Verses,* which gained him a wide and enthusiastic audience. A tireless worker and a brilliant conversationalist, he continued to write about Indian life and customs under the British Empire.

Returning to England via Japan, San Francisco, and New York, he wrote a number of novels—including *Kim* (1901), a colorful and dramatic picture of Indian social life—and collections of tales, including *Many Inventions* (1893), which introduced the character of Mowgli, and two *Jungle Books* (1894–5). His writings made him enormously popular and very wealthy, although his popularity diminished in later years. He was awarded the Nobel Prize for Literature in 1907.

The Mark of the Beast

*Your gods and my gods—do you
or I know which are the stronger?*
—Native proverb

East of Suez,[1] some hold, the direct control of providence ceases, man being there handed over to the power of the gods and devils of Asia, and the Church of England providence only exercising an occasional and modified supervision in the case of Englishmen.

This theory accounts for some of the more unnecessary horrors of life in India; it may be stretched to explain my story.

My friend Strickland of the police, who knows as much of natives of India as is good for any man, can bear witness to the facts of the case. Dumoise, our doctor, also saw what Strickland and I saw. The inference which he drew from the evidence was entirely incorrect. He is dead now; he died in a rather curious manner, which has been elsewhere described.

When Fleete came to India he owned a little money and some land in the Himalayas,[2] near a place called Dharmsala. Both properties had been left him by an uncle, and he came out to finance them. He was a big, heavy, genial and inoffensive man. His knowledge of natives was, of course, limited, and he complained of the difficulties of the language.

He rode in from his place in the hills to spend New Year in the station, and he stayed with Strickland. On New Year's Eve there was a big dinner at the club, and the night was excusably wet.[3] When men foregather from the uttermost ends of the Empire[4] they have a right to be riotous. The Frontier had sent down a continent o' Catch-'em-Alive-Os who had not seen twenty white faces for a year, and were used to ride

---

1. Suez: the area between the Mediterranean and Red Seas connecting Africa and Asia.
2. Himalayas: range of mountains in southern Asia between India and Tibet and through West Pakistan, Nepal, and Bhutan.
3. wet: that is, there was much drinking of alcohol.
4. Empire: the British Empire, which included India until 1947.

fifteen miles to dinner at the next fort at the risk of a Khyberee bullet where their drinks should lie. They profited by their new security, for they tried to play pool with a curled-up hedgehog found in the garden, and one of them carried the marker round the room in his teeth. Half a dozen planters had come in from the south and were talking 'horse' to the Biggest Liar in Asia, who was trying to cap all their stories at once. Everybody was there, and there was a general closing up of ranks and taking stock of our losses in dead or disabled that had fallen during the past year. It was a very wet night, and I remember that we sang 'Auld Lang Syne' with our feet in the Polo Championship Cup and our heads among the stars, and swore that we were all dear friends. Then some of us went away and annexed Burma, and some tried to open up the Sudan and were opened up by fuzzies[5] in that cruel scrub outside Suakim, and some found stars and medals, and some were married, which was bad, and some did other things which were worse, and the others of us stayed in our chains and strove to make money on insufficient experiences.

Fleete began the night with sherry and bitters, drank champagne steadily up to dessert, then raw, rasping Capri with all the strength of whisky, took Benedictine with his coffee, four or five whiskies and sodas to improve his pool strokes, beer and bones at half-past two, winding up with old brandy. Consequently, when he came out, at half-past three in the morning, into fourteen degrees of frost, he was very angry with his horse for coughing, and tried to leapfrog into the saddle. The horse broke away and went to his stables; so Strickland and I formed a guard of dishonor to take Fleete home.

Our road lay through the bazaar,[6] close to a little temple of Hanuman, the monkey-god, who is a leading divinity worthy of respect. All gods have good points, just as have all priests. Personally, I attach much importance to Hanuman, and am kind to his people—the great grey apes of the hills. One never knows when one may want a friend.

There was a light in the temple, and as we passed we could hear voices of men chanting hymns. In a native temple the priests rise at all hours of the night to do honor to their god. Before we could stop him, Fleete dashed up the steps, patted two priests on the back, and was

---

5. **fuzzies:** Sudanese tribesmen (British slang).
6. **bazaar:** street market.

gravely grinding the ashes of his cigar-butt into the forehead of the red stone image of Hanuman.

Strickland tried to drag him out, but he sat down and said solemnly: "Shee that? Mark of the B-beasht! *I* made it. Ishn't it fine?"

In half a minute the temple was alive and noisy, and Strickland, who knew what came of polluting gods, said that things might occur. He, by virtue of his official position, long residence in the country and weakness for going among the natives, was known to the priests and he felt unhappy. Fleete sat on the ground and refused to move. He said that "good old Hanuman" made a very soft pillow.

Then, without any warning, a Silver Man came out of a recess behind the image of the god. He was perfectly naked in that bitter, bitter cold, and his body shone like frosted silver, for he was what the Bible calls 'a leper as white as snow.'[7] Also he had no face, because he was a leper of some years' standing, and his disease was heavy upon him. We two stooped to haul Fleete up, and the temple was filling and filling with folk who seemed to spring from the earth, when the Silver Man ran in under our arms, making a noise exactly like the mewing of an otter, caught Fleete round the body and dropped his head on Fleete's breast before we could wrench him away. Then he retired to a corner and sat mewing while the crowd blocked all the doors.

The priests were very angry until the Silver Man touched Fleete. That nuzzling seemed to sober them.

At the end of a few minutes' silence one of the priests came to Strickland and said, in perfect English, "Take your friend away. He has done with Hanuman but Hanuman has not done with him." The crowd gave room and we carried Fleete into the road.

Strickland was very angry. He said that we might all three have been knifed, and that Fleete should thank his stars that he had escaped without injury.

Fleete thanked no one. He said that he wanted to go to bed. He was gorgeously drunk.

We moved on, Strickland silent and wrathful, until Fleete was taken with violent shivering fits and sweating. He said that the smells of the

---

7. "a leper . . . snow": A leper is a person afflicted with leprosy, a contagious disease that causes loss of sensation with eventual paralysis, and wasting of muscle and skin, with accompanying deformities and mutilations. The allusion is to II Kings, Chapter 5, verse 27.

bazaar were overpowering, and he wondered why slaughterhouses were permitted so near English residences. "Can't you smell the blood?" said Fleete.

We put him to bed at last, just as the dawn was breaking, and Strickland invited me to have another whisky and soda. While we were drinking he talked of the trouble in the temple, and admitted that it baffled him completely. Strickland hates being mystified by natives, because his business in life is to overmatch them with their own weapons. He has not yet succeeded in doing this, but in fifteen or twenty years he will have made some small progress.

"They should have mauled us," he said, "instead of mewing at us. I wonder what they meant. I don't like it one little bit."

I said that the managing committee of the temple would in all probability bring a criminal action against us for insulting their religion. There was a section of the Indian Penal Code which exactly met Fleete's offense. Strickland said he only hoped and prayed that they would do this. Before I left I looked into Fleete's room, and saw him lying on his right side, scratching his left breast. Then I went to bed, cold, depressed and unhappy, at seven o'clock in the morning.

At one o'clock I rode over to Strickland's house to inquire after Fleete's head. I imagined that it would be a sore one. Fleete was breakfasting and seemed unwell. His temper was gone, for he was abusing the cook for not supplying him with an underdone chop. A man who can eat raw meat after a wet night is a curiosity. I told Fleete this and he laughed.

"You breed queer mosquitoes in these parts," he said. "I've been bitten to pieces, but only in one place."

"Let's have a look at the bite," said Strickland. "It may have gone down since this morning."

While the chops were being cooked, Fleete opened his shirt and showed us, just over his left breast, a mark, the perfect double of the black rosettes—the five or six irregular blotches arranged in a circle—on a leopard's hide. Strickland looked and said, "It was only pink this morning. It's grown black now."

Fleete ran to a glass.

"By Jove!" he said, "this is nasty. What is it?"

We could not answer. Here the chops came in, all red and juicy, and Fleete bolted three in a most offensive manner. He ate on his right grinders[8] only, and threw his head over his right shoulder as he snapped the meat. When he had finished, it struck him that he had been behaving strangely, for he said apologetically, "I don't think I ever felt so hungry in my life. I've bolted like an ostrich."

After breakfast Strickland said to me, "Don't go. Stay here, and stay for the night."

Seeing that my house was not three miles from Strickland's, this request was absurd. But Strickland insisted, and was going to say something, when Fleete interrupted by declaring in a shamefaced way that he felt hungry again. Strickland sent a man to my house to fetch over my bedding and a horse, and we three went down to Strickland's stables to pass the hours until it was time to go out for a ride. The man who has a weakness for horses never wearies of inspecting them; and when two men are killing time in this way they gather knowledge and lies the one from the other.

There were five horses in the stables, and I shall never forget the scene as we tried to look them over. They seemed to have gone mad. They reared and screamed and nearly tore up their pickets;[9] they sweated and shivered and lathered and were distraught with fear. Strickland's horses used to know him as well as his dogs; which made the matter more curious. We left the stable for fear of the brutes throwing themselves in their panic. Then Strickland turned back and called me. The horses were still frightened, but they let us 'gentle' and make much of them, and put their heads in our bosoms.

"They aren't afraid of *us*," said Strickland. "D'you know, I'd give three months' pay if Outrage here could talk."

But Outrage was dumb, and could only cuddle up to his master and blow out his nostrils, as is the custom of horses when they wish to explain things but can't. Fleete came up when we were in the stalls, and as soon as the horses saw him, their fright broke out afresh. It was all that we could do to escape from the place unkicked. Strickland said, "They don't seem to love you, Fleete."

"Nonsense," said Fleete; "my mare will follow me like a dog." He went to her; she was in a loose-box; but as he slipped the bars she plunged, knocked him down, and broke away into the garden. I laughed, but Strickland was not amused. He took his moustache in both

---

8. **grinders**: molars.
9. **pickets**: stakes in the ground used as hitching posts.

fists and pulled at it till it nearly came out. Fleete, instead of going off to chase his property, yawned, saying that he felt sleepy. He went to the house to lie down, which was a foolish way of spending New Year's Day.

Strickland sat with me in the stables and asked if I had noticed anything peculiar in Fleete's manner. I said that he ate his food like a beast; but that this might have been the result of living alone in the hills, out of the reach of society as refined and elevating as ours for instance. Strickland was not amused. I do not think that he listened to me, for his next sentence referred to the mark on Fleete's breast, and I said that it might have been caused by blister-flies, or that it was possibly a birthmark newly born and now visible for the first time. We both agreed that it was unpleasant to look at, and Strickland found occasion to say that I was a fool.

"I can't tell you want I think now," said he, "because you would call me a madman; but you must stay with me for the next few days, if you can. I want you to watch Fleete, but don't tell me what you think till I have made up my mind."

"But I am dining out tonight," I said.

"So am I," said Strickland, "and so is Fleete. At least if he doesn't change his mind."

We walked about the garden smoking, but saying nothing—because we were friends, and talking spoils good tobacco—till our pipes were out. Then we went to wake up Fleete. He was wide awake and fidgeting about his room.

"I say, I want some more chops," he said. "Can I get them?"

We laughed and said, "Go and change. The ponies will be round in a minute."

"All right," said Fleete. "I'll go when I get the chops—underdone ones, mind."

He seemed to be quite in earnest. It was four o'clock, and we had had breakfast at one; still, for a long time, he demanded those underdone chops. Then he changed into riding clothes and went out into the veranda. His pony—the mare had not been caught—would not let him come near. All three horses were unmanageable—mad with fear—and finally Fleete said that he would stay at home and get something to eat. Strickland and I rode out wondering. As we passed the temple of Hanuman, the Silver Man came out and mewed at us.

"He is not one of the regular priests of the temple," said Strickland. "I think I should peculiarly like to lay my hands on him."

There was no spring in our gallop on the racecourse that evening. The horses were stale, and moved as though they had been ridden out.

"The fright after breakfast has been too much for them," said Strickland.

That was the only remark he made through the remainder of the ride. Once or twice, I think, he swore to himself; but that did not count.

We came back in the dark at seven o'clock, and saw that there were no lights in the bungalow. "Careless ruffians my servants are!" said Strickland.

My horse reared at something on the carriage drive, and Fleete stood up under its nose.

"What are you doing, grovelling about the garden?" said Strickland.

But both horses bolted and nearly threw us. We dismounted by the stables and returned to Fleete, who was on his hands and knees under the orange-bushes.

"What the devil's wrong with you?" said Strickland.

"Nothing, nothing in the world," said Fleete, speaking very quickly and thickly. "I've been gardening—botanizing, you know. The smell of the earth is delightful. I think I'm going for a walk—a long walk—all night."

Then I saw that there was something excessively out of order somewhere, and I said to Strickland, "I am not dining out."

"Bless you!" said Strickland. "Here, Fleete, get up. You'll catch fever there. Come in to dinner and let's have the lamps lit. We'll all dine at home."

Fleete stood up unwillingly, and said, "No lamps—no lamps. It's much nicer here. Let's dine outside and have some more chops—lots of 'em and underdone—bloody ones with gristle."

Now a December evening in Northern India is bitterly cold, and Fleete's suggestion was that of a maniac.

"Come in," said Strickland sternly. "Come in at once."

Fleete came, and when the lamps were brought, we saw that he was literally plastered with dirt from head to foot. He must have been rolling in the garden. He shrank from the light and went to his room. His eyes were horrible to look at. There was a green light behind them, not in them, if you understand, and the man's lower lip hung down.

Strickland said, "There is going to be trouble—big trouble—tonight. Don't you change your riding-things."

We waited and waited for Fleete's reappearance, and ordered dinner in the meantime. We could hear him moving about his own room, but there was no light there. Presently from the room came the long-drawn howl of a wolf.

People write and talk lightly of blood running cold and hair standing up, and things of that kind. Both sensations are too horrible to be trifled with. My heart stopped as though a knife had been driven through it, and Strickland turned as white as the tablecloth.

The howl was repeated, and was answered by another howl far across the fields.

That set the gilded roof on the horror. Strickland dashed into Fleete's room. I followed, and we saw Fleete getting out of the window. He made beast-noises in the back of his throat. He could not answer us when we shouted at him. He spat.

I don't quite remember what followed, but I think that Strickland must have stunned him with the long bootjack,[10] or else I should never have been able to sit on his chest. Fleete could not speak, he could only snarl, and his snarls were those of a wolf, not of a man. The human spirit must have been giving way all day and have died out with the twilight. We were dealing with a beast that had once been Fleete.

The affair was beyond any human and rational experience. I tried to say 'hydrophobia',[11] but the word wouldn't come, because I knew that I was lying.

We bound this beast with leather thongs of the punkah-rope, and tied its thumbs and big toes together, and gagged it with a shoe-horn, which makes a very efficient gag if you know how to arrange it. Then we carried it into the dining room, and sent a man to Dumoise, the doctor, telling him to come over at once. After we had dispatched the messenger and were drawing breath, Strickland said, "It's no good. This isn't any doctor's work." I, also, knew that he spoke the truth.

The beast's head was free, and it threw it about from side to side. Anyone entering the room would have believed that we were curing a wolf's pelt. That was the most loathsome accessory of all.

Strickland sat with his chin in the heel of his fist, watching the beast as it wriggled on the ground, but saying nothing. The shirt had been

---

10. **bootjack:** device for gripping the heel of a boot to aid in removing it.
11. **hydrophobia:** rabies.

torn open in the scuffle and showed the black rosette mark on the left breast. It stood out like a blister.

In the silence of the watching we heard without, mewing like a she-otter. We both rose to our feet, and, I answer for myself, not Strickland, felt sick, actually and physically sick. We told each other, as did the men in *Pinafore,* that it was the cat.[12]

Dumoise arrived, and I never saw a little man so unprofessionally shocked. He said that it was a heart-rending case of hydrophobia, and that nothing could be done. At least any palliative[13] measures would only prolong the agony. The beast was foaming at the mouth. Fleete, as we told Dumoise, had been bitten by dogs once or twice. Any man who keeps half a dozen terriers must expect a nip now and again. Dumoise could offer no help. He could only certify that Fleete was dying of hydrophobia. The beast was then howling, for it had managed to spit out the shoehorn. Dumoise said that he would be ready to certify to the cause of death, and that the end was certain. He was a good little man, and he offered to remain with us; but Strickland refused the kindness. He did not wish to poison Dumoise's New Year. He would only ask him not to give the real cause of Fleete's death to the public.

So Dumoise left, deeply agitated; and as soon as the noise of the cartwheels had died away Strickland told me, in a whisper, his suspicions. They were so wildly improbable that he dared not say them aloud; and I, who entertained all Strickland's beliefs, was so ashamed of owning to them that I pretended to disbelieve.

"Even if the Silver Man had bewitched Fleete for polluting the image of Hanuman, the punishment could not have fallen so quickly."

As I was whispering this the cry outside the house rose again, and the beast fell into a fresh paroxysm of struggling till we were afraid that the thongs that held it would give way.

"Watch!" said Strickland. "If this happens six times I shall take the law into my own hands. I order you to help me."

He went into his room and came out in a few minutes with the barrels of an old shotgun, a piece of fishing-line, some thick cord, and his heavy wooden bedstead. I reported that the convulsions had followed

---

12. **the men . . . cat:** In a comedy song in Gilbert and Sullivan's operetta *H.M.S. Pinafore,* the chorus asks what noise they heard, and someone in hiding assures them that all is well; what they heard was the cat.
13. **palliative** (pa´ lē ə tiv): easing; helpful.

the cry by two seconds in each case, and the beast seemed perceptibly weaker.

Strickland muttered, "But he can't take away the life! He can't take away the life!"

I said, though I knew that I was arguing against myself, "It may be a cat. It must be a cat. If the Silver Man is responsible, why does he dare to come here?"

Strickland arranged the wood on the hearth, put the gun-barrels into the glow of the fire, spread the twine on the table and broke a walking stick in two. There was one yard of fishing line, gut lapped with wire, such as is used for *mahseer*[14] fishing, and he tied the two ends together in a loop.

Then he said, "How can we catch him? He must be taken alive and unhurt."

I said that we must trust in providence, and go out softly with polo-sticks into the shrubbery at the front of the house. The man or animal that made the cry was evidently moving round the house as regularly as a night-watchman. We could wait in the bushes till he came by and knock him over.

Strickland accepted this suggestion, and we slipped out from a bathroom window into the front veranda and then across the carriage drive into the bushes.

In the moonlight we could see the leper coming round the corner of the house. He was perfectly naked, and from time to time he mewed and stopped to dance with his shadow. It was an unattractive sight, and thinking of poor Fleete, brought to such degradation by so foul a creature, I put away all my doubts and resolved to help Strickland from the heated gun-barrels to the loop of twine—from the loins to the head and back again—with all tortures that might be needful.

The leper halted in the front porch for a moment and we jumped out on him with the sticks. He was wonderfully strong, and we were afraid that he might escape or be fatally injured before we caught him. We had an idea that lepers were frail creatures, but this proved to be incorrect. Strickland knocked his legs from under him and I put my foot on his neck. He mewed hideously, and even through my riding-boots I could feel that his flesh was not the flesh of a clean man.

---

14. *mahseer:* a large Indian freshwater fish.

He struck at us with his hand- and feet-stumps. We looped the lash of a dog-whip round him, under the armpits, and dragged him backwards into the hall and so into the dining-room where the beast lay. There we tied him with trunkstraps. He made no attempt to escape, but mewed.

When we confronted him with the beast the scene was beyond description. The beast doubled backwards into a bow as though he had been poisoned with strychnine, and moaned in the most pitiable fashion. Several other things happened also, but they cannot be put down here.

"I think I was right," said Strickland. "Now we will ask him to cure this case."

But the leper only mewed. Strickland wrapped a towel round his hand and took the gun-barrels out of the fire. I put the half of the broken walking stick through the loop of fishing-line and buckled the leper comfortably to Strickland's bedstead. I understood then how men and women and little children can endure to see a witch burnt alive; for the beast was moaning on the floor, and though the Silver Man had no face, you could see horrible feelings passing through the slab that took its place, exactly as waves of heat play across red-hot iron—gun-barrels for instance.

Strickland shaded his eyes with his hands for a moment and we got to work. This part is not to be printed.

The dawn was beginning to break when the leper spoke. His mewings had not been satisfactory up to that point. The beast had fainted from exhaustion and the house was very still. We unstrapped the leper and told him to take away the evil spirit. He crawled to the beast and laid his hand upon the left breast. That was all. Then he fell face down and whined, drawing in his breath as he did so.

We watched the face of the beast, and saw the soul of Fleete coming back into the eyes. Then a sweat broke out on the forehead and the eyes —they were human eyes—closed. We waited for an hour, but Fleete still slept. We carried him to his room and bade the leper go, giving him the bedstead, and the sheet on the bedstead to cover his nakedness, the gloves and the towels with which we had touched him, and the whip that had been hooked round his body. He put the sheet about him and went out into the early morning without speaking or mewing.

Strickland wiped his face and sat down. A night-gong, far away in the city, made seven o'clock.

"Exactly four-and-twenty hours!" said Strickland. "And I've done enough to ensure my dismissal from the service, besides permanent quarters in a lunatic asylum. Do you believe that we are awake?"

The red-hot gun-barrel had fallen on the floor and was singeing the carpet. The smell was entirely real.

That morning at eleven we two together went to wake up Fleete. We looked and saw that the black leopard-rosettes on his chest had disappeared. He was very drowsy and tired, but as soon as he saw us, he said, "Oh! Confound you fellows. Happy New Year to you. Never mix your liquors. I'm nearly dead."

"Thanks for your kindness, but you're over time," said Strickland. "Today is the morning of the second. You've slept the clock round with a vengeance."

The door opened, and little Dumoise put his head in. He had come on foot, and fancied that we were laying out[15] Fleete.

"I've brought a nurse," said Dumoise. "I suppose that she can come in for . . . what is necessary."

"By all means," said Fleete cheerily, sitting up in bed. "Bring on your nurses."

Dumoise was dumb. Strickland led him out and explained that there must have been a mistake in the diagnosis. Dumoise remained dumb and left the house hastily. He considered that his professional reputation had been injured, and was inclined to make a personal matter of the recovery. Strickland went out too. When he came back, he said that he had been to call on the temple of Hanuman to offer redress for the pollution of the god, and had been solemnly assured that no white man had ever touched the idol, and that he was an incarnation of all the virtues laboring under a delusion. "What do you think?" said Strickland.

I said, "'There are more things . . .'"[16]

But Strickland hates that quotation. He says that I have worn it threadbare.

---

15. **laying out**: preparing for burial.
16. **"There . . . things"**: The quote is from Shakespeare's *Hamlet,* Act I, Scene 5: "There are more things in heaven and earth, Horatio, than are dreamt of in your philosophy."

One other curious thing happened which frightened me as much as anything in all the night's work. When Fleete was dressed he came into the dining-room and sniffed. He had a quaint trick of moving his nose when he sniffed. "Horrid doggy smell, here," said he. "You should really keep those terriers of yours in better order. Try sulphur, Strick."

But Strickland did not answer. He caught hold of the back of a chair, and, without warning, went into an amazing fit of hysterics. It is terrible to see a strong man overtaken with hysteria. Then it struck me that we had fought for Fleete's soul with the Silver Man in that room, and had disgraced ourselves as Englishmen for ever, and I laughed and gasped and gurgled just as shamefully as Strickland, while Fleete thought that we had both gone mad. We never told him what we had done.

Some years later, when Strickland was married and was a church-going member of society for his wife's sake, we reviewed the incident dispassionately and Strickland suggested that I should put it before the public.

I cannot myself see that this step is likely to clear up the mystery; because, in the first place, no one will believe a rather unpleasant story, and, in the second, it is well known to every right-minded man that the gods of the heathen are stone and brass, and any attempt to deal with them otherwise is justly condemned.

Discussion Questions

1. Describe the setting. Is it integral—that is, does it influence the events of the plot—or does it merely serve as background?

2. What does Fleete do to offend the Indians?

3. What part does the leper play in all these proceedings?

4. How do Strickland and the narrator reverse the "mark of the beast"?

5. What attitudes toward the natives and their customs do the three Englishmen, Strickland, Fleete, and the narrator, display in their words and deeds?

Suggestion for Writing

The narrator quotes from Shakespeare: "There are more things in heaven and earth, Horatio, than are dreamt of in your philosophy." Apparently Strickland thinks the narrator quotes it too often. How does it apply here? In the voice of the narrator, write a memoir or personal essay explaining how the truth of Shakespeare's words are borne out by the events in this story.

Guy de Maupassant (1850-1893)

Guy de Maupassant was born and raised in Normandy, a region in northwest France that formed the setting for many of his stories and novels. His father, an attractive dandy and amateur painter, and his mother, a brilliant, strong-willed woman, were incompatible and separated when he was young. Maupassant spent three unhappy years in religious school before transferring to a public school. To help his family earn a living, he worked for 10 years as a government clerk in Paris, a dreary job that increased his determination to write. The publication of his story "Ball of Fat" in 1880 was a sensation. He went on to write nearly 300 short stories and a half-dozen novels, as well as travelogs, plays, poems, and hundreds of articles in various magazines. At an early age he contacted syphilis, which later took its toll in the form of headaches and depression. He unsuccessfully sought relief in drugs. After two suicide attempts he was confined to an asylum in Paris, where he died raving mad. Maupassant developed an economical narrative technique that became a sort of trademark. His work had a profound effect on the development of the short story form.

Vendetta

Paolo Saverini's widow dwelt alone with her son in a small, mean house on the ramparts[1] of Bonifacio.[2] Built on a spur of the mountain and in places actually overhanging the sea, the town looks across the rock-strewn straits to the low-lying coast of Sardinia. On the other side, girdling it almost completely, there is a fissure in the cliff, like an immense corridor, which serves as a port, and down this long channel, as far as the first houses, sail the small Italian and Sardinian fishing-boats, and once a fortnight the broken-winded old steamer from Ajaccio. Clustered together on the white hillside, the houses form a patch of even more dazzling whiteness. Clinging to the rock, gazing down upon those deadly straits where scarcely a ship ventures, they look like the nests of birds of prey. The sea and the barren coast, stripped of all but a scanty covering of grass, are forever harassed by a restless wind, which sweeps along the narrow funnel, ravaging the banks on either side. In all directions the black points of innumerable rocks jut out from the water, with trails of white foam streaming from them, like torn shreds of cloth, floating and quivering on the surface of the waves.

The widow Saverini's house was planted on the very edge of the cliff and its three windows opened upon this wild and dreary prospect. She lived there with her son Antoine and their dog Sémillante, a great gaunt brute of the sheepdog variety, with a long rough coat, whom the young man took with him when he went out shooting.

One evening, Antoine Saverini was treacherously stabbed in a quarrel by Nicolas Ravolati, who escaped that same night to Sardinia.

At the sight of the body, which was brought home by passers-by, the old mother shed no tears, but she gazed long and silently at her dead son. Then, laying her wrinkled hand upon the corpse, she promised him the vendetta.[3] She would not allow anyone to remain with her, and shut herself up with the dead body. The dog Sémillante, who remained

---

1. **ramparts:** embankments of earth or natural stone surrounding a town and serving as a defensive barrier.
2. **Bonifacio:** town on the extreme southern tip of the French island of Corsica. The Italian island of Sardinia is directly south, across the Strait of Bonifacio.
3. **vendetta** (ven de′ tə): feud in which the relations of a murdered or wronged person seek revenge on the attacker or members of his family.

with her, stood at the foot of the bed and howled, with her head turned towards her master and her tail between her legs. Neither of them stirred, neither the dog nor the old mother, who was now leaning over the body, gazing at it fondly, and silently shedding great tears. Still wearing his rough jacket, which was pierced and torn at the breast, the boy lay on his back as if asleep, but there was blood all about him—on his shirt, which had been torn open in order to expose the wound, on his waistcoat, trousers, face and hands. His beard and hair were matted with clots of blood.

The old mother began to talk to him, and at the sound of her voice the dog stopped howling.

"Never fear, never fear, you shall be avenged, my son, my little son, my poor child. You may sleep in peace. You shall be avenged, I tell you. You have your mother's word, and you know she never breaks it."

Slowly she bent down and pressed her cold lips to the dead lips of her son.

Sémillante resumed her howling, uttering a monotonous, long-drawn wail, heart-rending and terrible. And thus the two remained, the woman and the dog, till morning.

The next day Antoine Saverini was buried, and soon his name ceased to be mentioned in Bonifacio.

He had no brother, nor any near male relation. There was no man in the family who could take up the vendetta. Only his mother, his old mother, brooded over it.

From morning till night she could see, just across the straits, a white speck upon the coast. This was the little Sardinian village of Longosardo, where the Corsican bandits took refuge whenever the hunt for them grew too hot. They formed almost the entire population of the hamlet. In full view of their native shores they waited for a chance to return home and regain the bush. She knew that Nicolas Ravolati had sought shelter in that village.

All day long she sat at her window gazing at the opposite coast and thinking of her revenge, but what was she to do with no one to help her, and she herself so feeble and near her end? But she had promised, she had sworn by the dead body of her son, she could not forget, and she dared not delay. What was she to do? She could not sleep at night; she knew not a moment of rest or peace, but racked her brains unceasingly. Sémillante, asleep at her feet, would now and then raise her head and emit a piercing howl. Since her master had disappeared, this had become a habit; it was as if she were calling him, as if she, too, were inconsolable and preserved in her canine soul an ineffaceable[4] memory of the dead.

One night, when Sémillante began to whine, the old mother had an inspiration of savage, vindictive ferocity. She thought about it till morning. At daybreak she rose and betook herself to church. Prostrate on the stone floor, humbling herself before God, she besought Him to aid and support her, to lend to her poor, worn-out body the strength she needed to avenge her son.

Then she returned home. In the yard stood an old barrel with one end knocked in, in which was caught the rain-water from the eaves. She turned it over, emptied it, and fixed it to the ground with stakes and stones. Then she chained up Sémillante to this kennel and went into the house.

With her eyes fixed on the Sardinian coast, she walked restlessly up and down her room. He was over there, the murderer.

The dog howled all day and all night. The next morning, the old woman brought her a bowl of water, but no food, neither soup nor bread. Another day passed. Sémillante was worn out and slept. The next morning her eyes were gleaming, and her coat staring, and she tugged frantically at her chain. And again the old woman gave her nothing to eat. Maddened with hunger, Sémillante barked hoarsely. Another night went by.

At daybreak, the widow went to a neighbor and begged for two trusses[5] of straw. She took some old clothes that had belonged to her husband, stuffed them with straw to represent a human figure, and made a head out of a bundle of old rags. Then, in front of Sémillante's kennel, she fixed a stake in the ground and fastened the dummy to it in an upright position.

The dog looked at the straw figure in surprise and, although she was famished, stopped howling.

The old woman went to the pork butcher and bought a long piece of black pudding.[6] When she came home she lighted a wood fire in the yard, close to the kennel, and fried the black pudding. Sémillante

---

4. **ineffaceable** (in i fās′ i bəl): incapable of being erased.
5. **trusses**: bundles or packs.
6. **black pudding**: blood sausage.

bounded up and down in a frenzy, foaming at the mouth, her eyes fixed on the gridiron with its maddening smell of meat.

Her mistress took the steaming pudding and wound it like a tie round the dummy's neck. She fastened it on tightly with string as if to force it inwards. When she had finished she unchained the dog.

With one ferocious leap, Sémillante flew at the dummy's throat and with her paws on its shoulders began to tear it. She fell back with a portion of her prey between her paws, sprang at it again, slashing at the string with her fangs, tore away some scraps of food, dropped for a moment, and hurled herself at it in renewed fury. She tore away the whole face with savage rendings and reduced the neck to shreds.

Motionless and silent, with burning eyes, the old woman looked on. Presently she chained the dog up again. She starved her another two days, and then put her through the same strange performance. For three months she accustomed her to this method of attack, and to tear her meals away with her fangs. She was no longer kept on the chain. At a sign from her mistress, the dog would fly at the dummy's throat.

She learned to tear it to pieces even when no food was concealed about its throat. Afterwards she was always given the black pudding her mistress had cooked for her.

As soon as she caught sight of the dummy, Sémillante quivered with excitement and looked at her mistress, who would raise her finger and cry in a shrill voice, "Tear him."

One Sunday morning when she thought the time had come, the widow Saverini went to confession and communion, in an ecstasy of devotion. Then she disguised herself as a tattered old beggar man, and struck a bargain with a Sardinian fisherman, who took her and her dog across to the opposite shore.

She carried a large piece of black pudding wrapped in a cloth bag. Sémillante had been starved for two days and her mistress kept exciting her by letting her smell the savory[7] food.

The pair entered the village of Longosardo. The old woman hobbled along to a baker and asked for the house of Nicolas Ravolati. He had resumed his former occupation, which was that of a joiner,[8] and he was working alone in the back of his shop.

---

7. **savory:** tasty.
8. **joiner:** workman who makes furniture and interior woodwork.

The old woman threw open the door and called: "Nicolas, Nicolas!"

He turned round. Slipping the dog's lead, she cried: "Tear him! Tear him!"

The maddened dog flew at his throat. The man flung out his arms, grappled with the brute and they rolled on the ground together. For some moments he struggled, kicking the floor with his feet. Then he lay still, while Sémillante tore his throat to shreds.

Two neighbors, seated at their doors, remembered having seen an old beggar man emerge from the house and, at his heels, a lean black dog, which was eating, as it went along, some brown substance that its master was giving it.

By the evening the old woman had reached home again.

That night she slept well.

Discussion Questions

1. How would you describe the author's style? What effect does this style have upon this tale of vendetta?

2. Why do you suppose the author doesn't develop the character of Antoine Saverini or show his quarrel with Nicolas Ravolati?

3. What does the vendetta mean to the widow Saverini?

4. How does the widow Saverini set about accomplishing her vendetta? How does she herself react to what she does?

Suggestion for Writing

There are only three bits of dialog in this short tale, and there is no dramatization of the quarrel between Antoine Saverini and Nicolas Ravolati or the subsequent killing. Imagine what might have passed between these two men. Write a scene of dialog in play form that dramatizes their quarrel. (You will have to imagine the subject of the quarrel and the incident that touches it off.) The narrator says that Ravolati stabbed Saverini "treacherously"; how do you interpret that description? Include stage directions if you wish.

Edith Nesbit (1858-1924)

Edith Nesbit was the last of six children; her father died when she was three or four years old. She was sent to boarding school, which she hated, and later was taken to Europe to be educated. The family then resettled in London, where she met Hubert Bland, whom she married in 1880. Because of her husband's illness and financial setbacks, she began writing stories and articles to support her family. The success of a children's book, *The Treasure Seekers,* gave her family some financial security. Nesbit went on to write dozens of books of fiction for children. Bridging the Victorian and the Edwardian Ages, she was one of the first writers of children's books who thought it was enough to entertain her readers without having to teach them lessons as well. In addition, she wrote plays and verse for children and novels, plays, and verse for adults, some of these with her husband, Bland, or with other collaborators. The couple associated with well-known writers, painters, and politicians of their time. They were founding members of the socialist organization that later became the Fabian Society. Many of her books for children remain in print. One critic compared her to Lewis Carroll, commenting that she was able to "create a world of magic and inverted logic that was entirely her own."

No. 17

I yawned. I could not help it. But the flat, inexorable[1] voice went on.

"Speaking from the journalistic point of view—I may tell you, gentlemen, that I once occupied the position of advertisement editor to the *Bradford Woollen Goods Journal*—and speaking from that point of view, I hold the opinion that all the best ghost stories have been written over and over again; and if I were to leave the road and return to a literary career I should never be led away by ghosts. Realism's what's wanted nowadays, if you want to be up-to-date."

The large commercial[2] paused for breath.

"You never can tell with the public," said the lean, elderly traveler; "it's like in the fancy[3] business. You never know how it's going to be. Whether it's a clockwork ostrich or Sometite silk or a particular shape of shaded glass novelty or a tobacco-box got up to look like a raw chop, you never know your luck."

"That depends on who you are," said the dapper man in the corner by the fire. "If you've got the right push about you, you can make a thing go, whether it's a clockwork kitten or imitation meat, and with stories, I take it, it's just the same—realism or ghost stories. But the best ghost story would be the realest one, *I* think."

The large commercial had got his breath.

"I don't believe in ghost stories, myself," he was saying with earnest dullness; "but there was rather a queer thing happened to a second cousin of an aunt of mine by marriage—a very sensible woman with no nonsense about her. And the soul of truth and honor. I shouldn't have believed it if she had been one of your flighty, fanciful sort."

"Don't tell us the story," said the melancholy man who traveled in hardware; "you'll make us afraid to go to bed."

The well-meant effort failed. The large commercial went on, as I had known he would; his words overflowed his mouth, as his person overflowed his chair. I turned my mind to my own affairs, coming back to the commercial room in time to hear the summing up.

---

1. **inexorable:** unrelenting.
2. **commercial:** commercial traveler; traveling salesman.
3. **fancy:** ornament; trinket.

"The doors were all locked, and she was quite certain she saw a tall, white figure glide past her and vanish. I wouldn't have believed it if—" And so on *da capo*,⁴ from "if she hadn't been the second cousin" to the "soul of truth and honor."

I yawned again.

"Very good story," said the smart little man by the fire. He was a traveler, as the rest of us were; his presence in the room told us that much. He had been rather silent during dinner, and afterwards, while the red curtains were being drawn and the red and black cloth laid between the glasses and decanters and the mahogany, he had quietly taken the best chair in the warmest corner. We had got our letters written and the large traveler had been boring for some time before I even noticed that there was a best chair and that this silent, bright-eyed, dapper, fair man had secured it.

"Very good story," he said; "but it's not what I call realism. You don't tell us half enough, sir. You don't say when it happened or where, or the time of year, or what color your aunt's second cousin's hair was. Nor yet you don't tell us what it was she saw, nor what the room was like where she saw it, nor why she saw it, nor what happened afterwards. And I shouldn't like to breathe a word against anybody's aunt by marriage's cousin, first or second, but I must say I like a story about what a man's seen *himself*."

"So do I," the large commercial snorted, "when I hear it."

He blew his nose like a trumpet of defiance.

"But," said the rabbit-faced man, "we know nowadays, what with the advance of science and all that sort of thing, we know there aren't any such things as ghosts. They're hallucinations; that's what they are—hallucinations."

"Don't seem to matter what you call them," the dapper one urged. "If you see a thing that looks as real as you do yourself, a thing that makes your blood run cold and turns you sick and silly with fear—well, call it ghost, or call it hallucination, or call it Tommy Dodd;⁵ it isn't the *name* that matters."

The elderly commercial coughed and said, "You might call it another name. You might call it—"

---

4. *da capo:* (Italian) in music, repeat from the beginning.
5. **call it Tommy Dodd:** (British slang) call the winner or loser when tossing coins.

"No, you mightn't," said the little man, briskly; "not when the man it happened to had been a teetotal[6] Bond of Joy for five years and is to this day."

"Why don't you tell us the story?" I asked.

"I might be willing," he said, "if the rest of the company were agreeable. Only I warn you it's not that sort-of-a-kind-of-a-somebody-fancied-they-saw-a-sort-of-a-kind-of-a-something-sort of a story. No, sir. Everything I'm going to tell you is plain and straightforward and as clear as a time-table—clearer than some. But I don't much like telling it, especially to people who don't believe in ghosts."

Several of us said we did believe in ghosts. The heavy man snorted and looked at his watch. And the man in the best chair began.

"Turn the gas down a bit, will you? Thanks. Did any of you know Herbert Hatteras? He was on this road a good many years. No? Well, never mind. He was a good chap, I believe, with good teeth and a black whisker. But I didn't know him myself. He was before my time. Well, this that I'm going to tell you about happened at a certain commercial hotel. I'm not going to give it a name, because that sort of thing gets about, and, in every other respect it's a good house and reasonable, and we all have our living to get. It was just a good ordinary old-fashioned commercial hotel, as it might be this. And I've often used it since, though they've never put me in that room again. Perhaps they shut it up after what happened.

"Well, the beginning of it was, I came across an old school-fellow; in Boulter's Lock one Sunday it was, I remember. Jones was his name, Ted Jones. We both had canoes. We had tea at Marlow, and we got talking about this and that and old times and old mates; and do you remember Jim, and what's become of Tom, and so on. Oh, you know. And I happened to ask after his brother, Fred by name. And Ted turned pale and almost dropped his cup, and he said, 'You don't mean to say you haven't heard?' 'No,' says I, mopping up the tea he'd slopped over with my handkerchief. 'No; what?' I said.

"'It was horrible,' he said. 'They wired for me, and I saw him afterwards. Whether he'd done it himself or not, nobody knows; but they'd found him lying on the floor with his throat cut.' No cause could be assigned for the rash act, Ted told me. I asked him where it had hap-

---

6. teetotal: complete, total.

pened, and he told me the name of this hotel—I'm not going to name it. And when I'd sympathized with him and drawn him out about old times and poor old Fred being such a good old sort and all that, I asked him what the room was like. I always like to know what the places look like where things happen.

"No, there wasn't anything specially rum[7] about the room, only that it had a French bed with red curtains in a sort of alcove; and a large mahogany wardrobe as big as a hearse, with a glass door; and, instead of a swing-glass,[8] a carved, black-framed glass screwed up against the wall between the windows, and a picture of 'Belshazzar's Feast' over the mantelpiece. I beg your pardon?" He stopped, for the heavy commercial had opened his mouth and shut it again.

"I thought you were going to say something," the dapper man went on. "Well, we talked about other things and parted, and I thought no more about it till business brought me to—but I'd better not name the town either—and I found my firm had marked this very hotel—where poor Fred had met his death, you know—for me to put up at. And I had to put up there too, because of their addressing everything to me there. And, anyhow, I expect I should have gone there out of curiosity.

"No. I didn't believe in ghosts in those days. I was like you, sir." He nodded amiably to the large commercial.

"The house was very full, and we were quite a large party in the room—very pleasant company, as it might be tonight; and we got talking of ghosts—just as it might be us. And there was a chap in glasses, sitting just over there, I remember—an old man on the road, he was; and he said, just as it might be any of you, 'I don't believe in ghosts, but I wouldn't care to sleep in Number Seventeen, for all that'; and, of course, we asked him why. 'Because,' said he, very short, 'that's why.'

"But when we'd persuaded him a bit, he told us.

"'Because that's the room where chaps cut their throats,' he said. 'There was a chap called Bert Hatteras began it. They found him weltering[9] in his gore.[10] And since that every man that's slept there's been found with his throat cut.'

---

7. **rum:** (British slang) bad; unfortunate.
8. **swing-glass:** hinged mirror.
9. **weltering:** rolling about; wallowing.
10. **gore:** blood, especially clotted blood.

"I asked him how many had slept there. 'Well, only two beside the first,' he said; 'they shut it up then.' 'Oh, did they?' said I. 'Well, they've opened it again. Number Seventeen's my room!'

"I tell you those chaps looked at me.

"'But you aren't going to *sleep* in it?' one of them said. And I explained that I didn't pay half a dollar for a bedroom to keep awake in.

"'I suppose it's press of business has made them open it up again,' the chap in spectacles said. 'It's a very mysterious affair. There's some secret horror about that room that we don't understand,' he said, 'and I'll tell you another queer thing. Every one of those poor chaps was a commercial gentleman. That's what I don't like about it. There was Bert Hatteras—he was the first, and a chap called Jones—Frederick Jones, and then Donald Overshaw—a Scotchman he was, and traveled in child's underclothing.'

"Well, we sat there and talked a bit, and if I hadn't been a Bond of Joy, I don't know that I mightn't have exceeded, gentlemen—yes, positively exceeded; for the more I thought about it the less I liked the thought of Number Seventeen. I hadn't noticed the room particularly, except to see that the furniture had been changed since poor Fred's time. So I just slipped out, by and by, and I went out to the little glass case under the arch where the booking-clerk sits—just like here, that hotel was—and I said:—

"'Look here, miss; haven't you another room empty except seventeen?'

"'No, she said; 'I don't think so.'

"'Then what's that?' I said, and pointed to a key hanging on the board, the only one left.

"'Oh,' she said, 'that's sixteen.'

"'Anyone in sixteen?' I said. 'Is it a comfortable room?'

"'No,' said she. 'Yes; quite comfortable. It's next door to yours—much the same class of room.'

"'Then I'll have sixteen, if you've no objection.' I said, and went back to the others, feeling very clever.

"When I went up to bed I locked my door, and, though I didn't believe in ghosts, I wished seventeen wasn't next door to me, and I wished there wasn't a door between the two rooms, though the door was locked right enough and the key on my side. I'd only got the one candle besides the two on the dressing table, which I hadn't lighted;

and I got my collar and tie off before I noticed that the furniture in my new room was the furniture out of Number Seventeen; French bed with red curtains, mahogany wardrobe as big as a hearse, and the carved mirror over the dressing-table between the two windows, and 'Belshazzar's Feast' over the mantelpiece. So that, though I'd not got the *room* where the commercial gentlemen had cut their throats, I'd got the *furniture* out of it. And for a moment I thought that was worse than the other. When I thought of what that furniture could tell, if it could speak—

"It was a silly thing to do—but we're all friends here and I don't mind owning up—I looked under the bed and I looked inside the hearse-wardrobe and I looked in a sort of narrow cupboard there was, where a body could have stood upright—"

"A body?" I repeated.

"A man, I mean. You see, it seemed to me that either these poor chaps had been murdered by someone who hid himself in Number Seventeen to do it, or else there was something there that frightened them into cutting their throats; and upon my soul, I can't tell you which idea I liked least!"

He paused, and filled his pipe very deliberately. "Go on," someone said. And he went on.

"Now, you'll observe," he said, "that all I've told you up to the time of my going to bed that night's just hearsay. So I don't ask you to believe it—though the three coroners' inquests would be enough to stagger most chaps, I should say. Still, what I'm going to tell you now's *my* part of the story—what happened to me myself in that room."

He paused again, holding the pipe in his hand, unlighted.

There was a silence, which I broke.

"Well, what *did* happen?" I asked.

"I had a bit of a struggle with myself," he said. "I reminded myself it was not that room, but the next one that it had happened in. I smoked a pipe or two and read the morning paper, advertisements and all. And at last I went to bed. I left the candle burning, though, I own that."

"Did you sleep?" I asked.

"Yes. I slept. Sound as a top. I was awakened by a soft tapping on my door. I sat up. I don't think I've ever been so frightened in my life. But I made myself say, 'Who's there?' in a whisper. Heaven knows I never expected anyone to answer. The candle had gone out and it was pitch-dark. There was a quiet murmur and a shuffling sound outside. And no one answered. I tell you I hadn't expected anyone to. But I cleared my throat and cried out, 'Who's there?' in a real out-loud voice. And 'Me, sir,' said a voice. 'Shaving-water, sir; six o'clock, sir.'

"It was the chambermaid."

A movement of relief ran round our circle.

"I don't think much of your story," said the large commercial.

"You haven't heard it yet," said the story-teller, dryly. "It was six o'clock on a winter's morning, and pitch-dark. My train went at seven. I got up and began to dress. My one candle wasn't much use. I lighted the two on the dressing table to see to shave by. There wasn't any shaving-water outside my door, after all. And the passage was as black as a coal-hole. So I started to shave with cold water; one has to, sometimes, you know. I'd gone over my face and I was just going lightly round under my chin, when I saw something move in the looking-glass. I mean something that moved was reflected in the looking-glass. The big door of the wardrobe had swung open, and by a sort of double reflection I could see the French bed with the red curtains. On the edge of it sat a man in his shirt and trousers—a man with black hair and whiskers, with the most awful look of despair and fear on his face that I've ever seen or dreamt of. I stood paralyzed, watching him in the mirror. I could not have turned round to save my life. Suddenly he laughed. It was a horrid, silent laugh, and showed all his teeth. They were very white and even. And the next moment he had cut his throat from ear to ear, there before my eyes. Did you ever see a man cut his throat? The bed was all white before."

The story-teller had laid down his pipe, and he passed his hand over his face before he went on.

"When I could look round I did. There was no one in the room. The bed was as white as ever. Well, that's all," he said, abruptly, "except that now, of course, I understood how these poor chaps had come by their deaths. They'd all seen this horror—the ghost of the first poor chap, I suppose—Bert Hatteras, you know; and with the shock their hands must have slipped and their throats got cut before they could stop themselves. Oh! by the way, when I looked at my watch it was two o'clock; there hadn't been any chambermaid at all. I must have dreamed that. But I didn't dream the other. Oh! and one thing more. It was the same room. They hadn't changed the room, they'd only changed the number. *It was the same room!*"

"Look here," said the heavy man; "the room you've been talking about. *My* room's sixteen. And it's got the same furniture in it as what you describe, and the same picture and all."

"Oh, has it?" said the story-teller, a little uncomfortable, it seemed. "I'm sorry. But the cat's out of the bag now, and it can't be helped. Yes, it *was* this house I was speaking of. I suppose they've opened the room again. But you don't believe in ghosts; *you'll* be all right."

"Yes," said the heavy man, and presently got up and left the room.

"He's gone to see if he can get his room changed. You see if he hasn't," said the rabbit-faced man; "and I don't wonder."

The heavy man came back and settled into his chair.

"I could do with a drink," he said, reaching to the bell.

"I'll stand some punch, gentlemen, if you'll allow me," said our dapper story-teller. "I rather pride myself on my punch. I'll step out to the bar and get what I need for it."

"I thought he said he was a teetotaler,"[11] said the heavy traveler when he had gone. And then our voices buzzed like a hive of bees. When our story-teller came in again we turned on him—half-a-dozen of us at once—and spoke.

"One at a time," he said, gently. "I didn't quite catch what you said."

"We want to know," I said, "how it was—if seeing that ghost made all those chaps cut their throats by startling them when they were shaving—how was it *you* didn't cut *your* throat when you saw it?"

"I should have," he answered, gravely, "without the slightest doubt—I should have cut my throat, only," he glanced at our heavy friend, "I always shave with a safety razor. I travel in them," he added, slowly, and bisected[12] a lemon.

"But—but," said the large man, when he could speak through our uproar, "I've gone and given up my room."

"Yes," said the dapper man, squeezing the lemon; "I've just had my things moved into it. It's the best room in the house. I always think it worth while to take a little pains to secure it."

---

11. **teetotaler:** person who drinks no alcoholic beverages.
12. **bisected:** cut in half.

Discussion Questions

1. Describe the setting. What are all the salesmen doing at the hotel?

2. All the characters are referred to by descriptions, such as "the large commercial," "the rabbit-faced man," or "the dapper man," instead of by name. Why do you suppose the author chose not to assign them names?

3. How would you describe the tone of this story? What elements contribute to that tone?

4. Explain the punch line of the story.

5. Is this a ghost story, or not? Explain your answer.

Suggestion for Writing

Take on the character of one of the salesmen in this story; for example, the heavy man who gives up his room. Imagine that it is another evening in another hotel with a different group of salesmen sitting around telling each other stories. Tell what happened here. If you are a different character, relate how much you enjoyed the joke played by the dapper man upon the heavy man. If you are the heavy man, have you come to accept with good grace the joke played on you?

Edgar Allan Poe (1809–1849)

At the age of two, Edgar Poe was left an orphan and was taken in by the childless couple John and Frances Allan. Poe came to hate his foster father, a wealthy Virginia merchant who wanted him to become a merchant and disowned him when Poe spoke of a literary career. He attended a boarding school in England and then the University of Virginia for less than a year before enlisting in the U.S. Army. In 1830 Poe entered West Point but was dismissed within the year for "gross neglect of duty."

In 1835 Poe married his frail cousin, Virginia. Moving to Philadelphia, he began to enjoy some success with his stories, poems, and criticisms. Virginia died in 1847. Poe had already suffered from emotional troubles and poverty; now he became haunted by her memory. His sense of persecution—and his problems with alcohol—increased. Poe disappeared on a business trip and was found later on the streets of Baltimore, battered and drunk. After four days of delirium, he died.

Poe's poems often achieve an effect of a haunting, musical melancholy, as in "The Raven," one of his best-known works. He constructed his stories to create a single effect—usually horror, madness, irony, or revenge—upon the reader, piling incident upon incident to build to a stirring climax.

The Facts in the Case of M. Valdemar

Of course I shall not pretend to consider it any matter for wonder, that the extraordinary case of M.[1] Valdemar has excited discussion. It would have been a miracle had it not—especially under the circumstances. Through the desire of all parties concerned, to keep the affair from the public, at least for the present, or until we had farther opportunities for investigation—through our endeavors to effect this—a garbled or exaggerated account made its way into society, and became the source of many unpleasant misrepresentations; and, very naturally, of a great deal of disbelief.

It is now rendered necessary that I give the facts—as far as I comprehend them myself. The are, succinctly, these:

My attention, for the last three years, had been repeatedly drawn to the subject of Mesmerism;[2] and, about nine months ago, it occurred to me, quite suddenly, that in the series of experiments made hitherto, there had been a very remarkable and most unaccountable omission: —no person had as yet been mesmerized *in articulo mortis*.[3] It remained to be seen, first, whether, in such condition, there existed in the patient any susceptibility to the magnetic influence; secondly, whether, if any existed, it was impaired or increased by the condition; thirdly, to what extent, or for how long a period, the encroachments of Death might be arrested by the process. There were other points to be ascertained, but these most excited my curiosity—the last in especial, from the immensely important character of its consequences.

In looking around me for some subject by whose means I might test these particulars, I was brought to think of my friend, M. Ernest Valdemar, the well-known compiler of the "Bibliotheca Forensica," author (under the *nom de plume*[4] of Issachar Marx) of the Polish

---

1. **M.:** (French) abbreviation for Monsieur (Mister).
2. **Mesmerism:** hypnotism, so called after F. A. Mesmer (1734–1815), a physician who practiced it in connection with his theory of animal magnetism, or the power to influence others in a physical way.
3. *in articulo mortis:* (Latin) at the moment of death.
4. *nom de plume:* (French) pen name.

versions of "Wallenstein" and "Gargantua." M. Valdemar, who has resided principally at Harlem, N.Y. since the year 1939, is (or was) particularly noticeable for the extreme spareness of his person—his lower limbs much resembling those of John Randolph; and, also, for the whiteness of his whiskers, in violent contrast to the blackness of his hair—the latter, in consequence, being very generally mistaken for a wig. His temperament was markedly nervous, and rendered him a good subject for mesmeric experiment. On two or three occasions I had put him to sleep with little difficulty, but was disappointed in other results which his peculiar constitution had naturally led me to anticipate. His will was at no period positively, or thoroughly, under my control, and in regard to *clairvoyance*,[5] I could accomplish with him nothing to be relied upon. I always attributed my failure at these points to the disordered state of his health. For some months previous to my becoming acquainted with him, his physicians had declared him in a confirmed phthisis.[6] It was his custom, indeed, to speak calmly of his approaching dissolution, as of a matter neither to be avoided nor regretted.

When the ideas to which I have alluded first occurred to me, it was of course very natural that I should think of M. Valdemar. I knew the steady philosophy of the man too well to apprehend any scruples from him; and he had no relatives in America who would be likely to interfere. I spoke to him frankly upon the subject; and, to my surprise, his interest seemed vividly excited. I say to my surprise; for although he had always yielded his person freely to my experiments. He had never before given me any tokens of sympathy with what I did. His disease was of that character which would admit of exact calculation in respect to the epoch[7] of its termination in death; and it was finally arranged between us that he would send for me about twenty-four hours before the period announced by his physicians as that of his decease.

It is now rather more than seven months since I received, from M. Valdemar himself, the subjoined[8] note:

---

5. **clairvoyance:** extrasensory perception.
6. **phthisis** (thī´ sis): a wasting disease, such as tuberculosis of the lungs.
7. **epoch:** point in time.
8. **subjoined:** attached below.

> My Dear P—— ,
> You may as well come now. D—— and F——, are agreed that I cannot hold out beyond tomorrow midnight; and I think they have hit the time very nearly.
>
> Valdemar.

I received this note within half an hour after it was written, and in fifteen minutes more I was in the dying man's chamber. I had not seen him for ten days, and was appalled by the fearful alteration which the brief interval had wrought in him. His face wore a leaden hue; the eyes were utterly lustreless; and the emaciation was so extreme, that the skin had been broken through by cheekbones. His expectoration[9] was excessive. The pulse was barely perceptible. He retained, nevertheless, in a very remarkable manner, both his mental power and a certain degree of physical strength. He spoke with distinctness—took some palliative medicines without aid—and, when I entered the room, was occupied in penciling memoranda in a pocket-book. He was propped up in the bed by pillows. Doctors D—— and F—— were in attendance.

After pressing Valdemar's hand, I took these gentlemen aside, and obtained from them a minute account of the patient's condition. The left lung had been for eighteen months in a semi-osseous or cartilaginous state, and was of course, entirely useless for all purposes of vitality. The right, in its upper portion, was also partially, if not thoroughly, ossified, while the lower region was merely a mass of purulent tubercles,[10] running one into another. Several extensive perforations existed; and, at one point, permanent adhesion of the ribs had taken place. These appearances in the right lobe were of comparatively recent date. The ossification had proceeded with very unusual rapidity; no sign of it had been discovered a month before, and the adhesion had only been observed during the three previous days. Independently of the phthisis, the patient was suspected of aneurysm of the aorta; but on this point the osseous symptoms rendered an exact diagnosis impossible. It was the opinion of both physicians that M. Valdemar would die about midnight on the morrow (Sunday). It was then seven o'clock on Saturday evening.

On quitting the invalid's bed-side to hold conversation with myself, D—— and F—— had bidden him a final farewell. It had not been

---

9. **expectoration:** saliva; spit.
10. **purulent tubercles:** nodules or swellings discharging pus.

their intention to return; but, at my request, they agreed to look in upon the patient about ten the next night.

When they had gone, I spoke freely with M. Valdemar on the subject of his approaching dissolution, as well as, more particularly, of the experiment proposed. He still professed himself quite willing and even anxious to have it made, and urged me to commence it at once. A male and female nurse were in attendance; but I did not feel myself altogether at liberty to engage in a task of this character with no more reliable witnesses than these people, in case of sudden accident, might prove. I therefore postponed operations until about eight the next night, when the arrival of a medical student, with whom I had some acquaintance (Mr. Theodore L— —l), relieved me from farther embarrassment. It had been my design, originally, to wait for the physicians; but I was induced to proceed, first, by the urgent entreaties of M. Valdmar, and secondly, by my conviction that I had not a moment to lose, as he was evidently sinking fast.

Mr. L— —l was so kind as to accede to my desire that he would take notes of all that occurred; and it is from his memoranda that what I now have to relate is, for the most part, either condensed or copied *verbatim*.

It wanted about five minutes of eight when, taking the patient's hand, I begged him to state, as distinctly as he could, to Mr. L— —l, whether he (M. Valdemar) was entirely willing that I should make the experiment of mesmerizing him in his then condition.

He replied feebly, yet quite audibly, "Yes, I wish to be mesmerized"—adding immediately afterwards, "I fear you have deferred it too long."

While he spoke thus, I commenced the passes which I had already found most effectual in subduing him. He was evidently influenced with the first lateral stroke of my hand across his forehead; but although I exerted all my powers, no farther perceptible effect was induced until some minutes after ten o'clock, when Doctors D— — and F— — called, according to appointment. I explained to them, in a few words, what I designed, and as they opposed no objection, saying that the patient was already in the death agony, I proceeded without hesitation—exchanging, however, the lateral passes for downward ones, and directing my gaze entirely into the right eye of the sufferer.

By this time his pulse was imperceptible and his breathing was stertorous,[11] and at intervals of half a minute.

This condition was nearly unaltered for a quarter of an hour. At the expiration of this period, however, a natural although a very deep sigh escaped the bosom of the dying man, and the stertorous breathing ceased—that is to say, its stertorousness was no longer apparent; the intervals were undiminished. The patient's extremities were of an icy coldness.

At five minutes before eleven, I perceived unequivocal signs of the mesmeric influence. The glassy roll of the eye was changed for that expression of uneasy inward examination which is never seen except in cases of sleep-waking, and which it is quite impossible to mistake. With a few rapid lateral passes I made the lids quiver, as in incipient sleep, and with a few more I closed them altogether. I was not satisfied, however, with this, but continued the manipulations vigorously, and with the fullest exertion of the will, until I had completely stiffened the limbs of the slumberer, after placing them in a seemingly easy position. The legs were at full length; the arms nearly so, and reposed on the bed at a moderate distance from the loins. The head was very slightly elevated.

When I had accomplished this, it was fully midnight, and I requested the gentlemen present to examine M. Valdemar's condition. After a few experiments, they admitted him to be in an unusually perfect state of mesmeric trance. The curiosity of both the physicians was greatly excited. Dr. D— — resolved at once to remain with the patient all night, while Dr. F— —took leave with a promise to return at daybreak. Mr. L— —l and the nurses remained.

We left M. Valdemar entirely undisturbed until about three o'clock in the morning, when I approached him and found him in precisely the same condition as when Dr. F— — went away—that is to say, he lay in the same position; the pulse was imperceptible; the breathing was gentle (scarcely noticeable, unless through the application of a mirror to the lips); the eyes were closed naturally; and the limbs were as rigid and as cold as marble. Still the general appearance was certainly not that of death.

As I approached M. Valdemar I made a kind of half effort to influence his right arm into pursuit of my own, as I passed the latter gently

---

11. **stertorous:** loud and labored.

to and fro above his person. In such experiments with this patient, I had never perfectly succeeded before, and assuredly I had little thought of succeeding now; but to my astonishment, his arm very readily, although feebly, followed every direction I assigned it with mine. I determined to hazard a few words of conversation.

"M. Valdemar," I said, "are you asleep?" He made no answer, but I perceived a tremor about the lips, and was thus induced to repeat the question again and again. At its third repetition, his whole frame was agitated by a very slight shivering; the eyelids unclosed themselves so far as to display a white line of a ball; the lips moved sluggishly, and from between them, in a barely audible whisper, issued the words:

"Yes;—asleep now. Do not wake me!—Let me die so!"

I here felt the limbs and found them as rigid as ever. The right arm, as before, obeyed the direction of my hand. I questioned the sleep-waker again:

"Do you still feel pain in the breast, M. Valdemar?"

The answer now was immediate, but even less audible than before:

"No pain—I am dying."

I did not think it advisable to disturb him farther just then, and nothing more was said or done until the arrival of Dr. F— —, who came a little before sunrise, and expressed unbounded astonishment at finding the patient still alive. After feeling the pulse and applying a mirror to the lips, he requested me to speak to the sleep-waker again. I did so, saying:

"M. Valdemar, do you still sleep?"

As before, some minutes elapsed ere a reply was made; and during the interval the dying man seemed to be collecting his energies to speak. At my fourth repetition of the question, he said very faintly, almost inaudibly:

"Yes; still asleep—dying."

It was now the opinion, or rather the wish, of the physicians, that M. Valdemar should be suffered to remain undisturbed in his present apparently tranquil condition, until death should supervene—and this, it was generally agreed, must now take place within a few minutes. I concluded, however, to speak to him once more, and merely repeated my previous question.

While I spoke, there came a marked change over the countenance of the sleep-waker. The eyes rolled themselves slowly open, the pupils disappearing upwardly; the skin generally assumed a cadaverous hue, resembling not so much parchment as white paper; and the circular hectic[12] spots which, hitherto, had been strongly defined in the center of each cheek, *went out* at once. I use this expression, because the suddenness of their departure put me in mind of nothing so much as the extinguishment of a candle by a puff of the breath. The upper lip, at the same time, writhed itself away from the teeth, which it had previously covered completely; while the lower jaw fell with an audible jerk, leaving the mouth widely extended, and disclosing in full view the swollen and blackened tongue. I presume no member of the party then present had been unaccustomed to death-bed horrors; but so hideous beyond conception was the appearance of M. Valdemar at this moment, that there was a general shrinking back from the region of the bed.

I now feel that I have reached a point of this narrative at which every reader will be startled into positive belief. It is my business, however, simply to proceed.

There was no longer the faintest sign of vitality in M. Valdemar; and concluding him to be dead, we were consigning him to the charge of the nurses, when a strong vibratory motion was observable in the tongue. This continued for perhaps a minute. At the expiration of this period, there issued from the distended and motionless jaws a voice—such as it would be madness in me to attempt describing. There are, indeed, two or three epithets[13] which might be considered as applicable to it in part; I might say, for example, that the sound was harsh, and broken and hollow; but the hideous whole is indescribable, for the simple reason that no similar sounds have ever jarred upon the ear of humanity. There were two particulars, nevertheless, which I thought then, and still think, might fairly be stated as characteristic of the intonation—as well adapted to convey some idea of its unearthly peculiarity. In the first place, the voice seemed to reach our ears—at least mine—from a vast distance, or from some deep cavern within the earth. In the second place, it impressed me (I fear, indeed that it will be impossible to make myself comprehended) as gelatinous or glutinous matters impress the sense of touch.

---

12. **hectic:** red or flushed, as with fever.
13. **epithets:** descriptive words or phrases.

I have spoken both of "sound" and of "voice." I mean to say that the sound was one of distinct—of even wonderfully, thrillingly distinct—syllabification. M. Valdemar *spoke*—obviously in reply to the question I had propounded to him a few minutes before. I had asked him, it will be remembered, if he still slept. He now said:

"Yes;—no;—*I have been* sleeping—and now—now—*I am dead.*"

No person present even affected to deny, or attempted to repress, the unutterable, shuddering horror which these few words, thus uttered, were so calculated to convey. Mr. L— —l (the student) swooned. The nurses immediately left the chamber, and could not be induced to return. My own impressions I would not pretend to render intelligible to the reader. For nearly an hour, we busied ourselves, silently—without the utterance of a word—in endeavors to revive Mr. L— —l. When he came to himself, we addressed ourselves again to an investigation of Valdemar's condition.

It remained in all respects as I have last described it, with the exception that the mirror no longer afforded evidence of respiration. An attempt to draw blood from the arm failed. I should mention, too, that this limb was no farther subject to my will. I endeavored in vain to make it follow the direction of my hand. The only real indication, indeed, of the mesmeric influence, was now found in the vibratory movement of the tongue, whenever I addressed M. Valdemar a question. He seemed to be making an effort to reply, but had no longer sufficient volition.[14] To queries put to him by any other person than myself he seemed utterly insensible—although I endeavored to place each member of the company in mesmeric *rapport* with him. I believe that I have now related all that's necessary to an understanding of the sleep-waker's state at this epoch. Other nurses were procured; and at ten o'clock I left the house with the two physicians and Mr. L— —l.

In the afternoon we all called again to see the patient. His condition remained precisely the same. We had now some discussion as to the propriety and feasibility of awakening him; but we had little difficulty in agreeing that no good purpose would be served by so doing. It was evident that, so far, death (or what is usually termed death) had been arrested by the mesmeric process. It seemed clear to us all that to awaken M. Valdemar would be merely to insure his instant, or at least his speedy dissolution.

---

14. **volition:** willpower.

From this period until the close of last week—*an interval of nearly seven months*—we continued to make daily calls at M. Valdemar's house, accompanied, now and then, by medical and other friends. All this time the sleep-waker remained *exactly* as I have last described him. The nurses' attentions were continual.

It was on Friday last that we finally resolved to make the experiment of awakening, or attempting to awaken him; and it is the (perhaps) unfortunate result of this latter experiment which has given rise to so much discussion in private circles—to so much of what I cannot help thinking unwarranted popular feeling.

For the purpose of relieving M. Valdemar from the mesmeric trance, I made use of the customary passes, these for a time, were unsuccessful. The first indication of revival was afforded by a partial descent of the iris. It was observed, as especially remarkable that this lowering of the pupil was accompanied by the profuse out-flowing of a yellowish ichor[15] (from beneath the lids) of a pungent and highly offensive odor.

It was now suggested that I should attempt to influence the patient's arm, as heretofore. I made the attempt and failed. Dr. F—— then intimated a desire to have me put a question. I did so, as follows:

"M. Valdemar, can you explain to us what are your feelings or wishes now?"

There was an instant return of the hectic circles on the cheeks; the tongue quivered, or rather rolled violently in the mouth (although the jaws and lips remained rigid as before); and at length the same hideous voice which I have already described, broke forth:

"For God's sake!—quick!—quick!—put me to sleep—or, quick!—waken me!—quick!—*I say to you that I am dead!*"

I was thoroughly unnerved, and for an instant remained undecided what to do. At first I made an endeavor to re-compose the patient; but, failing in this through total abeyance[16] of the will, I retraced my steps and as earnestly struggled to awaken him. In this attempt I soon saw that I should be successful—or at least soon fancied that my success would be complete—and I am sure that all in the room were prepared to see the patient awaken.

For what really occurred, however, it is quite impossible that any human being could have been prepared.

---

15. **ichor** (ī´ kôr): a watery discharge.
16. **abeyance** (ə bā´ əns): suspension; inactivity.

As I rapidly made the mesmeric passes, amid ejaculations of "dead! dead!" absolutely *bursting* from the tongue and not from the lips of the sufferer, his whole frame at once—within the space of a single minute, or even less, shrunk—crumbled—absolutely *rotted* away beneath my hands. Upon the bed, before that whole company, there lay a nearly liquid mass of loathsome—of detestable putrescence.[17]

---

17. putrescence (pyu tres´ ns): rotting matter.

Discussion Questions

1. Explain the experiment the narrator proposes. What three things, especially, does he hope to learn from it?

2. Why is Ernest Valdemar a good candidate for this experiment?

3. Why is the narrator not willing to begin the experiment until the medical student, Theodore L— —l, arrives?

4. Describe M. Valdemar's condition while he is in the "mesmeric trance."

5. Explain what happens at the end.

Suggestion for Writing

Imagine that you are the medical student, Theodore L— —l, or the male or female nurse who is in attendance on that final night—as you have been continually for seven months. Write a journal entry of what you witnessed. You needn't go into any medical detail; just be personal and immediate. Include, if you wish, your personal feelings about the experiment and about the man (the narrator; give him a name) who conducts it.

Robert Louis Stevenson (1850–1894)

Robert Louis Stevenson was born in Edinburgh, Scotland, into a strict and religious family. He attended various private schools, but his formal education was much interrupted by illness. His father—a famous lighthouse builder—wanted him to follow in the family tradition as an engineer, but young Stevenson was more interested in writing. He spent some time in an artists' colony in France, where he met the woman he would marry years later; during this time his literary career began with essays published in various magazines.

His novels *Treasure Island* (first published as a serial in a young people's magazine), *Dr. Jekyll and Mr. Hyde,* and *Kidnapped* enjoyed great success. He traveled twice to America; then he traveled with his wife, mother, and stepson to the South Seas, where they settled on the island of Samoa. Though ill with the tuberculosis that would eventually kill him, Stevenson worked industriously. He became known locally as *Tusitala* ("the teller of tales"), and he made use of local settings and legends for some of the stories in *Island Nights Entertainments,* part of his *New Arabian Nights* series of collections of tales.

The Isle of Voices

Keola was married with Lehua, daughter of Kalamake, the wise man of Molokai,[1] and he kept his dwelling with the father of his wife. There was no man more cunning than that prophet; he read the stars, he could divine[2] by the bodies of the dead, and by the means of evil creatures: he could go alone into the highest parts of the mountain, into the region of the hobgoblins, and there he would lay snares to entrap the spirits of the ancient.

For this reason no man was more consulted in all the Kingdom of Hawaii. Prudent people bought, and sold, and married, and laid out their lives by his counsels; and the King had him twice to Kona to seek the treasures of Kamehameha.[3] Neither was any man more feared: of his enemies, some had dwindled in sickness by virtue of his incantations, and some had been spirited away, the life and the clay both, so that folk looked in vain for so much as a bone of their bodies. It was rumored that he had the art of the gift of the old heroes. Men had seen him at night upon the mountains, stepping from one cliff to the next; they had seen him walking in the high forest, and his head and shoulders were above the trees.

This Kalamake was a strange man to see. He was come of the best blood in Molokai and Maui, of a pure descent; and yet he was more white to look upon than any foreigner: his hair the color of dry grass, and his eyes red and very blind, so that "Blind as Kalamake, that can see across tomorrow," was a byword in the islands.

Of all of these doings of his father-in-law, Keola knew a little by the common repute, a little more he suspected, and the rest he ignored. But there was one thing troubled him. Kalamake was a man that spared for nothing whether to eat or to drink, or to wear; and for all he paid in bright new dollars. "Bright as Kalamake's dollars," was another saying in the Eight Isles. Yet he neither sold, nor planned, nor

---

1. Molokai: one of the eight principle islands in the chain of Pacific islands that at one time formed the Kingdom of Hawaii. Maui, mentioned later, is another.
2. divine: prophesy.
3. Kamehameha: chief who united the Hawaiian islands in 1795 and became its first king. At the time of the story, Kamehameha V, who ruled 1863–1872, was in power.

took hire—only now and then from his sorceries—and there was no source conceivable for so much silver coin.

It chanced one day Keola's wife was gone upon a visit to Kaunakakai, on the lee[4] side of the island, and the men were forth at the sea fishing. But Keola was an idle dog, and he lay in the verandah and watched the surf beat on the shore and the birds fly about the cliff. It was a chief thought with him always—the thought of the bright dollars. When he lay down to bed he would be wondering why there were so many, and when he woke at morn he would be wondering why they were all new; and the thing was never absent from his mind. But this day of all days he made sure in his heart of some discovery. For it seems he had observed the place where Kalamake kept his treasure, which was a lock-fast desk against the parlor wall, under the print of Kamehameha the Fifth, and a photograph of Queen Victoria with her crown; and it seems again that, no later than the night before, he found occasion to look in, and behold the bag lay there empty. And this was the day of the steamer; he could see her smoke off Kalaupapa; and she must soon arrive with a month's goods, tinned salmon and gin, and all manner of rare luxuries for Kalamake.

"Now if he can pay for his goods to-day," Keola thought, "I shall know for certain that the man is a warlock, and the dollars come out of the Devil's pocket."

While he was so thinking, there was his father-in-law behind him, looking vexed.

"Is that the steamer?" he asked.

"Yes," said Keola. "She has but to call at Pelekunu, and then she will be here."

"There is no help for it then," returned Kalamake, "and I must take you in my confidence, Keola, for the lack of anyone better. Come here within the house."

So they stepped together into the parlor, which was a very fine room, papered and hung with prints, and furnished with a rocking chair and a table and a sofa in the European style. There was a shelf of books besides, and a family Bible in the midst of the table, and the lock-fast writing desk against the wall, so that anyone could see it was the house of a man of substance.

---

4. **lee:** sheltered from the weather.

Kalamake made Keola close the shutters of the windows, while he himself locked all the doors and set open the lid of the desk. From this he brought forth a pair of necklaces hung with charms and shells, a bundle of dried herbs, and the dried leaves of trees, and a green branch of palm.

"What I am about," said he, "is a thing beyond wonder. The men of old were wise; they wrought marvels, and this among the rest; but that was at night, in the dark, under the fit stars and in the desert. The same will I do here in my own house and under the plain eye of day."

So saying, he put the Bible under the cushion of the sofa so that it was all covered, brought out from the same place a mat of a wonderfully fine texture, and heaped the herbs and leaves on sand in a tin pan. And then he and Keola put on the necklaces and took their stand upon the opposite corners of the room.

"The time comes," said the warlock,[5] "be not afraid."

With that he set flame to the herbs, and began to mutter and wave the branch of palm. At first the light was dim because of the closed shutters; but the herbs caught strongly afire, and the flames beat upon Keola, and the room glowed with the burning, and next the smoke rose and made his head swim and his eyes darken, and the sound of Kalamake muttering ran in his ears. And suddenly, to the mat on which they were standing came a snatch or twitch, that seemed to be more swift than lightning. In the same wink the room was gone and the house, the breath all beaten from Keola's body. Volumes of light rolled upon his eyes and head, and he found himself transported to a beach of the sea, under a strong sun, with a great surf roaring; he and the warlock standing there on the same mat, speechless, gasping and grasping at one another, and passing their hands before their eyes.

"What was this?" cried Keola, who came to himself the first, because he was the younger. "The pang of it was like death."

"It matters not," panted Kalamake. "It is now done."

"And in the name of God, where are we?" cried Keola.

"That is not the question," replied the sorcerer. "Being here we have matter in our hands, and that we must attend to. Go, while I recover my breath, into the borders of the wood, and bring me the leaves of such and such a herb, and such and such a tree, which you will find to grow there plentifully—three handfuls of each. And be speedy. We

---

5. **warlock:** sorcerer.

must be home again before the steamer comes; it would seem strange if we had disappeared." And he sat on the sand and panted.

Keola went up the beach, which was of shining sand and coral, strewn with singular shells; and he thought in his heart—

"How do I not know this beach? I will come here again and gather shells."

In front of him was a line of palms against the sky; not just the palms of the Eight Islands, but tall and fresh and beautiful, and hanging out withered fans like gold among the green, and he thought in his heart—

"It is strange I should not have found this grove. I will come here again, when it is warm, to sleep." And he thought, "How warm it has grown suddenly!" For it was winter in Hawaii, and the day had been chill. And he thought also, "Where are the gray mountains? And where is the high cliff with the hanging forest and the wheeling birds?" And the more he considered, the less he might conceive in what quarter of the islands he was fallen.

In the border of the grove, where it met the beach, the herb was growing, but the tree further back. Now, as Keola went toward the tree, he was aware of a young woman who had nothing on her body but a belt of leaves.

"Well!" thought Keola, "they are not very particular about their dress in this part of the country." And he paused, supposing she would observe him and escape; and seeing that she still looked before her, stood and hummed aloud. Up she leaped at the sound. Her face was ashen, she looked this way and that, and her mouth gaped with the terror of her soul. But it was a strange thing that her eyes did not rest upon Keola.

"Good day," said he. "You need not be so frightened; I will not eat you." And had scarce opened his mouth before the young woman fled into the bush.

"These are strange manners," thought Keola. And, not thinking what he did, ran after her.

As she ran, the girl kept crying in some speech that was not practiced in Hawaii, yet some of the words were the same, and he knew she kept calling and warning others. And presently he saw more people running—men, women, and children, one with another, all running and crying like people at a fire. And with that he began to grow afraid himself, and returned to Kalamake bringing the leaves. Then he told what he had seen.

"You must pay no heed," said Kalamake. "All this is like a dream and shadows. All will disappear and be forgotten."

"It seemed none saw me," said Keola.

"And none do," replied the sorcerer. "We walk here in the broad sun invisible by reasons of these charms. Yet they hear us, and therefore it is well to speak softly, as I do."

With that he made a circle round the mat with stones, and in the midst he set the leaves.

"It will be your part," said he, "to keep the leaves alight, and feed the fire slowly. While they blaze (which is but for a little moment) I must do my errand; and before the ashes blacken, the same power that brought us carries us away. Be ready now with the match; and do you call me in good time lest the flames burn out and I be left."

As soon as the leaves caught, the sorcerer leaped like a deer out of the circle, and began to race along the beach like a hound that has been bathing. As he ran, he kept stooping to snatch shells, and it seemed to Keola that they glittered as he took them. The leaves blazed with a clear flame that consumed them swiftly; and presently Keola had but a handful left, and the sorcerer was far off, running and stopping.

"Back!" cried Keola. "Back! The leaves are near done."

At that Kalamake turned, and if he had run before, now he flew. But fast as he ran, the leaves burned faster. The flame was ready to expire when, with a great leap, he bounded on the mat. The wind of his leaping blew it out; and with that the beach was gone, and the sun and the sea, and they stood once more in the dimness of the shuttered parlor, and were once more shaken and blinded; and on the mat between them lay a pile of shining dollars. Keola ran to the shutters; and there was the steamer tossing in the swell close in.

The same night Kalamake took his son-in-law apart, and gave him five dollars in his hand.

"Keola," said he, "if you are a wise man (which I am doubtful of) you will think you slept this afternoon on the verandah, and dreamed as you were sleeping. I am a man of few words, and I have for my helpers people of short memories."

Never a word more said Kalamake, nor referred again to that affair. But it ran all the while in Keola's head—if he were lazy before, he would now do nothing.

"Why should I work," thought he, "when I have a father-in-law who makes dollars of sea-shells?"

Presently his share was spent. He spent it all upon fine clothes. And then he was sorry.

"For," thought he, "I had done better to have bought a concertina, with which I might have entertained myself all day long." And then he began to grow vexed with Kalamake.

"This man has the soul of a dog," thought he. "He can gather dollars when he pleases on the beach, and he leaves me to pine for a concertina! Let him beware: I am no child. I am as cunning as he, and hold his secret." With that he spoke to his wife Lehua, and complained of her father's manners.

"I would let my father be," said Lehua. "He is a dangerous man to cross."

"I care that for him!" cried Keola and snapped his fingers. "I have him by the nose. I can make him do what I please." And he told Lehua the story.

But she shook her head.

"You may do what you like," said she; "but as sure as you thwart my father, you will be no more heard of. Think of this person and that person; think of Hua, who was a noble of the House of Representatives, and went to Honolulu every year; and not a bone or a hair of him was found. Remember Kamau, and how he wasted to a thread, so that his wife lifted him with one hand. Keola, you are a baby in my father's hands; he will take you with his thumb and finger and eat you like a shrimp."

Now Keola was truly afraid of Kalamake, but he was vain too; and these words of his wife's incensed him.

"Very well," said he, "if that is what you think of me, I will show how much you are deceived." And he went straight to where his father-in-law was sitting in the parlor.

"Kalamake," said he, "I want a concertina."

"Do you, indeed?" said Kalamake.

"Yes," said he, "and I may as well tell you plainly, I mean to have it. A man who picks up dollars on the beach can certainly afford a concertina."

"I had no idea you had so much spirit," replied the sorcerer. "I thought you were a timid, useless lad, and I cannot describe how much pleased I am to find I was mistaken. Now I begin to think I may have found an assistant and successor in my difficult business. A concertina? You shall have the best in Honolulu. And tonight, as soon as it is dark, you and I will go and find the money."

"Shall we return to the beach?" asked Keola.

"No, no!" replied Kalamake; "you must begin to learn more of my secrets. Last time I taught you to pick shells; this time I shall teach you to catch fish. Are you strong enough to launch Pili's boat?"

"I think I am," returned Keola. "But why should we not take your own, which is afloat already?"

"I have a reason which you will understand thoroughly before tomorrow," said Kalamake. "Pili's boat is the better suited for my purpose. So, if you please, let us meet there as soon as it is dark; and in the meanwhile, let us keep our own counsel, for there is no excuse to let the family into our business."

Honey is not more sweet than was the voice of Kalamake, and Keola could scarce contain his satisfaction.

"I might have had my concertina weeks ago," thought he, "and there is nothing needed in this world but a little courage."

Presently he spied Lehua weeping, and was half in a mind to tell her all was well.

"But no," thinks he; "I shall wait till I can show her the concertina; we shall see what the chit[6] will do then. Perhaps she will understand in the future that her husband is a man of some intelligence."

As soon as it was dark father and son-in-law launched Pili's boat and set the sail. There was a great sea, and it blew strong from the leeward; but the boat was swift and light and dry, and skimmed the waves. The wizard had a lantern, which he lit and held with his finger through the ring; and the two sat in the stern and smoked cigars, of which Kalamake had always a provision, and spoke like friends of magic and the great sums of money they could make by its exercise, and what they should buy first, and what second; and Kalamake talked like a father.

Presently he looked all about, and above him at the stars, and back at the island, which was already three parts sunk under the sea, and he seemed to consider ripely his position.

"Look!" says he, "there is Molokai already far behind us, and Maui like a cloud; and by the bearing of these three stars I know I am come where I desire. This part of the sea is called the Sea of the Dead. It is in this place extraordinarily deep, and the floor is all covered with the bones of men, and in the holes of this part gods and goblins keep their

---

6. chit: impudent girl.

habitation. The flow of the sea is to the north, stronger than a shark can swim, and any man who shall here be thrown out of a ship it bears away like a wild horse into the uttermost ocean. Presently he is spent and goes down, and his bones are scattered with the rest, and the gods devour his spirit."

Fear came on Keola at the words, and he looked, and by the light of the stars and the lantern, the warlock seemed to change.

"What ails you?" cried Keola, quick and sharp.

"It is not I who am ailing," said the wizard; "but there is one here very sick."

With that he changed his grasp upon the lantern, and, behold! as he drew his finger from the ring, the finger stuck and the ring was burst, and his hand was grown to be of the bigness of three.

At that sight Keola screamed and covered his face.

But Kalamake held up the lantern. "Look rather at my face," said he—and his head was huge as a barrel, and still he grew and grew as a cloud grows on a mountain, and Keola sat before him screaming, and the boat raced on the great seas.

"And now," said the wizard, "what do you think about that concertina? and are you sure you would not rather have a flute? No?" says he; "that is well, for I do not like my family to be changeable of purpose. But I begin to think that I had better get out of this paltry boat, for my bulk swells to a very absurd degree, and if we are not the more careful, she will presently be swamped."

With that he threw his legs over the side. Even as he did so, the greatness of the man grew thirty-fold and forty-fold as swift as sight or thinking, so that he stood in the deep sea to the armpits, and his head and shoulders rose like a high isle, and the swell beat and burst upon his bosom, as it beats and breaks against a cliff. The boat ran still to the north, but he reached out his hand, and took the gunwale by the finger and thumb, and broke the side like a biscuit, and Keola was spilled into the sea. And the pieces of the boat the sorcerer crushed in the hollow of his hand and flung miles away into the night.

"Excuse me for taking the lantern," said he, "for I have a long wade before me, and the land is far, and the bottom of the sea uneven, and I feel the bones under my toes."

And he turned and went off walking with great strides; and as often as Keola sank in the trough he could see him no longer; but as often as he was heaved upon the crest, there he was striding and dwindling, and he held the lamp high over his head, and the waves broke white about him as he went.

Since first the islands were fished out of the sea, there was never a man so terrified as this Keola. He swam indeed, but he swam as puppies swim when they are cast in to drown, and knew not wherefore. He could not but think of the hugeness of the swelling of the warlock, of that face which was as great as a mountain, of those shoulders that were broad as an isle, and of the seas that beat on them in vain. He thought, too, of the concertina—and shame took hold upon him; and of the dead men's bones, and fear shook him.

Of a sudden he was aware of something dark against the stars that tossed, and a light below, and a brightness of the cloven sea; and he heard speech of men. He cried out aloud and a voice answered, and in a twinkling the bows of a ship hung above him on a wave like a thing balanced, and swooped down. He caught with his two hands in the chains of her, and the next moment was buried in the rushing seas, and the next hauled on board by seamen.

They gave him gin and biscuits and dry clothes, and asked him how he came where they found him, and whether the light they had seen was the lighthouse, Lae o Ka Laau. But Keola knew white men are like children and only believe their own stories; so about himself he told them what he pleased, and as for the light (which was Kalamake's lantern) he vowed he had seen none.

This ship was a schooner bound for Honolulu, and then to trade in the low islands; and by a very good chance for Keola she had lost a man off the bowsprit in a squall. It was no use talking. Keola durst not stay in the Eight Islands. Word goes so quickly, and all men are so fond to talk and carry news, that if he hid in the north end of Kauai or in the south end of Kaü, the wizard would have wind of it before a month, and he must perish. So he did what seemed most prudent, and shipped sailor in the place of the man who had been drowned.

In some ways the ship was a good place. The food was extraordinarily rich and plenty, with biscuits and salt beef every day, and pea soup and puddings made of flour and suet twice a week, so that Keola grew fat. The captain also was a good man, and the crew no worse than other whites. The trouble was the mate, who was the most difficult man to please Keola had ever met with, and beat and cursed him daily, both for what he did and what he did not. The blows that he dealt were very sore, for he was strong; and the words he used were very unpalatable, for Keola was come of a good family and accustomed to respect. And what was the worst of all, whenever Keola found a chance to sleep, there was the mate awake and stirring him up with a rope's end. Keola saw that it would never do; and he made up his mind to run away.

They were about a month out from Honolulu when they made the land. It was a fine starry night, the sea was smooth as well as the sky fair; it blew a steady trade; and there was the island on their weather bow, a ribbon of palm trees lying flat along the sea. The captain and the mate looked at it with the night glass, and named the name of it, and talked of it, beside the wheel where Keola was steering. It seemed it was an isle where no traders came. By the captain's way, it was an isle besides where no man dwelt; but the mate thought otherwise.

"I don't give a cent for the directory," said he. "I've been past here one night in the schooner *Eugenie*; it was just such a night as this; they were fishing with torches, and the beach was thick with lights like a town."

"Well, well," says the captain, "its steep-to, that's the great point; and there ain't any outlying dangers by the chart, so we'll just hug the lee side of it. Keep her romping full, don't I tell you!" he cried to Keola, who was listening so hard that he forgot to steer.

And the mate cursed him, and swore that Kanaka[7] was for no use in the world, and if he got started after him with a belaying pin, it would be a cold day for Keola.

And so the captain and the mate lay down on the house together, and Keola was left to himself.

"This island will do very well for me," he thought; "if no traders deal there, the mate will never come. And as for Kalamake, it is not possible he can ever get as far as this."

With that he kept edging the schooner nearer in. He had to do this quietly, for it was the trouble with these white men, and above all with the mate, that you could never be sure of them; they would all be sleeping sound, or else pretending, and if a sail shook, they would jump to their feet and fall on you with a rope's end. So Keola edged her up little by little, and kept all drawing. And presently the land was close on board and the sound of the sea on the sides of it grew loud.

With that, the mate sat up suddenly upon the house.

---

7. **Kanaka:** native Hawaiian.

"What are you doing?" he roars. "You'll have the ship ashore!"

And he made one bound for Keola, and Keola made another clean over the rail and plump into the starry sea. When he came up again, the schooner had played off on her true course, and the mate stood by the wheel himself, and Keola heard him cursing. The sea was smooth under the lee of the island; it was warm besides, and Keola had his sailor's knife, so he had no fear of sharks. A little way before him the trees stopped; there was a break in the line of the land like the mouth of a harbor; and the tide, which was then flowing, took him up and carried him through. One minute he was without, and the next within: had floated there in a wide shallow water, bright with ten thousand stars, and all about him was the ring of the land, and its string of palm trees. And he was amazed, because this was a kind of island he had never heard of.

The time of Keola in that place was in two periods—the period when he was alone, and the period when he was there with the tribe. At first he sought everywhere and found no man; only some houses standing in a hamlet, and the marks of fires. But the ashes of the fires were cold and the rains had washed them away; and the winds had blown, and some of the huts were overthrown. It was here he took his dwelling, and he made a fire drill, and a shell hook, and fished and cooked his fish, and climbed after green coconuts, the juice of which he drank, for in all the isle there was no water. The days were long to him, and the nights terrifying. He made a lamp of cocoa shell, and drew the oil of the ripe nuts, and made a wick of fiber; and when evening came, he closed up his hut, and lit his lamp, and lay and trembled till morning. Many a time he thought in his heart he would have been better in the bottom of the sea, his bones rolling there with the others.

All this while he kept by the inside of the island, for the huts were on the shore of the lagoon and it was there the palms grew best; and the lagoon itself abounded with good fish. And to the outer side he went once only, and he looked but the once at the beach of the ocean, and came away shaking. For the look of it, with its bright sand, and strewn shells, and strong sun and surf, went sore against his inclination.

"It cannot be," he thought, "and yet it is very like. And how do I know? These white men, although they pretend to know where they are sailing, most take their chance like other people. So that after all we may have sailed in a circle, and I may be quite near to Molokai, and this may be the very beach where my father-in-law gathers his dollars."

So after that he was prudent, and kept to the land side.

It was perhaps a month later, when the people of the place arrived—the fill of six great boats. They were a fine race of men, and spoke a tongue that sounded very different from the tongue of Hawaii, but so many of the words were the same that it was not difficult to understand. The men besides were very courteous, and the women very towardly, and they made Keola welcome, and built him a house, and gave him a wife; and what surprised him the most, he was never sent to work with the young men.

And now Keola had three periods. First he had a period of being very sad, and then he had a period when he was pretty merry. Last of all came the third, when he was the most terrified man in the four oceans.

The cause of the first period was the girl he had to wife. He was in doubt about the island, and he might have been in doubt about the speech, of which he had heard so little when he came there with the wizard on the mat. But about his wife there was no mistake conceivable, for she was the same girl that ran from him crying in the wood. So he had sailed all this way, and might as well have stayed in Molokai and had left home and wife and all his friends for no other cause than to escape his enemy, and the place he had come to was that wizard's hunting ground, and the shore where he walked invisible. It was at this period when he kept the most close to the lagoon-side, and as far as he dared, abode in the room of his hut.

The cause of the second period was talk he heard from his wife and the chief islanders. Keola himself said little. He was never so sure of his new friends, for he judged they were too civil to be wholesome, and since he had grown better acquainted with his father-in-law the man had grown more curious. So he told them nothing of himself, but only his name and descent, and that he came from the Eight Islands, and what fine islands they were; and about the king's palace in Honolulu, and how he was a chief friend of the king and the missionaries. But he put many questions and learned much. The island where he was was called the Isle of Voices; it belonged to the tribe, but they made their home upon another, three hours' sail to the southward. There they lived and had their permanent houses, and it was a rich island, where were eggs and chickens and pigs, and ships came trading with rum and tobacco. It was there the schooner had gone after Keola deserted; there, too, the mate had died, like the fool of a white man he was;. It seems, when the ship came, it was the beginning of the sickly season in that isle, when the fish of the lagoon are poisonous, and all who eat of them swell up and die. The mate was told of it; he saw the boats preparing, because in that season the people leave that island and sail to the Isle of Voices; but he was a fool of a white man, who would believe no stories but his own, and he caught one of these fish, cooked it and ate it, and swelled up and died, which was good news to Keola. As for the Isle of Voices, it lay solitary the most part of the year; only now and then a boat's crew came for copra,[8] and in the bad season, when the fish at the main isle were poisonous, the tribe dwelt there in a body. It had the name from a marvel, for it seemed the seaside of it was all beset with invisible devils; day and night you heard them talking one with another in strange tongues; day and night little fires blazed up and were extinguished on the beach; and what was the cause of these doings no man might conceive. Keola asked them if it were the same in their own island where they stayed, and they told him no, not there; nor yet in any other of some hundred isles that lay all about them in that sea; but it was a thing peculiar to the Isle of Voices. They told him also that these fires and voices were ever on the seaside and in the seaward fringes of the wood, and a man might dwell by the lagoon two thousand years (if he could live so long) and never be any way troubled; and even on the seaside the devils did no harm if let alone. Only once a chief had cast a spear at one of the voices, and the same night he fell out a coconut palm and was killed.

Keola thought a good bit with himself. He saw he would be all right when the tribe returned to the main island, and right enough where he was, if he kept by the lagoon, yet he had a mind to make things righter if he could. So he told the high chief he had once been in an isle that was pestered the same way, and the folk had found a means to cure the trouble.

"There was a tree growing in the bush there," says he, "and it seems these devils came to get the leaves of it. So the people of the isle cut down the tree whenever it was found, and the devils came no more."

They asked what kind of tree this was, and he showed them the tree of which Kalamake burned the leaves. They found it hard to believe,

---

8. **copra:** dried coconut meat.

yet the idea tickled them. Night after night the old men debated it in their councils, but the high chief (though he was a brave man) was afraid of the matter, and reminded them daily of the chief who cast a spear against the voices and was killed, and the thought of that brought all to a stand again.

Though he could not yet bring about the destruction of the trees, Keola was well enough pleased, and began to look about him and take pleasure in his days; and, among other things he was the kinder to his wife, so that the girl began to love him gently. One day he came to the hut, and she lay on the ground lamenting.

"Why," said Keola, "what is wrong with you now?"

She declared it was nothing.

The same night she woke him. The lamp burned very low, but he saw by her face she was in sorrow.

"Keola," she said, "put your ear to my mouth that I may whisper, for no one must hear us. Two days before the boats begin to be got ready, go you to the sea side of the isle and lie in a thicket. We shall choose that place beforehand, you and I, and hide food, and every night I shall come nearby there singing. So when a night comes and you do not hear me, you shall know we are clean gone out of the island, and you may come forth again in safety."

The soul of Keola died within him.

"What is this?" he cried. "I cannot live among devils. I will not be left behind upon the isle. I am dying to leave it."

"You will never leave it alive, my poor Keola," said the girl; "for to tell the truth, my people are eaters of men; but this they keep secret. And the reason they will kill you before we leave is because in our island ships come, and Donat-Kimaran comes and talks for the French, and there is a white trader there in the house with a verandah, and a catechist.[9] Oh, that is a fine place indeed! The trader has barrels filled with flour, and a French warship once came in the lagoon and gave everybody wine and biscuits. Ah, my poor Keola, I wish I could take you there, for great is my love to you, and it is the finest place in the seas except Papeete."

So now Keola was the most terrified man in the four oceans. He had heard tell of eaters of men in the south islands, and the thing had always been a fear to him; and here it was knocking at his door. He

---

9. **catechist:** teacher, especially of religion.

had heard besides, by travelers, of their practices, and how when they are in a mind to eat a man, they cherish and fondle him like a mother with a favorite baby. And he saw this must be his own case; and that was why he had been housed, and fed, and wived, and liberated from all work; and why the old men and the chiefs discoursed with him like a person of weight. So he lay on his bed and railed upon his destiny; and the flesh curdled on his bones.

The next day the people of the tribe were very civil, as their way was. They were elegant speakers, and they made beautiful poetry, and jested at meals, so that a missionary must have died laughing. It was little enough Keola cared for their fine ways, all he saw was the white teeth shining in their mouths, and his gorge rose[10] at the sight; and when they were done eating, he went and lay in the bush like a dead man.

The next day it was the same, and then his wife followed him.

"Keola," she said, "if you do not eat, I tell you plainly you will be killed and cooked tomorrow. Some of the old chiefs are murmuring already. They think you are fallen sick and must lose flesh."

With that Keola got to his feet, and anger burned in him.

"It is little I care one way or the other," said he. "I am between the devil and the deep sea. Since die I must, let me die the quickest way; and since I must be eaten at the best of it, let me rather be eaten by hobgoblins than by men. Farewell," said he, and he left her standing, and walked to the sea side of that island.

It was all bare in the strong sun; there was no sign of man, only the beach was trodden, and all about him as he went, the voices talked and whispered, and the little fires sprang up and burned down. All tongues of the earth were spoken there; the French, the Dutch, the Russian, the Tamil, the Chinese. Whatever land knew sorcery, there were some of its people whispering in Keola's ear. That beach was thick as a cried fair, yet no man seen; and as he walked he saw the shells vanish before him, and no man to pick them up. I think the devil would have been afraid to be alone in such a company; but Keola was past fear and courted death. When the fires sprang up, he charged for them like a bull. Bodiless voices called to and fro; unseen hands poured sand upon the flames; and they were gone from the beach before he reached them.

---

10. **his gorge rose:** he felt nauseated.

"It is plain Kalamake is not here," he thought, "or I must have been killed long since."

With that he sat him down in the margin of the wood, for he was tired, and put his chin upon his hands. The business before his eyes continued: the beach babbled with voices, and the fires sprang up and sank, and the shells vanished and were renewed again even while he looked.

"It was a by-day when I was here before," he thought, "for it was nothing to this."

And his head was dizzy with the thought of these millions and millions of dollars, and all these hundreds and hundreds of persons culling them upon the beach and flying in the air higher and swifter than eagles.

"And to think how they have fooled me with their talk of mints," says he, " and that money was made there, when it is clear that all the new coin in all the world is gathered on these sands! But I will know better the next time!" said he.

And at last, he knew not very well how or when, sleep fell on Keola, and he forgot the island and all his sorrows.

Early the next day, before the sun was yet up, a bustle woke him. He awoke in fear, for he thought the tribe had caught him napping; but it was no such matter. Only, on the beach in front of him, the bodiless voices called and shouted one upon another, and it seemed they all passed and swept beside him up the coast of the island.

"What is afoot now?" thinks Keola, And it was plain to him it was something beyond ordinary, for the fires were not lighted nor the shells taken, but the bodiless voices kept posting up the beach, and hailing and dying away, and others following, and by the sound of them these wizards should be angry.

"It is not me they are angry at," thought Keola, "for they pass me close."

As when hounds go by, or horses in a race, or city folk coursing to a fire, and all men join and follow after, as it was now with Keola; and he knew not what he did, nor why he did it, but there, lo and behold! he was running with the voices.

So he turned one point of the island, and this brought him in view of a second; and there he remembered the wizard trees to have been growing by the score together in a wood. From this point there went up a hubbub of men crying not to be described; and by the sound of them, those that he ran with shaped their course for the same quarter. A little nearer, and there began to mingle with the outcry the crash of many axes. And at this a thought came at last into his mind that the high chief had consented; that the men of the tribe had set to cutting down these trees; that word had gone about the isle from sorcerer to sorcerer, and these were all now assembling to defend their trees. Desire of strange things swept him on. He posted with the voices, crossed the beach, and came into the borders of the wood, and stood astonished. One tree had fallen, others were part hewed away. There was the tribe clustered. They were back to back, and bodies lay, and blood flowed among their feet. The hue of fear was on all their faces; their voices went up to heaven shrill as a weasel's cry.

Have you seen a child when he is all alone and has a wooden sword, and fights, leaping and hewing with the empty air? Even so the man-eaters huddled back to back, and heaved up their axes, and laid on, and screamed as they laid on, and behold! no man to contend with them! only here and there Keola saw an axe swinging over against them without hands; and time and again a man of the tribe would fall before it, clove in twain or burst asunder, and his soul sped howling.

For a while Keola looked upon this prodigy[11] like one that dreams, and then fear took him by the midst as sharp as death, that he should behold such doings. Even in that same flash the high chief of the clan espied him standing, and pointed and called out his name. Thereas the whole tribe saw him also, and their eyes flashed, and their teeth clashed.

"I am too long here," thought Keola, and ran further out of the wood and down the beach, not caring whither.

"Keola!" said a voice close by upon the empty sand.

"Lehua! is that you?" he cried, and gasped, and looked in vain for her; but by the eyesight he was stark alone.

"I saw you pass before," the voice answered; "but you would not hear me. Quick! get the leaves and the herbs, and let us free."

"You are here with the mat?" he asked.

"Here, at your side," said she. And he felt her arms about him. "Quick! the leaves and the herbs, before my father can get back."

So Keola ran for his life, and fetched the wizard fuel; and Lehua guided him back, and set his feet upon the mat, and made the fire. All

---

11. **prodigy:** extraordinary happening.

the time of its burning, the sound of the battle towered out of the wood; the wizards and the man-eaters hard at fight; the wizards, the viewless ones, roaring out aloud like bulls upon a mountain, and the men of the tribe replying shrill and savage out of the terror of their souls. And all the time of the burning, Keola stood there and listened, and shook, and watched how the unseen hands of Lehua poured the leaves. She poured them fast, and the flame burned high, and scorched Keola's hands; and she speeded and blew the burning with her breath. The last leaf was eaten, the flame fell, and the shock followed, and there were Keola and Lehua in the room at home.

Now, when Keola could see his wife at last he was mighty pleased, and he was mighty pleased to be home again in Molokai and sit down beside a bowl of poi[12]—for they make no poi on board ships, and there was none in the Isle of Voices—and he was out of the body with pleasure to be clean escaped out of the hands of the eaters of men. But there was another matter not so clear, and Lehua and Keola talked of all night and were troubled. There was Kalamake left upon the isle. If, by the blessing of God, he could but stick there, all were well; but should he escape and return to Molokai, it would be an ill day for his daughter and her husband. They spoke of his gift of swelling, and whether he could wade the distance in the seas. But Keola knew by this time where that island was—and that is to say, in the Low or Dangerous Archipelago. So they fetched the atlas and looked upon the distance in the map, and by what they could make of it, it seemed a far way for an old gentleman to walk. Still, it would not do to make too sure of a warlock like Kalamake, and they determined at last to take counsel of a white missionary.

So the first one that came by Keola told him everything. And the missionary was very sharp on him for taking the second wife in the low island; but for all the rest, he vowed he could make neither head nor tail of it.

"However," says he, "if you think this money of your father's ill-gotten, my advice to you would be, give some of it to the lepers and some to the missionary fund. And as for this extraordinary rigmarole, you cannot do better than keep it to yourselves."

But he warned the police at Honolulu, by all he could make out, Kalamake and Keola had been coining false money, and it would not be amiss to watch them.

---

12. **poi:** food made of taro root pounded to a paste.

Keola and Lehua took his advice, and gave many dollars to the lepers and the fund. And no doubt the advice must have been good, for from that day to this, Kalamake has never more been heard of. But whether he was slain in the battle by the trees, or whether he is still kicking his heels upon the Isle of Voices, who shall say?

Discussion Questions

1. What kind of person is Keola? How does he bring trouble on himself?

2. What is supposed to be the cause of the voices on the beach? Summarize what is happening in the real world and in the world of magic when invisible voices are heard.

3. How does Lehua save Keola? What does she risk to do so?

4. What attitudes toward Europeans ("white men") are expressed by native characters in the story or by the narrator? How do you account for these attitudes?

5. What elements of a folk tale do you find in this story?

Suggestion for Writing

"Who shall say," the story ends, whether Kalamake was killed or remained stuck on the Isle of Voices? Certainly Lehua and Keola are troubled by the thought: her father is a powerful sorcerer. Suppose Kalamake does escape (any way you choose) and comes looking for his daughter and son-in-law. Write a scene that describes their encounter. What revenge will he take on Keola? Will he spare Lehua for her treachery in abandoning him? You have seen some of Kalamake's powers—what other powers might he have that are not described in the story?

H. G. Wells (1866-1946)

Herbert George Wells was the son of domestic servants turned small shopkeepers. He escaped a life of poverty by winning a scholarship at the Normal School of Science, the first college in England to offer a science education for teachers. His first published book was a biology textbook, but with the publication of his first novel, *The Time Machine* (1896), he began a series of science-fiction novels that proved to be enormously popular. Many of them, such as *The War of the Worlds* (1898) have been dramatized and filmed several times. Some of Wells's science fiction seems today eerily prophetic. Eventually Wells abandoned science fiction for comic novels of lower middle-class life. He developed a passionate concern for human beings and society, and his fiction took a turn toward satire and social criticism. He believed that people could advance through knowledge and education, and he attempted to help the process through works of public education, such as *The Outline of History* (1920). Although a sense of world catastrophe underlies much of his work, he is thought of as a liberal optimist, and his writing contains a vigor that continues to impress readers today.

The Story of the Late Mr. Elvesham

I set this story down, not expecting it will be believed, but, if possible, to prepare a way of escape for the next victim. He may perhaps profit by my misfortune. My own case, I know, is hopeless, and I am now in some measure prepared to meet my fate.

My name is Edward George Eden. I was born at Trentham, in Staffordshire, my father being employed in the gardens there. I lost my mother when I was three years old and my father when I was five, my uncle, George Eden, then adopted me as his own son. He was a single man, self-educated, and well-known in Birmingham as an enterprising journalist; he educated me generously, fired my ambition to succeed in the world, and at his death, which happened four years ago, left me his entire fortune, a matter of about five hundred pounds after all outgoing charges were paid. I was then eighteen. He advised me in his will to expend the money in completing my education. I had already chosen the profession of medicine, and through his posthumous[1] generosity, and my good fortune in a scholarship competition, I became a medical student at University College, London. At the time of the beginning of my story I lodged at 11A University Street, in a little upper room, very shabbily furnished, and draughty, overlooking the back of Shoolbred's premises. I used this little room both to live in and sleep in, because I was anxious to eke out my means to the very last shillingsworth.

I was taking a pair of shoes to be mended at a shop in the Tottenham Court Road when I first encountered the little old man with the yellow face, with whom my life has now become so inextricably[2] entangled. He was standing on the kerb, and staring at the number on the door in a doubtful way, as I opened it. His eyes—they were dull gray eyes, and reddish under the rims, fell to my face and his countenance immediately assumed an expression of corrugated[3] amiability.

"You come," he said, "apt to the moment. I had forgotten the number of your house. How do you do, Mr. Eden?"

---

1. **posthumous** (päs´ chü məs): after death.
2. **inextricably:** so that it cannot be undone.
3. **corrugated:** wrinkled.

I was a little astonished at the familiar address, for I had never set eyes on the man before. I was annoyed, too, at his catching me with my boots under my arm. He noticed my lack of cordiality.

"Wonder who the deuce I am, eh? A friend, let me assure you. I have seen you before, though you haven't seen me. Is there anywhere where I can talk to you?"

I hesitated. The shabbiness of my room upstairs was not a matter for every stranger. "Perhaps," said I, "we might walk down the street. I'm unfortunately prevented—" My gesture explained the sentence before I had spoken it.

"The very thing," he said, and faced this way and then that. "The street? Which way shall we go?" I slipped my boots down in the passage. "Look here!" he said abruptly; "this business of mine is a rigmarole.[4] Come and lunch with me, Mr. Eden. I'm an old man, a very old man, and not good at explanations, and what with my piping voice and the clatter of the traffic—"

He laid a persuasive skinny hand that trembled a little upon my arm.

I was not so old that an old man might not treat me to a lunch. Yet at the same time I was not altogether pleased at this abrupt invitation. "I had rather—" I began. "But I had rather," he said, catching me up, "and a certain civility is surely due to my gray hairs," and so I consented, and went away with him.

He took me to Blavitski's; I had to walk slowly to accommodate myself to his paces; and over such a lunch as I had never tasted before, he fended off my leading questions, and I took a better note of his appearance. His clean-shaven face was lean and wrinkled, his shriveled lips fell over a set of false teeth, and his white hair was thin and rather long; he seemed small to me—and his shoulders were rounded and bent. And, watching him, I could not help but observe that he, too, was taking note of me, running his eyes, with a curious touch of greed in them, over me from my broad shoulders to my sun-tanned hands and up to my freckled face again. "And now," said he, as we lit our cigarettes, "I must tell you of the business in hand."

"I must tell you, then, that I am an old man, a very old man." He paused momentarily. "And it happens that I have money that I must presently be leaving, and never a child have I to leave it to." I thought of the confidence trick, and resolved I would be on the alert for the

---

4. **rigmarole:** a fussy, involved procedure.

vestiges[5] of my five hundred pounds. He proceeded to enlarge on his loneliness, and the trouble he had to find a proper disposition of his money. "I have weighed this plan and that plan, charities, institutes, and scholarships, and libraries, and I have come to this conclusion at last,"—he fixed his eyes on my face,—"that I will find some young fellow, ambitious, pure-minded, and poor, healthy in body and healthy in mind, and, in short, make him my heir, give him all that I have." He repeated, "Give him all that I have. So that he will suddenly be lifted out of all the trouble and struggle in which his sympathies have been educated, to freedom and influence."

I tried to seem disinterested. With a transparent hypocrisy, I said, "And you want my help, my professional services maybe, to find that person."

He smiled and looked at me over his cigarette, and I laughed at his quiet exposure of my modest pretense.

"What a career such a man might have!" he said. "It fills me with envy to think how I have accumulated that another man may spend—

"But there are conditions, of course, burdens to be imposed. He must, for instance, take my name. You cannot expect everything without some return. And I must go into all the circumstances of his life before I can accept him. He *must* be sound. I must know his heredity, how his parents and grandparents died, have the strictest inquiries made into his private morals—"

This modified my secret congratulations a little. "And do I understand," said I, "that I—?"

"Yes," he said, almost fiercely. "You. *You.*"

I answered never a word. My imagination was dancing wildly, my innate skepticism was useless to modify its transports. There was not a particle of gratitude in my mind—I did not know what to say nor how to say it. "But why me in particular?" I said at last.

He had chanced to hear of me from Professor Haslar, he said, as a typically sound and sane young man, and he wished, as far as possible, to leave his money where health and integrity were assured.

That was my first meeting with the little old man. He was mysterious about himself; he would not give his name yet, he said, and after I had answered some questions of his, he left me at the Blavitski portal. I noticed that he drew a handful of gold coins from his pocket when it

---

5. vestiges: remaining traces.

came to paying for the lunch. His insistence upon bodily health was curious. In accordance with an arrangement we had made I applied that day for a life policy in the Loyal Insurance Company for a large sum, and I was exhaustively overhauled by the medical advisers of that company in the subsequent week. Even that did not satisfy him, and he insisted I must be reexamined by the great Doctor Henderson. It was Friday in Whitsun[6] week before he came to a decision. He called me down quite late in the evening—nearly nine it was,—from cramming chemical equations for my Preliminary Scientific examination. He was standing in the passage under the feeble gas-lamp, and his face was a grotesque interplay of shadows. He seemed more bowed than when I had first seen him, and his cheeks had sunk in a little.

His voice shook with emotion. "Everything is satisfactory, Mr. Eden," he said. "Everything is quite, quite satisfactory. And this night of all nights, you must dine with me and celebrate your—accession."[7] He was interrupted by a cough. "You won't have long to wait, either," he said, wiping his handkerchief across his lips, and gripping my hand with his long bony claw that was disengaged. "Certainly not very long to wait."

We went into the street and called a cab. I remember every incident of that drive vividly, the swift, easy motion, the contrast of gas and oil and electric light, the crowds of people in the streets, the place in Regent Street to which we went, and the sumptuous dinner we were served with there. I was disconcerted at first by the well-dressed waiter's glances at my rough clothes, but as the champagne warmed my blood, my confidence revived. He had already told me his name in the cab; he was Egbert Elvesham, the great philosopher, whose name I had known since I was a lad at school. It seemed incredible to me that this man, whose intelligence had so early dominated mine, this great abstraction should suddenly realize itself as this decrepit, familiar figure. I dare say every young fellow who has suddenly fallen among celebrities has felt something of my disappointment. He told me now of the future that the feeble streams of his life would presently leave dry for me, houses, copyrights, investments; I had never suspected that philosophers were so rich. He watched me drink and eat with a touch of envy. "What a capacity for living you have!" he said; and

---

6. **Whitsun:** Pentecost, a Christian festival that follows seven weeks after Easter.
7. **accession:** act of coming into power.

then, with a sigh, a sigh of relief I could have thought it, "It will not be long."

"Ay," said I, my head swimming now with champagne; "I have a future perhaps—of a fairly agreeable sort, thanks to you. I shall now have the honor of your name. But you have a past. Such a past as is worth all my future."

He shook his head and smiled, as I thought with half-sad appreciation of my flattering admiration. "That future," he said, "would you in truth change it?" The waiter came with liqueurs. "You will not perhaps mind taking my name, taking my position, but would you indeed—willingly—take my years?"

"With your achievements," said I gallantly.

He smiled again. "Kümmel[8]—both," he said to the waiter, and turned his attention to a little paper packet he had taken from his pocket. "This hour," said he, "this after-dinner hour is the hour of small things. Here is a scrap of my unpublished wisdom." He opened the packet with his shaking yellow fingers, and showed a little pinkish powder on the paper. "This," said he—"well, you must guess what it is, but Kümmel—put but a dash of this powder in it—is Himmel."[9] His large grayish eyes watched mine with an inscrutable expression.

It was a bit of a shock to me to find this great philosopher gave his mind to the flavor of liqueurs. However, I feigned a great interest in his weakness, for I was drunk enough for such small sycophancy.[10]

He parted the powder between the little glasses, and rising suddenly with a strange unexpected dignity, held out his hand toward me. I imitated his action, and the glasses rang. "To a quick succession," said he, and raised his glass towards his lips.

"Not that," said I hastily. "Not that."

He paused, with the liqueur at the level of his chin, and his eyes blazing into mine.

"To a long life," said I.

He hesitated. "To a long life," said he, with a sudden bark of laughter, and with eyes fixed on one another we tilted the little glasses. His eyes looked straight into mine, and as I drained the stuff off, I felt a curiously intense sensation. The first touch of it set my

---

8. **Kümmel:** a German liqueur with caraway and other flavorings.
9. **Himmel:** (German) Heaven.
10. **sycophancy** (sik´ ə fən sē): act of a flattering servant.

brain in a furious tumult; I seemed to feel an actual physical stirring in my skull, and a seething humming filled my ears. I did not notice the flavor in my mouth, the aroma that filled my throat; I saw only the gray intensity of his gaze that burnt into mine. The draught, the mental confusion, the noise and stirring in my head, seemed to last an interminable time. Curious vague impressions of half-forgotten things danced and vanished on the edge of my consciousness. At last he broke the spell. With a sudden explosive sigh he put down his glass.

"Well?" he said.

"It's glorious," said I, though I had not tasted the stuff.

My head was spinning. I sat down. My brain was chaos. Then my perception grew clear and minute as though I saw things in a concave mirror. His manner seemed to have changed into something nervous and hasty. He pulled out his watch and grimaced at it. "Eleven-seven! Still tonight I must—Seven—twenty-five. Waterloo! I must go at once." He called for the bill, and struggled with his coat. Officious waiters came to our assistance. In another moment I was wishing him good-bye, over the apron of a cab, and still with an absurd feeling of minute distinctness, as though—how can I express it?—I not only saw but felt through an inverted opera-glass.

"That stuff," he said. He put his hand to his forehead. "I ought not to have given it to you. It will make your head split tomorrow. Wait a minute. Here." He handed me out a flat little thing like a seidlitz powder. "Take this in water as you are going to bed. The other thing was a drug. Not till you're ready to go to bed, mind. It will clear your head. That's all. One more shake—Futurus!"[11]

I gripped his shriveled claw. "Good-bye," he said, and by the droop of his eyelids I judged he, too, was a little under the influence of that brain-twisting cordial.

He recollected something else with a start, felt in his breast-pocket, and produced another packet, this time a cylinder the size and shape of a shaving stick. "Here," said he, "I'd almost forgotten. Don't open this until I come tomorrow—but take it now."

It was so heavy that I well-nigh dropped it. "All ri'!" said I, and he grinned at me through the cab window, as the cabman flicked his horse into wakefulness. It was a white packet he had given me, with red seals

---

11. **Futurus:** to the Future (as a toast).

at either end and along its edge. "If this isn't money," said I, "it's platinum or lead."

I stuck it with elaborate care into my pocket, and with a whirling brain walked home through the Regent Street loiterers and the dark back streets beyond Portland Road. I remember the sensations of that walk very vividly, strange as they were. I was still so far myself that I could notice my strange mental state, and wonder whether this stuff I had had was opium—a drug beyond my experience. It is hard now to describe the peculiarity of my mental strangeness—mental doubling vaguely expresses it. As I was walking up Regent Street I found in my mind a queer persuasion that it was Waterloo station, and had an odd impulse to get into the Polytechnic as a man might get into a train. I put a knuckle in my eye, and it was Regent Street. How can I express it? You see a skillful actor looking quietly at you, he pulls a grimace, and lo!—another person. Is it too extravagant if I tell you that it seemed to me as if Regent Street had, for the moment, done that? Then, being persuaded it was Regent Street again, I was oddly muddled about some fantastic reminiscences that cropped up. "Thirty years ago," thought I, "it was here that I quarreled with my brother." Then I burst out laughing, to the astonishment and encouragement of a group of night prowlers. Thirty years ago I did not exist, and never in my life had I boasted a brother. The stuff was surely liquid folly, for the poignant regret for that lost brother still clung to me. Along Portland Road the madness took another turn. I began to recall vanished shops, and to compare the street with what it used to be. Confused, troubled thinking was comprehensible enough after the drink I had taken, but what puzzled me were these curiously vivid phantasmal[12] memories that had crept into my mind; and not only the memories that had crept in, but also the memories that had slipped out. I stopped opposite Stevens', the natural history dealer's, and cudgeled[13] my brains to think what he had to do with me. A 'bus went by, and sounded exactly like the rumbling of a train. I seemed to be dipped into some dark, remote pit for the recollection. "Of course," said I, at last, "he has promised me three frogs tomorrow. Odd I should have forgotten."

Do they still show children dissolving views?[14] In those I remember one view would begin like a faint ghost, and grow and oust another. In

---

12. **phantasmal** (fan taz′ məl): ghostly.
13. **cudgeled:** pounded.
14. **dissolving views:** an early form of slide show.

just that way it seemed to me that a ghostly set of new sensations was struggling with those of my ordinary self.

I went on, through Euston Road to Tottenham Court Road, puzzled, and a little frightened, and scarcely noticed the unusual way I was taking, for commonly I used to cut through the intervening network of back streets. I turned into University Street, to discover that I had forgotten my number. Only by a strong effort did I recall 11A, and even then it seemed to me that it was a thing some forgotten person had told me. I tried to steady my mind by recalling the incidents of the dinner, and for the life of me I could conjure up no picture of my host's face; I saw him only as a shadowy outline, as one might see oneself reflected in a window through which one was looking. In his place, however, I had a curious exterior vision of myself sitting at a table, flushed, bright-eyed, and talkative.

"I must take this other powder," said I. "This is getting impossible."

I tried the wrong side of the hall for my candle and the matches, and had a doubt of which landing my room might be on. "I'm drunk," I said, "that's certain," and blundered needlessly on the staircase to sustain the proposition.

At first glance my room seemed unfamiliar. "What rot!" I said, and stared about me. I seemed to bring myself back by the effort and the odd phantasmal quality passed into the concrete familiar. There was the old looking-glass, with my notes on the albumens[15] stuck in the corner of the frame, my odd everyday suit of clothes pitched about the floor. And yet it was not so real, after all. I felt an idiotic persuasion trying to creep into my mind, as it were, that I was in a railway carriage in a train just stopping, that I was peering out of the window at some unknown station. I gripped the bed-rail firmly to reassure myself. "It's clairvoyance, perhaps," I said. "I must write to the Psychical Research Society."

I put the rouleau[16] on my dressing-table, sat on my bed and began to take off my boots. It was as if the picture of my present sensations was painted over some other picture that was trying to show through. "Curse it!" said I; "my wits are going or am I in two places at once?" Half-undressed, I tossed the powder into a glass and drank it off. It

---

15. albumens (al byü′ mənz): photographic papers.
16. rouleau (rü lo′): (French) a small roll of something. In this story it probably refers to the packet Elvesham gave to Eden in the restaurant.

effervesced, and became a fluorescent amber color. Before I was in bed my mind was already tranquilized. I felt the pillow at my cheek, and thereupon I must have fallen asleep.

I awoke abruptly out of a dream of strange beasts, and found myself lying on my back. Probably everyone knows that dismal emotional dream from which one escapes, awake indeed but strangely cowed. There was a curious taste in my mouth, a tired feeling in my limbs, a sense of cutaneous[17] discomfort. I lay with my head motionless on my pillow, expecting that my feeling of strangeness and terror would probably pass away, and that I should then doze off again to sleep. But instead of that, my uncanny sensations increased. At first I could perceive nothing wrong about me. There was a faint light in the room, so faint that it was the very next thing to darkness, and the furniture stood out in it as vague blots of absolute darkness. I stared with my eyes just over the bedclothes.

It came to my mind that someone had entered the room to rob me of my rouleau of money, but after lying for some moments, breathing regularly to stimulate sleep, I realized this was mere fancy. Nevertheless, the uneasy assurance of something wrong kept fast hold of me. With an effort I raised my head from the pillow, and peered about me at the dark. What it was, I could not conceive. I looked at the dim shapes around me, the greater and lesser darknesses that indicated curtains, table, fireplace, bookshelves, and so forth. Then I began to perceive something unfamiliar in the forms of the darkness. Had the bed been turned round? Yonder should be the bookshelves, and something shrouded and pallid rose there, something that would not answer to the bookshelves, however I looked at it. It was far too long to be my shirt thrown on a chair.

Overcoming a childish terror, I threw back the bedclothes and thrust my leg out of the bed. Instead of coming out of my truckle-bed upon the floor, I found my feet scarcely reached the edge of the mattress. I made another step, as it were, and sat up on the edge of the bed. By the side of my bed should be the candle, and the matches upon the broken chair. I put out my hand and touched—nothing. I waved my hand in the darkness, and it came against some heavy hanging, soft and thick in texture, which gave a rustling noise at my touch. I grasped this

---

17. **cutaneous** (kyü tā nē əs): of the skin.

and pulled it; it appeared to be a curtain suspended over the head of my bed.

    I was now thoroughly awake, and beginning to realize that I was in a strange room. I was puzzled. I tried to recall the overnight circumstances, and I found them now, curiously enough, vivid in my memory: the supper, my reception of the little packages, my wonder whether I was intoxicated, my slow undressing, the coolness to my flushed face of my pillow. I felt a sudden distrust. Was that last night, or the night before? At any rate, this room was strange to me, and I could not imagine how I had got into it. The dim, pallid outline was growing paler, and I perceived it was a window, with the dark shape of an oval toilet-glass against the weak intimation of the dawn that filtered through the blind. I stood up, and was surprised by a curious feeling of weakness and unsteadiness. With trembling hands outstretched, I walked slowly towards the window, getting, nevertheless, a bruise on the knee from a chair by the way. I fumbled round the glass, which was large, with handsome brass sconces, to find the blind-cord. I could not find any. By chance I took hold of the tassel, and with the click of a spring the blind ran up.

    I found myself looking out upon a scene that was absolutely strange to me. The night was overcast, and through the flocculent[18] gray of the heaped clouds there filtered a faint half-light of dawn. Just at the edge of the sky, the cloud-canopy had a blood-red rim. Below, everything was dark and indistinct, dim hills in the distance, a vague mass of buildings running up into pinnacles, trees like spilt ink, and below the window a tracery of black bushes and pale gray paths. It was so unfamiliar that for a moment I thought myself still dreaming. I felt the toilet-table; it appeared to be made of some polished wood, and was rather elaborately furnished—there were little cut-glass bottles and a brush upon it. There was also a queer little object, horseshoe-shaped, it felt, with smooth, hard projections, lying in a saucer. I could find no matches nor candle-stick.

    I turned my eyes to the room again. Now the blind was up, faint specters of its furnishing came out of the darkness. There was a huge curtained bed, and the fireplace at its foot had a large white mantel with something of the shimmer of marble.

    I leant against the toilet-table, shut my eyes and opened them again, and tried to think. The whole thing was far too real for dreaming. I

18: **flocculent:** wooly.

was inclined to imagine there was still some hiatus[19] in my memory as a consequence of my draught of that strange liqueur; that I had come into my inheritance, perhaps, and suddenly lost my recollection of everything since my good fortune had been announced. Perhaps if I waited a little, things would be clearer to me again. Yet my dinner with old Elvesham was now singularly vivid and recent. The champagne, the observant waiters, the powder, and the liqueurs—I could have staked my soul it all happened a few hours ago.

And then occurred a thing so trivial and yet so terrible to me that I shiver now to think of that moment. I spoke aloud. I said: "How the devil did I get here?" . . . *And the voice was not my own.*

It was not my own, it was thin, the articulation was slurred, the resonance of my facial bones was different. Then to reassure myself, I ran one hand over the other and felt loose folds of skin, the bony laxity of age. "Surely," I said in that horrible voice that had somehow established itself in my throat, "surely this thing is a dream!" Almost as quickly as if I did it involuntarily, I thrust my fingers into my mouth. My teeth had gone. My finger-tips ran on the flaccid surface of an even row of shriveled gums. I was sick with dismay and disgust.

I felt then a passionate desire to see myself, to realize at once in its full horror the ghastly change that had come upon me. I tottered to the mantel, and felt along it for matches. As I did so, a barking cough sprang up to my throat, and I clutched the thick flannel nightdress I found about me. There were no matches there, and I suddenly realized that my extremities were cold. Sniffing and coughing, whimpering a little perhaps, I fumbled back to bed. "It is surely a dream," I whimpered to myself as I clambered back, "surely a dream." It was a senile repetition. I pulled the bedclothes over my shoulders, over my ears, I thrust my withered hand under the pillow, and determined to compose myself to sleep. Of course it was a dream. In the morning the dream would be over, and I should wake up strong and vigorous again to my youth and studies. I shut my eyes, breathed regularly, and, finding myself wakeful, began to count slowly through the powers of three.

But the thing I desired would not come. I could not get to sleep. And the persuasion of the inexorable reality of the change that had happened to me grew steadily. Presently I found myself with my eyes wide open, the powers of three forgotten, and my skinny fingers upon my

---

19. hiatus: gap.

shriveled gums. I was indeed, suddenly and abruptly, an old man. I had in some unaccountable manner fallen through my life and come to old age, in some way I had been cheated of all the best of my life, of love, of struggle, of strength and hope. I groveled into the pillow and tried to persuade myself that such hallucination was possible. Imperceptibly, steadily, the day grew clearer.

At last, despairing of further sleep, I sat up in bed and looked about me. A chill twilight rendered the whole chamber visible. It was spacious and well-furnished, better furnished than any room I had ever slept in before. A candle and matches became dimly visible upon a little pedestal in a recess. I threw back the bedclothes, and shivering with the rawness of the early morning, albeit it was summer-time, I got up and lit the candle. Then, trembling horribly so that the extinguisher rattled on its spike, I tottered to the glass and saw—*Elvesham's face!* It was none the less horrible because I had already feared as much. He had already seemed weak and physically pitiful to me, but seen now, dressed only in a coarse flannel nightdress that fell apart and showed the stringy neck, seen now as my own body, I cannot describe its desolate decrepitude. The hollow cheeks, the straggling tail of dirty gray hair, the rheumy bleared eyes, the quivering, shriveled lips, the lower displaying a gleam of the pink interior lining, and those horrible dark gums showing. You who are mind and body together at your natural years cannot imagine what this fiendish imprisonment meant to me. To be young and full of the desire and energy of youth, and to be caught, and to presently be crushed in this tottering ruin of a body. . . .

But I wander from the course of my story. For some time I must have been stunned at this change that had come upon me. In some inexplicable way, I had been changed, though how, short of magic, the thing had been done, I could not say. And as I thought, the diabolical ingenuity of Elvesham came home to me. It seemed plain to me that as I found myself in his, so he must be in possession of *my* body, of my strength that is, and my future. But how to prove it? Then as I thought, the thing became so incredible even to me that my mind reeled, and I had to pinch myself, to feel my toothless gums, to see myself in the glass, and touch the things about me before I could steady myself to face the facts again. Was all life hallucination? Was I indeed Elvesham, and he me? Had I been dreaming of Eden overnight? Was there any Eden? But if I was Elvesham, I should remember where I was on the previous morning, the name of the town in which I lived, what happened before the dream began. I struggled with my thoughts. I recalled the queer doubleness of my memories overnight. But now my mind was clear. Not the ghost of any memories but those proper to Eden could I raise.

"This way lies insanity!" I cried in my piping voice. I staggered to my feet, dragged my feeble, heavy limbs to the wash-hand stand, and plunged my gray head into a basin of cold water. Then, toweling myself, I tried again. It was no good. I felt beyond all question that I was indeed Eden, not Elvesham. But Eden in Elvesham's body.

Had I been a man of any other age, I might have given myself up to my fate as one enchanted. But in these skeptical days miracles do not pass current. Here was some trick of psychology. What a drug and a steady stare could do, a drug and a steady stare, or some smaller treatment, could surely undo. Men have lost their memories before. But to exchange memories as one does umbrellas! I laughed. Alas! not a healthy laugh, but a wheezing, senile titter. I could have fancied old Elvesham laughing at my plight, and a gust of petulant anger, unusual to me, swept across my feelings. I began dressing eagerly in the clothes I found lying about on the floor, and only realized when I was dressed that it was an evening suit I had assumed. I opened the wardrobe and found some ordinary clothes, a pair of plaid trousers, and an old-fashioned dressing gown. I put a venerable smoking-cap on my venerable head, and coughing a little from my exertions, tottered out upon the landing.

It was then perhaps a quarter to six, and the blinds were closely drawn and the house quite silent. The landing was a spacious one, a broad, richly-carpeted staircase went down into the darkness of the hall below, and before me a door ajar showed me a writing-desk, a revolving bookcase, the back of a study chair, and a fine array of bound books, shelf upon shelf.

"My study," I mumbled, and walked across the landing. Then at the sound of my voice a thought struck me, and I went back in the bedroom and put in the set of false teeth. They slipped in with the ease of old habit. "That's better," said I, gnashing them, and so returned to the study.

The drawers of the writing-desk were locked. Its revolving top was also locked. I could see no indications of the keys, and there were none in the pockets of my trousers. I shuffled back at once to the bedroom, and went through the dress-suit, and afterwards the pockets of all the garments I could find. I was very eager; and one might have imagined that burglars had been at work, to see my work when I had done. Not only were there no keys to be found, but not a coin, not a scrap of paper—save only the receipted bill of the overnight dinner.

    A curious weariness asserted itself. I sat down and stared at the garments flung here and there, their pockets turned inside out. Every moment I was beginning to realize the immense intelligence of the plans of my enemy, to see more and more clearly the hopelessness of my position. With an effort I arose and hurried into the study again. On the staircase was a housemaid pulling up the blinds. She stared, I think, at the expression of my face. I shut the door of the study behind me, and, seizing a poker, began an attack upon the desk. That is how they found me. The cover of the desk was split, the lock smashed, the letters torn out of the pigeon-holes and tossed about the room. In my senile rage I had flung about the pens and other such light stationery, and overturned the ink. Moreover, a large vase upon the mantel had got broken—I do not know how. I could find no cheque-book, no money, no indications of the slightest use for the recovery of my body. I was battering madly at the drawers, when the butler, backed by two women-servants, intruded upon me.

That simply is the story of my change. No one will believe my frantic assertions. I am treated as one demented, and even at this moment I am under restraint. But I am sane, absolutely sane, and to prove it I have sat down to write this story minutely as the thing happened to me. I appeal to the reader, whether there is any trace of insanity in the style or method of the story he has been reading. I am a young man locked away in an old man's body. But the clear fact is incredible to everyone. Naturally I appear demented to those who will not believe this, naturally I do not know the names of my secretaries, of the doctor who came to see me, of my servants and neighbors, of this town (wherever it is) where I find myself. Naturally I lose myself in my own house, and suffer inconveniences of every sort. Naturally I ask the oddest questions. Naturally I weep and cry out, and have paroxysms[20] of despair. I have no money and no cheque-book. The bank will not recognize my signature, for I suppose that, allowing for the feeble muscles I now have, my handwriting is still Eden's. These people about me will not let

---

20. paroxysms (pâr´ ek siz´ mz): fits; spasms.

me go to the bank personally. It seems, indeed, that there is no bank in this town, and that I have taken an account in some part of London. It seems that Elvesham kept the name of his solicitor secret from all his household—I can ascertain nothing. Elvesham was, of course, a profound student of mental science, and all my declarations of the facts of the case merely confirm the theory that my insanity is the outcome of overmuch brooding upon psychology. Dreams of the personal identity indeed! Two days ago I was a healthy youngster, with all life before me; now I am a furious old man, unkempt and desperate and miserable, prowling about a great luxurious strange house, watched, feared, and avoided as a fanatic by everyone about me. And in London is Elvesham: beginning life again in a vigorous body, and with all the accumulated knowledge and wisdom of threescore and ten. He has stolen my life.

What has happened I do not clearly know. In the study are volumes of manuscript notes referring chiefly to the psychology of memory, and parts of what may be either calculations or ciphers in symbols absolutely strange to me. In some passages there are indications that he was also occupied with the philosophy of mathematics. I take it he has transferred the whole of his memories, the accumulation that makes up his personality, from this old withered brain of his to mine, and, similarly, that he has transferred mine to his discarded tenement. Practically, that is, he has changed bodies. But how such a change may be possible is without the range of my philosophy. I have been a materialist for all my thinking life, but here, suddenly, is a clear case of man's detachability from matter.

One desperate experiment I am about to try. I am writing here before putting the matter to issue. This morning, with the help of a table-knife that I had secreted at breakfast, I succeeded in breaking open a fairly obvious secret drawer in this wretched writing-desk. I discovered nothing save a little green glass phial containing a white powder. Round the neck of the phial was a label, and thereon was written this one word, *"Release."* This may be—is most probably, poison. I can understand Elvesham placing poison in my way, and I should be sure that it was his intention so to get rid of the only living witness against him were it not for this careful concealment. The man has practically solved the problem of immortality. Save for the spite of chance, he will live in my body until it has aged, and then, again, throwing that aside, he will assume some other victim's youth and strength. When one remembers his heartlessness, it is terrible to think of the ever-growing experience that . . . How long has he been leaping from body to body? . . . But I tire of writing. The powder appears to be soluble in water. The taste is not unpleasant.

There the narrative found upon Mr. Elvesham's desk ends. His dead body lay between the desk and the chair. The latter had been pushed back, probably by his last convulsion. The story was written in pencil, and in a crazy hand quite unlike his usual minute characters. There remain only two curious facts to record. Indisputably there was some connection between Eden and Elvesham, since the whole of Elvesham's property was deeded to the young man. But he never inherited. When Elvesham committed suicide, Eden was, strangely enough, already dead. Twenty-four hours before, he had been knocked down by a cab and killed instantly, at the crowded crossing at the intersection of Gower Street and Euston Road. So that the only human being who could thrown light upon this fantastic narrative is beyond the reach of questions.

Discussion Questions

1. What does Mr. Elvesham tell Edward Eden he will do for the young man, and what conditions does he demand?

2. What does Eden find has happened to him after his dinner with Elvesham?

3. How does Eden explain Elvesham's scheme?

4. Why does Eden write this story?

5. Explain the terrible irony revealed in the final paragraph.

Suggestion for Writing

Put yourself in Egbert Elvesham's place. If you had the ability to change places with another person, would you do it? If so, with whom would you change, and why? Write a brief essay discussing these questions. Also discuss this: How do you justify to yourself the morality of tampering with another person's life without his or her knowledge or permission?

Edith Wharton (1862-1937)

Born into a wealthy and distinguished New York City family, Edith Wharton made use of this genteel, formal society as the setting for many of her novels and short stories. At age 23 she married a banker, and the couple spent much time in Europe before settling permanently in France; they divorced in 1913. Writing was considered unladylike in Wharton's society, and she was over forty before she published her first novel. In 1920 she was awarded the Pulitzer Prize for *The Age of Innocence,* which explores the moral hypocrisy that can underlie the foundations of a life of luxury.

One of her best-known works is *Ethan Frome* (1911), a tale of frustrated love set in a stark, New England village. Of her 86 stories, many are simple, chilling ghost stories, but they don't always contain ghostly apparitions; instead, the characters themselves may become ghostlike.

The Lady's Maid's Bell

I

It was the autumn after I had the typhoid. I'd been three months in hospital, and when I came out I looked so weak and tottery that the two or three ladies I applied to were afraid to engage me. Most of my money was gone, and after I'd boarded for two months, hanging about the employment agencies, and answering any advertisement that looked any way respectable, I pretty nearly lost heart, for fretting hadn't made me fatter, and I didn't see why my luck should ever turn. It did thoug—or I thought so at the time. A Mrs. Railton, a friend of the lady that first brought me out to the States, met me one day and stopped to speak to me: she was one that had always a friendly way with her. She asked me what ailed me to look so white, and when I told her, "Why, Hartley," says she, "I believe I've got the very place for you. Come in tomorrow and we'll talk about it."

The next day, when I called, she told me the lady she'd in mind was a niece of hers, a Mrs. Brympton, a youngish lady, but something of an invalid, who lived all the year round at her country-place on the Hudson, owing to not being able to stand the fatigue of town life.

"Now, Hartley," Mrs. Railton said, in that cheery way that always made me feel things must be going to take a turn for the better—"now understand me; it's not a cheerful place I'm sending you to. The house is big and gloomy; my niece is nervous, vaporish;[1] her husband—well, he's generally away; and the two children are dead. A year ago I would as soon have thought of shutting a rosy active girl like you into a vault; but you're not particularly brisk yourself just now, are you? and a quiet place, with country air and wholesome food and early hours, ought to be the very thing for you. Don't mistake me," she added, for I suppose I looked a trifle downcast; "you may find it dull but you won't be unhappy. My niece is an angel. Her former maid, who died last spring, had been with her twenty years and worshipped the ground she walked on. She's a kind mistress to all, and where the mistress is kind, as you know, the servants are generally good-humored, so you'll probably get on well enough with the rest of the household. And you're the very

---

1. **vaporish:** having low spirits.

woman I want for my niece: quiet, well-mannered, and educated above your station. You read aloud well, I think? That's a good thing; my niece likes to be read to. She wants a maid that can be something of a companion: her last was, and I can't say how she misses her. It's a lonely life . . . Well, have you decided?"

"Why, ma'am," I said, "I'm not afraid of solitude."

"Well, then, go; my niece will take you on my recommendation. I'll telegraph her at once and you can take the afternoon train. She has no one to wait on her at present, and I don't want you to lose any time."

I was ready enough to start, yet something in me hung back; and to gain time I asked, "And the gentleman, ma'am?"

"The gentleman's almost always away, I tell you," said Mrs. Railton, quick-like—"and when he's there," says she suddenly, "you've only to keep out of his way."

I took the afternoon train and got out at D— — station at about four o'clock. A groom in a dog-cart was waiting, and we drove off at a smart pace. It was a dull October day, with rain hanging close overhead, but by the time we turned into Brympton Place woods the daylight was almost gone. The drive wound through the woods for a mile or two, and came out on a gravel court shut in with thickets of tall black-looking shrubs. There were no lights in the windows, and the house *did* look a bit gloomy.

I had asked no questions of the groom, for I never was one to get my notion of new masters from their other servants: I prefer to wait and see for myself. But I could tell by the look of everything that I had got into the right kind of house, and that things were done handsomely. A pleasant-faced cook met me at the back door and called the house-maid to show me up to my room. "You'll see madam later," she said. "Mrs. Brympton has a visitor."

I hadn't fancied Mrs. Brympton was a lady to have many visitors, and somehow the words cheered me. I followed the house-maid upstairs, and saw, through a door on the upper landing, that the main part of the house seemed well furnished, with dark paneling and a number of old portraits. Another flight of stairs led us up to the servants' wing. It was almost dark now, and the house-maid excused herself for not having brought a light. "But there's matches in your room," she said, "and if you go careful you'll be all right. Mind the step at the end of the passage. Your room is just beyond."

I looked ahead as she spoke, and half-way down the passage I saw a woman standing. She drew back into a doorway as we passed and the house-maid didn't appear to notice her. She was a thin woman with a white face, and a darkish stiff gown and apron. I took her for the housekeeper and thought it odd that she didn't speak, but just gave me a long look as we went by. My room opened into a square hall at the end of the passage. Facing my door was another which stood open: the house-maid exclaimed when she saw it:

"There—Mrs. Blinder's left that door open again!" said she, closing it.

"Is Mrs. Blinder the housekeeper?"

"There's no housekeeper: Mrs. Blinder's the cook."

"And is that her room?"

"Laws, no," said the house-maid, cross-like. "That's nobody's room. It's empty, I mean, and the door hadn't ought to be open. Mrs. Brympton wants it kept locked."

She opened my door and led me into a neat room, nicely furnished, with a picture or two on the walls; and having lit a candle she took leave, telling me that the servants'-hall tea was at six, and that Mrs. Brympton would see me afterward.

I found them a pleasant-spoken set in the servants' hall, and by what they let fall I gathered that, as Mrs. Railton had said, Mrs. Brympton was the kindest of ladies; but I didn't take much notice of their talk, for I was watching to see the pale woman in the dark gown come in. She didn't show herself, however, and I wondered if she ate apart; but if she wasn't the housekeeper, why should she? Suddenly it struck me that she might be a trained nurse, and in that case her meals would of course be served in her room. If Mrs. Brympton was an invalid it was likely enough she had a nurse. The idea annoyed me, I own, for they're not always the easiest to get on with, and if I'd known I shouldn't have taken the place. But there I was and there was no use pulling a long face over it; and not being one to ask questions I waited to see what would turn up.

When tea was over the house-maid said to the footman: "Has Mr. Ranford gone?" and when he said yes, she told me to come up with her to Mrs. Brympton.

Mrs. Brympton was lying down in her bedroom. Her lounge stood near the fire and beside it was a shaded lamp. She was a delicate-looking lady, but when she smiled I felt there was nothing I wouldn't do for her. She spoke very pleasantly, in a low voice, asking me my name and age and so on, and if I had everything I wanted, and if I wasn't afraid of feeling lonely in the country.

"Not with you I wouldn't be, madam," I said, and the words surprised me when I'd spoken them, for I'm not an impulsive person; but it was just as if I'd thought aloud.

She seemed pleased at that, and said she hoped I'd continue in the same mind; then she gave me a few directions about her toilet,[2] and said Agnes the house-maid should show me next morning where things were kept.

"I am tired tonight, and shall dine upstairs," she said. "Agnes will bring me my tray, that you may have time to unpack and settle yourself; and later you may come and undress me."

"Very well, ma'am," I said. "You'll ring, I suppose?"

I thought she looked odd.

"No—Agnes will fetch you," says she quickly, and took up her book again.

Well—that was certainly strange: a lady's maid having to be fetched by the house-maid whenever her lady wanted her! I wondered if there were no bells in the house; but the next day I satisfied myself that there was one in every room, and a special one ringing from my mistress's room to mine; and after that it did strike me as queer that, whenever Mrs. Brympton wanted anything, she rang for Agnes, who had to walk the whole length of the servants' wing to call me.

But that wasn't the only queer thing in the house. The very next day I found out that Mrs. Brympton had no nurse; and then I asked Agnes about the woman I had seen in the passage the afternoon before. Agnes said she had seen no one, and I saw that she thought I was dreaming. To be sure, it was dusk when we went down the passage, and she had excused herself for not bringing a light; but I had seen the woman plain enough to know her again if we should meet. I decided that she must have been a friend of the cook's, or of one of the other woman-servants; perhaps she had come down from town for a night's visit, and the servants wanted it kept secret. Some ladies are very stiff about having their servants' friends in the house overnight. At any rate, I made up my mind to ask no more questions.

In a day or two another odd thing happened. I was chatting one afternoon with Mrs. Blinder, who was a friendly disposed woman, and

---

2. **toilet:** process of dressing and grooming.

had been longer in the house than the other servants, and she asked me if I was quite comfortable and had everything I needed. I said I had no fault to find with my place or with my mistress, but I thought it odd that in so large a house there was no sewing-room for the lady's maid.

"Why," says she, "there *is* one: the room you're in is the old sewing-room."

"Oh," said I; "and where did the other lady's maid sleep?"

At that she grew confused, and said hurriedly that the servants' rooms had all been changed about last year, and she didn't rightly remember.

That struck me as peculiar, but I went on as if I hadn't noticed: "Well, there's a vacant room opposite mine, and I mean to ask Mrs. Brympton if I mayn't use that as a sewing-room."

To my astonishment, Mrs. Blinder went white, and gave my hand a kind of squeeze. "Don't do that, my dear," said she, trembling-like. "To tell you the truth, that was Emma Saxon's room, and my mistress has kept it closed ever since her death."

"And who was Emma Saxon?"

"Mrs. Brympton's former maid."

"The one that was with her so many years?" said I, remembering what Mrs. Railton had told me.

Mrs. Blinder nodded.

"What sort of woman was she?"

"No better walked the earth," said Mrs. Blinder. "My mistress loved her like a sister."

"But I mean—what did she look like?"

Mrs. Blinder got up and gave me a kind of angry stare. "I'm no great hand at describing," she said; "and I believe my pastry's rising." And she walked off into the kitchen and shut the door after her.

II

I had been near a week at Brympton before I saw my master. Word came that he was arriving one afternoon, and a change passed over the whole household. It was plain that nobody loved him below stairs. Mrs. Blinder took uncommon care with the dinner that night, but she snapped at the kitchen-maid in a way quite unusual with her; and Mr. Wace, the butler, a serious, slow-spoken man, went about his duties as if he'd been getting ready for a funeral. He was a great Bible-reader,

Mr. Wace was, and had a beautiful assortment of texts at his command; but that day he used such dreadful language, that I was about to leave the table, when he assured me it was all out of Isaiah; and I noticed that whenever the master came Mr. Wace took to the prophets.

About seven, Agnes called me to my mistress's room; and there I found Mr. Brympton. He was standing on the hearth; a big fair bull-necked man, with a red face and little bad-tempered blue eyes: the kind of man a young simpleton might have thought handsome, and would have been like to pay dear for thinking it.

He swung about when I came in, and looked me over in a trice. I knew what the look meant, from having experienced it once or twice in my former places. Then he turned his back on me, and went on talking to his wife; and I knew what *that* meant, too. I was not the kind of morsel[3] he was after. The typhoid had served me well enough in one way: it kept that kind of gentleman at arm's-length.

"This is my new maid, Hartley," says Mrs. Brympton in her kind voice; and he nodded and went on with what he was saying.

In a minute or two he went off, and left my mistress to dress for dinner, and I noticed as I waited on her that she was white, and chill to the touch.

Mr. Brympton took himself off the next morning, and the whole house drew a long breath when he drove away. As for my mistress, she put on her hat and furs (for it was a fine winter morning) and went out for a walk in the gardens, coming back quite fresh and rosy, so that for a minute, before her color faded, I could guess what a pretty young lady she must have been, and not so long ago, either.

She had met Mr. Ranford in the grounds, and the two came back together, I remember, smiling and talking as they walked along the terrace under my window. That was the first time I saw Mr. Ranford, though I had often heard his name mentioned in the hall. He was a neighbor, it appeared, living a mile or two beyond Brympton, at the end of the village; and as he was in the habit of spending his winters in the country he was almost the only company my mistress had at that season. He was a slight tall gentleman of about thirty, and I thought him rather melancholy-looking till I saw his smile, which had a kind of surprise in it, like the first warm day in spring. He was a great reader, I heard, like my mistress, and the two were for ever borrowing books

---

3. **morsel:** little bit; here, a desirable female.

of one another, and sometimes (Mr. Wace told me) he would read aloud to Mrs. Brympton by the hour, in the big dark library where she sat in the winter afternoons. The servants all liked him, and perhaps that's more of a compliment than the masters suspect. He had a friendly word for every one of us, and we were all glad to think that Mrs. Brympton had a pleasant companionable gentleman like that to keep her company when the master was away. Mr. Ranford seemed on excellent terms with Mr. Brympton, too; though I could but wonder that two gentlemen so unlike each other should be so friendly. But then I knew how the real quality[4] can keep their feelings to themselves.

As for Mr. Brympton, he came and went, never staying more than a day or two, cursing the dullness and the solitude, grumbling at everything, and (as I soon found out) drinking a deal more than was good for him. After Mrs. Brympton left the table he would sit half the night over the old Brympton port and madeira, and once, as I was leaving my mistress's room rather later than usual, I met him coming up the stairs in such a state that I turned sick to think of what some ladies have to endure and hold their tongues about.

The servants said very little about their master; but from what they let drop I could see it had been an unhappy match from the beginning. Mr. Brympton was coarse, loud and pleasure-loving; my mistress quiet, retiring, and perhaps a trifle cold. Not that she was not always pleasant-spoken to him: I thought her wonderfully forbearing;[5] but to a gentleman as free as Mr. Brympton I daresay she seemed a little offish.

Well, things went on quietly for several weeks. My mistress was kind, my duties were light, and I got on well with the other servants. In short, I had nothing to complain of; yet there was always a weight on me. I can't say why it was so, but I know it was not the loneliness that I felt. I soon got used to that; and being still languid[6] from the fever, I was thankful for the quiet and the good country air. Nevertheless, I was never quite easy in my mind. My mistress, knowing I had been ill, insisted that I should take my walk regular, and often invented errands for me:—a yard of ribbon to be fetched from the village, a letter posted, or a book returned to Mr. Ranford. As soon as I was out of doors my spirits rose, and I looked forward to my walks

---

4. **the real quality:** the upper class.
5. **forbearing:** self-controlled.
6. **languid:** lacking energy.

through the bare moist-smelling woods; but the moment I caught sight of the house again my heart dropped down like a stone in a well. It was not a gloomy house exactly, yet I never entered it but a feeling of gloom came over me.

Mrs. Brympton seldom went out in winter; only on the finest days did she walk an hour at noon on the south terrace. Excepting Mr. Ranford, we had no visitors but the doctor, who drove over from D—— about once a week. He sent for me once or twice to give me some trifling direction about my mistress, and though he never told me what her illness was, I thought, from a waxy look she had now and then of a morning, that it might be the heart that ailed her. The season was soft and unwholesome, and in January we had a long spell of rain. That was a sore trial to me, I own, for I couldn't go out, and sitting over my sewing all day, listening to the drip, drip of the eaves, I grew so nervous that the least sound made me jump. Somehow, the thought of that locked room across the passage began to weigh on me. Once or twice, in the long rainy nights, I fancied I heard noises there; but that was nonsense, of course, and the daylight drove such notions out of my head. Well, one morning Mrs. Brympton gave me quite a start of pleasure by telling me she wished me to go to town for some shopping. I hadn't known till then how low my spirits had fallen. I set off in high glee, and my first sight of the crowded streets and the cheerful-looking shops quite took me out of myself. Toward afternoon, however, the noise and confusion began to tire me, and I was actually looking forward to the quiet of Brympton, and thinking how I should enjoy the drive home through the dark woods, when I ran across an old acquaintance, a maid I had once been in service with. We had lost sight of each other for a number of years, and I had to stop and tell her what had happened to me in the interval. When I mentioned where I was living she rolled up her eyes and pulled a long face.

"What! The Mrs. Brympton that lives all the year at her place on the Hudson? My dear, you won't stay there three months."

"Oh, but I don't mind the country," says I, offended somehow at her tone. "Since the fever I'm glad to be quiet."

She shook her head. "It's not the country I'm thinking of. All I know is she's had four maids in the last six months, and the last one, who was a friend of mine, told me nobody could stay in the house."

"Did she say why?" I asked.

"No—she wouldn't give me her reason. But she says to me, *Mrs. Ansey, she says, if ever a young woman as you know of thinks of going there, you tell her it's not worth while to unpack her boxes.*"

"Is she young and handsome?" said I, thinking of Mr. Brympton.

"Not her! She's the kind that mothers engage when they've gay young gentlemen at college."

Well, though I knew the woman was an idle gossip, the words stuck in my head, and my heart sank lower than ever as I drove up to Brympton in the dusk. There *was* something about the house—I was sure of it now . . .

When I went in to tea I heard that Mr. Brympton had arrived, and I saw at a glance that there had been a disturbance of some kind. Mrs. Blinder's hand shook so that she could hardly pour the tea, and Mr. Wace quoted the most dreadful texts full of brimstone.[7] Nobody said a word to me then, but when I went up to my room Mrs. Blinder followed me.

"Oh, my dear," says she, taking my hand, "I'm so glad and thankful you've come back to us!"

That struck me, as you may imagine. "Why," said I, "did you think I was leaving for good?"

"No, no, to be sure," said she, a little confused, "but I can't a-bear to have madam left alone for a day even." She pressed my hand hard, and, "Oh, Miss Hartley," says she," be good to your mistress, as you're a Christian woman." And with that she hurried away, and left me staring.

A moment later Agnes called me to Mrs. Brympton. Hearing Mr. Brympton's voice in her room, I went round by the dressing-room, thinking I would lay out her dinner-gown before going in. The dressing-room is a large room over the portico[8] that looks toward the gardens. Mr. Brympton's apartments are beyond. When I went in, the door into the bedroom was ajar, and I heard Mr. Brympton saying angrily:— "One would suppose he was the only person fit for you to talk to."

"I don't have many visitors in winter," Mrs. Brympton answered quietly.

"You have *me!*" he flung at her sneeringly.

---

7. **brimstone:** hellfire.
8. **portico:** a covered porch, usually with columns.

"You are here so seldom," said she.

"Well—whose fault is that? You make the place about as lively as the family vault—"

With that I rattled the toilet-things, to give my mistress warning, and she rose and called me in.

The two dined alone, as usual, and I knew by Mr. Wace's manner at supper that things must be going badly. He quoted the prophets something terrible, and worked on the kitchen-maid so that she declared she wouldn't go down alone to put the cold meat in the ice-box. I felt nervous myself, and after I had put my mistress to bed I was half tempted to go down again and persuade Mrs. Blinder to sit up awhile over a game of cards. But I heard her door closing for the night so I went on to my own room. The rain had begun again, and the drip, drip, drip seemed to be dropping into my brain. I lay awake listening to it, and turning over what my friend in town had said. What puzzled me was that it was always the maids who left . . .

After a while I slept; but suddenly a loud noise wakened me. My bell had rung. I sat up, terrified by the unusual sound, which seemed to go on jangling through the darkness. My hands shook so that I couldn't find the matches. At length I struck a light and jumped out of bed. I began to think I must have been dreaming; but I looked at the bell against the wall, and there was the little hammer still quivering.

I was just beginning to huddle on my clothes when I heard another sound. This time it was the door of the locked room opposite mine softly opening and closing. I heard the sound distinctly, and it frightened me so that I stood stock still. Then I heard a footstep hurrying down the passage toward the main house. The floor being carpeted, the sound was very faint, but I was quite sure it was a woman's step. I turned cold with the thought of it, and for a minute or two I dursn't breathe or move. Then I came to my senses.

"Alice Hartley," says I to myself, "someone left that room just now and ran down the passage ahead of you. The idea isn't pleasant, but you may as well face it. Your mistress has rung for you, and to answer her bell you've got to go the way that other woman has gone."

Well—I did it. I never walked faster in my life, yet I thought I should never get to the end of the passage or reach Mrs. Brympton's room. On the way I heard nothing and saw nothing: all was dark and quiet as the grave. When I reached my mistress's door the silence was so deep that

I began to think I must be dreaming, and was half minded to turn back. Then panic seized me, and I knocked.

There was no answer, and I knocked again, loudly. To my astonishment the door was opened by Mr. Brympton. He started back when he saw me, and in the light of my candle his face looked red and savage.

"You?" he said, in a queer voice. *"How many of you are there, in God's name?"*

At that I felt the ground give under me; but I said to myself that he had been drinking, and answered as steadily as I could: "May I go in, sir? Mrs. Brympton has rung for me."

"You may all go in, for what I care," says he, and, pushing by me, walked down the hall to his own bedroom. I looked after him as he went, and to my surprise I saw that he walked as straight as a sober man.

I found my mistress lying very weak and still, but she forced a smile when she saw me, and signed to me to pour out some drops for her. After that she lay without speaking, her breath coming quick, and her eyes closed. Suddenly, she groped out with her hand, and *"Emma,"* says she, faintly.

"It's Hartley, madam," I said. "Do you want anything?"

She opened her eyes wide and gave me a startled look.

"I was dreaming," she said. "You may go, now, Hartley, and thank you kindly. I'm quite well again, you see." And she turned her face away from me.

III

There was no more sleep for me that night, and I was thankful when daylight came.

Soon afterward, Agnes called me to Mrs. Brympton. I was afraid she was ill again, for she seldom sent for me before nine, but I found her sitting up in bed, pale and drawn-looking, but quite herself.

"Hartley," says she quickly, "will you put on your things at once and go down to the village for me? I want this prescription made up—" here she hesitated a minute and blushed—" and I should like you to be back again before Mr. Brympton is up."

"Certainly, madam," I said.

"And—stay a moment—" she called me back as if an idea had just struck her—"while you're waiting for the mixture, you'll have time to go on to Mr. Ranford's with this note."

It was a two-mile walk to the village, and on my way I had time to turn things over in my mind. It struck me as peculiar that my mistress should wish the prescription made up without Mr. Brympton's knowledge; and, putting this together with the scene of the night before, and with much else that I had noticed and suspected, I began to wonder if the poor lady was weary of her life, and had come to the mad resolve of ending it. The idea took such hold on me that I reached the village on a run, and dropped breathless into a chair before the chemist's counter. The good man, who was just taking down his shutters, stared at me so hard that it brought me to myself.

"Mr. Limmel," I says, trying to speak indifferent, "will you run your eye over this, and tell me if it's quite right?"

He put on his spectacles and studied the prescription.

"Why, it's one of Dr. Walton's," says he. "What should be wrong with it?"

"Well—is it dangerous to take?"

"Dangerous—how do you mean?"

I could have shaken the man for his stupidity.

"I mean—if a person was to take too much of it—by mistake of course—" says I, my heart in my throat.

"Lord bless you, no. It's only lime water. You might feed it to a baby by the bottleful."

I gave a great sigh of relief and hurried on to Mr. Ranford's. But on the way another thought struck me. If there was nothing to conceal about my visit to the chemist's, was it my other errand that Mrs. Brympton wished me to keep private? Somehow, that thought frightened me worse than the other. Yet the two gentlemen seemed fast friends, and I would have staked my head on my mistress's goodness. I felt ashamed of my suspicions, and concluded that I was still disturbed by the strange events of the night. I left the note at Mr. Ranford's, and hurrying back to Brympton, slipped in by a side door without being seen, as I thought.

An hour later, however, as I was carrying in my mistress's breakfast, I was stopped in the hall by Mr. Brympton.

"What were you doing out so early?" he says, looking hard at me.

"Early—me, sir?" I said, in a tremble.

"Come, come," he says, an angry red spot coming out on his forehead, "didn't I see you scuttling home through the shrubbery an hour or more ago?"

I'm a truthful woman by nature, but at that a lie popped out ready-made. "No, sir, you didn't," said I and looked straight back at him.

He shrugged his shoulders and gave a sullen[9] laugh. "I suppose you think I was drunk last night?" he asked suddenly.

"No, sir, I don't," I answered, this time truthfully enough.

He turned away with another shrug. "A pretty notion my servants have of me!" I heard him mutter as he walked off.

Not till I had settled down to my afternoon's sewing did I realize how the events of the night had shaken me. I couldn't pass that locked door without a shiver. I knew I had heard someone come out of it, and walk down the passage ahead of me. I thought of speaking to Mrs. Blinder or to Mr. Wace, the only two in the house who appeared to have an inkling of what was going on, but I had a feeling that if I questioned them they would deny everything, and that I might learn more by holding my tongue and keeping my eyes open. The idea of spending another night opposite the locked room sickened me, and once I was seized with the notion of packing my trunk and taking the first train to town; but it wasn't in me to throw over a kind mistress in that manner, and I tried to go on with my sewing as if nothing had happened. I hadn't worked ten minutes before the sewing machine broke down. It was one I had found in the house, a good machine but a trifle out of order: Mrs. Blinder said it had never been used since Emma Saxon's death. I stopped to see what was wrong, and as I was working at the machine a drawer which I had never been able to open slid forward and a photograph fell out. I picked it up and sat looking at it in a maze.[10] It was a woman's likeness, and I knew I had seen the face somewhere—the eyes had an asking look that I had felt on me before. And suddenly I remembered the pale woman in the passage.

I stood up, cold all over, and ran out of the room. My heart seemed to be thumping in the top of my head, and I felt as if I should never get away from the look in those eyes. I went straight to Mrs. Blinder. She was taking her afternoon nap, and sat up with a jump when I came in.

"Mrs. Blinder," said I, "who is that?" And I held out the photograph.

She rubbed her eyes and stared.

"Why, Emma Saxon," says she. "Where did you find it?"

---

9. **sullen:** ill-humored.
10. **maze:** bewilderment.

I looked hard at her for a minute. "Mrs. Blinder," I said, "I've seen that face before."

Mrs. Blinder got up and walked over to the looking-glass. "Dear me! I must have been asleep," she says. "My front[11] is all over one ear. And now do run along, Miss Hartley, dear, for I hear the clock striking four, and I must go down this very minute and put on the Virginia ham for Mr. Brympton's dinner."

IV

To all appearances, things went on as usual for a week or two. The only difference was that Mr. Brympton stayed on, instead of going off as he usually did, and that Mr. Ranford never showed himself. I heard Mr. Brympton remark on this one afternoon when he was sitting in my mistress's room before dinner:

"Where's Ranford?" says he. "He hasn't been near the house for a week. Does he keep away because I'm here?"

Mrs. Brympton spoke so low that I couldn't catch her answer.

"Well," he went on, "two's company and three's trumpery;[12] I'm sorry to be in Ranford's way, and I suppose I shall have to take myself off again in a day or two and give him a show." And he laughed at his own joke.

The very next day, as it happened, Mr. Ranford called. The footman said the three were very merry over their tea in the library, and Mr. Brympton strolled down to the gate with Mr. Ranford when he left.

I have said that things went on as usual; and so they did with the rest of the household; but as for myself, I had never been the same since the night my bell had rung. Night after night I used to lie awake, listening for it to ring again, and for the door of the locked room to open stealthily. But the bell never rang, and I heard no sound across the passage. At last the silence began to be more dreadful to me than the most mysterious sounds. I felt that *someone* was cowering there, behind the locked door, watching and listening as I watched and listened, and I could almost have cried out, "Whoever you are, come out and let me see you face to face, but don't lurk there and spy on me in the darkness!"

---

11. **front:** an article of clothing worn over the breast, such as a dickey.
12. **trumpery:** deceit; trickery.

Feeling as I did, you may wonder I didn't give warning. Once I very nearly did so; but at the last moment something held me back. Whether it was compassion for my mistress, who had grown more and more dependent on me, or unwillingness to try a new place, or some other feeling that I couldn't put a name to, I lingered on as if spell-bound, though every night was dreadful to me, and the days but little better.

For one thing, I didn't like Mrs. Brympton's looks. She had never been the same since that night, no more than I had. I thought she would brighten up after Mr. Brympton left, but though she seemed easier in her mind, her spirits didn't revive, nor her strength either. She had grown attached to me, and seemed to like to have me about; and Agnes told me one day that, since Emma Saxon's death, I was the only maid her mistress had taken to. This gave me a warm feeling for the poor lady, though after all there was little I could do to help her.

After Mr. Brympton's departure, Mr. Ranford took to coming again, though less often than formerly. I met him once or twice in the grounds, or in the village, and I couldn't but think there was a change in him, too; but I set it down to my disordered fancy.

The weeks passed, and Mr. Brympton had now been a month absent. We heard he was cruising with a friend in the West Indies, and Mr. Wace said that was a long way off, but though you had the wings of a dove and went to the uttermost parts of the earth, you couldn't get away from the Almighty. Agnes said that as long as he stayed away from Brympton the Almighty might have him and welcome; and this raised a laugh, though Mrs. Blinder tried to look shocked, and Mr. Wace said the bears would eat us.

We were all glad to hear that the West Indies were a long way off, and I remember that, in spite of Mr. Wace's solemn looks, we had a very merry dinner that day in the hall. I don't know if it was because of my being in better spirits, but I fancied Mrs. Brympton looked better, too, and seemed more cheerful in her manner. She had been for a walk in the morning, and after luncheon she lay down in her room, and I read aloud to her. When she dismissed me I went to my own room feeling quite bright and happy, and for the first time in weeks walked past the locked door without thinking of it. As I sat down to my work I looked out and saw a few snow-flakes falling. The sight was pleasanter than the eternal rain, and I pictured to myself how pretty the bare gardens would look in their white mantle. It seemed to me as if the snow would cover up all the dreariness, indoors as well as out.

The fancy had hardly crossed my mind when I heard a step at my side. I looked up, thinking it was Agnes.

"Well, Agnes—" said I, and the words froze on my tongue; for there, in the door, stood Emma Saxon.

I don't know how long she stood there. I only know I couldn't stir or take my eyes from her. Afterward I was terribly frightened, but at the time it wasn't fear I felt, but something deeper and quieter. She looked at me long and long, and her face was just one dumb[13] prayer to me—but how in the world was I to help her? Suddenly she turned, and I heard her walk down the passage. This time I wasn't afraid to follow—I felt that I must know what she wanted. I sprang up and ran out. She was at the other end of the passage, and I expected her to take the turn toward my mistress's room; but instead of that she pushed open the door that led to the backstairs. I followed her down the stairs, and across the passageway to the back door. The kitchen and hall were empty at that hour, the servants being off duty, except for the footman, who was in the pantry. At the door she stood still a moment, with another look at me; then she turned the handle, and stepped out. For a minute I hesitated. Where was she leading me to? The door had closed softly after her, and I opened it and looked out, half expecting to find that she had disappeared. But I saw her a few yards off hurrying across the courtyard to the path through the woods. Her figure looked black and lonely in the snow, and for a second my heart failed me and I thought of turning back. But all the while she was drawing me after her; and catching up an old shawl of Mrs. Blinder's I ran out into the open.

Emma Saxon was in the wood-path now. She walked on steadily, and I followed at the same pace, till we passed out of the gates and reached the highroad. Then she struck across the open fields to the village. By this time the ground was white, and as she climbed the slope of a bare hill ahead of me I noticed that she left no foot-prints behind her. At sight of that my heart shriveled up within me, and my knees were water. Somehow, it was worse here than indoors. She made the whole countryside seem lonely as the grave, with none but us two in it, and no help in the wide world.

Once I tried to go back; but she turned and looked at me, and it was as if she had dragged me with ropes. After that I followed her like a

---

13. **dumb:** mute; silent.

dog. We came to the village and she led me through it, past the church and the blacksmith's shop, and down the lane to Mr. Ranford's. Mr. Ranford's house stands close to the road: a plain old-fashioned building, with a flagged[14] path leading to the door between box-borders. The lane was deserted, and as I turned into it I saw Emma Saxon pause under the old elm by the gate. And now another fear came over me. I saw that we had reached the end of our journey, and that it was my turn to act. All the way from Brympton I had been asking myself what she wanted of me, but I had followed in a trance, as it were, and not till I saw her stop at Mr. Ranford's gate did my brain begin to clear itself. I stood a little way off in the snow, my heart beating fit to strangle me, and my feet frozen to the ground; and she stood under the elm and watched me.

I knew well enough that she hadn't led me there for nothing. I felt there was something I ought to say or do—but how was I to guess what it was? I had never thought harm of my mistress and Mr. Ranford, but I was sure now that, from one cause or another, some dreadful thing hung over them. *She* knew what it was; she would tell me if she could; perhaps she would answer if I questioned her.

It turned me faint to think of speaking to her; but I plucked up heart and dragged myself across the few yards between us. As I did so, I heard the house-door open and saw Mr. Ranford approaching. He looked handsome and cheerful, as my mistress had looked that morning, and at sight of him the blood began to flow again in my veins.

"Why, Hartley," said he, "what's the matter? I saw you coming down the lane just now, and came out to see if you had taken root in the snow." He stopped and stared at me. "What are you looking at?" he says.

I turned toward the elm as he spoke, and his eyes followed me; but there was no one there. The lane was empty as far as the eye could reach.

A sense of helplessness came over me. She was gone, and I had not been able to guess what she wanted. Her last look had pierced me to the marrow; and yet it had not told me! All at once, I felt more desolate than when she had stood there watching me. It seemed as if she had left me all alone to carry the weight of the secret I couldn't guess. The snow went round me in great circles, and the ground fell away from me.

---

14. **flagged:** covered with flagstones.

A drop of brandy and the warmth of Mr. Ranford's fire soon brought me to, and I insisted on being driven back at once to Brympton. It was nearly dark, and I was afraid my mistress might be wanting me. I explained to Mr. Ranford that I had been out for a walk and had been taken with a fit of giddiness[15] as I passed his gate. This was true enough; yet I never felt more like a liar than when I said it.

When I dressed Mrs. Brympton for dinner she remarked on my pale looks and asked what ailed me. I told her I had a headache, and she said she would not require me again that evening, and advised me to go to bed.

It was a fact that I could scarcely keep on my feet; yet I had no fancy to spend a solitary evening in my room. I sat downstairs in the hall as long as I could hold my head up; but by nine I crept upstairs, too weary to care what happened if I could but get my head on a pillow. The rest of the household went to bed soon afterward; they kept early hours when the master was away, and before ten I heard Mrs. Blinder's door close, and Mr. Wace's soon after.

It was a very still night, earth and air all muffled in snow. Once in bed I felt easier, and lay quiet, listening to the strange noises that come out in a house after dark. Once I thought I heard a door open and close again below: it might have been the glass door that led to the gardens. I got up and peered out of the window; but it was in the dark of the moon, and nothing visible outside but the streaking of snow against the panes.

I went back to bed and must have dozed, for I jumped awake to the furious ringing of my bell. Before my head was clear I had sprung out of bed, and was dragging on my clothes. *It is going to happen now, I heard myself saying;* but what I meant I had no notion. My hands seemed to be covered with glue—I thought I should never get into my clothes. At last I opened my door and peered down the passage. As far as my candle-flame carried, I could see nothing unusual ahead of me. I hurried on, breathless; but as I pushed open the baize[16] door leading to the main hall my heart stood still, for there at the head of the stairs was Emma Saxon, peering dreadfully down into the darkness.

For a second I couldn't stir; but my hand slipped from the door, and as it swung shut the figure vanished. At the same instant there came

---

15. **giddiness:** dizziness.
16. **baize** (bāz): a thick felt, traditional for covering doors to servants' quarters.

another sound from below stairs—a stealthy mysterious sound, as of a latchkey turning in the house-door. I ran to Mrs. Brympton's room and knocked.

There was no answer, and I knocked again. This time I heard someone moving in the room; the bolt slipped back and my mistress stood before me. To my surprise I saw that she had not undressed for the night. She gave me a startled look.

"What is this, Hartley?" she says in a whisper. "Are you ill? What are you doing here at this hour?"

"I am not ill, madam; but my bell rang."

At that she turned pale, and seemed about to fall.

"You are mistaken," she said harshly; "I didn't ring. You must have been dreaming." I had never heard her speak in such a tone. "Go back to bed," she said, closing the door on me.

But as she spoke I heard sounds again in the hall below: a man's step this time, and the truth leaped out on me.

"Madam," I said, pushing past her, "there is someone in the house—"

"Someone—?"

"Mr. Brympton, I think—I hear his step below—"

A dreadful look came over her, and without a word, she dropped flat at my feet. I fell on my knees and tried to lift her: by the way she breathed I saw it was no common faint. But as I raised her head there came quick steps on the stairs and across the hall: the door was flung open, and there stood Mr. Brympton, in his traveling-clothes, the snow dripping from him. He drew back with a start as he saw me kneeling by my mistress.

"What the devil is this?" he shouted. He was less high-colored than usual, and the red spot came out on his forehead.

"Mrs. Brympton has fainted, sir," said I.

He laughed unsteadily and pushed by me. "It's a pity she didn't choose a more convenient moment. I'm sorry to disturb her, but—"

I raised myself up aghast at the man's action.

"Sir," said I, "are you mad? What are you doing?"

"Going to meet a friend," said he, and seemed to make for the dressing-room.

At that my heart turned over. I don't know what I thought or feared; but I sprang up and caught him by the sleeve.

"Sir, sir," said I, "for pity's sake look at your wife!"

He shook me off furiously.

"It seems that's done for me," says he, and caught hold of the dressing-room door.

At that moment I heard a slight noise inside. Slight as it was, he heard it too, and tore the door open; but as he did so he dropped back. On the threshold stood Emma Saxon. All was dark behind her, but I saw her plainly, and so did he. He threw up his hands as if to hide his face from her; and when I looked again she was gone.

He stood motionless, as if the strength had run out of him; and in the stillness my mistress suddenly raised herself, and opening her eyes fixed a look on him. Then she fell back, and I saw the death-flutter pass over her . . .

We buried her on the third day, in a driving snowstorm. There were few people in the church, for it was bad weather to come from town, and I've a notion my mistress was one that hadn't many near friends. Mr. Ranford was among the last to come, just before they carried her up the aisle. He was in black, of course, being such a friend of the family, and I never saw a gentleman so pale. As he passed me, I noticed that he leaned a trifle on a stick he carried; and I fancy Mr. Brympton noticed it, too, for the red spot came out sharp on his forehead, and all through the service he kept staring across the church at Mr. Ranford, instead of following the prayers as a mourner should.

When it was over and we went out to the graveyard, Mr. Ranford had disappeared, and as soon as my poor mistress's body was underground, Mr. Brympton jumped into the carriage nearest the gate and drove off without a word to any of us. I heard him call out, "To the station," and we servants went back alone to the house.

Discussion Questions

1. What effect is gained by having the story narrated by Alice Hartley—instead of Mrs. Blinder, for example, or an anonymous narrator?

2. Of what does Mr. Brympton suspect his wife? Does there seem to be any basis for his suspicion?

3. The ghost of Emma Saxon appears only irregularly, and the bell rings only twice. What seem to be the occasions for her appearance and for the ringing of the bell?

4. Do you think other members of the Brympton household have seen Emma Saxon's ghost? Explain the reasons for your answer.

5. What do you suppose the ghost of Emma Saxon is trying to communicate to Alice Hartley?

Suggestion for Writing

What do you imagine is in the note that Mrs. Brympton sends to Mr. Ranford? Consider what happens in the story previous to this incident and write a note to Mr. Ranford in the voice of Mrs. Brympton. (You will have to decide on the nature of the relationship between them.) Then write a return note in the voice of Mr. Ranford.